Beyond Those Distant Stars

By John B. Rosenman

He sucked in his breath, glanced at the panel. "Only two more decks. I've got to say this. I've been meaning to ever since…"

But they had reached the docking bay, and the door opened. Stella exited first, followed by George. "Stella," he shouted, "I've got to tell you something! I tried to do it earlier at the meeting."

She glanced over her shoulder. "No time. Tell me later if we make it." And if we make it, maybe I'll tell Jason how much I've come to care about him. How much I think about him even when I'm not alone.

She marched across the docking bay, which was tinged by the smell of blood and medicines she couldn't identify. Several soldiers had escaped the alien vessel and were being attended by medtechs. Stella passed them, heading straight toward the dark mouth of the Scaleys' boarding tube.

"Commander, are you here?"

She turned, scanning their faces and seeing looks of amaze¬ment among the dazed, ravaged expressions. She gripped her plasma jet, held it up for all to see.

"Yes, I am here," she shouted. "Are you with me, comrades?"

A few rose to their feet. A man with a bloody shoulder pushed aside his gutted suit and tottered upright. "You're going in there?"

"Both of us are," George rumbled.

His confirmation brought more of them to their feet, some of whom she recognized. Nick Flynn, a gunnery specialist, stepped forward. He had been a phenomenal runner in the last Olympiad. Brett Duvall joined him, a soft-featured woman with extensive combat experience.

"Are you with me, comrades?" Stella shouted again.

This time a frail chorus answered. More soldiers rose.

Teeth clenched, Stella closed and sealed her faceplate. Then she turned and led her followers into the alien ship.

No novel just writes itself.
My hearty thanks and appreciation go to
the Oceanfront Writers' Group,
especially to my friends Richard Rowand,
Jacqueline Falkenhan, Jean Klein,
and Alan Bryden, who read and commented on the novel.

Above all, I want to thank my editor, Jody Wallace,
for her tireless help and brilliant suggestions.
At one point she stayed up to three a.m. for three straight nights,
working on yet another of my revisions.
I consider myself extremely lucky to have had her for an editor.

PROLOGUE

Emergency!

"Why do they call me?" Supervisor Stella McMasters muttered as she ran down the circular metal stairs of the turbine building on the planet Warren. "The crew knows more about reactor plants than I do!" She raced past each landing's flashing red lights that warned of out-of-control readouts in the pit below.

Radiation Protection Supervisor...Hah! I'm a nav-comm officer, not a bloody tank sniffer. I belong on a ship fighting the aliens. Dammit, I always hoped to command my own ship. Now look at me-given a soft job as a reward for loyal service.

Reaching the bottom, Stella headed for where Jack Faust bent over one of the filter tanks, the headset he was required to wear dangling from a back pocket. He was studying the panel on number 4, apparently still trying to dislodge the resin he'd mentioned earlier.

"Still constipated?" she called, thinking that she'd have to put him on report again for not wearing his headphones.

"Tighter than a Scaley's asshole," he half-shouted over the hum of massive pipes welded to the wall. "I've used air, steam, gas, solvent, but the bitch hasn't budged. I tell ya, Sup, I'm worried."

She nodded at the readout. "It's only 200. That's within accepted limits."

Faust straightened and rubbed a slender, lined face. "Doesn't feel right, somehow. And I've been doing this a long time, even worked in the asteroid belt and at Solax out near the galactic rim."

"Have you checked the sight port?"

"Yeah, just five minutes ago." He shrugged. "Maybe I oughta take another look."

She watched him climb the ladder fixed to the tank and squint at the sight port.

"Hey, it's steamed up now. I can't see a thing."

Steamed. Her face froze at the word. She removed her cap and ran a hand through her blonde hair. What had she read recently about a blocked filter tank whose temperature registered normal?

A dull cough echoed through the pipe overhead. She raised her hand.

"Jack, get down!"

He turned on the ladder and looked down at her. "What?"

More sounds thrummed through the conduit. This time he heard it. She saw his mouth open.

"Get down!" she shouted. "It's-"

Like a giant snake, the pipe exploded from its mounts. Struts and valve controls rained like hail. But worst of all was the steaming water that covered Faust as he fell to the floor.

Suddenly every alarm light on tank four started flashing. She stood, gazing down at the still body. In just seconds it had been transformed into something she didn't recognize.

Searing water sprinkled her side, licking her boot heels.

Somewhere a klaxon shrieked.

Arms pulled her back from behind. Doug Shane, a man on her crew, spoke into the comlink on his headset.

"Turbine trip. Tank 4, level 1." He grabbed her elbow. "C'mon," he shouted, "let's get out before the reactor blows."

She nodded, knowing it would take at least an hour for a meltdown to develop over in the reactor building. What she had to do now was evacuate her crew from the upper levels, then report to command, who would be trying to stop it.

"All right," she ordered, "let's clear the place; make sure everyone's got the word."

She watched Doug head toward the ladder she had just descended, and then followed. Of course, all her crew must know there was a problem, but it was her job to make sure even though a high-pitched oscillating warble now filled the building. Why didn't Jack move? If he'd just got off when I told him, he'd be alive now. Why hadn't the fool listened?

Forcing the image of Jack's frozen figure on the ladder from her mind, she picked up her pace to catch Doug. Mustn't think of that. What I've got to do now-

Ahead of Doug, a salmon-colored pipe overhead abruptly shook. And Doug was...

There was no time to shout, as she'd had with Jack. Dashing forward, she slammed him hard to the side, sending his body flying. Above her, the pipe punctured, spewing a flood of steaming liquid. Trying to duck, she barely had time to turn her head before a cloud of radioactive iodine settled over her like an invisible cloak. One breath shriveled her lungs and drove her to her knees, where she teetered briefly before collapsing to the floor. Desperately, she tried to rise, to escape the death that even now descended upon her, but her body seemed distant, as unreachable as the stars.

The last thing Stella remembered before she lost consciousness was a voice calling her name.

CHAPTER ONE

A year later, Stella McMasters' duroplast heart beat faster as she gazed up at the sleek tower of the *Spaceranger*-her first command. Over a hundred meters tall, it contained twenty-six levels, 1100 crew, and pointed toward the stars like a silver spear. To her, it was more beautiful by far than any lover she had ever known, any creed or dream.

Well, it's about time, she thought. After all, I'm only thirty-seven.

"Ready to board, Commander?"

She turned to her first officer, a bald, smiling man. "Patch us aboard, Sloan," she said.

Sloan nodded and pressed the comlink on his collar. "Williams here. Commander McMasters is ready to board."

"Aye, aye, ser," a voice answered.

She watched a ramp descend and started toward it across the bleak plain of New Mars, followed closely by Sloan. As she climbed, she felt her insides squirm as if she were in null-gee but ignored the sensation. It was an illusion, like the itch in amputated limbs. After the meltdown on Warren, rad contamination had necessitated the removal of her viscera, not to mention her heart, lungs, arms, face and eyes. She couldn't feel such sickness anymore. The unit that pumped and circulated her synblood would be good for 300 years yet, assuming it didn't short out.

Her mouth twisted at the mordant humor, and-thanks to synthetic tear ducts-she blinked back some moisture.

Once through the airlock, she and Sloan rode a tube up toward the bow, and then entered the bridge where her systems officers waited. Besides Sloan, who was in charge of navigation and communications, there was George Darron, the ship's immense, bearded psyche-physician; Carol Wayne, the engineer and weapons control officer, a small woman with alert eyes; and Myles Uxman, the expressionless director of internal security. Jason, the pilot, whose detached brain was interfaced directly with the ship, was not visible, but his clear computer-synthesized voice greeted her promptly when Sloan introduced them.

When the amenities were over, she smiled. "Please sit."

After they did, she squared her shoulders, self-conscious and determined to look like a commander. General Chen had been quite blunt after her promotion. Though she was not the first cyborg, she was the first physically enhanced cyborg commander, the experiment of a medical unit that faced considerable opposition for its director's radical theories. One of these theories was that cyborg humans would make superior soldiers who would play a crucial role in the war effort. Stella had been chosen as the prototype because of her stable military record and official regret concerning her accident. Because she was experimental, she should expect considerable skepticism and prejudice, even outright hatred. He had warned that she would need a damned tough skin.

Stella, whose skin was a fibrous polymer resistant to temperatures up to 500 degrees, stretched her lips in a smile that she had practiced endlessly before a mirror. With most of her facial nerves gone, she'd had to painfully reacquire expressions she had once made without thinking.

"People, we've been given our orders. We are to rendezvous with General Loran's forces a light-day away from Cygnus X-1 in preparation for doing battle with the enemy."

"X-1?" the engineer/weapons control officer said. "That's halfway across the galaxy."

"Technically it's only 8,000 light-years. Just three jumps, I'd say."

"I believe I can do it in two, ser," the pilot said.

Stella frowned. The disembodied voice made it difficult to know where to look. She settled for straight ahead.

"Two jumps," she finally said. "Explain."

"Commander, Central reports a new wormie they call Charbydis near Loran Base where we have to report. Indications are it has a narrow horizon, but I should have no trouble accessing it."

"Excellent." She found herself drawn by the deep soft voice, though she knew it was only a computer translation of the pilot's brain waves.

"Tell me...Commander," the psyche-physician said. "We're to play second fiddle to the good general, aren't we? Essentially our purpose is to mop up behind him after he's had his glorious victory and saved us all from extinction."

Second fiddle. Mop up. Gazing at the huge, bearded man, Stella recalled hearing that besides psychiatry and space medicine, Darron specialized in ancient Terran languages and idioms.

"Dr. Darron, if you mean by those terms that our mission will be 'back up,' then your guess is as good as mine."

He smiled, folding brawny arms. "With all due respect... Commander, none of this is exactly top secret."

"What do you mean?"

"Simply that speculation about just such an offensive against the invaders has been rampant for weeks. Good old X-1 has often been mentioned as an ideal place for Loran and his fawning support team to reverse the losses of the past five years and rescue humanity."

Uxman, the internal security officer, stiffened in his chair. Darron was edging toward treason. Within the rigid hierarchy of the Empire, such insubordination to a superior, especially during this war, could lead to a death sentence. Equally alarming to Stella, though, was the subtle pause before 'Commander.'

"Our job is not to question, but to carry out orders."

"Yes, but we can discuss-"

"I prefer not to." She raised her eyes to the bridge's central command chair, and then glanced out the plexiport at the great dark. "But I will say this: in my opinion, General Loran is over criticized. He's far too astute a leader to think he can defeat the Scaleys solely by a core attack force. I hardly think we've been sent on this mission just for show."

"Then how do you explain yourself?" Darron spread his huge hands. "Ser, I don't mean to be rude, but isn't your presence here somewhat unorthodox?"

"Unorthodox?"

"Yes. Or to use your own words, mainly 'for show'?"

"I don't follow, Dr. Darron."

He frowned. "Ser, correct me if I'm wrong, but isn't Academy training usually required in order to achieve Commander status? Yet I don't believe you ever attended."

It was very quiet on the bridge. Stella felt a hard knot of anger. The condescending bastard had insulted her and challenged her qualifications. Short of a harsh reprimand or requesting a court-martial, what could she do? She couldn't let it pass, yet knew of only one other way to establish her authority.

"Dr. Darron," she said, "would you please stand?"

"I beg your pardon?"

She smiled. "That's an order, Doctor."

Darron looked at the others, and then slowly rose.

"Please come to me."

He hesitated, and then moved toward her, stopping half a meter away.

"Closer."

Nervously, he complied. Almost touching his body, she stood staring up at him. Despite her height, Darron was a head taller and weighed twice as much. His massive body loomed over her, seemingly invincible.

Stella raised her hands overhead. "Slip your fingers through mine."

His hairy paws engulfed her slender, synthetic ones.

"Now press," she ordered. "Use all your strength. Drive me to the floor."

"Commander," Sloan said, "perhaps-"

"I'm waiting, Dr. Darron."

He shook his head like a confused bear. "What's the point of this? Prosthetic surgery isn't my specialty, but even with new advances, I'll still crush you."

"Do it!"

His heavy chest swelled. Then she felt his hands press

against hers, their force increasing as they met resistance. He grunted in surprise, and then pressed harder.

"When are you going to start?" she said. "I'm tired of waiting."

He stiffened, and then bore down with all his might.

Gasps. Sounds of disbelief. Stella smiled.

"Dr. Darron, is that the best you can do? Then it's my turn."

She monitored the pressure carefully, but still drove him down to his knees so hard that the deck shook. He moaned.

"Do you still think I'm here only 'for show'?" she asked. "And if so, would you like to see what I can really do?"

His face twisted in pain. "No!"

"Very well." Releasing her pressure, she helped him up.

"Perhaps, Commander," Sloan said smoothly, "We should defer this matter and entertain a report on the *Spaceranger's* status."

Stella nodded, grateful for the ploy as Darron resumed his seat. "Well taken, Sloan." She smiled at the engineer. "I'm especially interested in our capacity, Carol. Just how many mega joules can this crate pump out?"

As Carol answered, Stella glanced at Darron. The huge man, she saw, was glaring at her with rage.

Later, alone with Sloan on the bridge, she decided to risk a little candor. "I was pretty bad, wasn't I?"

Sloan rubbed his bald head. "Why do you say that, Commander?"

"Look at me, Sloan, and drop the commander shit, all right? You're second-in-command and we have to work together."

Sloan straightened the green shirt of his uniform. "You want me to go into it here?"

"Please."

"All right," he said. "To begin with, you let Darron run on too long, draw you in. The moment he questioned our orders, you should have slammed the hatch shut."

"What else?"

He shrugged. "You defended General Loran against Darron's charges. I know morale's suffered in the fleet because of continued setbacks, and there's chatternet about corruption and depravity at the top, including the Emperor's court, but you shouldn't do that, Stella. In the service, people have been routinely executed for insubordination and dereliction of duty. Our physician is your subordinate. He answers to you, not the other way around."

She nodded as Sloan went to the wall. "What's your pleasure, ser?"

"Coffee, please. Black."

He keyed a panel and a moment later handed her a squeeze bulb.

Sloan selected a drink for himself and returned. "Mine's hot cocoa," he grinned. "Been crazy for it ever since-"

Suddenly he slipped on something and dropped it. Stella's hand shot out and caught the container before it fell ten centimeters.

"Bloody damned Scaley!" He blinked at her hand, and then stooped to pick up the offending object-a silver pen.

"Must have dropped it earlier," he said, accepting the bulb from her. "My God, it's not just strength, is it? I never saw anyone move so fast."

She thumbed off the lid on her straw. "The servos respond instantly to the brain's signal. I've been told it's nine times quicker than normal."

"I believe it." He took a sip, and then rubbed his large nose. "We haven't talked about your, uh, condition."

"Go ahead."

"I've never met anyone as...synthetic as you. About sixty percent?"

"Nearly seventy. They couldn't clone me-something wrong with my DNA. And while they did manage to save half my bones, I'm basically high tech. Strictly state of the art, you might say."

"Well, you sure surprised George and the rest of us. Prosthetic surgery must have come a long way lately. You're obviously faster, stronger, and more efficient than any of us."

She swallowed some coffee. Faster and stronger, yes. Certainly more efficient. Unlike her facial expressions, she had mastered her new body's fine and gross motor skills within a month. But she could barely taste the coffee and only faintly feel the sun on her 'skin' or the wind on her back. If she was careless with a laser knife, she could cut off a hand without even knowing it.

And I haven't felt anything sexual since even before the surgery, she thought. Even if a man wanted me, I'd be like stone.

"What about you, Sloan?" Her mouth curved in a good imitation of a smile. "How long have you been getting a space tan at the Emperor's expense?"

He grinned at the old joke of enlisted personnel. "Thirty-two years, man and boy. Came up the hard way. I've been a loader, a ship's steward, a shuttle station maintenance Johnny, you name it. Finally earned a run at one of the systems guilds in nav and com."

Stella found herself liking this homely man. "According to records, you've been a first officer for nine years but never applied to the Academy to command your own ship. I was a first officer too, and did apply, though they kept turning me down." She paused. "If you don't mind my asking, was it money or connections that kept you from applying? I know they're important."

Sloan dropped the container in a wall disposal unit. "Important? Stella, without them, there's no chance at all they'll let an enlisted grunt like me enter the Academy and command his own ship. That's the way it is in this caste-ridden empire, no matter how good you are. Everybody has their station, and there's no rising above it." He shook his head. "But the truth is, a man's got to know what he's cut out for. Being the one at the top who makes all the decisions and bears all the responsibilities- I'm just not suited for that. But you are."

"Even after my recent performance?"

"Shaky performances are common for new commanders. I've served under several, and believe me, you're already far from the worst. Besides, the meeting wasn't that bad, especially the way you tamed George."

"Thanks, Sloan."

"Sure." He stifled a yawn. "I'm zacked, think I'll turn in."

He headed toward the door, and then stopped. "Just out of curiosity, do you still sleep?"

She nodded. "About three hours a night. It used to be six."

"Commander, I need only one," a voice said.

"Jason?" She stiffened, remembering.

"I tried to warn you," Sloan said gently. "Remember? I asked if you wanted to speak here on the bridge, but you wouldn't listen."

She watched him leave, and then turned to the wall above the holovid screens.

"I would have patched out, Commander," Jason's rich voice said from everywhere, "but except for the officers' personal quarters, I'm programmed to have continual and full access to the ship and its instruments."

"I didn't know that."

"Forgive me for asking, but weren't you supplied with op specs for this craft? My schematics should be among them."

She turned away, and then realized his 'eyes' were everywhere. Embarrassed, she touched the padded command chair located in the center of the bridge. "The files I was given were vast. I didn't have time." She knew that was no excuse, for she was the one in command. At the moment it seemed she couldn't stop making mistakes.

Jason was silent. Stella turned back to the wall above the holovid screens. "You seem different from the implant pilots we had on other ships. They were limited, interfaced only with the drive systems. And they..."

"Had bodies?" Jason's voice permeated the room from all directions. "With all due respect, I am a much improved model. You see, Commander, I am the ship."

You ARE the ship? My God, Stella suddenly realized, he's even more artificial than me. Except for his brain, he's all metal.

"Tell me about it, Jason," she said. "What's it like being an implant pilot?"

"What's it like? Ser, I'm not only much more efficient than earlier models. I feel different."

"Feel different? How?"

"Commander, I'm afraid it will sound strange."

"Tell me anyway. How do you feel different?"

"How?" Jason hesitated, and then grew enthusiastic. "When I'm in space, I can feel the solar wind on my skin; feel the power surge through my engines. I...I'm no longer just a little man with a limited body who's trapped in a dull routine. I'm far more than that. You see, I *am* the ship, and all of you are like living cells within me."

Bloody Scale-face, Stella thought. He not only sounds strange, he sounds half-mad.

"Commander, do you see the stars?"

She gazed out the plexiport at the glittering vastness of space.

"Aren't those lights beautiful?" he almost sang. "When I'm thrusting at full power, I hunger for them, and all I want is to race beyond those distant stars. I want to devour the void, consume it forever."

For once, Stella was glad her face did not easily reflect emotion. Troubled, she studied the stars, feeling as if they formed some mystic pattern she must solve.

"Commander," Jason said, "may I make an observation about one of your main systems officers?"

"Proceed," she said. Jason now sounded subdued, no longer filled with pride and manic joy. At the same time, the resonant tones stirred something inside her.

"After our meeting, I'm more concerned than ever about psyche-physician Darron," Jason said. "To be honest, I'm worried."

"Please get on with it," she ordered, slipping fully into the role of command. "If you have any information at all, you must share it."

"Yes, Commander. Dr. Darron on two occasions has told crewmen that this mission is stupid and reckless."

"As he did at our meeting."

"Yes, but he went further, and both incidents involved engine techs. I don't have to tell you how improper that is."

"No, you don't. What else did he say?"

There was a pause. "That we're a decadent, corrupt empire past our prime and the Scaleys have not only crushed us in every single battle, but will ultimately destroy us completely. That General Loran is old and no longer capable of leading."

"I see," she said.

"And ser, at your meeting, Dr. Darron challenged you. If you'll pardon my saying, ser, your officers should support you in your difficult task, not try to tear you down."

"Thank you, Jason."

"Ser, I just want you to know that I will always be here for you, even when others aren't. You can count on me."

She felt moved by Jason's warm support and pledge of loyalty. Then she recalled she was talking to a disembodied voice. What was happening to her, and why was it happening on her very first command? She had been ordered to launch in twelve hours. Should she delay on such hearsay? For God's sake, grumbling and complaints were common on every ship she had served on.

But what if Darron was sowing sedition among those who maintained the engines?

Still, what kind of observer was Jason? Could she really believe someone who had sounded so emotional? What did anyone really know about the effects of being an implant pilot? The procedure was so new.

"Commander," Jason said, "is everything all right?"

This time, despite her concerns, his voice stirred her, reminding her of desire she had forgotten. But she couldn't feel desire; all her organs and hormones were artificial.

"Commander?"

"Thank you for informing me," she said with an effort. "Please continue to do so if you observe anything suspicious."

"Aye, aye, ser."

She nodded. "Good night, Jason." Even as she left the bridge, she heard his soft parting words.

"Good night, Commander. Rest well."

Oh God, she thought, what a voice! I wonder what he looks like.

CHAPTER TWO

Pain.

She writhed in agony, trying not to scream. Something pressed against her arm. She heard clicking.

"Shit. She's over a thousand rem. We'll have to isolate her."

"Right. Let's go."

Sounds, footsteps. Something touched her. "Okay, Tom...ready? One, two, three...LIFT."

She seemed to soar, weightless in a bubble of her own torment. A disembodied voice wafted through her dream.

"Shane okay?"

"Yeah. Says she saved him. Knocked him on his ass to the side and took it full blast herself."

"Shit, look at her skin. All the scrubbing in the world ain't gonna help. The stuff's in her bones by now."

"Well, we can try parts."

"Or clone."

"Have to see a gene scan first."

Suddenly a rift opened and she was more aware. She heard the wheels of a gurney turning beneath her. Above, a ceiling with bright lighting raced by. She could just make out two men moving quickly at the foot of the gurney. They were dressed in green rad suits and the light gleamed on their transparent face guards so she couldn't see their features.

"Any word yet?"

"Hear it went solid. They couldn't get any coolant into the reactor loop."

"So it's blown?"

"Any time now."

Something slammed behind her head, and double doors burst open and then closed behind the figures. She couldn't see them, and they were unaware of her. Angry, awash in pain and struggling to breathe, she tried to sit up, but hands lifted and glided her into an enclosure. Bleary, sinking into semi-consciousness again, she peered about.

"There, there, dear," a woman said from behind a protective window. She looked a million kilometers away.

A steel arm extended a hypo held in metallic fingers. Another arm swabbed her arm with disinfectant, as if procedures must be followed at all costs.

"Don't!" she cried, but so weakly she barely heard it. Oh God, why couldn't she breathe? Why did her chest hurt? "Don't cut! Please don't cut anything off!"

The needle slid into her arm, withdrew.

"No pros...prosthe..." She tried to remember a word but felt herself fade. Soon all that remained were faces watching her from behind windows. That, and the pain.

Soon, no pain. No faces.

Only her pounding, pounding heart.

She came awake in the middle of her cabin. The heart she had felt racing in her dream beat calmly in her chest as always, sixty-two times a minute. All the terrors or physical strain in the world wouldn't increase its pace by one beat.

Yes, she was efficient.

Removing her sleeping gown, she stepped naked to the full-length mirror, seeing a tall, slender blonde woman with a stiff face. She forced her lips to smile. How easily and naturally she had smiled once. Now, unless she was careful, her face resembled a frozen, expressionless mask.

Her hand rose, cupped a small, synthetic breast, which she could barely feel.

I should have told them to go all the way, make me like

Jason. Only a brain with no frail legacy of flesh to confuse me.

She sighed. Even if she had renounced her flesh, would she have been any happier? Perhaps she'd be even more miserable.

Going to her desk comconsole she made two calls, ordering the officers to be in her cabin in ten minutes. Then she started to dress. Halfway through, though, she made another call. The person who answered seemed surprised but said she'd be glad to show Commander McMasters around her department in half an hour. No trouble at all.

Now why did I call her? Stella thought afterward. What possible purpose would my visit there serve?

But the appointment was made, and she used the time before her officers' arrival to call up Jason's schematics. A blue holo outline of the ship appeared, overlaid by red lines emanating from the bow where Jason's brain was located. The lines seemed to go everywhere except for a few private quarters.

After she finished reading the specs, Myles Uxman arrived, followed shortly by Sloan.

"The first thing I want to ask," she said closing the door, "is whether Jason has access to this particular cabin? Myles, that should fall under Internal Security. I've studied Jason's schems and he does seem to be excluded from a few places."

Myles and Sloan shared a look of surprise. "That's correct, ser. While he has virtually complete access to this ship, he is excluded from the cabins of main systems officers."

"You're sure?"

Myles' round, plump face frowned. "I've examined the interface specs personally, Commander. There's no way he can patch into restricted territory."

"So he can't override? He can't listen to us now?"

Myles and Sloan shared another look. "What is it, Stella?" Sloan asked.

Folding her arms, Stella told them of Jason's excitement, of his concern about Dr. Darron.

When she was finished, both men looked worried. "I didn't know Jason was acting like that," Myles said.

"You see the problem, don't you?" Stella coaxed. "I can't have an unstable pilot in charge of the ship."

"There shouldn't be any danger of that," Sloan said. He glanced at Myles. "We went over Jason's schems together. In related ways, we're both responsible for his operation. Myles is concerned about his effect on security, me with Jason's nav instructions. We've both found nothing to worry about."

"But he's a new development, isn't he? A high-tech breakthrough. We haven't really had time to find out what effect it will have on one's sanity to be totally removed from the body for an extended period. I know Jason's not supposed to be on-line for more than three months without being relieved, but the fact is, he could become mad or delusional within a single day, couldn't he? He referred to us all as being like cells inside him, and said he wanted to 'devour the void forever.'"

Sloan shrugged. "I've talked a lot with Jason. He's had two short missions like this before. Besides that, he's got a good sense of humor and impresses me as being very dedicated to his position."

"The Empire shares your optimism," Stella said. "Especially since a disembodied brain is more practical, able to use the ship's systems more quickly and efficiently."

"Surely," Sloan said, "the Empire wouldn't rashly sanction his use without...Bloody damned Scaley, do you realize half the ships in the fleet have similar pilots?"

"What did he say about the stars?" Myles said. "That he 'hungered' for them?"

"Yes," Stella said. "And while we're considering Jason's possible godlike delusions, let's not forget that he may also be paranoid."

"But his suspicions about Darron make sense," Sloan said. "Stella, that's another reason Jason interfaces with most of the ship-so he can check human circuits as well as mechanical ones and report dangerous conduct to head systems officers. It's another way he's cost-effective."

"I think I see what Commander McMasters means," Myles said. "He-"

"Call me Stella, Myles."

Myles hesitated, and then smiled. "All right. It's conceivable that Jason's near-omniscience could lead to delusions that he's..." He shook his head. "But I can't believe it. Like Sloan says, the Empire-"

"Did Jason inform you of Dr. Darron?" Stella said.

Myles blinked. "No."

"Shouldn't he have? I just scanned his schems, Myles. Jason is supposed to report directly to you, the Director of Internal Security. Not to the commander."

Myles pursed his lips. "That was irregular, I admit. I'll speak to him."

"There's another possibility too," Sloan said. "Dr. Darron could be the security risk. His conduct at the meeting bordered on insult and insubordination." He rubbed his bald head, which gleamed in the overhead light. "Perhaps he's trying to get the engine techs to strike-or worse."

Myles puffed out his plump cheeks. "If I knew that, I'd ask Stella to cold tank him." He sighed. "Listen, you've heard how low morale has sunk in the ranks because of our recent losses to the Scaleys. Incidents of insubordination have trebled just this year alone, and there are signs it will get even worse. If I panicked over every suspicious case, where would I stop?"

"But Dr. Darron is in position to do a great deal of harm," Sloan said. "My God, he's our psyche-physician!"

"Enough," Stella said. "We have two possible security risks on board the *Spaceranger*, and I have only nine hours to decide. If I ask that one or both be removed it could delay our departure for weeks, perhaps forever. Do either of you have anything to add?"

Silence. Finally, Sloan gave her a rueful smile. "Stella, this is one reason I never wanted your job."

Stella nodded. "Thank you both for your time."

She watched them leave, waited briefly, then left herself, careful to palm lock the door against trespassers.

She slipped down the corridor, glancing behind her to see if she was being watched. Perhaps Jason's paranoia was contagious. Summoning a tube, she entered and descended.

Her destination was amidships, sixteen levels below, where an armed guard at a station checked her features against those on her badge before snapping her a salute. A metal door opened and she passed through.

"Commander McMasters?" A stunningly beautiful woman in a white lab coat greeted her. Shaking hands, Stella noted with bitter envy the lustrous auburn hair, soft, even features, and curves that the shapeless coat couldn't quite conceal.

"Dr. Wynn. I appreciate your seeing me on such short notice."

"Not at all, Commander. How may I be of service?"

"I'd like to see our pilot."

"Of course." Dr. Wynn hesitated, obviously hoping for some explanation, but Stella didn't provide one. "If you'll come this way."

They moved down a path bordered on both sides by cryotanks. "How many crew do you have here?"

"Two at present." Dr. Wynn pointed at a corpulent man working on a nearby cryotank. "That's Jason's replacement pilot, Peter."

Stella glanced at him, and then followed Wynn to a chamber on the other side.

"He's in here," Dr. Wynn said.

Stella stepped up to the viewport and looked inside, seeing another male. This one was beautiful, endowed with a muscular, well-formed body and limbs. Tight raven curls framed a handsome face.

"That's Jason," Dr. Wynn said. "He wears his hair long." She touched Stella lightly, laughter in her voice. "He said he came from a long line of Greek heroes. That a distant ancestor of his piloted the *Argonaut*."

Stella looked at her, but Dr. Wynn was gazing raptly through the port at her side. Despite the coolness of this section, her cheeks were flushed.

"Have you known Jason long?"

This time Dr. Wynn looked at her. "Only two days. He reported here from the *Valiant* and Dr. Darron and a team of us performed the procedure."

"It went well?"

"Oh yes. His brain was extracted through the back of the skull, transferred to a nutri-cell and interfaced with the ship. Reimplantation should also be routine."

Stella studied her expression. "Evidently he made an impression on you."

Dr. Wynn blushed. "You might say that. He has quite a way about him."

You can say that again. Stella turned back to Jason, her eyes passing over the molded contours of his body. Below his waist, black curls clustered about his sex. Oh yes, she thought. Such a man must be good at many things.

What had she expected to find here? A clue that would tell her what to do? All she had discovered was something she should have known: that unlike her, Jason had a body he could return to and someone who would care.

"Thank you for your time, Dr. Wynn," she said. "I believe I'll go back now."

It was time. She strapped herself into the commander's purple chair and leaned back. The chair was not only located in the center of the bridge at a slight distance from others, but came with screens that could be activated for privacy. During her career she had wondered about the isolation. Now, for the first time, it was driven home. The separation stressed the loneliness of command, its terrible and awful burdens. On this craft no one could make decisions or take the blame but herself.

Click. The screens rose about her, called forth by Jason.

"Well, Jason," she said, feeling a new intimacy. "It looks like it's just you and me."

"Yes, Commander," Jason's voice responded. "As I said before, I will always be here for you, even when others aren't." A moment later: "Ser, I have Control on hold. Should I patch them through to you?"

Though required, the question was a formality. Stella held back a moment. "Jason, can you see what I look like?"

"Ser?"

Why am I asking this? "Can you see my...face?"

A brief pause. "Yes, Commander. Your signature is quite clear."

Signature? "You mean you can't actually see what I look like?"

"Commander, present technology doesn't quite permit that. Beyond and within the ship's parameters, I distinguish objects by spectroscopic patterns. It's not quite the same as seeing with my eyes, but I assure you, I've been extensively trained, and it's just as accurate and efficient."

Stella smiled at his defensive tone, and then found herself wondering if he could tell she was smiling. Of course he could. He just couldn't tell what she looked like.

"Get Control," she said.

"Yes, Commander."

A click. A moment later came a man's voice: "This is Control, Commander. We have you cleared to launch in two minutes. Will you lift off or abort?"

How many commanders had answered that question in the past three thousand years? She wet her lips with moisture that was not saliva and looked up at the bulkhead.

"*Ad astra*, Commander?" Jason said.

Ad astra. Oh yes, it was ancient Terran Latin and meant 'to the stars.' "Please stand by," she said to Control. She started to recline her chair.

"Allow me, Commander," Jason said. The chair shifted and she felt herself carefully tipped back. She gripped the chair arms, then relaxed and closed her eyes. Oddly, she imagined it was Jason's muscular arms that held her. She felt herself sink into his embrace as his voice caressed her.

"How is that?" he whispered, just centimeters away.

"Commander, this is Control. You have sixty seconds to liftoff."

Jason's arms gently cradled and cushioned her. Though she knew it was wrong, that the Empire had a rule against fraternization, it was as if she were under a spell. And was it truly fraternization when she couldn't even touch his body? She smiled, feeling his close presence almost on her face, her lips. *Shall we go see those distant stars together, Jason?*

A heartbeat later she opened her eyes, hardening herself. No more weakness. Damn it, decide. Do it now. Right or wrong, decide.

"Commander, this is Control. You have thirty-"

"McMasters here," she said, cutting him short. "Everything's fine at this end. Let's go for it."

CHAPTER THREE

After the roar of their engines and the cruel pressure she barely felt; after all systems checked out *go* and they reached five thousand kilometers per second; after the thrill of command was tamed by a week's routine and they slowed for a billion kilometers to reach their first jump-it was finally time to meet her crew and tell them of their mission.

Straightening her uniform, Stella glanced one last time at the black whirling funnel nine hundred kilometers away on the holovid display and left the bridge, followed by her officers.

"Commander, I've been meaning to speak to you."

She glanced at Darron's imposing bulk. "Not now, George. We've got a meeting."

The tube door opened, and they entered and descended. Darron, Carol, Myles, Sloan. Only Jason, she thought, was physically absent, and she would have liked him to be here more than anyone else. She thought of his voice, of how it changed ever so slightly when he spoke to her, as if they had an understanding. As if he thought of her too and dreamed as she did, of the day he could reach out and touch her hand. She knew it was foolish to think such things and to agonize about her sexuality and attractiveness to men. It was even more foolish to think of Jason restored to his body and naked in her cabin. After all, she had a ship to run and a mission to perform. She must not be distracted from that.

Still, she couldn't get rid of the feeling that she and Jason shared a bond, one she yearned to explore and deepen, to find out if their feelings were as real as she hoped. She imagined them together, his lips burning against hers as he moved inside her.

She cleared her throat and glanced about, wondering if anyone could tell what she was thinking. Beside her, Darron fidgeted. Then his eyes settled on hers, and he smiled.

Why don't I feel at ease with Darron? Stella thought. Is it that he baited me earlier, or that I feel guilty for having humiliated him?

The door opened, and they left, entering Assembly, the largest room on the ship. Two levels aft of the bridge, it was dotted here and there by miniature gardens of flowers and shrubs. Stella saw glorious red, white, and pink blossoms that, as always, struck her as incongruous. "We talk of war/Amid the scents of heaven," she recalled an anti-war poet writing, "And scatter lives like petals/Throughout the universe of time."

Leading her officers, she marched down the central aisle toward the platform at the front. Though her crew stood at attention on both sides, some couldn't resist looking at her. Look at the freak, she imagined them whispering. That's not her real face and body. They grew them in a lab vat.

Shoulders back, Stella mounted the platform and stood erect behind the rostrum. Perhaps two hundred crew faced her. On vidscreens, she saw nine hundred other souls watching from stations about the ship. Stella turned to the large hologram suspended three meters high in the room's center. Kolanera, the twelve-year-old Emperor, gazed back at her with soft, guileless eyes as if thinking of his parents, who had died in a tragic accident a year before. Malik, the Regent-Protector chosen to rule in trust until Kolanera reached his majority at nineteen, was not shown. Stella recalled with unease the rumors she'd heard about his dishonesty and corruption.

"In the name of our Emperor, Kolanera the Fifth," she intoned, "let us raise every voice and heart and sing our Imperial Anthem."

She began singing and two hundred voices immediately followed, obedient to a thousand-year-old tradition. Glancing about, Stella saw that those on the screens held their hands clasped over their hearts and were singing too.

Raise every voice and heart

That we true soldiers play our part.
Our Emperor's will shall be our way,
To serve and die-glorious pay!
Though comrades perish at our side,

We shall fight on bravely-not abide
The foe who scorns His sacred crown.
We strike him boldly-cast him down!

Even though the anthem's meter and rhyme scheme were deficient, she loved and was true to it, just as her soldiers were. As they sang together, she felt very close to them, united by a common goal and purpose, by a commitment to something larger than herself. Her eyes teared, and for once even her terrible accident seemed joyful, an unexpected benediction.

The last voice faded in the chamber, leaving it strangely silent.

"In the Emperor's name," she said, "you may sit."

They did so, and she was aware again of her difference from them, of her terrible apartness. But one glance at her Emperor's trusting features strengthened her resolve and she started to speak.

She greeted and told them of their mission, which she knew they already suspected. "Comrades, as you have no doubt guessed, we have been assigned an important mission. We have been ordered to rendezvous with General Loran's forces and support him in the greatest engagement yet in the war effort, one that may ultimately decide its course."

A few faint cheers greeted her words. She waited, then, punctuating her remarks with forceful gestures, tried to present their role in the best possible light. They were a valuable force essential to General Loran's campaign, she said, and the combat readiness of ships like theirs would make a crucial difference in the coming battle. She informed them of the two wormholes ahead before they reached their goal some 8268 light-years distant, of how their first jump would be undertaken in just a few hours.

Her last statement caused a few in the audience to murmur. Evidently, they had not expected to face the rigors of a jump so soon.

When she was finished, she folded her hands on the rostrum. "Are there any questions?" she asked.

She waited, half-expecting someone to rise and expose her as an impostor. But they all sat cowed. Rank is rank, she thought, touching a gold commander's wing on her collar.

"That being the case," she said, "I now turn the proceedings over to Dr. Darron, who will share with you some recent findings and, uh, meaty tidbits about the enemy. Again, I wish you well, and I look forward to working with you on this most vital enterprise."

Returning to her seat amid applause, she was met halfway by Dr. Darron. "Commander," he whispered, "there aren't any new 'tidbits' about the Scaleys. It's the same old stew!"

She patted his shoulder. "Then spice it up, George, but make them care."

When she was seated, Carol smiled and gave her an approving nod. Stella smiled back and turned her attention to the rostrum, where Darron nodded at a tech operating a holo projector. A moment later an image equal in size to the Emperor's appeared facing it in the air.

A Scaley.

Scattered curses, sounds of shock. Stella leaned forward, wondering if her plan to motivate the crew would work or backfire. Admittedly, the symbolism was heavy-handed, but this juxtaposition of good and evil, of beloved Emperor and despised enemy was having an impact.

As the crew settled down, the tech slowly rotated the three-dimensional image so they could see it from all sides. For perhaps the thousandth time, Stella studied the face and form of the enemy.

Vaguely reptilian, the size of a large human, a Scaley seemed at first almost beautiful, with delicate features and mottled, silver-blue scales. The longer you stared at one, though, the more disquieting it seemed. There was something intangible in a Scaley's face or appearance that was deeply disturbing to humans. Scientists, xenologists, and philosophers had endlessly debated, but all anyone knew was that humans instinctively felt it and that the Scaleys were deadly, intent on devouring the stars.

Merely five years before, when the Empire of United Worlds was enjoying an unequalled period of conquest and expansion, the Scaleys had invaded this part of the galaxy. Where they'd come from, no one knew, nor whether they had any real culture, beliefs, or language as humans understood them. None of their ships had ever been captured, and the few Scaleys taken prisoner had somehow self-destructed or willed themselves to die, leaving only rapidly deteriorating corpses for analysis.

If only we could speak to one, Stella thought. Establish contact in some way. At the rostrum, Darron was warming to his subject, trotting out an old theory. Indications were that the Scaleys were a hive-like species and mentality, like bees and ants. That would explain their implacable efficiency. He raised his eyes to the Scaley revolving above. "If so," he said, "we may have to emulate and even surpass their ferocity in the service of our Emperor."

There was robust applause, followed by Darron's call for questions. Several hands rose; Darron picked one.

"Ser," said a crewman, "why do Scaleys always die after we capture them?"

"Apparently," Darron rumbled, "it's a genetic trait to prevent them from disclosing military secrets or compromising their security."

A woman rose, a dietician Stella recognized. "Dr. Darron, based on the fact that we've lost every battle against the Scaleys, do you really think we have a chance to win this war?"

Dr. Darron waved to quiet the resulting outburst, and then seemed lost for words. Watching him, Stella remembered Jason reporting that Darron felt the Empire was weak and already beaten. If he believed that, how could he possibly respond?

On the other hand, if he was a traitor, appearing to be tongue-tied might be an excellent way to sow doubt and undermine their mission.

Darron's apparent inability to speak was having an effect.

Murmurs rose, a rising crest that would soon-

Stella reached the rostrum in five strides. "Of course we'll win!" she shouted. "We'll win because a free-thinking race that can love and serve a cause will always prevail over a mechanical one, however cruel and efficient."

Her eloquent words stilled the assembly, but the woman seemed unimpressed. "Commander, that hasn't been proven. This is the first conflict we've had with any alien race."

Stella glanced up at the Emperor's boyish face, then at their alien nemesis. "True," she said, "but-"

Suddenly brilliant red lights began flashing at the four corners of the hall. A moment later, a piercing shriek rent the air. "Battle stations! Report to Battle Stations!"

Sloan was already leaping from the platform. In the sudden commotion, the packed crew struggled to avoid collision as they left for different stations. Stella, knowing her speed would enable her to reach the bridge first, saw many crew glance fearfully at the vidscreens.

She was watching when the displayed scene changed, became that of open space, which rushed toward her in a close-up. When it stopped, the black maw of the wormhole was clearly visible.

As was the sleek length of the Scaley warship positioned directly beside it.

CHAPTER FOUR

Though she'd trailed Sloan and her other officers from the platform, Stella gained the bridge first. Ignoring the tubes, she tackled the utility stairs that climbed the ship's length.

Her feet a blur, she remembered other stairs, those descending to the turbine building floor on Warren. Would this be another disaster? Would she once again be too late?

Fighting panic, she willed herself to go even faster, willed her straining body to be on the bridge.

At last she burst onto it, rushing toward crew and holovid displays with her heart calmly beating as if in mockery of her thoughts.

"Commander." A tight-faced junior officer turned to her. "They just popped out of nowhere. One moment there was a wormie; the next, they were sitting right next to it!"

"Relax, Lee," Stella said, scanning the readouts. How could the Scaleys maintain a position so close to the funnel? The pull there had to be almost infinite!

Rapid footsteps sounded behind as her main officers arrived.

"It can't be reverse thrusters," Carol said. "No drive system could resist that pull. They've got to have something new. An anti-grav shield, maybe. Or a space-dislocation device."

"Negative," Sloan said. "We've tried both."

"The important concern right now is not their tech breakthrough," Stella said, though that itself was alarming enough, since the Scaleys had already almost won the war. "The enemy has blocked us, people. They're here because they don't want us to go through."

"What if they're doing this at other wormies?" George said. "The scale-heads could block half our forces from Loran."

I thought you WANTED that, Stella thought. She watched Carol, who barely reached George's sternum, look up at him with flashing eyes. "Shouldn't you be in med? If there're any injuries, you'll be needed there."

Stella had no time for the personality clash developing between the two. "Right now we need him here, Carol. He's our expert on the Scaleys. If things get rough, what he knows about them could make the difference."

"Knows, hell. No one knows a nit about them."

Stella ignored her and glanced out the plexiport. Jason was keeping them end-on to the warship, conceding the enemy only the smallest possible target. Scanning the command console, she saw the Nero Force Shield up, the plasma and laser beam systems placed on code red. Good. Jason was a damned fine pilot who didn't need to be told things. Her eyes darted to Sloan, standing at the command console.

"Should I tightbeam a message?" he asked.

"Go ahead," she said. "They never answer, but it's SOP."

Sloan spread his hands. "What'll I say, Stella?"

She sighed. Sloan excelled at nav and com, but lacked initiative in other areas. "Ask them what they're doing here. Tell 'em we love them."

Sloan's eyebrows went up and he turned to adjust a dial. "*Spaceranger* calling. Identify yourself and state your mission." He repeated the message and switched off. No answer. After thirty seconds he went on-line again. "Maybe a different frequency…"

"Don't bother," Stella said. "The Scale-faces never communicate anyway. For all we know, they can't." She fought down her frustration and turned to Carol. "Our orders are to meet Loran near X-1. This wormie is the only route. It would take years to go around."

"Approximately three-point-seven years," Jason said.

"Unacceptable!" She eyed the wormhole.

"You aren't thinking of charging it, are you?" Carol said, her eyes fixed on Stella. "They'd fire a deflector beam and we'd enter it off-line. We'd be torn apart, Commander."

"She's right," Myles pitched in. "They've done it before."

"I'm aware of that." Stella fought the temptation to snap at her security director. It's not your area of expertise, she itched to say, but then, Carol had been right: no one really knew what to do with the Scaleys. Whatever they had tried in the past had invariably failed against their resourceful enemy.

Carol's eyes hadn't left her. "You're not thinking of charging the gate, which means...Oh God. You're not thinking of shooting it out with them, are you? A Scaley warship has three times our shielding and firepower, fifty percent more acceleration and maneuverability."

"I disagree, Carol," Jason's voice interrupted. "My schems suggest the *Spaceranger* is now equal in maneuverability to anything they can throw against us." Jason's voice rose. "They may be faster, but I can match any close-encounter moves they try, out-step them at any dance."

"Makes no difference," Carol snapped, her fine, sharp features hard. "We can absorb their hits only so long, and then our shields crumble. Be light on your feet all you want, Jason. Try dodging a plasma jet."

The bridge fell silent while Stella reviewed their situation. While both sides possessed mirror shielding that would bounce plasma and laser beams back at each other, the Scaleys' shielding, whose nature was unknown, was far superior. If the *Spaceranger* chose to swap artillery blasts, it would be rendered defenseless. Their obliteration would be assured.

Stella met Carol's gaze. "We have to go through that hole. My orders are explicit. They give us no choice."

"Can't we contact Command?" George asked. "See if Scaleys are at other wormholes?"

"Even if our message got through, it would take much too long," Stella said. "Besides, my orders give us no choice."

"Even if we all die?" George said.

Stella's eyes flashed. "Even if we all die, George. Unless you counsel treason and insubordination."

George colored and looked at the image of the Scaley warship. "I can accept dying," he growled, his strong, bearded chin pointed defiantly at the enemy. "But I can't embrace *kamikaze* suicide."

Though the reference was unknown to the other officers, Stella saw that the gist of George's words was not lost on Myles, who unsnapped his holster and withdrew his plasma jet. "Are you advising mutiny, Dr. Darron?" he said softly.

The psyche-physician's cheeks twitched. "No, of course not. It's just-"

"People," Stella said, "we have no time to feud. Myles: holster your sidearm; George: don't question our orders." She looked up at the wall above the vid displays. "Jason, can you approach fifty kilometers and maintain our distance against the wormie?"

"Aye, aye, ser."

"Then do so."

There was a faint sensation of speed and the Scaley ship loomed up in the screen. Jason's voice crackled: "Commander, now eight hundred fifty-one kilometers from their vessel."

"Good," she said. "Now steer to port broadside on. Give them a look at our pedigree lines."

Verniers fired, turning the ship till it presented the broadest possible target. Stella glanced about, seeing that all faces were drawn. At the battle stations console to Sloan's right, Lee Song's face had turned pale.

"Stella," Sloan said, crouching over a vid display, "the energy sig on their ship has darkened. It's...Oh shit, here they come."

Stella smiled tightly. "Maybe they'll ask us to dance."

George started to speak, and then reconsidered at a sharp look from Myles. Stella waited.

Finally Jason's voice filled the bridge again. "Stella, they've matched us, leveled off at fifty kilometers."

She nodded. "How much closer can you get without being sucked in?"

"I've already computed. I can maintain thrust against the wormie for twenty minutes at one hundred fifty kilometers closer. If I go two hundred kilometers, the time would be a third of that."

"Very well, vector to point-on and approach one hundred more kilometers, and then steer port to broadside again."

Carol sucked in her breath as Jason complied. When her order was completed, the Scaley warship echoed their movements.

"Enemy's one hundred kilometers closer," Jason reported. "We're six hundred kilometers apart."

Stella fought a surge of doubt.

Carol stepped toward her. "What are you doing, Commander? With all due respect, are you courting disaster?"

Stella swung around. "What difference does it make? With their speed and power, they can run us down any time they want and hammer us to bits. Our only chance is to outflank them and make a run for the hole."

"'Run for the hole'?" Sloan said.

"Yes. If we get to the wormie, there's a chance we'll pop out the other side a light-hour away from them. Even if it's less, they might never find us."

"What I want to know," George said, "is why they're toying with us. Why not just blast away?"

Myles' plump features produced a wry smile. "As our resident Scaley expert, Doctor, you seem to have missed a point. What better way to demoralize an opponent and erode their collective will than to 'toy' with them? It shows overweening confidence, the belief that you can destroy them at your pleasure."

Darron sighed. "Believe me; such tactics have had their effect throughout our ranks."

"Shh," Stella ordered, and an instant later, Jason spoke up. "Five hundred ninety kilometers...five hundred eighty... Enemy moving toward us again, Commander."

"They won't stop," Carol said. "I'm needed in munitions."

No one glanced at her as she left the bridge. They all watched the monitors on the command console. Five hundred fifty kilometers...five hundred forty...

"When they reach four hundred," Stella said, "begin taking evasive action without getting too close to the wormie, Jason."

"Should I fire first, Commander?"

Stella licked her lips. "No. Give them first crack, then respond."

"Stella," Sloan hissed. "You can't!"

"That's all, Jason," she said.

"Very good, ser," Jason said. "I'll send up the combat harness."

Panels in the deck opened and seats rose on tripods whose legs widened as they slid along grooves. Stella sat down and strapped herself in, then lowered the affixed helmet. When finished, she had limited mobility without the rigidity of a chair. Sloan and Lee, she saw, were pulling in telemetry at their stations, sliding in their harness through cogs in the deck that clicked fast.

Stella leaned back. Good or bad, the battle was joined. If Jason was demented…well, then she was trusting everything to him. But deep down she knew she had no choice the moment the warship appeared. Even if they'd run, they'd have been caught. Besides, from the beginning Jason had been the one crewman who had pledged his support. Now she felt she could trust him with anything, perhaps even her feelings.

"Stella."

She looked at George, who was strapped in harness to her right. Tense laughter boiled up inside her as she thought of what he resembled: a gigantic, bearded baby bird about to peck free of his egg.

"What is it, George?"

He swallowed. "I've been meaning…"

"Three hundred kilometers, Stella," Sloan reported.

Stella turned, watching the warship swell in the vid display. It looked so small there, but she knew its sleek finned structure was half again as long as the *Spaceranger*. She studied its blue-gray surface, wondering what the beings inside were like, what drove them, and what they really wanted. Was it just ruthless conquest as so many authorities claimed? Single-minded rapacious hunger? She remembered Jason's desire to "devour the void" and wondered if there was any similarity between him and them, or if humans resembled the enemy in any way. She trembled.

Closer…closer…two hundred fifty kilometers…two hundred… She felt useless and cursed herself for making this reckless decision. At the moment, Sloan, Lee, and the techs at other consoles were far more necessary than she.

One hundred kilometers...ninety...eighty...

At seventy-one kilometers, blinding white blips shot toward them. Jason evaded them easily, leaping aside like a dancer. They swung around with him in their harness as Jason swerved, nudged forward and closed to sixty kilometers...fifty...

I AM the ship, he had said. Oh God, let it be true.

"Why in the hell doesn't he shoot?" Myles growled. "We're just floating here like turds in a barrel!"

No one answered, including Jason, who didn't retaliate when the Scaley warship closed to forty kilometers. The ship bobbed and weaved, darted and corkscrewed up, down, sideways, and back with rear, front, and side thrusters. Then they were side-on and firing for the first time. In the monitor, Stella saw a molten plasma arc strike the warship just behind the bow. Gleaming fire instantly washed back, missing them and continuing on into space as Jason ducked and streaked beneath the course of the oncoming intruder.

Suddenly Jason's laughter filled the bridge. He was enjoying this!

In the display, the arrow-shaped bow of the warship was clearly visible, showing the scythe like slit of the plexiport sweeping across its front. Light from a distant sun flashed briefly on its surface.

At fifteen kilometers, the alien vessel halted. Jason slipped one way, then another, trying to outflank the ship and dart past, but the warship countered, then countered again. A pencil beam lanced out, laser fire that caught the *Spaceranger's* stern and was shot back. On the display, Stella saw it miss the warship by a wide margin. Another spear of light came, and she heard Lee's console signal a direct hit, hard.

"Shit," George said. "That's two straight and we didn't even muss their hair."

But then Jason speared them four straight times, alternating plasma and laser, testing their shields' resistance to both as he evaded their sallies. Rising over them, Jason laughed in triumph as he strafed the enemy a fifth time with two beams, one at stern, and the other amidships. Stella and all on the bridge cheered him on.

"Way to go!"

"Give it to 'em, Jason!"

As good as the enemy was, Jason was better. In fact, he had a clear edge. Still, she couldn't deny the inevitable conclusion. Two particularly wicked plasma bursts from different locations on the enemy ship brought a shrill cry from Lee at the battle monitors.

"Ser, that last hit took nearly twelve percent of our shields!"

"What are we down to now?" Stella asked.

"About half." Lee's eyes darted among the screens. "There's some residual loss of power too. We're draining."

George shifted in his harness. "'Bout down to the last grab in our bag of tricks," he said.

As the ship heaved and twisted and wheeled, Stella reviewed their options. George was right. They were approaching their last grab. "All right, Jason," she shouted, "activate the kaleidoscope. Let's see if we can lose them."

"Aye, aye, ser. I was about to do that."

Moments later, dozens of *Spacerangers* surrounded their own, projected by a prismatic field generator. For kilometers on all sides, exact copies of their craft darted, changed positions, and turned about a central axis. Though it had worked well in tests, it merited them a volley of shots that accurately found the true *Spaceranger*. Within seconds they took brutal hits at both the bow and stern. The bridge shook, and the crew swung hard in their harness.

A final burst scorched their side and rocked the entire ship. "Another hit, ser!" Lee called. "A bad one!"

"Deactivate," she shouted, "we'll only drain more power!" As a hundred *Spacerangers* winked out of existence about them, she wracked her brain for an escape, anything that could outwit and deceive the Scaleys. "Jason, we've lost over half our shields! Can you retreat, see if the enemy will hold?"

It was senseless, of course. She knew that any enemy, particularly one with superior muscle would seize the advantage and come down their throats. But amazingly, as the *Spaceranger* withdrew, the enemy didn't follow. At three hundred kilometers, Stella told Jason to level off. Slipping out of her harness, she joined Lee at the battle monitors.

"Why didn't they pursue us?" she said. "Keep firing till we'd had it?"

George joined them at the displays. "It's the old game of 'cat and mouse.' They're having too much fun playing with us."

She studied George as he in turn examined the monitors. Shield capacity was barely thirty-eight percent, yet damage to the ship was negligible. As George moved his head, red and green light bathed his features, projecting images onto them. The enemy warship itself appeared on his cheek like an omen.

Stella raised her head. "Well done, Jason! I'm going to recommend you for a Battle Wings Citation when we reach a base."

"Let's not decant the champagne just yet," Jason said. Stella could tell he was pleased from his voice, for in the past week she had grown familiar with every nuance of his intonation. Sometimes, in fact, when she closed her eyes, she felt his voice resonate through every fiber of her being, animate even tissue that had never known the spark of life.

She closed her eyes, thinking of Jason lying in his cold sleep with ebony curls caressing his nakedness.

"Commander."

She opened her eyes. Lee was pointing to the three-dimensional image of the warship poised above a vidplate.

Stella leaned forward. Carol's voice came over the com from munitions. "Do you see that, Stella? Looks like they're extending a boarding tube!"

"Yes, I see, Carol." She glanced toward the command console and confirmed that Sloan and Myles had seen it too. Sloan raised his eyebrows.

"They want us to board," Myles said.

"I think he's right, Stella," George said beside her.

Reluctantly, she nodded. "Or else they want to board us."

"Does it really make a difference?" George said.

Stella scrutinized the warship's image. "But why? To add to

their pleasure by drawing it out? More 'cat and mouse'?"

"Exactly," Myles said. "They're whetting their anticipation for the kill."

She shook her head. "That doesn't square, Myles. Everything we know about the Scaleys indicates they're cold and functional. Emotion of any kind has no place."

"Stella," George whispered, "we know so little about them. Beneath all those blue scales, who knows what we'll find?"

She frowned. "An invitation to dance. Have we ever received one before?"

Sloan shrugged. "They've chased and boarded us a few times, wiped us out." He pointed at the screens. "But we've never been invited on one of their ships."

"Their invitation might not be the same as ours," Jason's voice said. "In my opinion, it's an offer to die brutally in hand-to-hand combat on board their ship. That may be a change to you, but it's not one I appreciate."

Stella rubbed the back of her neck. "You would advise we continue as before, and with over sixty percent of our shields down? Jason, think. You're better than whoever is at their helm, but do you really think you can win?"

Jason sighed, his exhalation an unfelt wind. "I can give them a damned tough fight." Then: "No. Damn it, I can't."

Stella nodded, and then looked at those on the bridge. After a moment, she patted Lee's slender shoulder and smiled at her nav and com officer. "What have we got to lose? Sloan, connect me to the ship's crew. I believe we're going to accept."

CHAPTER FIVE

As Stella expected, her announcement to the *Spaceranger's* crew was received with fear and dismay. But almost immediately she was heartened by another reaction, a frenetic eagerness to fight motivated by desperation and relief. After the tension of the Scaley assault, taking things into their own hands rather than just sitting by was cathartic. At the very least, it burned away the pent-up anxiety that threatened to destroy them.

Sipping coffee in an effort to give her decision some element of sanity, Stella watched the *Spaceranger's* docking bay on one of the screens. It was a hubbub of activity, of crew suiting up, securing helmets, checking side arms. She saw a dek-path of soldiers help each other with their distinctive blue suits. Biochemically conditioned to be empaths and reared together to think almost as one, they consisted half of men, half of women. All were heavily decorated and bore insignia designating the Emperor's Arm, the highest rank of combat-tested soldiers. Stella gazed at a patch showing Kolanera, the boy emperor-to-be, against the background of a burning lightning bolt.

Dear God, she thought, what have I done?

There were perhaps eighty crew in the docking area, with nearly three times that many suiting up in adjacent corridors. She had ordered it that way, throwing everyone with combat experience into the assault. If they were lost, the *Spaceranger's* personnel would be reduced to a skeleton crew, but then, of course, it wouldn't matter.

On a nearby screen, the enemy's boarding tube loomed. To Stella, it resembled a dark mouth. Next to her, George scowled.

"'Will you walk into my parlor?' said the spider to the fly,'" he murmured.

The reference meant nothing to her, but beside her, Lee Song shuddered as if he understood. She looked at him in sympathy. Barely twenty-one, the slender battle tech had never experienced combat before. He looked at her in return and managed a wan smile. "Don't worry about me, ser."

"I won't, Lee. I know you'll be fine."

Elsewhere, Sloan and Myles leaned intently over the command console, receiving data from other sectors of the ship as well as the docking bay, informing Stella periodically of the status of different departments. Sickbay was at code red, fully ready, and security was prepared to seal off decks One through Twenty-Three in case of invasion. It was all very efficient and strictly SOP, but one glance at the suppressed terror in Lee's eyes confirmed the hopelessness of it all. These were not rebels or pirates they were about to encounter, but the Scaleys, against whom no humans had ever prevailed.

I've got to believe. And we have to believe in ourselves.

And now, barely five minutes after she had given her order, the docking bay hatch lowered to meet the aliens' boarding tube and form a bridge between the ships. Would the Scaleys surprise them and charge through themselves, taking the battle to them?

No. Somehow she felt that it was an invitation. An invitation to the oldest dance of all, the dance of death.

The hatch was down now, and the Scaleys' boarding tube waited, a dark tunnel leading to-what?

She squared her shoulders, knowing they had no choice. "Patch me through," she said.

Lee clicked a switch. She stepped forward and raised her voice. "This is your commander. In the name of the Emperor, I order you to attack."

In the docking bay, the dek-path marched forward, followed by perhaps thirty other combat-tested troops. They all wore infra-red displays inside their helmets which reported back to Lee's battle monitors. From where Stella stood, she and her bridge crew could see and hear everything this vanguard attack force did, as well as monitor their vital signs. If need be, Lee could even override the suits' automatic servos and take control.

But the system had its limitations. One was that most soldiers were hidden from view once they disappeared down the boarding tube-that is, unless they were caught in the advance guard's displays.

"Wish our battle station could process them all," Stella said.

"Wouldn't help, ser," Lee said. "Even current tech can't make the fast decisions needed for one soldier, let alone three hundred. There's still no substitute for an alert, trained human brain on the scene." He sighed. "Let's just hope their displays continue to work. We don't know what that ship is made of."

Suddenly those at the front of the attack force began to sing.

Stella didn't recognize it at first, but as the chorus spread back over the rest of the crew in the docking bay, the words became clear. Listening to them, she felt her eyes moisten.

Raise every voice and heart

That we true soldiers play our part....

The leaders entered the tube now, and their voices echoed like thunder as they advanced. Watching the monitors, she saw soldier after soldier wade forward into darkness, enclosed by curving walls on both sides.

Our Emperor's will shall be our way,

To serve and die-glorious pay!

Plasma jets and laser pistols appeared in their soldiers' arms as the tube lightened. It was getting brighter now. Soon...

Though comrades perish at our side,

We shall fight on bravely-not abide...

Closer and closer, the light of the alien ship loomed. And still they sang, sang even as they entered the vessel and started down a stark white corridor, the first view ever of what was inside a Scaley ship.

The foe who scorns His sacred crown.

We strike him boldly-cast him...

And suddenly the enemy was there, emerging from side corridors ten meters ahead. They waited, larger and taller than the humans, suited and helmeted and gripping firearms which weren't lasers or plasma jets or even driven-mass-projectile weapons but something else, something which tore open duroplast armor like tin and secreted a gas which brought almost instant death. Stella remembered the twisted, distorted faces of corpses that had fallen before it, bulging eyes that had almost burst from their sockets.

There was no singing now, only wary silence as her crew studied the Scaleys. Beside her, George's breath rasped. He clenched his hands.

As if on cue, they sprang at each other, Human against Scaley, Scaley against Human. Scanning the monitors, Stella saw a member of the dek-path fire at a Scaley, duck a shrill burst of fire in return, and close to grapple hand-to-hand. The Scaley picked him up like a child and smashed him against the wall. Smashed again and again.

Stella glanced at another display, and another. They all showed overlapping views of action and transmitted the strident sounds and cries of battle, and as she watched, she admired Lee's ability to coordinate all the channels and respond to individual situations. "Number Three, right behind you!" Lee barked, and a soldier spun, drilling a Scaley who had been about to fire. Nudging George, Stella backed away from the monitors, for there was only room for Lee at the controls.

"Number seven," he snapped, "left!", and the soldier whirled, spraying the enemy and receiving a blast in return almost at pointblank range.

On the displays, fighting was at such close quarters, firearms were rarely used. But Stella saw a Scaley's beam sear a soldier's breastplate and the soldier's eyes roll up in agony as gas flooded his helmet. She looked at a different screen.

One Scaley hurled a soldier against a wall, and then did the same with another. A nimble human climbed astride his back and was ripped off, his neck broken by a powerful twist of the alien's hands. For a moment, Stella saw the Scaley's delicate, beautiful face through its faceplate. It was as cold and dispassionate as a distant moon.

Two soldiers held a Scaley down while a third burned its helmet to pieces. Most of the time, though, the enemy destroyed her crew. Human faces screamed behind their faceplates, and their suits were savagely punctured. Weapons dropped from their hands or speared at the ceiling as they collapsed, clutching triggers in death-grips.

Within minutes, most of the *Spaceranger's* attack forces were down. Some who fought on were surrounded and quickly dispatched. From one vid display lying against the floor, Stella caught glimpses of survivors fleeing deeper into the ship. Some looked back in terror as the aliens pursued them.

It was carnage, slaughter, massacre. And one glance at her chronex confirmed it had all occurred in less than five minutes.

Turning, Stella went to the wall next to the refreshment panel and keyed open her locker. Ignoring the gaudy, tricorn Commander's hat which hung on a hook, she removed the combat suit below it and began to strip.

"What are you doing?" George said.

She lay down, slid inside, and rose. The thick duroplast armor contributed most of the suit's weight, and with the helmet added, many soldiers found themselves burdened and slow even with practice. Stella didn't. She activated her servos, zipped herself in and sealed. Then she took her helmet from the locker's shelf.

"Stella, don't!" Jason's voice echoed urgently throughout the bridge. "It's stupid, you can't go. You'll be killed!"

We'll all be killed if I don't even try, she thought. And you'll be killed too, Jason, with your beautiful body and generous heart. If I don't do something, I will never share your passion for life and explore your vital, far-reaching spirit. Don't you see? For your sake, and mine, and for all the others, I at least have to try to fight back.

She tore her eyes from her Commander's hat, symbol of power and responsibility, and shut the locker. No time for such thoughts. Lifting her head sharply, she summoned George. "Come here, George. I need you to attach my comm leads."

George lumbered forward. "He's right, this is crazy. You will get yourself killed! What do you hope to achieve?"

She waved her hand at the displays. "We're finished, can't you see that? I have to do something. I've got to try."

"Try? What for?" George's bearded face scrunched up as if he were about to cry. "Stella, you can't go. You're our commander!"

She glanced at Sloan, who, like Myles, stood frozen at the console. "If I don't return, Sloan, you're in command. That is, if there's anything left."

George reached to stop her; she swatted his hand away. "Damn it, can you think of another way?"

He flinched, his spurned hand suspended between them. "No, you're..." He nodded. "Very well, then."

Quickly, he opened his locker and yanked out a suit. "Come on," he shouted as he stripped, "we don't have much time!"

Stella blinked. "What the hell do you think you're doing?"

"Isn't it obvious?" George flopped on his broad back as Sloan and Myles moved forward and helped him slip into his suit.

"I'm ordering you to stay," Stella said. "That's a direct order."

"Tell you what you can do," George grunted as Sloan helped his right hand into an arm. "You can court-martial me for insubordination right here on the bridge if you like. Or put me on report."

She clutched her helmet, remembering Jack Faust at the turbine building, a man who hadn't liked orders. "I can stop you," she warned.

George ignored the threat. "You said it yourself," he wheezed as Sloan helped him to his feet. "We're finished. What the hell difference does it make what we do?"

Stella fumbled for a response as Myles took her helmet and placed it on her head. Gently, he reached inside her open faceplate to connect the comm leads.

Lee Song watched with stricken eyes from his station of death. Stella forced a smile and raised her thumb in a victory sign.

"Don't worry, I'll be back."

Myles patted her shoulder and before she knew it, she and George were moving to the lift tube with plasma jets in their hands. They entered it and George keyed the panel.

"You're a damned fool," she said. "You're a pill peddler, a middle-aged brain washer. What the hell do you know about fighting? You'll get us both killed."

"I've had more hand-to-hand than you. Check your compfiles if you like. As a young man, I graduated from the warriors' guild. Believe me; I killed my fair share of rebs before I saw the error of my ways."

"Even if that's true, I don't want you with me."

"Stella," he said gently. "It's not your fault."

His words ripped through her. She gazed blankly through the transparent door of the tube as deck after deck passed by.

"I'm the one who was in command when it happened." She shut her eyes, thinking of the brave crew she had sent to their deaths. In her mind she saw the punctured suits, the screaming faces.

A metal hand took hers. "There wasn't anything else you could do, and you know it." He sucked in his breath, glanced at the panel. "Only two more decks. I've got to say this. I've been meaning to ever since…"

But they had reached the docking bay, and the door opened. Stella exited first, followed by George. "Stella," he shouted, "I've got to tell you something! I tried to do it earlier at the meeting."

She glanced over her shoulder. "No time. Tell me later if we make it." *And if we make it, maybe I'll tell Jason how much I've come to care about him. How much I think about him even when I'm not alone.*

She marched across the docking bay, which was tinged by the smell of blood and medicines she couldn't identify. Several soldiers had escaped the alien vessel and were being attended by medtechs. Stella passed them, heading straight toward the dark mouth of the Scaleys' boarding tube.

"Commander, are you here?"

She turned, scanning their faces and seeing looks of amazement among the dazed, ravaged expressions. She gripped her plasma jet, held it up for all to see.

"Yes, I am here," she shouted. "Are you with me, comrades?"

A few rose to their feet. A man with a bloody shoulder pushed aside his gutted suit and tottered upright. "You're going in there?"

"Both of us are," George rumbled.

His confirmation brought more of them to their feet, some of whom she recognized. Nick Flynn, a gunnery specialist, stepped forward. He had been a phenomenal runner in the last

Olympiad. Brett Duvall joined him, a soft-featured woman with extensive combat experience.

"Are you with me, comrades?" Stella shouted again.

This time a frail chorus answered. More soldiers rose.

Teeth clenched, Stella closed and sealed her faceplate. Then she turned and led her followers into the alien ship.

CHAPTER SIX

The boarding tube surface felt dead and heavy beneath Stella's feet as she advanced into darkness which her photocell eyes soon lightened into day. Behind her the others followed, guided by their suits' optics.

As she moved, she felt a new concern. Why had George chosen to come with her? It seemed incredible when she stopped to think about it. She knew she shouldn't consider such doubts now, but she had suspected him of treason, and at the moment he was right behind her.

Jason she had suspected too, of instability. How wrong she had been to confuse his passion for paranoia! For the first time, she was glad he was not in his body, for she had no doubt he would have insisted on accompanying her to a horrible, inevitable death.

She gripped the plasma jet, forcing herself to concentrate only on the wide corridor ahead. White, featureless walls enclosed her. Below, the floor was blue metal of some sort which possessed a dull glow, as if a deep and distant fire lurked in its depths.

I'm in the aliens' ship, she thought. Actually in it.

The bodies covering the floor proved this was not a fantasy. There had to be hundreds of them, and she moaned at the torn and mangled corpses that stretched for fifty or sixty meters before her. Who knew how many more of her crew had retreated deeper into the ship only to perish, like those she had seen fleeing?

Grimly, she glanced behind her. Besides George, there were eight others, which meant their group totaled ten. Ten against how many thousands?

"Movement at nine o'clock," Lee's voice whispered in her ear.

She turned her head and saw that one of her own soldiers was making a feeble attempt to catch her attention. He lay on the floor, half covered by dead bodies. As she watched, his hand stirred, struggled up a few centimeters, then fell to the floor. Behind his faceplate, pale lips pleaded.

She moved cautiously forward, followed by the others. When she reached him, his hand crawled toward her foot. She stepped aside, gazing down into his desperate, pain-filled eyes.

We'll be back, she mouthed so he could see. But the hand labored toward her again, a stricken animal that knew only its agony.

WE'LL BE BACK. I PROMISE!

The hand continued, uncomforted by her assurance. The man's gaze bore dinto hers—begging, beseeching.

She felt George gently pull her arm. Turning, she nodded at him and continued. Much as she wanted, they couldn't afford to help the soldier or any others that might be alive. At least not now.

The bodies stretched before her, a gory landscape of human rubble. At some points they were packed so close that she and the others had to proceed slowly while stepping over crew who might still be alive. Sometimes, no matter how careful they were, it was necessary to force their way, to squeeze past twisted metal and faces grotesquely distorted by the Scaleys' death gas. Here, an entire arm had been burned off, the armor encasing it seemingly as fragile as an eggshell. There, a soldier's chest was a hollow, gaping ruin. Moving on, Stella made the mistake of meeting the eyes of a dead man she knew who had a wife and two children. She glanced away and pressed forward.

Not all the bodies were human, of course. A small minority were the enemy. Even in the ten minutes or so since they had died, their faces had come to display the same quick deterioration of the few aliens the Empire had captured. Most were little more than mush, their features dissolving even as she watched.

Eventually she reached a comparatively clear area near the first of the side corridors from which the Scaleys had emerged. She leaned against the wall and peered quickly around it.

Twenty-five meters away stood a group of Scaleys in glittering black armor.

The others joined her, keeping close to the wall just behind. "Commander," a voice whispered in her ear, "where's the enemy? Do you see any?"

"Yeah," Brett Duvall said. "This place should be packed."

She looked at them. "There's about ten of them twenty-five meters down the corridor," she said.

George's eyes widened. "What are they doing?"

She risked another glance, turned back. "Just looking at each other."

"That's freakin' queer," Brett said, her lips a bloodless slash behind her faceplate.

"Yes, it is," Stella said. Puzzled, she looked down the vacant corridor ahead of them. Come to think of it, it was freakin' queer. The Scaley ship was still joined to hers, and not only hadn't the enemy attempted to invade the *Spaceranger*, but they had left this corridor completely unprotected. There were no guards, no...

Surveillance?

She looked for cameras, but didn't see any. That meant nothing. Any race that could park their ship at the lip of a singularity like it was a docking station was capable of anything. Even of seeing through walls.

Carefully, she took another glance. They were still there.

Stella looked at her crew-at George, Nick, Brett and the others. She gripped her plasma jet, deciding.

"I'm going to charge 'em," she said. "The rest of you follow fast as you can."

"Are you crazy?" George and Brett hissed simultaneously. Nick moved up to her. "Ser, why don't you let me do it? I took first place at the Olympiad."

"Thanks, Nick," she said. "But with all due respect, you're not as fast as me."

Brett stepped closer. "Ser, why don't we step out and just burn them from here? It's safer, more efficient!"

"What if we miss just one and it runs and alerts the others?" Stella shook her head. "No, it's got to be clean or it's no good. We've got to kill them all." She gripped Brett's shoulder. "I'll try to stun them, catch them unprepared. The rest of you burn them when you get close."

Brett's face twitched. "It's twenty-five meters-you said so yourself! There's no way you can reach those Scaleheads without them hearing you. Our suits aren't exactly nightgowns, you know. Hell, they'll probably hear you soon as you step 'round that corner."

Stella smiled. "If I run fast enough, maybe it won't matter."

Brett's face was doing interesting things. "Run? You'd have to be shot out of a plasma tube to have a chance. Even you can't move that fast."

"Then you'll finish the job for me, all right?"

Her voice was hard, ending debate. She could tell from their faces they knew she meant it.

Having terminated the discussion, she saw that they not only accepted her decision but were warming to its execution. Brett licked her lips in anticipation. George, whom she had doubted and doubted again, gave her a hard grin. "I'll be right behind you, Stella." The others were preparing themselves, checking weapons and shifting their weight. It was, Stella thought, as if there came a time when even the near certainty of death was better than doing nothing.

She glanced around the corner and secured her weapon in her bracket holster.

"See you in hell," she said with a smile, and whispered a prayer.

Then she was off, the servos at heel, calf, thigh and elsewhere quickening the augmented ability of her cyborg body. Arrowed forward, she drove herself hard, striving for every scintilla of speed to reach them before they heard her and carved her apart.

She saw the first Scaley turn and then another, saw their hands reach for their weapons as she drove herself still harder. Their weapons rose and she left the floor, twisting her body as she shot out her foot with all her strength. It caught the first Scaley flush on the helmet and drove it back against the wall, reducing its skull to pulp. She landed and sprang up; struck aside a weapon whose fire grazed her helmet. Again she charged, a blur of movement.

Rage blazed within her, rage at her crew dead, at all the comrades' lives so senselessly slaughtered, and she seized a Scaley and cast it up against the wall. She whirled, seized another and dashed it to the floor, smashing it once twice three times to pieces inside its suit. Then she straightened and reached for her weapon.

A Scaley arm circled her neck from behind, pulling her off-balance as another aimed its weapon directly at her. Blinding light struck her chest and carved upward, nicking her faceplate. Her helmet flooded with gas.

Then a hand seized the arm of the alien with the weapon while another clamped about its throat from behind. George. She saw the barrel tilt upward, its beam impaling the ceiling as the psyche-physician fought to wrest the weapon free.

She had no time to watch. The rest of her crew arrived and the corridor erupted with laser and plasma fire. She rammed her elbow back into the Scaley holding her and whipped around, freeing herself.

She faced it.

Clutching its side, the Scaley's hand shot toward its side arm, faster by far than any normal human. Stella caught its hand midway and stepped forward, a silent snarl twisting her lips as she peered through the gas. Slowly, she raised the alien's hand before its face.

And crushed it.

The Scaley's face contorted, its toothless mouth gaping. So you can feel pain, she thought, and hurled it viciously against the wall.

She whirled, just in time to see Brett's beam impale a Scaley's faceplate. Five of her crew, she saw, were down, but two others had cornered a Scaley and were stitching a line of white fire up both sides.

That left George, who had long since renounced being a soldier. He grappled with the Scaley, still trying to force the weapon from its grip. Stella's sonic cleaners had cleared most of the gas from her helmet; the rest had seeped through her cracked faceplate. She could see clearly now and raised her plasma jet, aiming at the alien's chest.

"No," Brett said. She pressed her hand against Stella's arm. "Let him do it."

Stella frowned. It made no sense. Just one long pull of her trigger and the Scaley would be worm meat. She couldn't risk...

Another member of her crew approached, a man named Morner who was as young as Lee. "Please, ser," he said. "Let Dr. Darron finish it."

She glanced up and down the corridor, knowing she should fire. If the alien started to win, she would shoot.

Equally massive, George and his opponent struggled-a microcosm, perhaps, of the entire Scaley-Human war? But that was absurd. No human who had not been technologically enhanced could prevail against a Scaley, exceed its strength and endurance.

George's face had darkened to purple behind his faceplate. Grunting, he spun the alien, trying to dislodge its grip, but his foe would not give ground. Then, Stella saw that George was slowly, slowly bending the weapon back toward the Scaley's face. Millimeter by millimeter it turned, trembling in both their hands. His features a rictus of effort, George forced the barrel back toward the other's head till it pointed at the side of its helmet.

A beam lanced out, smashing the alien's faceplate, devouring its face. With a grunt, the Scaley relinquished its grip and collapsed to the floor.

A moment later George joined it, sliding slowly down the wall in exhaustion Stella feared might lead to a heart attack. Though George was only a few years older than she, he was soft, not used to exertion. She watched him sit gasping against the wall, and then glanced again up and down the corridor. Incredibly, their clash here had drawn no response. Where was the enemy? Were they in a bloody ghost ship?

Despite the danger, Brett seemed ecstatic. "Commander! Goddamnit, you were right to rush them. Do you know what we've done?" She gulped. "We've...we've beat them! For the first time ever, we've mother-humped the freakin' bastards!"

Stella felt less exalted. The five dead comrades on the floor had perished in a minor skirmish, not Armageddon. Turning, she saw that the young soldier was gaping at her.

"What is it, Morner?"

He pointed. "Ser, your helmet's broke. I saw gas go in."

"So?"

"It's Scaley death gas, ser. If you take just one small whiff, you're dead!"

"Yeah? Well, I'm different, soldier." She shook her plasma jet, knowing she should do something. They couldn't just stand here. But it all seemed so unreal. Here they were, the first humans ever to breach an alien ship and walk its unknown corridors, and she found herself distracted by a growing itch low down on her left thigh, on the human part of her. At that moment she would have given nine kingdoms just to scratch it.

No. She had to get her thoughts straight, make a plan.

"You, Brett," she said. "Take Morner and recon the far corridor up toward the bow. Comm us on channel B." She motioned at a corridor just a few meters away that appeared to run down the middle of the ship. "Nick and I will take this one and head the same way. Keep in contact. Let us know if you find anything."

Nick moved forward. "We're splitting up? What about Dr. Darron?"

She studied George, whose color had improved only slightly. "Dr. Darron will stay here. He's had enough. We'll collect him when we come back." She gripped her weapon, knowing they probably wouldn't be able to return. "That makes two groups of two apiece," she said. "I figure it'll improve our chances."

"What do you mean, I've 'had enough'?" Against the wall, George was struggling to his feet. He swayed briefly, and then braced himself. "I'm going."

She eyed him skeptically. "You sure? You look pretty beat."

"Hell, yes, I'm sure. I'm the doc, remember? I'm fine."

She nodded. "All right, you can come with me. Now come on, we've got to go."

"I've got an idea," George said. He pointed at the enemy's bodies. "These fellows are pretty big. What say I swap suits with one?"

Brett was the first to get it. "You could be a semblant, mix with the Scaleys!"

George stooped over a corpse. "I prefer to call it a 'wild card,' something that adds a little interest, an extra factor." He began struggling with the corpse's helmet. "C'mon and help before it turns to muck inside."

Brett flashed her a look. "Ser?"

George's jaw hardened. He continued to wrench at the corpse's black suit.

She hesitated. "This is crazy. What do you hope to accomplish? If they find out…"

George yanked the helmet free. "Don't you think they already know? I'm just trying to throw a monkey wrench into their plans."

She frowned, not knowing what a 'monkey wrench' was. "All right," she said. George took his suit's breather tube from the med compartment, opened his faceplate, and inserted the tube between his lips. Then he started to remove his armor. Along with the others, Stella moved forward to help him.

They solved the sealing apparatus and pulled the already softening corpse from the suit. A minute more passed as they maneuvered George back and forth so he could squirm and force himself inside. Another thirty seconds. The red numbers changed swiftly on Stella's inside helmet cronex as she worked, knowing that they had to hurry, that they must move.

Two minutes, ten seconds…two minutes, twenty…

At two and a half minutes, they hauled George upright and put on the helmet. He moved tentatively around, testing the suit. Its black surface flashed with light.

"How is it, Dr. Darron?" Morner said.

George grunted. "A bit snug but it's lighter than ours. Feels better too." He placed the breather tube between his lips, then closed the faceplate and sealed it. "Helmet's not too different from ours. Say, can you still hear me?"

They nodded, answered yes.

"Huh. So they've got audio. Guess the Scaleys do communicate with each other. That's an interesting fact to take back to Command."

George moved around some more, then returned to his suit and took a syringe of some kind from its med compartment. He rose with it in his hand and went to the weapon he had fought so fiercely for. Stooping, he picked it up.

"Hey," he said, "their servos are smooth. Don't overkick like ours." He examined the weapon, turning it in his hands. "Might as well make the disguise complete, right? To quote an old saying, 'When in Rome, do as the Romans do.'"

"You know, George," Stella said, "I'm getting pretty fricked at your old sayings."

George winked, his eyes gleaming. Suddenly Stella found herself staring at a stranger, or perhaps the George Darron who had graduated from the warriors' guild before he discovered he had no taste for death. He marched past her as if he had been born in the alien's suit.

"Hey," Nick said, "you're headed the wrong way. That's the stern you're going to."

George turned. "I'm an extra variable, I hope. A bit of the unpredictable. It's a variation on something I remember from the guild. An ancient countryman of yours from Terra once said, *'Divide et impera,'* which means, 'Divide and rule.'"

He waved his hand and left, striding quickly toward the stern.

"All right," Stella snapped, "let's go!"

Brett and Morner immediately headed for the far corridor on the other side of the ship. She lifted her weapon, and then motioned Nick into the middle corridor. It appeared to be similar to the one they'd entered by, about six meters wide with a floor of blue metal.

She advanced carefully down the right side, alert for attack, for a trap of some kind. Nick took the left side and turned into what looked like a large alcove. Seeing colored lights fluctuate and shift, Stella decided to investigate with him.

"Uh, Commander," Lee's voice said in her ear, "I don't think you should go there."

"Why not?" she said.

"It's...I'm looking at it through Nick's vid. He..."

In the alcove, Nick's body had twisted as if he were trying to break away from something. She heard him shout, then moan and babble gibberish. In her earphones, Lee's voice faltered. "D-Don't go there, ser. It's...Oh my dear sweeeeet God. Such b-beautiful lights and patterns!"

Ignoring the warning, she rushed to free Nick from whatever held him. When she reached his side, his face seemed swathed in ecstasy.

"Stella, this is Sloan. Lee is hypnotized. Be careful. Do not look at the thing! It's got a narcotic effect of some kind."

Nick's face bore eloquent testimony to the truth of Sloan's words. Clearly, he was in rapture, and Stella remembered the expressions of fanatic, 'New Son' worshippers she had seen. Compared to Nick, they seemed almost rational.

"Don't worry, Nick," she said. "I'll get you out."

She reached for him, keeping her eyes averted from whatever had bewitched him, and felt something caress the corner of her eye. Despite her resolve, she felt her head turn. Before her glowed a gigantic transparent globe containing multi-colored fluids which swayed and flowed and rippled back and forth, back and forth. She tried to turn away but somehow her head wouldn't move.

As her med unit pumped stimulants into her system in a massive effort to combat what registered as a deepening stupor, Sloan's voice shouted in her ear. Gradually, though, its pleas grew ever more distant, ever more unreal, as if the voice itself belonged to a realm infinitely unrelated to hers. And now the swaying, rippling, flowing, ever-changing waters of eternity brought forth miracles of creation from their womb, silvery-gold tesseracts of incarnate form and rectangles that were circles and a polygon with a million sides which she could actually count.

"COMMANDER, SNAP OUT OF IT!"

The cry was a crimson helix, a flaming sword, then a ripple of myriad wonders which undulated toward her in a dream which had been her own even when she had been million-year-old carbon spewed forth from the monobloc that had blossomed into creation. She saw the ripple unfold and beckon at her feet in a kaleidoscope of glorious, sublime, and ineffable patterns, opening endlessly like a cosmic flower of which she herself was the bud. The ripple retreated and returned, extending an ambrosia-scented crystal column even as some feeble voice that could not possibly have any relation to her, moaned "no" over and over again in her soul. Waving it aside, she laughed and stepped lightly onto the shining pedestal, letting it waft her to eternity as she waited to be born.

CHAPTER SEVEN

Paradise.

It was all senses rolled into one, and more, a synesthesia of the mind. Her satin skin sang, and the wind's scent was exquisite green music caressing her eyelids. She soared and crested on a wave of sublime contentment, lilac-tinged visions flavoring her mouth. And always, always, her glorious destiny lay just ahead. She knew that soon she would see it, a splendor beyond all others.

Something jarred her universe, and then jarred it again. The intricate facets of her jeweled inner sun developed a hairline crack. Jarred again, and the warm shimmering spray turned cold upon her skin. Then something, a hand, appeared and rapped against her helmet as another hand unsealed and opened her faceplate. A face swam into focus-black and aquiline, the eyes dark shining pools in which she saw...herself.

"Commander, wake up! We've got to move!"

"I..." Her lips felt coated with gum, as if she'd slept a thousand years. "What hap...?"

"You looked at that thing! Almost got me too but I caught on. Come on now, up!"

She felt herself pulled into a sitting position. The soldier, whose blue armor indicated he belonged to the dek-path, slipped her weapon into her holster and patted her armored shoulder. "Are you all right? Stay here, ser, while I try to rouse him. And please don't turn around. You don't want to look at it again."

She nodded, staring dully down at blue metal and infinite depths that...

Don't think of it or it'll happen again. But her entire being yearned for half-remembered ecstasies which faded even as she tried to recapture them. Such a divine dream. How could it hurt to take just one look?

NO.

She forced herself to rise, the part of her that was flesh prickling with pins and needles. How long had she been under? Keeping her back to the deadly lure, she checked her helmet cronex. Oh God, she'd lost twenty minutes!

A light lit on her vid. She pressed a button with her chin, accessing channel B.

"Commander?"

She opened her lips, wet them. "McMasters here."

"Thank God you are!" Brett's sharp voice responded. "I've called you twice but you didn't answer."

"There was...some trouble," Stella said, dimly hearing the soldier work on Nick behind her. "I'm all right now. We both are."

"Good. Ser, we're in some kind of utility room, maybe twenty meters aft of the bow. There's been Scaley activity."

"Activity?"

"Yes. Dozens of them, marchin' up to the bow. Something's up there, ser. I feel it. Have they marched your way too?"

"I'm not sure."

A brief pause. "Not sure? What do-"

"Never mind. Just don't look at any bright light displays, all right? They've got some kind of device that does odd things, mucks up your mind."

"Device? What do you mean?"

"There's no time to explain. Just do as I say: don't look at it."

"Yes, Commander."

"Good. Report back in ten minutes. Out."

Pressing the button with her chin again, she heard Nick's dazed voice on the other channel as the soldier helped him up. Taking Stella's arm, he steered them both toward the bow.

And not a moment too soon, for the floor was vibrating. Footsteps coming their way! She searched for a place to hide, but there was nothing, only clear, featureless walls and a floor that resonated with the enemy's approach.

She and the man who had rescued them saw it at the same time: an oval portal the same color as the wall, so easy to miss. Where did it lead? What if it were locked? Knowing they had no choice, she darted to it. Spotting a recessed handle, she turned it left, then right.

It was locked.

The enemy's footsteps echoed like thunder now. She glanced behind, seeing the black soldier's taut, alert face as he supported Nick under one arm. She turned back, braced herself.

The handle resisted, and then turned with a sharp crack. Slipping inside, she held the door open as they entered, then closed it.

They waited in a large dim chamber as the footsteps rose to a crescendo.

Through a wide slit in the door, they could see the corridor. At first it was empty. Then the Scaleys marched past in three neat rows, their heads held to the front as they moved with a precision no humans could match. Finally they were gone, their sound fading.

"I'll be a Scaley whore's mama," the black soldier whispered.

Stella looked up at him. "Which one are you?"

"Thunderheart, ser."

"I see. The others?"

He dropped his eyes. "Dead."

"I'm sorry," she said. "How do you know? Did you…" She let the sentence die.

"I just know," Thunderheart told her. "I feel it. Emperor's Arm. Silverwing, Launchblast, Spaceleaper and all the others. They're gone. The Scaleys spilled their souls' blood."

"My sympathy, Thunderheart," she said softly. As the Empire's most elite society of soldiers, The Emperor's Arm made service to the Sovereign a fierce, semi-mystical calling that incorporated equal parts ascetic self-denial and grueling, constant practice of arcane martial arts. Any of them would feel blessed to lay down their lives for the boy emperor and that to lose even one in combat was tragic. But to lose nine…

Stella sighed. What must it be like to lose nine of your

brothers and sisters, siblings conditioned since infancy to be as close as your own heartbeat? To be alone for the first time with no empathetic web to connect you to your family and define your selfhood? She glanced away, feeling a wave of shame. This soldier had lost so much, and yet, unlike her, he hadn't been conquered by a gaudy booby trap. Instead, he had saved those who were.

"How are you, Nick?" she ventured, avoiding Thunderheart's eyes.

"Much better, ser." His cheek twitched. "I mucked up."

"So did I. Let's forget it," she said.

"Commander," Thunderheart said. "The walls."

They were lightening. Or rather, darkening and lightening at the same time. Black interstellar reaches appeared, glittering with stars. And something was rising from the middle of the floor! Her plasma jet leapt into her hand as Thunderheart and Nick less quickly followed suit.

The column rose and unfolded, expanding throughout the chamber. Spheres of different sizes, different hues assumed orbits about a large central globe.

An orrery.

"What is it?" Nick said.

"Humanity's solar system," Thunderheart said, confirming Stella's suspicion. He pointed. "I think that one's Terra."

Nick squinted. "What's it for?"

The orrery changed. They watched as the sun, planets, and moons collapsed and dwindled toward the center. The gulf between the stars appeared, then Alpha Centauri and other bodies. More reaches swept by, leading in time to a blazing pinpoint situated before the black speck of a singularity.

"My God," Nick whispered, "that's us!"

"I think they're doing it for our benefit," Stella said.

"Benefit, hell," Thunderheart snarled. "They're playing with us. They know we're in here."

George said as much, Stella thought, wondering where he was. Seeing a light flash on her vid, she nudged the channel button with her chin.

"Commander," Brett's voice said, "we're still bunkered

down. The last Scaleys just passed. Traffic's been heavy."

"Read you clear," Stella answered. "What do you plan?"

"Thought as long as it's clear we'd recon up to the bow," Brett said. "They haven't noticed us yet and-"

The channel went dead.

Great, Stella thought. An instant later another voice came on, one tinged with panic.

"Stella, what happened to them? Lee's still a bit dazed."

"Don't know, Sloan," she said. "Just try to relax." She accessed channel A again. "Looks like they got them," she told her crew. "Their comm went dead."

Thunderheart began to swear softly, uttering imprecations in which Stella heard more obscenely imaginative observations about Scaleys and their body parts than she had ever thought possible. After an especially pungent phrase, she raised her hand.

"Enough. Okay, they know we're here, and they're biding their time. Let's try to do the same, shall we?"

Discipline settled in Thunderheart's eyes as the trained warrior returned. "Yes, my Commander."

Nick gestured past him. "Look."

The walls were changing again. They saw stars approach and vanish, approach and vanish as some unseen camera sped forward, traveling ever faster until light-years swept by in seconds. Red dwarves and white giants, quasars and nebulae passed, thousands of light-years now, all of it rushing so fast the eye could no longer follow.

Finally, at some great distance from them, the camera started to slow. Soon, they could see discrete solar systems, planets with continents and polar caps. Slower and slower they went, until...

A planet approached, and even from outer space they could tell it was raped and ravaged, cold and utterly lifeless. As they grew closer, they could see winds tear across its pitted sienna surface.

"Maybe that's where they live, or used to," Nick whispered in awe.

"Hope it's not an invitation," Stella said. "If it is, I'll pass."

There was a knock behind them.

They whirled, plasma jets trained on the door whose lock she had broken.

Slowly it opened, opened wider and wider as the chamber lightened. Stella waited, listening to the quiet, immutable beating of her heart.

A Scaley stood in the doorway, unsuited and unarmed. It held out its hand to them and started to sing.

Beautiful sounds enveloped them, notes melodious and pure and joyful. Notes that could stir the heart, make even a monster cry.

And Thunderheart burned it to rubble, and then forged past its crumbled remains into the corridor. They followed him, only to see other aliens waiting, all of them suited and armed. Thunderheart spun to meet them.

Stella caught his weapon. "No. Holster it." She looked at Nick. "You too."

Nick obeyed, but Thunderheart froze. "Holster my weapon, ser?"

Stella holstered her own. "Sometimes resistance is pointless, soldier."

He looked at his plasma jet, and then at the Scaleys, who stood motionless. How hard it must be to obey her when all his training had been devoted to killing the enemy, the same despised enemy that had just slain his brothers and sisters. To meekly lay down his weapon when he could take a Scaley or two with him must seem incredible, the height of folly and even treason. But resistance would only lead to their deaths and accomplish nothing.

Or was she wrong? At least Thunderheart's way would mean they died with honor and covered with enemy blood. What point could there be in surrendering?

Changing her mind, she opened her mouth to give a new order, but Thunderheart holstered his plasma jet. "Yes, Commander," he said.

Moving in, the Scaleys took their weapons and nudged them toward the bow. As they walked, Thunderheart's glances stung her conscience. She could almost hear his thoughts. *We surrendered like cowards when we could still fight. I saved you for THIS.* No, that was guilt speaking, for she knew Thunderheart was sworn never to question his superiors. What his looks signified was a question: What do you know that I don't that made you surrender?

She didn't know what to say and had only a vague feeling this was the wiser course. A commander shouldn't give an order on such a flimsy basis, should she?

Sloan's voice came through her earplugs. "Commander."

She sighed. "Pray for us, Sloan. It's too late to change my mind."

She could almost see his homely face scrunch with emotion. "God bless you, ser."

Stella recalled Sloan's statement that their 'caste-ridden empire' prevented poor and enlisted personnel from becoming commanders, never giving them a chance despite their qualifications. "For the record," she answered, "you were wise not to apply for this job. It's no tea-party, Sloan."

"Yes, ser. We're tracking you well," he said, obviously trying to find something positive. "We have a complete record of everything you've seen and heard on their ship. It should keep our experts busy for months."

A sound rose from somewhere. Her imagination? Audio feedback? It was coming from ahead of her, from rows of Scaleys standing against the wall on both sides of the corridor before what must be the bow. They were-there was no other word for it-singing.

Nick glanced at her in astonishment. Even Thunderheart's grim features looked puzzled.

"Stella," Sloan murmured, "what the bloody hell are they doing?"

She remembered Brett saying that she felt something was up there in the bow and keyed the volume louder so he could hear over the Scaleys' voices. "You know something, Sloan? We've given you a nice guided tour so far, but I've got a feeling you ain't seen nothing yet. It's what's up ahead in the bow you should watch for."

Sloan didn't reply, not even when they reached the first

aliens and it became clear to her what their song was. Though she didn't understand the words, there was no doubt that the Scaleys sang of adoration and of worship, of prayer and transcendence. Their faces looked transfigured, as if it were a church or cathedral they paid homage in, and as if they were glorified and exalted by doing so.

A shiver branched through Stella's body. I wonder what's waiting at the altar, she thought, and found herself remembering Jason for the first time since she'd entered the alien ship. Despite her fear, she hoped he was watching.

Clutching her empty holster, she passed through an arched portal with her crew and finally entered the bow of the ship.

CHAPTER EIGHT

One step inside and Stella felt a strange sensation, one she tried desperately to define. Hesitantly, she took a second step. Another.

Alien.

The air breathed it, the walls screamed it. She blinked, marching slowly toward dazzling mist that hovered ten meters ahead.

ALIEN.

Not the alienness of the sand tarqt on V'on, a ferocious two-headed lizard that attacked from below with an ear-splitting hiss its victims heard too late. Stella had seen one in a game preserve, and though it was frightening, what she sensed now was of a different magnitude entirely. Her pulse rate seemed to double as she approached, though she knew her heart beat as placidly as ever.

A meter from the mist, she looked back at Nick and Thunderheart.

"Are you ready, comrades?"

Thunderheart nodded. "Lead on, Commander."

She turned back, wishing she had someone to follow. As she proceeded, wisps of shining, shimmering mist clung to her suit before drifting past. With every step, the sense of alienness, of wrongness intensified.

Abruptly white nothingness surrounded her, and she groped her way through a soundless void reminiscent of the godless gulfs between the stars. Except this mist emitted branching scintillations of light. They reminded her of the electrical impulses within a brain.

The concept made her gasp. Could she be in a giant brain? Was this what propelled the enemy's ships: enormous mentalities as insubstantial as mist?

"Stella," Sloan's voice rasped in her earplugs. "I can't see anything."

"Wait," she said. "I have a feeling the main attraction's just ahead."

Before her, rifts appeared in the mist. She saw Brett and Morner standing without their helmets. Instead of perishing without air, they were rapturously moving their lips.

Singing.

Their voices broke suddenly upon her, the dampening effect of the mist nullified by their proximity. Stella froze, her crew stopping behind her as they listened.

It was the same singing as the Scaleys, vibrant with praise and transcendent joy. Whatever the aliens had worshipped, so now did Brett and Morner. Both had been twisted, transformed into converts.

And the object of their adoration waited just meters away, on the other side of the mist.

She gritted her teeth and marched forward, anxious to confront whatever it was even if it meant her death. What could the thing be?

For a moment, after she reached Brett and Morner, she had eyes only for the rapt expressions on their faces. Even when they abruptly stopped singing, their faces remained ecstatic, transfigured by sublime joy. Stella sensed that their sworn duties were ashes to them, that they did not even exist. Whatever her two crew had become, it was something wholly new.

She wrenched her gaze away, faced the being before which they stood.

Her first impression was of an enormous, glistening white slug three meters high. Repugnant, yes, but not awesome. Surely it wasn't something to mesmerize and steal her comrades' allegiance. Then she noticed the thing was writhing and shifting, fluctuating like the hypnotic light display that had ensnared her mind. There were intricate contours on the massive form, whorls and designs created by its bulges and indentations. The configurations on this being were analogous to the forms she had seen in the light display and would have the same effect if she weren't careful.

"Don't look at it!" she shouted to her crewmen. "Take only glances or it'll put you under just like them." She pointed at Brett and Morner.

A slash opened midway up the lustrous, white, protean body. "You have learned," a voice issued from it. It was like Jason's voice, everywhere at once and all-pervasive. Yet at the same time it was unspeakably alien.

Stella stepped forward, Sloan's faint breathing in her ears. "Who are you? What do you want?"

"First, to see you. Remove your helmets and surrender them to your captors. As with your friends, you will find this area breathable."

She started to refuse but several Scaleys stepped forward. Looking at her crew, she nodded.

After they obeyed and found they could breathe, dark, malignant laughter swept over them. As if teasing, a giant, incongruously beautiful eye opened where before there had been only a slug-like skin. Stella gazed at it, and then shifted her eyes. Like a sun, this thing had to be looked at obliquely, and only in snatches.

"Excellent," the voice said as its body flowed and changed in restless currents. "You have profited from experience and alerted your companions. Unfortunately, you cannot assist my two acolytes." Its laugh unfolded like an evil flower. "Nor, I am afraid, can you aid your other companion."

A large holoscreen materialized in the air between them, showing one of the ship's corridors. In the foreground what looked like a Scaley warrior stood rigid before the pattern chamber that had ensnared Stella.

"My amusement, or what I call my 'imager,' has only a benign effect on me," it said, "but I am afraid it has entrapped your friend. It is a pity, for I enjoyed his contest with my pawn all the more because he prevailed." Something like a sigh passed through the bow, and Stella saw an enormous red tongue move within the alien's mouth. "I was hoping he would prove to be a more resourceful adversary, that in my little game, he would pose at least a theoretic challenge."

We're like flies to it, Stella thought. And it pulls off our wings for sport. We never even had a ghost of a chance.

"I did find your companion's efforts mildly diverting," the being continued. "Disguising himself in one of my pawn's suits was amusing, however futile. And he did score a few points."

The holoscreen's view changed to another corridor, showing several Scaley bodies strewn here and there. "My pawns are efficient fighters but lack the ability to distinguish an opponent armored just as they. Your friend's strategy caught them off guard. In truth, because he moved so quickly and blended in so well, I thought even I had lost him briefly."

Pawns...amusement...score a few points...strategy... Reviewing the enemy's words, Stella was struck by how much they suggested a "game," a word the alien had actually used. She glanced again at the figure frozen before the hypnotic pattern device, at George, who had been caught just as surely as she.

Only for George, she knew, there would be no rescue. No one would save him from the mind trap which this thing casually called an "amusement" and "imager."

"What do you want?" she said, her voice sounding feeble in the gigantic bow.

"What do you think I want?" it whispered.

She glanced about at the Scaleys, and then at Brett and Morner, who stood with expressions of vacant adoration. "I think you want to be worshipped," she said. "You want mindless robots to make you feel important."

Laughter broke upon them in dark, myriad waves. "And so you shall. Within a small spacetime indeed you shall all worship me as your God."

"NEVER!" Thunderheart stepped forward, shaking his fist at the huge, beautiful eye in the flowing slug-like body. "My oath is sworn to Emperor Kolanera, who holds my life in his trust. You are offal, excrement that deserves only to be despised!"

Laughter sounded again but this time, to Stella, it sounded angry. "Your group's primary and secondary languages are so odd to me, so thoroughly irrational. I find your species' interest in games and strategy fascinating and commendable, yet they coexist with such maudlin and functionless sentiments. Sentiments, of course, which have already proven hollow. As you see, your companions quickly found a new icon for their devotions."

It must be telepathic, able to absorb our knowledge without our even knowing. Stella reached out to stop Thunderheart, but he stepped closer to the alien's shifting, ever-changing form.

"Nothing in this universe could compel me to forswear my sacred trust," he said. "Kolanera is my Lord. To me, and to all his sworn liegemen, you are a base, cowardly, depraved maggot. You are Scaley shit spawned by a degenerate race of bastard mutants whose diseased sons cohabit with your blind whore-mothers to produce a plague of abominations."

The words went on, a rich, elaborate, and seemingly endless litany of epithets used by the Emperor's Arm to denounce the enemy and show their contempt. Thunderheart, in his anger, apparently did not see that this thing had created the Scaleys and was something entirely different.

When Thunderheart finally ceased speaking, the voice that answered seemed higher and less intense. It took Stella a moment to determine what the change meant, which was that for the first time, the alien sounded excited and expectant.

"So, you think that nothing can weaken your allegiance, compromise your lofty principles?" It laughed, a skin-crawling sound that filled Stella with a crushing sense of loss. She thought of her father's funeral, when she and her mother had watched him lowered into the ground forever.

As the Scaleys watched, Thunderheart took another step forward, halting less than a meter away. "Let me just touch you, and I'll show you what honor is."

A susurration, like midnight wind or ice on graves. "I am waiting," it said, its body for the moment still.

Thunderheart took another step. Reached out.

And then the alien's pearl-white skin changed, seemed to roil.

Kolanera appeared, his delicate, childish features forming out of nothing on the alien's body, a three-dimensional image as real as life itself. Thunderheart caught his breath in disbelief.

"My Lord!"

"He's stealing it from your mind!" Stella said. "Ignore it."

She stopped as the boy emperor's features broadened and aged. Within seconds he was a young man in his prime. Then he was middle-aged and growing older.

"Such a short-lived race," the alien said as Kolanera withered into senility, his wrinkled features pleading for help.

Then, from the holoscreen of the alien's skin, the aged emperor laughed in contempt at Thunderheart, a cruel, soundless cackle, and spat in his face.

"Is this what you worship?" the alien mocked in turn. "Your race has terms for such frail, ephemeral creatures. I believe one is 'mayfly.' You will find that my glorious wings are immortal."

It's insane, thinks it's divine, Stella thought. But with such power to transmute others' thoughts and transmit them from its own body, why shouldn't it think so?

"Touch me," the alien coaxed, its tone soft, mesmerizing.

Thunderheart complied, placing his hand directly upon the alien's bloated white surface.

"What are you hiding, my brave soldier who insults me so courageously?" it said. "What secret wound does my gallant warrior harbor even now that seeks to destroy him? Let us see more clearly."

The nacreous skin roiled and changed again. Thunderheart stared, and then snatched his hand away.

On the alien's skin, Thunderheart's empath-family fought and died. One by one, Stella saw their deaths reenacted just as Thunderheart had glimpsed or perhaps sensed them. An enemy beam carved through a faceplate, and a mouth silently screamed.

"What will you be, my empty orphan, without them?" the alien said. "Even now, you begin to wonder. That is your secret, deepest, growing fear, for you suspect that you are already nine-tenths dead."

"NO!"

On, or in the alien's body, a soldier fell to his knees. Stella saw him look up and recognized his features through his faceplate.

Thunderheart.

"Join me," the alien whispered, its voice a silken caress. "Swear allegiance to me and I shall give you a new closeness to humble and eclipse what you've lost. I promise you the stars and all the galaxies you can count. We'll see them together, Thunderheart."

Two meters before her, Thunderheart trembled. The enemy was using all its will against Thunderheart's in an effort to usurp it. Slowly, Thunderheart turned to look at her. He looked like a man poised on the brink of damnation.

As Sloan's tense breathing sounded in her ears from the *Spaceranger*, Stella opened her lips. "Send it back to hell where it came from, Thunderheart. Kill it."

Thunderheart moaned, and then whirled. Leaping into the air, he shot his foot out with the lethal precision of the emperor's trained, elite corps. The blow struck the alien cleanly....

And passed through!

Incredibly, the alien opened to receive him, then closed behind, swallowing him whole. Through its translucent milky surface, Stella could see Thunderheart fight in its bowels, lash out with expert thrusts of arms and feet.

Then the alien's surface turned opaque, and Thunderheart was gone.

"What the hell ARE you?" Stella shouted. "WHY do you do this?"

"Shall I show you?" She saw its swollen red tongue slither in its gaping mouth. "Then come."

Something touched her mind, a presence. *Come into me.* Stella shivered and stepped back. She tried to repel it, only to feel its essence invade her mind. As they joined, she realized her mistake.

The alien wasn't an "It." Nor, despite one of Thunderheart's insults, was it an hermaphrodite.

What the alien was, despite his urging her to come into him, was clearly and undeniably male.

More gently this time, the alien reached out and touched her mind. *Don't resist me. You have sensed and understood me from the first time you saw me there has been a bond between us.*

No! She screamed inside.

Not with your conscious mind, perhaps, he answered, but at some deeper level.

In her mind, she opened her mouth and tore at his body, ripping whole chunks free.

You will come into me as your companion has, only closer. As close and deep as my thoughts of you.

Fiercely, she spat out gobbets of his flesh, his alien flesh, and fed him her hate in return.

Come into me. Come with me. I will take you to the All-Mother.

She gripped her fists. I'll tear the bitch's heart out!

Impatient laughter like the death of worlds. She does not have a heart but is as different from me as I am from you.

She's still a bitch! she screamed even as he began to stir her. Everything Thunderheart said about you goes double for HER.

You are wrong, he whispered. Let me show you.

And he did.

Aeons passed as a vital race called the Seeds of Time climbed up from the primordial mud and reached its proud pinnacle. She saw...

Oh God.

Decline. Over a billion years, two billion, and then three as evolution took them, a race primarily consisting of males, back to their origins. Limbs turned vestigial, and then disappeared. Families and culture withered. Though their numbers dwindled, their brains didn't atrophy. They continued to develop in profound if narrow ways, reaching supreme heights as their technology achieved for them virtual immortality. There was only one problem.

The great dark opened in her mind, seeded by distant stars. Space awaited, and there was all the time they could want to explore it, with the All-Mother as their guide and general, as their queen bee-hive master who alone was not decadent, who alone was not infinitely bored by the prospect of eternal life.

Do you see? he told her. You can join us, the Seeds of Time, and share these wonders with me.

His mind lay over hers like the casual arm or leg of a lover, possessive but loose enough so she could do as she wanted.

She felt a touch like soothing fire in every cell. Close to him, intimate in a way beyond words, Stella realized he was giving her a choice, that he wanted her to accept him of her own free will.

Be in and with me forever. We will explore this universe and others. I shall show you eternity, Stella!

Her name on his mental lips drove her to her knees. She swayed there as her body approached orgasm and beyond, a new pleasure that transcended description. Oh God, what was happening to her?

I want you to come willingly, Stella. Say you will come. Say you will come with me.

Her thighs opened before his vast plea. All those galaxies… to be with him forever.

No.

With an inner curse she cast him off. "No. You're dead inside. Tired and bored with your endless existence. You can't make me save you by being a plaything, a new diversion for your jaded mind. I won't! Your race is finished, has lived its span and must pass." She rose to her feet and chiseled her words with contempt. "Even if your race could rule the stars, you are still pathetic. I pity all of you, especially your precious All-Mother!"

She felt him withdraw, a lover whose rejection embraced his entire race.

"You cannot say that of her. She is blessed."

"Then why do you want to die?" she screamed. "Why is your deepest wish only to escape this life you hate? You called Thunderheart nine-tenths dead. What are you?"

"No. You do not understand."

"Don't lie to me. You said it yourself. We share a bond," she said. "I know what you are."

"No! Come with me and I shall show you that you are wrong," the alien said. "Together, we will share the universe."

"You're ashes inside," Stella snarled, "a desolate wasteland. You have only your pitiable emptiness to offer me. I spit on it."

Silence. She waited.

"You know nothing," he finally answered. "I was wrong to think we shared anything. You are of an inferior race doomed to extinction. Between us there can be no relationship save that of conqueror to conquered. In the future we shall crush you with even greater ease than we have already."

"You shall be crushed," Stella challenged. "You're old, once mighty but now wasted and worn out. Accept it. Find some cemetery and bury yourselves in it. We are a young, vital race and this galaxy belongs to us."

Silence followed again while Stella wondered how and why and in what way she understood this being. Despite her reluctance to admit she shared anything with him at all, she knew he had been right. There was a bond of some kind between them.

"It isn't wise to play games with a master gamesman," the alien said. "I have given you a look at me; now let us share your secrets. Perhaps we can determine if they justify your arrogance."

Stella glanced away at Nick, then at Brett and Morner, who stood in catatonic calm, waiting for their master's summons. Last, she scanned the dozens of Scaleys who surrounded her. What had the alien called them: Pawns? It was a word stolen from their own human language to define her crew's future slavery.

"So you won't speak, even though I know your thoughts? Even though I know your fears, what you dread most to have exposed?" Harsh laughter grated in her ears. "Then let me share it with your followers, see if it inspires their admiration."

"Stella," Sloan whispered in her ear from the *Spaceranger*, "what is he going to do?"

She swallowed, remained silent.

The alien's body changed again, and new images formed. She saw herself descend the circular stairs on Warren and join Jack Faust at the filter tank, saw the tank explode with Faust falling through the air in a rain of scalding death. Then Doug Shane joined her and spoke into his comlink. As they left, they approached a salmon-colored pipe overhead.

No.

She tried to close her eyes but couldn't. The alien held her, and as she watched, her old self died again. She saw the radioactive iodine descend in a lethal shroud, and though there was no sound, it was real to her, it was the very thing. She experienced it again just as it had happened, powerless as the alien raped her mind for all to see. She relived the painful operations that had saved her life and made her a freak, endured her recovery in the weeks that followed. And as she watched, one thought above all seared her mind: Please, Please, don't let him show that. Please, don't let them KNOW.

"Still so haughty, my stubborn one?" the alien said, his voice rising. "Then behold."

Slowly, teasingly, the one scene she did not want them to see appeared on the alien's skin. She saw her cabin on the *Spaceranger*. She was standing in it, beside her open berth. And she was...naked.

NO.

Another figure appeared, also naked. Male and tall. Dark-haired, muscular, and beautiful.

Jason.

"You think he'll want you, Stella?" the alien mocked. "Someone who is not even a woman? An artificial construct, a cyborg lie? Do you think he will love you, come into you with lust and desire as I asked you to come into me, and do so without loathing, without despising you?"

She watched the scene unfold, knowing that Jason was watching from the other ship, and that Sloan and Lee and so many others were observing her disgrace as well as her psychic defilement. Here, for all to see, were her innermost shames and desires laid bare for everyone to trample and wallow in, and above all, to pity.

In the scene, she was kissing Jason passionately and he was kissing back. She watched herself caress and stroke his back and firm buttocks, press herself against him. Then Jason was picking her up, carrying her lightly to her bed, placing her upon it. It was just as she'd imagined it when she was alone, lying in her bunk. Only now she wasn't alone.

Desperately Stella sought a way to resist this rape and invasion of her psyche. What could she possibly do? There was nothing to stop it!

Wait. What about…a paradox?

Tell me, she shouted in her mind, if you can refute Dahlmer's Paradox.

Dahlmer's Paradox?

Yes. She struggled to concentrate, to blot out her shame and terror. Dahlmer's Paradox. The concept formed, and then faded. She summoned all her strength and felt it coalesce again. Since between here and the most distant sun an infinite number of points exist, it must be impossible for you to reach it. Yet your ship can do so easily. HOW is that possible?

Amused contempt slapped her mind. I shall not be distracted by such a pathetic little trick, the alien thought, yet the images on his body faded and grew fuzzy. Within seconds Stella could no longer tell which figure was Jason's and which was hers.

HOW is that possible? Stella repeated. An infinite number of points must be passed, yet you can reach that sun easily.

On the alien's writhing, wavelike skin, the images wavered and their resolution blurred still more. Stella could feel the alien thrust the paradox forcibly from his mind and focus on her own. Instantly the images on his skin sharpened. Before her, Jason threw his head back and laughed. Though soundless, his scorn for her was clear. For Stella, gripped in the rigid vice of the alien's will, it was as if she actually stood in her cabin experiencing her disgrace. Jason gestured at her body, indicating its falseness, his own disgust and revulsion. She wanted to die.

Something happened to the display of her cabin. She saw the door shake, then shake again as if someone were striking it violently from the other side. As the images trembled, Stella felt the Scaleys press behind her in concern.

"What is this?" the alien said, somehow aware of the change on his skin. "Who is interfering? Is it the one called 'Nick'?"

Stella managed to turn and look at Nick. "No, it is not you," the alien said. "You lack the will. But there is no one else it can be."

The door broke and a figure burst through. He stood there breathing heavily, looking at Jason with hate-filled eyes.

George Darron.

"No, it cannot be. My imager trapped him!"

Stella glanced from George on the alien's skin to the 'imager' in the corridor before which George stood in his stolen armor. Or was it George?

"It cannot be," the alien said. "I only lost visual contact with him for a moment. He could not..."

Before her, Jason stared at George in surprise. She watched George step forward and viciously backhand Jason across the mouth, then seize him by the waist in his massive hands and hoist him against the wall so that his feet dangled in the air.

What's happening? Desperately she tried to make sense of the scene as George whirled and smashed Jason against the wall. He vanished in a puff of smoke.

As she watched, George Darron's eyes met those of her image and lingered. Then Stella saw him move forward and embrace her, press his lips passionately to hers.

"YOU HAVE DECEIVED ME," the alien screamed in outrage. "WHICH ONE ARE YOU? STEP FORWARD AND REVEAL YOURSELF AT ONCE."

Stella turned. The Scaleys were looking at each other in confusion, gesturing frantically in an effort to identify the impostor. She whirled back, just in time to see herself throw her arms around George Darron's broad neck as he swept her into his arms and carried her to the bed.

"HE'S CONCEALING HIMSELF AMONG YOU!" the alien roared, his astonishment changing to fear. "FIND HIM AT ONCE! DO NOT PERMIT HIM TO GET NEAR ME! HE INTENDS TO DESTROY US!"

One of the Scaleys moved forward and its weapon rose to send a beam narrowly past her. She heard a scream, a shrill, agonized one unlike any she had heard before, and turned to see the alien start to dissolve in bubbles of boiling protoplasm. Higher and higher the scream rose, a thread of hypersonic agony that threatened to snap as the beam probed and darted and sliced, seeking a core, an inner sanctum to breach.

Above, a device of some kind descended.

The Scaleys now looked crippled, their heads and limbs jerking like broken puppets as the figure in their midst swung its weapon from side to side. Turning back, she saw that the device above had now descended halfway to the floor, and that it was a shield.

She leapt forward and braced herself beneath it, pressing her hands against its dark surface. It continued relentlessly downward. If she didn't stop its descent, the alien would be saved, severely injured but intact. If that happened, all they had fought for would be lost.

She had to stop it.

She pushed back with all her might, her muscles straining as the weapon's beam swung and cut and the alien's scream rose still higher. Despite all her efforts, the now groaning shield continued to descend, forcing the Scaley to hold its fire. Centimeter by centimeter, Stella was driven to the deck.

On her knees, she remembered the wounded soldier in the corridor she had wanted to help. He had been in such pain, and she had promised him she would return. If she didn't stop this shield...

The soldier's eyes pleading in her mind, she found a cache of untapped strength and strained even harder, striving for just a millimeter of progress. Slowly, in agony, she felt the shield retreat before her fingers. She was forcing it back! Now she was off her knees, rising, pushing the shield still higher as the weapon whined and the alien's scream

Stopped.

An instant later, all the Scaleys ceased their movements and collapsed. The sound of their armor striking decks throughout the ship was deafening, a colossal din that ended as abruptly as it had begun.

Trembling, Stella released her grip on the shield locked in place above her. The tall figure deactivated the Scaley weapon by pressing something on its side and then raised its hands. Slowly, it removed its helmet.

George Darron looked at her, his gaze frank and direct, just as it had been in her cabin. Stunned, Stella met his eyes, seeing him as never before.

"George," she finally said, "I'm glad you could make it."

Then all seemed chaos as a thousand things happened at once. Nick peppered George with questions as George checked

Brett's and Morner's conditions. Stella herself was on the comlink to Sloan, ordering that units be deployed to secure all sectors of the enemy ship.

"You think the Scaleys are all dead, don't you, Stella?"

She glanced at George, who was bent over Brett, examining her eyes. "I think so, but assume otherwise. And Sloan?"

"Yes, Commander?" His voice quivered with excitement, barely restraining the triumph she herself fought to suppress.

"We have an enemy ship now, Sloan," she said. "Our very first. Since we can't control it from within the singularity, I want you and Jason to plot vector and coordinates for sending it through first." She grinned despite herself. "We're going to find a way to take this baby to Loran Base by ourselves, Sloan. Lay it right in their laps to study."

A pause, longer than she'd expected. "Are you all right, Sloan?" she finally said.

"Uh, yes. Great idea, Stella. Our whiz-heads can study the Scaley technology, suck it dry. Thanks to you, we can win this war!"

"Stella, they look fine," George said, rising from where Brett rested on the deck. "A good sleep and a little psy-con, and they'll be fit as a fiddle."

She met his eyes. Licked her lips. "That's great, George."

"Commander," Nick said.

Stella glanced at him, only to see that he was staring over her shoulder. "What is it, Nick?"

"Ser, I thought it was dead."

She turned and studied the huge, ruined pulp, which even now was beginning to smell. What did Nick mean? Of course the thing was dead. Anyone could see that.

Something stirred inside it, rippled across its ravaged surface.

"Stella," George said, "don't go any closer."

"Why not?" She glanced back and forth between them. "It's dead, isn't it? You killed it."

"I think I did. Let me make sure."

He stooped to pick up his weapon.

Stella nodded and turned back. Approaching, she knelt an

arm's length away from the alien's corpse and leaned forward for a last look. When she did, she saw it move again. As if it had been waiting, it surged forward and reared up over her face.

CHAPTER NINE

The alien came down, striking Stella and sending her flying, and even her quick reflexes weren't sufficient to keep her on her feet. She landed hard, her skull and arm rammed violently against the deck. Even before she finished skidding, George burned the alien at full power, searing deep grooves and gashes in the heaving protoplasm. Stunned from the impact, Stella struggled to her feet.

This can't be! her mind protested. The thing's dead. I know it!

At its now semi-dissolved, liquescent base, a slimy object appeared, writhing and struggling to get free. It reminded her of-a baby!

Could the alien be female?

No. That was impossible.

Fighting a headache, she activated all channels and turned to George. "Don't shoot!" she screamed. "Stop!"

George cut the power, and Stella clambered to the object, which continued to fight in its womblike prison. Kneeling, Stella took it in her hands and gently but forcefully wrested it free.

She wiped away the decomposing tissue that clung to the faceplate, seeing pleading eyes behind it.

"Bloody Scaley!" George said above her. "It's Thunderheart. He's still alive!"

"He won't be," she said, "if he doesn't get some air."

"What?" George knelt beside her, examining Thunderheart. "Damn, you're right. The ox unit must be damaged." His hands tried to open the faceplate and then turn the helmet. "Shit, plate's fused, and the lock's broken too!"

"Let me." As Thunderheart's mouth strained in agony, Stella gripped the helmet and tried to turn it. No good. She could do it but only by breaking the lock and Thunderheart's neck as well.

Beneath her, Thunderheart's body convulsed in its final crisis. She had only seconds left.

She must do something.

Clutching his helmet on both sides, she tried to pull it apart into two hemispheres. Too little force, and the helmet wouldn't open. Too much, and she knew the abrupt shock could kill him.

She closed her eyes, whispered a prayer.

With a clean snap, the helmet divided. George instantly pressed a hypospray against Thunderheart's carotid artery.

But his face didn't change. It remained calm and still, gripped by death.

"He's not responding."

"Give it a chance," George said.

She gazed down at the soldier. He had been so brave attacking the enemy with just his hands. Come on, damn you, breathe! She thought crazily of seizing Thunderheart by the ankles and holding him upside down, slapping his backside to make him breathe. If he didn't do something soon...

Suddenly Thunderheart's chest heaved and he gulped air. Another breath and he gave a lusty cry!

"Good," George said. "The peraxodine's taking effect. He should live."

George's prognosis proved conservative. Within thirty seconds Thunderheart pulled himself away and stood upright. Though shaky, he was clearly alert. Stella had heard reports of the phenomenal recuperative powers of the Emperor's Arm, but until now had not seen proof.

"Thunderheart, are you all right?"

"Yes, my Commander." He shuddered and shook his head. "As you command, ser. I am ready."

Brett and the others had recovered their helmets from the dead Scaleys and now Stella took hers from Nick. "You can wear mine, Thunderheart," she said, passing it over. "The plate's nicked, but you can use your breather tube. Beyond this bow, you'll need it."

"But ser..."

"I don't breathe," she said, glad for once that it was true.

Thunderheart looked at the helmet, then at her. "My life for yours, Commander. My soul's blood."

"All right," she said, turning away from his gaze, "let's vacate this area, get the hell back to our ship."

George put his Scaley helmet on and placed the breather tube between his lips. "That's the best damned idea I've heard all day," he said. "Just do me a favor, Sloan, will you?" he said, speaking now to the *Spaceranger*. "Tell the crewmen that if they see a live Scaley anywhere on this ship, not to fry it. Because it'll be me!"

Excited laughter burst through from the other end. "Duly noted and already done, Doctor! I've notified them to let you be. You're one damned Scaley everyone's gonna love!"

Stella laughed with the others, aware that her headache was almost gone and that she too sounded giddy and drunk. She fought to regain her composure.

"See you soon, Sloan."

"Aye, aye, ser."

"All right," she snapped. "Let's move."

The bow portals proved closed, and for a second Stella feared they would have to break out. But Morner stepped forward, turned the recessed handles, and pushed the doors open.

"Good work, comrade," she smiled.

He grinned. "Yes, ser!"

They entered the corridor and almost immediately reached the imager before which "George" stood. This time, Stella was careful not to look at it.

"Dr. Darron," Brett asked in awe. "How did you manage that?"

George grinned. "Easy. When the Scaleys didn't react to me, I figured they couldn't tell I was human. I just walked up to one who was alone, indicated it should open its faceplate, and juiced it in the snoot with this."

He held up a small hypospray.

"What's that, ser?" Nick asked.

"DL-Prime. I took it from my armor when I changed suits.

It causes death within two seconds and total somatic rigidity in ten. The Scaley was so stiff it couldn't collapse, so I propped it up in front of this thing."

"How did you know it would work?" Stella asked.

George looked at her, and then shrugged. "I didn't. But when it did, I tried it on some others. And I kept movin' fast as I could, hoping that whatever was watching would lose me like a needle in a haystack. We tried it with the kaleidoscope when we were on the *Spaceranger,* but the multiple images of the ship didn't fool the enemy. This time the method worked." He turned, glanced at the imager, then away. "It was all a lucky stunt, a stab in the dark. I had no reason to believe it would work, but I had to try something."

"An 'extra variable,' I think you called it," Stella said. "Why weren't you caught by this thing?" Her eyes averted, she gestured blindly at the imager.

Sounds came to them-crewmen from the *Spaceranger* were approaching. "I almost was," George said gently, "but my training helped. It's a variation on the Sensory Multi-phase Amplifier or what we call 'Mind Maze,' which we use to extract information from criminals. This thing here"-he smiled at the swirling, ever-changing device, then looked away, slightly disoriented-"This, uh, thing here is a very elaborate, supremely refined version of the principle."

He turned to it again.

"Careful, ser," Thunderheart said, pulling him away.

"You're right," George laughed in embarrassment. "It does lock onto you, doesn't it? See, Stella," he said, giving her a sidelong glance. "Anyone can be mucked up by this, even me, and I know how these things work."

They headed down the corridor, meeting soldiers who nodded at her and gaped at George. Stella smiled at their uncertainty. One part of their minds was conditioned to hate and fire at the enemy on sight; the other respected George as their main health officer and now, surprisingly, as a fellow soldier in his own right.

The best moment of all was when George, dressed in Scaley armor, stopped a medtech and told him the alien's remains were just ahead in the bow. "I want a complete workup," he ordered. "An A through R2 series. Blood, bone, brain, balls, you name it. Have a report on that Slug on my desk in twelve hours."

"Yes, s-ser," the medtech sputtered as he struggled to cope with George's appearance.

"What the freaking hell are you waiting for?" George shouted. "An engraved invitation from the Emperor? Get your ass in gear."

"Yes, ser!" The medtech shambled away, clanking in the unfamiliar armor.

"I wish I could see that look on his face again," Stella said. "It was priceless."

George looked at her, and then shifted his eyes. "You can," he said. "The ship's recorders got it from both our scanners."

They continued on, turning left into a side corridor, the same one where they had killed a group of Scaleys while losing five of their own. Soldiers poured past them, and a few medtechs examined her dead crew and loaded their bodies onto suspension cribs. Others took samples from Scaleys, inserting silvery-blue skin tissue and thin green blood into plastic tubes.

They turned left again, into the main corridor by which they'd entered. Human and Scaley bodies stretched ahead, medtechs and others milling around them, looking for survivors. Their approach, especially George's, drew a few stares, but Stella was glad to see that the slain and wounded comrades constituted their first concern.

Halfway to the entrance, she remembered the wounded soldier who had pled for help and her promise that she would return. Now, unbelievably, she had.

Through the shifting figures of her crew, she spotted him. Yes, it was the same one, his body half buried under others, and his hand outstretched as before on the floor. Could he still be alive?

Leaping nimbly where she could, she maneuvered her way to the soldier and lightly pressed his shoulder. Pale eyelids fluttered open.

She smiled at him. "I told you I'd be back."

She beckoned to George and Thunderheart. "I want the

bodies on top of this soldier removed so I can carry him to the ship."

George frowned. "Why not let our crew do it?"

"Because I made a promise." She looked at Thunderheart, who had been staring at her as if mesmerized.

Thunderheart stiffened. "At once!"

She watched George determine that the two bodies covering the soldier were indeed dead before they removed them. Then she stooped to pick up the soldier.

"Wait, Stella," George said. "Moving him's dangerous. I'll get a suspension crib."

"He's already got one," she said.

Carefully, she maneuvered her fingers beneath the soldier's body and rose to her feet. Gently, with a smooth precision, she bore him toward the portal by which they'd entered, and into the *Spaceranger's* docking bay.

Perhaps a hundred soldiers waited for her there, and when she saw them, she remembered her shame. Jason and half her crew must have witnessed her disgrace, seen her most secret fantasy stripped bare for the humiliation it was. She shifted her fingers on the soldier she carried and defiantly raised her chin.

As George and the others followed her, those in the docking bay stepped forward, but instead of the laughter she half expected, they spontaneously started to shout. It took several moments to recognize what they were saying, over and over again.

"*McMASTERS! McMASTERS! McMASTERS!*"

On and on it went as the full significance of their accomplishment sank in. For the first time ever in the Human-Scaley War, humans had prevailed in battle. And not only prevailed, but completely routed and destroyed the enemy. She wanted to turn, to tell them that they were the heroes, not just she, but knew there would be time for that later.

With the thunderous syllables of her name chanted in praise behind her, she carried the promise she had kept to sickbay.

After the soldier was taken to surgery, a hundred things seemed to happen at once. Sloan and half the navigational crew arrived at sickbay soon after, and a spontaneous victory cheer rang out. People kissed and embraced each other indiscriminately, several fastening on Stella until Thunderheart, backed by George, pushed them off.

"Let her rest," George shouted. "Can't you see she's exhausted?"

Thunderheart's ebony features gleamed in the bright room, glowering at those who still sought to embrace Stella. When his expression registered, they withdrew, and Thunderheart assumed a post at the entrance to prevent other visitors.

"Stella," Sloan said, "Jason and I have already charted a course for sending the Slug ship through the hole. We've secured it for transport."

Slug? Where did that come from?

"Excellent," she said. "I want to send it through within twelve hours. The sooner we get it to Loran Base, the better. Also, we'll all need to meet as soon as possible so we can determine just what we've learned about the Scaleys-or Slugs-so we can present it to Command."

"I agree." With a subdued air, Sloan glanced away, rubbing his large nose. Well, she told herself, after victory comes the realization of more tasks. As the man in charge of getting not one but two ships through a singularity, Sloan had good reason to act pensive, even peculiar. She recalled Sloan's pause when she first mentioned this assignment.

"I'll see you later, Stella," he said, patting her armored hand.

"Wait a minute. I'll go with you, soon as I shake this suit."

"No, you won't," George announced. He took Stella's arm and directed her to a bed where he made her sit before pointing to the jagged tear in her armor. "That Slug's stooge carved you proper. Let's see if you're ship worthy."

"It's mostly the armor's that's damaged," she protested, watching Sloan go. "I have two other suits."

"Humor me," George said. "Please?"

Stella sighed and nodded. When her suit was removed, she felt embarrassed that she was clad only in underwear. Then she gasped, noticing the wound in her side. Thirty centimeters long, it was deep enough to insert a fingernail all the way in.

"I didn't think it was that bad. I barely felt it."

"That's not surprising," George said. "Your skin's synthetic." He went to a cabinet and returned with a green tube.

"What's that?"

"Synderm healant. It'll help your skin close." He smiled at her. "You won't even have a scar."

She shook her head in amazement. "How about that? I thought I'd have to protect you on this mission and you end up tending to me." She studied him. "Why did you go, anyway? I thought you were against the war and didn't like fighting. Hell, I even suspected..." She watched George's eyes drop and pressed her advantage. "Something happened to you once, didn't it? Something that turned you against war."

George turned the tube in his hands. "Yes."

"Why did you go with me?"

He stroked his beard. "I couldn't let you hop that tug alone." He raised his eyes to hers. "I tried to tell you twice today, but we were always in a hurry. When I realized the Slug was a vid empath of sorts, I projected my libido onto its hide. In the confusion that followed, I was able to get close and have a clear shot."

"Oh, George." She rested her hand on his shoulder. "I'm not worth it."

"You're beautiful," he said, "and I'm not the only one who thinks that way."

"But I'm fake, a-"

The hand with the tube covered her lips. "You're Stella," George whispered. "If you were one hundred percent certified lab rat, you'd still be no less."

Such fervor dazed her, and she glanced about sickbay in confusion. After all that had happened, this was the most amazing thing of all. "You can't mean that."

"It's Jason, isn't it?" he said. "You don't think you're worthy of him. You think-"

This time she silenced him. Just because Jason hadn't spoken to her yet didn't mean he wasn't listening or observing her. George's warm breath on her bare skin reminded her that she was sitting on this bed almost naked, exposed to him as well. She pulled away.

"Listen to me, Stella," he said, gripping her shoulders then removing his hands when she tensed. "I knew about Jason before we met the alien. Uh, everyone on the bridge did."

She stared at him in renewed shame. Was there nothing her crew didn't know about her?

George went to a closet and returned with a lilac sleeping gown, which he held open for her. After a moment she rose and slipped into it.

"How?" she demanded, tying the cord about her waist.

He quirked an eyebrow. "A hundred little things you did gave you away. Like your gestures and the tone of your voice, the way you sat in your seat talking to Jason about your childhoods and hobbies. You didn't get that personal with any of the rest of us." He straightened her collar. "Don't feel embarrassed. Believe me, there's not one person aboard who doesn't love and admire you, Stella. If there were any Doubting Thomases left, you've converted them, including me."

"You?"

He smiled. "Before, I didn't think we had a chance in this stupid war. Hell, I thought war itself was pointless and futile, the product of pride, greed, cruelty, and a love of destruction. Now, because of the insane thing you made us try, I think we not only have a snowball's chance in hell to win this war, but we can actually make a difference."

Stella gazed at him, concerned about an earlier statement. "What about Jason? Do you think he loves and admires me too?"

George sighed. "Maybe admire, but I don't know about love." He softened his tone. "I know Jason. He likes women but uses them. There's stories in the corps that he...well, let's just say he's got a history, a reputation for sweet words and hasty exits."

She narrowed her eyes. "Just another hot-wired jump pilot, right? Love 'em and leave 'em. A dumb slit in every port."

"He'll only hurt you, Stella," he said. "I've seen a hundred like him. The best thing that could happen to you is that he doesn't like you at all."

"Perhaps I need someone more dependable." She reached up and stroked his cheek. "But that wouldn't-"

"You talk too much," he said, leaning down to kiss her.

His lips covered hers, soft and warm, moving and molding her flesh. To Stella, they felt mildly pleasant, but little more. Still, it was good to be held, to have someone want to hold her, even if it wasn't Jason. Behind George, Thunderheart's armor creaked as he stiffened, but he didn't protest. After a while George's lips left hers and gently settled on her left eyelid, then her right before withdrawing.

"One more thing," he said, "and this I kept trying to tell you more than anything else. I've wanted to apologize for being such a dumb muck that day you assumed command. Baiting you, questioning your competence. I was a complete and total jerk."

She smiled at the unfamiliar reference and tapped his nose. "Isn't there an ancient saying to cover that, George?"

His eyes widened. "Say, there should be. I'm supposed to be the expert in that area." He pondered a moment, and then shrugged. "I give up. Do you know one?"

"How about, 'let's bury the howitzer'?"

He stared, then threw his head back and roared. "You mean 'Let's bury the hatchet,'" he choked out. "The United States of America, circa 1800."

"Whatever."

George's laughing gaze rested on hers and he raised his hand. "Friends?"

She pressed his hand with her own, feeling her throat tighten with emotion. "Friends."

"Good, but don't squeeze too hard, huh? I'm not as strong as you."

"Agreed," she smiled.

George nodded, and then stepped back. "Enough small talk. I better treat that cut of yours."

"I think I'll do without it."

He blinked. "Why?"

She sought an explanation, a reason why she'd do such a thing. Could it be that having a scar would link her with the frail, breakable bodies of her crew, that she'd still be in some way 'human'?

"Just because," she said.

He glanced at the tube in his hand, and then swung to Thunderheart as if seeking his support. Thunderheart's dark, bright gaze was fixed on her.

"It won't hurt anything, will it?" Her head began to throb. "After all, it can't get infected."

George's thick brows bunched in a frown. "At least let me clean it and monitor it later," he said. "As for now, I want you to rest here for a while. That was a mean spill you took when you hit the deck, and you ought to lie down. Doctor's orders, okay?" He went to the cabinet for another tube before she could protest.

After George and Thunderheart left sickbay, she slipped under the covers while a nurse drew a white curtain around her bed for privacy. She closed her eyes, trying for calm, a respite from all the excitement.

"Stella."

It was Jason. Finally. She kept her eyes shut and tried to control her voice so he didn't hear the fear and anxiety George's words had caused. "Yes?"

The voice moved closer, modulated and directed to her ears alone. "I want you to know I'd never do what George said. You mean too much to me."

She smiled. She wanted to believe Jason, believe that someone like him could care at least a little about someone like her, even though they'd never even touched. But she couldn't forget George's warning. "I bet you say that to all the fems, Jason. Dr. Wynn, for example. She seems quite taken with you."

A heartbeat passed. Then another. "She means nothing to me, Stella. Please, I think of you always here between the stars and feel you close inside me."

A cold chill. "Can you actually feel me?"

"As close as you are to me now," he whispered.

She rocked her head from side to side on the pillow. "George is right. You're one smooth talker. Honey's bitter lemon compared to you."

"Please don't judge me," Jason pleaded, his soft, rich voice caressing her cheek.

"You're right. I should judge myself instead. It's wrong for a commander even to think about fraternizing with one of her officers." She thought of how she'd been led astray by the mere sound of Jason's voice, feeling it implied a promise, a shared understanding.

"I can't believe that what I feel is wrong," Jason whispered. "I can only hope you feel the same way." He sighed. "We have to do something in this terrible war to survive, something to make life worth living." He paused. "Anyway, it didn't stop George, did it? Was he wrong to kiss you like that?"

Stella kept her eyes shut, not knowing what to answer. All she knew was that she didn't want to spoil the illusion or question her sudden hope. As long as she didn't open her eyes and look, Jason lay right on the bed beside her, as true and loving as he claimed.

"All right," she whispered. "I'll wait till we actually meet before making up my mind. But you'd better be as good as your talk."

"I will be," Jason murmured, and this time she thought she could actually feel his lips brush her skin. "I'll let you rest now, Commander. But before I go, congratulations. I'm proud to serve under your command."

It was almost time.

She took another turn about her cabin, puttering about with this and that to make the seconds pass. Any moment Sloan would come as they agreed, and they would march to the bridge. There, perched in the very nose of this ship she had somehow come to command, she would sit in her chair and give the order to send the aliens' ship and then their own down the devil's Stygian gorge-to what? Would it be to victory, to an eventual end of the war? Or, since it was impossible to send a message through the turbulence of a singularity, would Imperial sentinels on the other side blast the Slug ship to pieces out of fear before the *Spaceranger* could even arrive to dissuade them?

Dear Lord, what, exactly, was going to happen?

Ay, there's the rub, as George would say, quoting some ancient play. George: the memory of his lips on hers troubled her briefly, as did Thunderheart's worshipful gaze. Then both were swept away by the towering thought of Jason. If only she could speak to him! But Jason, she knew, was absorbed in the myriad details of this double launch and shouldn't be disturbed.

She took another turn about her quarters, stopping before a holocube of her mother, a widow since her father's death fourteen years before. The white-haired image served only to remind her she had not paid her mother a visit in four years. But then, would her mother really want to see her as she was now?

A knock.

She turned. "Come in."

The door opened and Sloan entered and closed it behind him. He nodded. "Commander."

"Well. Sloan." Nervously, she picked at her uniform. "This was a good idea you had to go together." She smiled to cover the tension. "Might set a precedent, don't you think? From now on, every time our side catches an alien ship and prepares to plop down a black hole with it, the commander and first officer will march in parade toward the bridge."

"Yes, Stella. Perhaps that will happen." Sloan scratched his bald head, evidently more nervous than she. But then, why shouldn't he be, considering the amazing and unprecedented operation he was handling?

She forced her lips to smile. "Lighten up, Sloansy. You look like you're going to a funeral."

"Ah, no, ser." He gestured behind her. "Won't you, uh, need your hat?"

Her tricorn Commander's hat. So far she had avoided this showy and pretentious part of her uniform. But perhaps it was only proper that she wear it.

"Thanks," she said, turning. It was only when she had her hat in her hand that she felt something was wrong. Something about the way Sloan had sounded when he'd asked about the hat. Curious, she turned back.

Before her, Sloan's face was a cold mask above the laser that pointed directly at her heart. "I'm afraid I can't let you wear it, ser," he said. "You see, there's been a change of command."

CHAPTER TEN

She stared at the dark, round nozzle for what seemed like minutes, and then raised her eyes to his.

"You're really doing this, aren't you, Sloan?"

"Yes, ser." The barrel didn't waver.

She thought of his recent behavior-hesitancy in responding over the comlink followed by excessive praise and a quiet reserve. The reserve she had attributed to his serious appreciation of new responsibilities. Obviously she had been wrong.

She turned the Commander's hat in her hands. "Why, Sloan?"

Sloan raised his free hand and rubbed his mouth. "Remember when I told you I didn't want your job? That I was happy with nav and com? I lied."

"You said a man had to know his limitations," she said, "that you weren't right for command."

Sloan shook with anger. "More lies. I would have made a good commander, but I was never given a chance. I applied six times to the Academy but was denied!"

Stella frowned, remembering Sloan criticizing the Empire for refusing to promote the poor. "But you said you didn't apply, and I checked your compfiles for promotion specs just as I did those of my other officers. There was nothing there about it."

Sloan smirked. "I didn't want anyone on board to know. Also, you forget I'm the nav and com chief. It was easy for me to remove that information."

She fought to keep calm. While Sloan had been advising her about her mistakes in conducting her first meeting, she had been making the biggest error of all by trusting him.

"I don't seem to be able to stop making mistakes, do I, Sloan?" she asked, determined to keep him talking, to use his anger against him. "God, how you must have laughed when I called you in about my suspicions concerning George and Jason. What a joke. They turn out to be loyal while my first officer proves a traitor!"

"I'm not a traitor!" The laser's barrel snapped up a few centimeters. "I'm not selling the Empire to the bloody Slugs. When we met in your cabin I wasn't even thinking of doing this. It was only when we took the Slug's ship that-"

"You saw a chance to grab the glory for yourself?"

"Listen. Damn you, I deserve it, have it coming." He shook the laser. "Enough talk. I have a right to do this. I was born poor. Dirty, lice-ridden poor."

"So what? You told me how you struggled...climbed the ladder...finally earned your way into a nav and com guild."

"But not the Academy," Sloan stressed. "The hypocrites only take rich 'comrades' for that."

"But I'm not rich...." She stopped.

"No, you aren't," Sloan said triumphantly. "You got in through a fluke, because of that one-in-a-billion blowup on Warren. That was the only way you could become a commander, Stella. And you know it."

Yes, she did know it, as well as the hypocrisy and class consciousness concerning the commander's calling. Sloan was right. Despite the lip service paid to equality and a common cause, admittance to the Academy would be difficult indeed for a poor boy without connections.

She watched him, realizing he still hadn't fired.

"I want you to understand," Sloan said. "It's important to me. All my life I've dreamed about having my own ship. To be in charge, to give the orders! I've wanted and wanted it and suffered a dozen stupid, humiliating jobs while clawing my way up. But no matter how hard I climbed, no matter how well I did, they never gave this garbage-poor son of a Cleotian mine worker a chance!"

"And now you see it," she said. "Your one-in-ten-trillion opportunity to have all you've ever wanted. All you have to do is take it from me." Stella shook her head. "And you say you're not a traitor?"

"It's only a squaring of accounts. I'll make a damned good commander, and I'll serve the Emperor well!"

She glanced at her comconsole, so near and yet so far. Her quarters were off-limits to Jason, who would have alerted someone to help.

"It won't work, you know," she said. "How will you explain my burned body?"

"No problem," Sloan said. "I came here as we'd agreed, found you distraught, overwhelmed by events. That, plus your accident on Warren, took their toll. You babbled, then snatched my weapon and burned yourself to pieces."

And they'll believe you, she thought, because of your reputation and all that's happened. Here and there, maybe some will doubt, but it won't matter.

"I promise you'll receive all the honors," Sloan continued, "all the recognition you deserve. I won't deny you anything. I swear to you I'll do my best to make you immortal within the Empire."

That's supposed to make me happy about dying? Her eyes burned into Sloan's.

"Damn it, Sloan, I liked you."

He flinched, and then resettled, his hand tightening on his weapon. "Stella-"

"I liked you, damn it. You were part of our team, helped me get started." She shook her head. "You poor fool. There was glory enough for everyone, if that was what you wanted."

"It wasn't enough for what they took from me! I wanted..."

"This?" She held up the tricorn Commander's hat. "Is this what you want?"

He stared, mesmerized by the gaudy object. So pretentious and pompous. But to him it represented everything he'd been denied.

She shook it. "It'll be a lie, don't you see that?" she said. "You'll hate yourself for it the rest of your life. The hat will become a symbol of what you betrayed."

He braced himself as the ship's position suddenly shifted. "No, it won't."

"No? Then take it."

And she tossed the hat to his left.

Sloan turned, and then caught himself. Stella was already diving through the air at his chest. She saw the barrel swing back and, even as she struck, knew that he had time to fire despite her great speed.

She drove him to the floor, where she easily removed the laser from his hand. Then she lay with her arms around him as he trembled.

"Sloan," she said, "we don't have time."

He nodded. "I know. You'll have to arrest me, Stella."

"Is that what you want for you and your family?" she said. "Disgrace? Contempt? Believe me, it'll be a thousand times worse than merely being poor, Sloan."

"What else can you do?" he said. "Be honest. You couldn't trust me again after this. Every time you turned your back, gave an order... And you know what a problem loyalty's become. The Emperor himself decreed the death penalty for offenses far less than mine. Even a well-meaning soldier who fails an assignment is stigmatized."

"I know." As usual, Sloan was right. And yet she needed him. Sloan had personally inspected the only controls they'd found on the alien ship's bridge. He knew best which choices were most likely to unanchor the craft and propel it into the singularity. Though it was refined guesswork, she must have him do it.

"Lee can do it just as well," Sloan said, reading her thoughts. "Remember? He toured the Slug ship with me."

Lee Song? "But he's so young. A good battle tech with fair nav skills, but he needs seasoning. We need someone like Merritt or O'Bannion."

Sloan shook his head. "No, Lee. Trust me on this, Stella. I trained him myself. He's brilliant." He swallowed. "And he's a poor boy like myself. Comes from servant stock."

She looked down at him, wondering if she were about to make another mistake. Trust Lee?

"Because you didn't fire," she finally said, "I'll consider it." She hesitated. "I'll also make it right for you. You slipped, Sloan, when the ship lurched. Hit your head."

"My wife...family."

"Yes. A hero's pension."

He sighed, briefly closed his eyes. "Better than I deserve. Sorry. I've served and loved the Emperor all my life. Stella..."

"Yes, Sloan."

He smiled faintly. "I like you too."

She closed her eyes. "Goodbye," she whispered.

And broke his neck.

She lay there, still feeling the sharp, short snap of his neck in her arms, and started to cry. Tears, synthetic ones that always felt a bit oily, fell on Sloan's face and hands. *Oh, damn you!* She trembled, thinking of her secret shame, and how it paled beside his. Would she ever be able to trust anyone again?

"Commander McMasters, we're waiting for you on the bridge. Is everything all right?"

She wiped her eyes and quickly rose to press a switch on her comconsole. "There's been an accident. Send Dr. Darron to my cabin at once."

In two minutes, she heard a knock and opened the door. George entered with a medbag, followed unexpectedly by Thunderheart, who closed the door behind him.

George knelt quickly beside Sloan and deftly examined his neck, eyes, pulse before speaking into his comlink. "Cancel backup. It's too late."

"He slipped when the ship moved," Stella said, "hit his head on the wall. When I reached him, he was dead."

She saw George find something on Sloan's cheek and delicately rub it between his fingers.

Her tears.

George sniffed the substance, and then raised his eyes to hers. "He slipped?"

"Yes, when the ship moved a while ago."

"I see. He lost his balance and broke his neck?"

Why is he doing this? She motioned at Sloan's body. "I liked Sloan, George. He was my first officer."

Why was George looking at her that way? She knew her face couldn't give her away. Unless she controlled it, it remained impassive.

Still, something, perhaps the tone of her voice or the unlikely manner in which she said Sloan had died, betrayed her to Thunderheart. He moved forward, his eyes darting between Sloan and her. Though not wearing battle armor, he looked every bit as formidable as before, moving like a coiled, muscular spring.

"He tried to hurt you!"

"No, Thunderheart," she said. "He slipped on the floor."

Thunderheart's jaw hardened. Unwilling to contradict her, he turned to George. "I should have been here."

"That's enough, Thunderheart," George said, rising. He ushered him to the door and opened it. "Please wait outside."

George closed the door behind him. Turned.

"Mind telling me what happened?"

"Perhaps when you tell me what made you quit being a warrior. As for now, I want Sloan put with the other casualties." She headed for the door.

He pressed her arm, stopping her. "All right, we'll talk later." He inhaled deeply. "So much is happening, and we don't have time. Look, Stella, there's another problem: Thunderheart. He shouldn't even be here. When you talked to the bridge, they relayed it to sickbay and he joined me in the corridor en route. I told him not to come."

"I don't have time right now," she said.

"Listen." George took her shoulders in his massive hands. "Thunderheart's an orphan, the last piece of a broken puzzle. His nine brothers and sisters are dead. He's the only member of the Emperor's Arm left on ship."

"Make it fast," she said. "What's your point?"

"I wish I had time to do a psyche-scan on him," George said. "Right now I don't, but it doesn't take much insight to see the man's becoming fixated on you as the core of his new world. You saw what the Slug revealed about him: he fears he's nine-tenths dead. You can't afford that type of unstable dependency around you. You've replaced the Emperor in his allegiances, and he obviously wants to be your bodyguard."

She removed George's hands from her shoulders. "A while ago, I could have used one." She glanced down at Sloan, and then looked away. "Couldn't you be overreacting? You know as well as I the Emperor's Arm swears allegiance not only to the Emperor but to their superiors."

"Damn it, Stella, he's a lit powder keg! There's no telling what the man might do. He could become paranoid and refuse to let others see you for fear you might be hurt, as evidently happened here. Or he could do worse. The point is, there's no telling. Please, for your own safety, let me isolate him for a complete workup."

"Thanks," she said. "I'll take it under advisement. As for now, George, let's go."

After they left her cabin, Thunderheart accompanied them. A few minutes later, when she reached the bridge, she found her officers and tech personnel waiting.

"Comrades," she said, "there's been a tragic accident. When the ship lurched, Sloan Williams slipped in my cabin and lost his life. I've directed Dr. Darron to have his remains taken to the ship morgue, where they will be kept with those of his comrades, who, like him, courageously gave their lives in the Emperor's service."

She squared her shoulders, and then continued.

"If this were peacetime, we'd have the luxury of pausing to honor our comrades and show them the respect they deserve. Unfortunately, a most pressing and unprecedented challenge awaits us, one which may prove historic because it could turn the tide against the enemy. Therefore, we have to defer our mourning to a more suitable time."

She paused, aware that some on the bridge had disagreed with her decision to proceed to Loran Base even before Sloan's death. Take time to regroup and mourn the dead, Carol had advised her. Return to New Mars and let the experts handle it. But Stella knew her delay could cost them months. Even the Empire's famous scientists might press the wrong thing on the alien ship and blow them all to hell.

She raised her chin. "That does it, people, except for one thing. I want to make an announcement. As of now, Lee Song is promoted to the rank of chief Navigation and Communications officer. As such, he will be answerable to me alone."

First officer. As several crewmen gasped, Lee Song's features froze in disbelief at the battle monitors. A few techs looked disappointed, especially the strawberry-haired O'Bannion.

"That's all, comrades," Stella said. "Return to your duties." Moving forward, she pinned George with her eyes. "I want Thunderheart to sit in the chair next to you," she ordered, turning away before he could object.

As her crew busied themselves at their stations, Stella marched toward Lee, who stiffened at the monitors and started to salute. Catching himself, he grinned sickly.

"Relax, Lee." She watched his expression. Only twenty-one, and catapulted to the number-two position without warning. Yet Sloan had said he was the one to handle the assignment.

"Commander," Lee said, "are you sure?" He wobbled on his feet and touched the monitors to steady himself. "I come from a long line of livery bondsfolk, servant class. Besides, I've barely had three years experience and..."

"Go ahead."

His eyes met hers. "Commander, I failed you on the Slug ship. When you saw that thing..."

"The imager."

Lee's head bobbed. "Yes, the imager. It caught me, ser. I was totally wiped by it."

Stella watched his head dip in embarrassment and took a half-step forward. Choices. Decisions. That was all life was. You trusted a traitor like Sloan and didn't listen to a friend like George who gave you professional advice designed to protect you.

"Listen to me, Lee," she said, her face just centimeters from his. "That thing wiped me too, and I'm in charge of this ship. How do you think I felt?" She lowered her voice. "You can't go back and change things. You never can. All you can do is go forward and learn from your mistakes."

She watched Lee's boyish face absorb her words, and then continued. "If you can't do it, say so. I won't be disappointed. But I saw you at the monitors when our crew boarded the Slug ship. You were brilliant, Lee. I don't care if you come from sixty generations of latrine scrubbers or have only three months experience, I saw you save several lives no one else could."

Lee's chin rose. She fired her last volley.

"Before the accident, Sloan praised you. He even said you'd be a good replacement for him."

Lee blinked. "He said that? Sloan did?"

"Yes. He had great admiration for you, Lee. Just as I do."

Now. Now was the moment when he would either meet the challenge or succumb to it. If he declined this charge, he would have a long time to regret it.

She saw him pull back his shoulders. A smile slowly split his face from ear to ear.

"I won't let you down, ser!"

She smiled back. "Then get your ass in gear and help me get both these boats to Loran Base."

She sat down in her command chair and strapped herself in.

"Stella?"

She adjusted her headset. "Yes, Jason."

"Prepared to interface with enemy bridge."

"Proceed."

On monitors directly ahead appeared different views of the alien's bridge a hundred kilometers away, the distance she had ordered established between the two craft. The alien himself was conspicuously absent, his remains the responsibility of George's pathology unit. In his place stood five chairs welded to the floor and reinforced by duroplast braces. They were occupied by nav and com personnel, a tiny skeleton crew that would ride the alien ship through the singularity.

That is, if they managed to decipher the strange control panel located before the chairs.

For the second time in three hours, Stella studied it in puzzlement. Concealed before by the alien's bulk, the panel's display offered no clues to its operation. Two meters square, it consisted of ninety-eight multihued polyhedrons and two crystal, disk-shaped levers located in the center. No writing or markings appeared anywhere.

She tapped her chair in frustration. At a meeting two hours before, George had pointed out that ninety-eight polyhedrons + two levers = one hundred, a perfect number in certain ancient Terran cultures. This fact suggested a similarity between the alien's thinking and their own.

Stella had objected that such thought was anthropocentric and led to mystical-religious babble. In fact, they knew nothing about the alien's belief system and how it might affect the control panel.

Sloan, Myles, Lee, and those in nav and com had also rejected George's musings. Sloan (plotting treachery) had cautioned that they could speculate endlessly about the Slugs' inner nature, but it made more sense to focus on the efficient ordering of the ship's instruments. Whatever the species, a practical arrangement must follow certain principles.

"But," Stella said, "doesn't it all depend on the alien's physiology? Since he possessed only vestigial organs," (she said nothing about the mysterious All-Mother) "he apparently manipulated the panel by thought waves alone. In that case, wouldn't all parts of the panel be equally accessible?"

Her question had opened an even murkier realm. How, indeed, could anyone determine the mechanical preferences of an alien race that lacked even a means of locomotion? Sloan conceded they couldn't, but since humans had never encountered another intelligent species, they could only resort to what they knew, which was the way humans thought. "On that basis," he'd said, "the right-hand preference of most humans is the best guide. If pressed, the right lever should nullify the force that keeps the Slug ship in place and direct it through the singularity."

"Assuming it isn't something else that needs to be pressed," Stella had said, "what does the left lever do?"

"We, uh, think it holds the ship in place despite the gravity well. If it doesn't, we'll just have to try the other." Sloan had shrugged. "What else can we do, Stella? As well as we can determine, there are no other navigational devices aboard the ship."

Lee's voice interrupted her memories of that meeting. "Commander, shall we proceed?"

This is madness. Maybe Carol and others were right and she should return to let the Imperial High Command handle the Slug ship. Let them muck up and take the blame, not her.

"Commander?"

"Proceed, Lee," she ordered, her mouth brassy with fear.

Lee relayed the order to O'Bannion, one of the crew seated on the alien bridge. He acknowledged it and, leaning forward, carefully pushed the right lever.

Stella watched it sink inward, and then return to its original position.

Nothing.

The alien ship remained in place, some seven hundred fifteen kilometers away from the whirling black funnel of the singularity.

"Permission to press the left lever, Commander," Lee said.

Desperately, Stella sorted through what she knew. She had met the alien, fought him, and even shared his mind. There was no one who should know one-tenth as much as she about the enemy. Yet she had no idea what to do, no idea what the panel did or how the alien steered his ship.

"Commander..."

She cleared her throat. "Permission granted," she rasped.

On the enemy bridge, O'Bannion leaned forward again. She watched the left lever sink beneath his fingers. This one didn't return to its original position. Nor, she realized, had she expected it to. Why did this all seem so familiar?

She stiffened, sudden knowledge screaming through her body.

On the monitors, the bridge began to vibrate. The five-member crew shimmered and grew dim.

"Commander," Lee said, "something's happening!"

Of course it is, dammit. The ship's going to explode!

Somehow, she knew that. And she knew too that the hundred kilometers distance she had ordered was less than half of what was needed. It wouldn't save or protect them at all.

In just seconds, unless she did something, the Slug craft would blow up and take them all with it.

CHAPTER ELEVEN

Stella spoke quickly. "Press the left one again!"

Tense with horror, she waited as Lee relayed the order. The process seemed to pass in agonizing slow motion. Surely she was too late. Surely there was time for the ship to have been destroyed a dozen times over. She continued to stare as O'Bannion's hand crept toward the left lever and finally pressed it.

The lever returned to its original position. The alien bridge stilled; the vibrations passed.

If Stella had had lungs, she would have expelled her breath. She found herself wishing she still possessed this form of release as relief washed over her. Instead, she relaxed her grip on the chair.

"Commander," Lee gasped, "the situation appears to have stabilized."

"Lee," she said, "I'm taking charge on this. My orders go direct to O'Bannion."

"Uh, yes, ser."

Aware of Lee's disappointment, she made a mental note to assure him that he hadn't failed her. In fact, no one, including Sloan, had failed her in this operation. There was only one person, she knew, who could possibly help her fathom the alien ship.

Herself.

You have sensed and understood me from the beginning, the alien had said. >there has been a bond between us.

Yes, the alien had said that to her. But he had lied. Perhaps some perverted, partial bond had indeed been established after he had forced her to experience his mind, but to say that a bond had been forged the very first moment she had seen him? It was impossible.

She started to dismiss the thought, but some part of her that would not flinch from even the most odious truth made her reconsider. Assuming the Slug had not been lying, how could he possibly have been telling the truth?

A seemingly irrelevant question occurred to her then. Why had the alien extended his boarding tube when he had them all at his mercy? What purpose could it have served?

The answer came quickly. He did it because he was bored and lonely, banished from his fellows who were scattered throughout space. *Just as I feel-have felt-banished from the fellowship of my own race because I am no longer human.*

The truth struck. The alien had been right. They shared a terrible loneliness, a mutual understanding. THAT was the bond he had spoken of.

But she sensed a still greater bond, the one the alien had created in making her share his mind. That was the bond she needed to use. How could she do it?

On the monitors, ninety-eight multi-hued polyhedrons and two crystal, disk-shaped levers faced her. George had said that to the ancients, the sum of ninety-eight and two represented some divine form of perfection. Ninety-eight and two equaled one hundred, and one hundred was everything, all there was.

She stiffened in her chair. One hundred was all. It represented the All-Mother.

She leaned toward O'Bannion's image. "Dan, do you hear me? This is McMasters."

"Yes, Commander."

"I want you and your crew to press all ninety-eight facets of the panel before you but not the two levers. Understand?"

O'Bannion turned to his companions in perplexity. "All ninety-eight? Not the levers?"

"Yes," she said, putting steel in her voice. "Do it!"

Despite their armor, the five figures leapt to obey. When pressed, each polyhedron blazed with light, and after the order was completed, the effect was mesmerizing. As Stella gazed at the dazzling array, it was as if something she had once known had returned to her.

All praise to the All-Mother.

The two levers in the center now scintillated with light, and she knew that the left one was different. If pressed alone, it would destroy the ship and inform the All-Mother that one of her sons had been conquered and had chosen to take his life.

Stella shuddered. So the All-Mother knew. That was the very last thing she had needed, for the Queen Bitch Commander to come down their throats.

She couldn't worry about that now. She had to decide what to do next.

As she sat there, endless space seemed to unfold before her eyes, and she felt the boredom of eternal life, of loneliness beyond despair.

Come into me. Come with me. I will take you to the All-Mother.

No!

Be in and with me forever. We will explore this universe and others. I shall show you eternity, Stella!

"D-Dan," she stammered, "I want you to listen carefully."

"Yes, Commander."

"Good. I want you to press both levers simultaneously, at the exact same instant."

"Yes, ser." She watched him turn, place his hands against the two levers, and carefully press them.

Nothing.

"You were non-sync," she told him when he turned back. "It has to be together. No deviation at all."

She watched him approach the dazzling panel again and place his hands carefully on the levers, trying to accomplish what the alien himself had done so effortlessly through thought alone.

She watched him flex his fingers, prepare himself.

Then push.

Instantly the panel changed, opened out and wheeled up as if into a new dimension, towering over the crew who backed off in alarm. Beneath a large globe that floated in the center appeared complex panels consisting of strange gauges and differently colored, fluctuating ovals that resembled the singularity. From the remnants of her bond with the Slug, she knew they were electromagnetic force fields, vortexes that interrelated within an immensely intricate system.

It was the drive and navigation center. Her bond with the dead alien had not only enabled her to solve the mechanism, but would enable her to control the ship.

"Lee," Stella barked, "tell Thunderheart to suit up with me at once. And have a shuttle pod ready. We're taking the Slug ship through the hole together."

Minutes later, as Myles attached her comm leads, George was still trying to dissuade her from going. His greatest objection, she suspected, was her chosen companion. Despite her haste she could tell he was also envious of Thunderheart, and when Jason voiced his concern, she felt a fleeting pleasure. Could Jason begrudge her the man's company too?

"Stella, think!" George expostulated. "Even to go near that ship-"

The arrival of Thunderheart's armor from his locker amidships ignited new activity as several officers moved to assist him. In the commotion, Stella slipped free of George's remonstrations and faced Lee.

"I'm sending our crew back. There'll be just the two of us on the Slug ship. We're going to change the whole plan, Lee. When you receive my order, you take the *Spaceranger* through first, comm the guard ships on the other side and prepare them for our appearance so they won't launch an attack. We'll follow you thirty minutes after you disappear down the hole's throat. Copy?"

Lee nodded. No frantic questions, no opposition, just prompt support. "Yes, thirty minutes."

"Good."

She wheeled about, anxious to be gone before she reconsidered and lost her nerve. As if sensing her impatience, those helping Thunderheart quickened their efforts, and he soon rose.

"Ready, Commander."

They marched to the lift tube and descended with George's last verbal barrage reaching her ears. Twelve levels below, they left the tube and went to the shuttle port. There a pod waited, chambered into the projector tube that pointed out into space.

At its helm, Brett Duvall grinned mischievously. "Hi, Stella."

Stella looked twice, and then grinned back. She glanced at Thunderheart, who beamed in delight.

"We First Contact Heroes gotta stick together, don't you think?" Brett said. "Wish we could take the others, though. Be like old times."

Stella forced a laugh and boarded the pod, wondering if that was what the six-member crew who had first encountered a Slug would be called. In the far future, when they were long dead, would people sing of their exploits and remember their names?

Vanity, she told herself. All any of us have is now. Think of that alone or you'll kill them all.

When they were seated, Brett fired the thrusters and they shot down the tube into space. Covered by a plastene dome, the shuttle pod provided a clear view of space and remote, twinkling stars. To one side, Stella discerned a white dwarf, which seemed to symbolize the vanity of all hopes of immortality. In the end, everything was finite and died. Even the universe would grind to a halt one day.

"I want to thank you, ser," Thunderheart said.

She snapped out of her reverie. "What for?"

He looked down at his hands. "When my family died, I felt lost." He squirmed in shame, and then forged on. "In just minutes I felt empty and alone, cut off from my strength. It was something I'd never imagined before."

In just minutes? Stella had heard of the close psychic bond among empaths but hadn't known its severance could have such a quick effect. "You had us, the rest of the crew," she said. For the first time she wondered if Thunderheart's combat-tested, gene-engineered abilities were the only reason she had taken him with her. Perhaps she was also drawn by the fact that like her, he was different and alone.

"It's not the same," Thunderheart responded. "We grew

up together, slept together, ate together, had sex together, and sensed what each was thinking. On a few occasions, we even had trouble telling each other apart or determining who we were. There was no I or you, you see. Only we."

"So you didn't need anyone else? The other crew were strangers?"

Starlight glistened on Thunderheart's faceplate. "Not strangers, but not comrades either." He rolled his shoulders, searching for words. "More like distant companions, members of the same army."

Stella nodded, noting with a covert glance that they were halfway to their destination. "The Emperor too?" she prodded.

Thunderheart looked down. "Not distant, but not near either. Our spiritual star, the one that brought us even closer. When my family died, that too was lost. I was lost. It was like..."

"Like being terribly alone?" she finished. "No longer belonging anywhere or with anyone? A freak in a universe where everyone except you had a place? Is that how you felt, Thunderheart?"

Thunderheart's head rose in surprise. "Yes! When I faced the enemy and he tempted me, I saw a way both to die with honor and to escape this growing emptiness which I felt would soon destroy me. With my dying breath, I could still serve you and my Emperor and damage the foe. So I attacked and the enemy took me, and I fought until my last breath was gone. And then..."

"You died."

Thunderheart nodded, gazing past her into eternity. "But then, something very strange happened. Instead of endless nothing, there was your face, you bringing me back, only different now, everything different, and new." His eyes shifted, and she saw herself register in their depths. "It was like being..."

"Reborn?" she said.

He drew a tremulous breath. "Like being reborn," he said. "With you there to guide me."

Stella smiled and touched his shoulder, understanding at last the main reason she had chosen Thunderheart to go with her.

As Brett Duvall fired the retros and the colossal bulk of the alien ship loomed up, doubt returned to Stella with crushing abruptness. Had she really solved this alien conundrum? Just because she had bonded with the enemy and prevented the craft's destruction didn't mean she could fly it, let alone take it successfully down a singularity.

What a fool she was!

Thunderheart's trusting gaze discouraged self-reproach. Feigning confidence, she rose briskly and strode across the egress ramp into the alien's boarding tube as Brett hovered alongside.

"Brett," she called over the whine of the engine, "I'm sending the crewmen back. Sorry I can't ask you aboard."

Brett's delicate, bright face grinned and she held up her hand as Thunderheart crossed the ramp. "Thanks for everything, Commander. I wouldn't have missed it for a shovelful of worlds."

Stella and Thunderheart marched down the boarding tube. It seemed strange, for while the crew who had accompanied her the first time were absent, she felt she could still hear their footsteps beside her.

Turning left, they proceeded down the corridor where most of the fighting had occurred. All the bodies, both Scaleys and Human, had been transported to George's department, yet to her it was as if the battle still raged. A laser fired and a faceplate shattered. Screams of agony pursued her as they continued.

Turning right, they headed down the corridor where they had defeated the Scaleys and where George, in single combat, had bested one of the enemy. Right again, down the vaulted corridor where the imager continued to unfold its dark magic- through the portal-and onto the alien bridge.

The five-member crew stood at attention as Stella entered the room and stopped before them.

"Comrades," she said, "you may return to the *Spaceranger.* A pod's waiting at the boarding tube to take you there."

The crew traded glances, and then O'Bannion nodded. "Yes, Commander."

As they left, Stella approached the drive center's glittering, intricate array. Beyond it, the sweeping plexiport window yawned into space, revealing the swirling black mouth of the singularity. She gazed at it, and then returned her attention to the machinery.

To her horror it looked different, confusing. She saw odd-looking, swirling ovals that resembled whirlpools and intricate gauges and scales. All were meaningless, mechanical gibberish. It was an alien Gordian knot she could never hope to untie.

Thunderheart waited behind her. She turned and met his bright gaze, which she knew would see no fault or flaw in her even if she slunk away in defeat and returned to the ship. Yet her crew would not be so charitable, for she had brashly announced that she would personally thread this ship through a cosmic needle. Now she would have to admit she couldn't.

Thunderheart smiled, and somehow it both calmed her and hardened her resolve, made her feel more capable. Though he couldn't help her pilot this ship, his presence strengthened her. She watched him sit down and strap himself into one of the welded chairs.

When she turned back to the drive center, everything became familiar again. The ship was activating her link with the deceased alien. She could, in part, perceive her surroundings through the Slug's senses. Swallowing her fear and aversion, Stella struggled to accept the transformation and use it to her advantage.

The panels no longer looked complex but rudimentary and as familiar as the contours of her slug-like body. Stepping forward, she felt the heritage and memory of her new race sink into her, recreating, with the lore of a billion centuries, every cell and fiber. Stars beckoned, and the gulfs called-called with a voice that had once been young and eagerly answered.

No longer one race but two, Stella reached out and inserted her hand/mind into a gold, oval force field, savoring the electric tingle and warm flow of current in her fingers/body. All that was missing was a final component of the alien mind-link and she would be able to pilot the craft by thought alone, just as the Slug had.

On the panel, a display appeared. O'Bannion and the

others boarded the shuttle pod. Moments later the egress ramp withdrew and the pod looped off into space.

Pressing her hand into two more force fields-a green one and a gray-Stella retracted the boarding tube and sealed the hatch. Then, as if she were seeing with the Slug's single, Cyclopean eye, she watched her hands blur as they flew over the panels, disappearing into vortexes, accessing and adjusting their interplay and systemic balance, preparing her ship for the leap ahead.

When all was ready, she strapped herself in beside Thunderheart. Before her, one swirling red oval stood out, commanding her attention. It alone, she knew, would free this vessel for its plunge down the singularity.

Rubbing her chin, Stella spoke into her comlink. "Time to go, Lee."

"Aye, aye, ser," came the reply. "See you in thirty minutes."

Shortly afterward, the *Spaceranger* streaked past them. In the plexiport, she saw it whoosh down the maelstrom as if sucked to perdition. There was a glint of silver hull, a flash of fin, and then nothing.

Glancing about, Stella focused on familiarizing herself with the ship. Thank God she could fly it. Maybe things were going their way at last.

Her thoughts turned to Jason, and she remembered how close he had seemed in sickbay, how his voice had sounded when he said, "I can only hope you feel the same way." She regretted not telling him of her love, but then, could she really be sure of her feelings? What if the ache in her heart, this yearning, was only a sick need born from loneliness?

When a half hour had elapsed, she smiled at Thunderheart. Then she reached out for the red oval vortex that would propel them through the singularity.

My son, Wind-of-the-Stars-what has happened to him?

The voice was an exhalation from far away. Words in an alien language breathed through her mind.

Stella clutched her chair in shock. Wind-of-the-Stars is dead, she thought. I have blown him out, All-Mother.

Gone, this fruit of my fertile womb? The astonished response seemed to come from a great distance. *His ship, the Pregnant Song, abides still, and yet he has spun his death song?*

I myself spun it for him, Stella answered. And I alone will guide the Pregnant Song.

Brief silence. *And what are YOU called?*

Though she did not have to speak, Stella's lips formed the words. "If you choose to know, share with your other bastards this truth: I, Stella Singlethorne McMasters, sang your child to death and claimed his craft."

And what are you?

She savored her response. I am a human.

Even greater astonishment reached her across the void. Then hate beyond description raged and staggered her will. Before it, her son's power over minds was as nothing. Before it, even the close bond of empaths was an insubstantial dream. Even from a great distance, Stella felt her determination falter. What could possibly stand against this monster?

Stella Singlethorne McMasters, the silent voice whispered, *I will await your arrival and spin your death myself. It will be a song like none I have ever spun, and I will sing it not only for you but for all your inferior species.*

Stella fought to quell her rage. As she did, something passed through across the infinite sea of space, a glimpse of some great secret the All-Mother possessed that she didn't want to reveal. What was it? Even as she searched, it was gone.

I myself will spin your death song, she countered, and every note shall be a dirge.

She reached for an oval.

Phantom laughter. *Are you sure it is THAT one, frail human?*

She snatched her hand back, an ice pick of realization making her gasp. Suddenly, she no longer knew into which force field she should insert her hand. While she had been sparring with the All-Mother, her opponent had been playing a far deadlier game without her notice.

It is I who shall sing for you! Malignant, labyrinthine laughter.

Stella tore her eyes from the panels and glanced at

Thunderheart, who tensed at her distress. "Commander, are you all right?"

She ignored him and turned back.

You have lost! Triumph, distant glee.

No. She studied the mazelike configuration. She must concentrate. Could it be the blue oval, or the green? She moved her hand in that direction. One of the purple ones, perhaps? Again, she moved her hand.

You have lost!

No!

Part of the Slug's memory returned. The oval force field she must use was located directly before her. Which one was it? Could it be the one with the star-like, changing cluster, the orange one that seemed to endlessly iris shut, or the gray? Yes. No. She had to decide.

Distant laughter, needle-sharp and cold.

Then she remembered, or thought she did, and moved her hand for the last time. All right, you motherfreakin' bitch. Get ready, 'cause I'm coming to get you!

With a silent scream, Stella leaned forward and plunged her hand into a force field.

CHAPTER TWELVE

The floor of existence fell and she dropped through.

Into the black maelstrom, whirlpool down falling forever and *her seventh birthday, strawberry shortcake and whipped cream sweet gooey in her mouth*...down...*her first kiss at twelve like spring fire on her lips*...down and round forever...her heart falling through *her warm feet on sun-baked sand, the delicious crystal cold ocean curling about her toes*...round and round forever down, a soundless roar, falling...

Her first attack of space sickness at seventeen-clutching her stomach, not wanting other crew to laugh...

Falling forever, time a Mobius strip of never-ending thought; a serpent swallowing its own tail; causality wrenched asunder, yesterday following tomorrow.

Straining, she gives birth to her mother.

Hears dirt clumps fall on his coffin as his daughter Stella weeps above...

down

down

down

The lethal gas descends, swallows her whole as a klaxon shrieks a death knell for all she's ever been.

No no no no no

And she was through, waking to a mystic gestalt of stars whose secret she for a moment knew. Unbuckling her harness, she rose and gazed out the plexiport at space three thousand light-years from where they had jumped.

She had done it!

Laughing in triumph, she wanted to strut and rub the All-Mother's nose in her victory. But then, she didn't really know if the bitch had a nose, did she? Whether she did or not, more urgent matters came first.

The *Spaceranger* was flanked on opposite sides by vigilants-rugged, twenty-meter guard ships with considerable fire power. Stella assumed that Lee had commed them, told them of her imminent arrival.

There was only one problem: the Slug ship was still moving, heading directly at them.

Quickly, she moved to alter her course. Inserting her hand into a yellow force field, she reached too deep and increased their speed. Thunderheart stirred in the chair beside her as the vigilant on the *Spaceranger's* port side loomed. How did the alien stop this ship? She tried vainly to remember as they streaked toward the guard ship, seeing it move as the pilot became aware of the danger. Thank God. Maybe they were going to miss it.

They didn't. The Slug ship's force field struck the vigilant's a glancing blow just astern. Feeling the Slug's memory return, Stella pulled back her hand, managing to brake and swing the ship around as the guard ship spun off into space. A rear section spewed debris into the void. Yet the ship itself remained essentially intact. If she could comm them, make clear it was an accident caused by her inexperience....

In silent splendor, the vigilant exploded. For a moment, its death was glorious, a brilliant vermilion flower that unfolded ragged blossoms into space. Then the fireworks winked out, and there was only a graveyard of dark debris.

Through it came the guard ship's companion. In the plexiport, she saw the other vigilant streak directly at them. A spear of plasma fire lashed out, striking their bow. Above, a monitor wailed.

They were being attacked!

The Slug's memory strengthened. Stella accessed the artillery board, which unfolded from the central panel and hovered directly above it. Another barrage struck the ship as the vigilant swept past and rounded upon them. There came another hit. Another.

Stella steered the ship around, centering her hand/mind above a whirling dark vortex on the artillery board. All she had to do was use it, plunge her consciousness as no other human could into its depths, and destroy their attacker.

But she couldn't. She couldn't fire on an Imperial vessel.

Summoning a screen, she gazed at the *Spaceranger's* bridge, where Lee bent over a comm panel, desperately trying to reason with the surviving guard ship.

"...Repeat, there must have been a malfunction. The destruction of your comrades' ship was an accident, not an act of aggression! Our pilot has now regained control of the alien ship. Repeat, there's no need..."

The other guard ship wasn't listening. It swerved and swooped, rounding again and again on the Slug ship with blinding bolts of plasma. Superb as her shielding and damage-control system was, it couldn't endlessly absorb such punishment.

On the screen, Lee tensed. "They won't listen, ser! I can't make them stop!"

An instant later, after another hit, the screen went dark.

Stella started to reach into a multicolored vortex on her left to reestablish equilibrium among the system's force-field components and reconstruct the comm connection.

No. Better to run, outrace this pesky tormentor and let Lee plead for reason. As she accelerated, the guard ship stung her again and again. In time, she would outrace it easily, but for now, the hull absorbed and shot back dozens of lethal plasma streams into space. Above, the damage monitors shrilled a constant chorus as the shields drained.

Still, damage remained limited: barely thirty percent. Smiling in admiration at the Slug's (her?) defense technology, she missed the bright laser jet as the *Spaceranger* opened fire on her attacker. Two steady beams, bright as novas, impaled the guard ship's hull.

When she looked up, it was just in time to see the vigilant explode into a trillion pieces.

Before she reestablished contact with the *Spaceranger*, Stella glanced at Thunderheart, who stared in wonder at a display of the black whirlpool as seen from the other side. A readout below it in alien numbers indicated they were well over two hundred thousand kilometers away.

But it was the debris floating in space that was important, and she reflected on the accident's cruel irony. They hadn't been reduced to a bunch of quarks like the one in two thousand that jump through a wormie, but they did take out an Imperial guard ship by accident. Damn it, the chances of that happening were so remote!

Speaking of unexpected catastrophes, what if the All-Mother pounced and invaded her mind again across the vastness of space? But then, there was no need for her to do so, was there? The bitch had said it herself: *I will await your arrival....*

In the meantime, she struggled to reach Lee, which meant that she had to infiltrate the entire drive and interrelated communications system. Without the limbless alien's memory, it would have been impossible, for the machinery required an intelligence that could adjust the extremely complex, multiple force-field network by sight/thought alone. While she did feel as if she could interface her mind with the system, some vital link was still missing, requiring her to use her synthetic, woefully inefficient hands.

At last Lee's face appeared and he poured out regret at what he'd done. "I hated to do it, ser. But I'd lost you on vid, and they were spraying you at will." He rubbed his forehead. "There must have been at least six comrades on board that guard ship."

"Don't worry about it, Lee," she said. "You did the right thing." He couldn't have known her shields were still seventy percent intact and the Pregnant Song was in no real danger. She moved quickly to forestall the guilt rising in his eyes. "You had to make a quick decision with little data and it was the right one. Lee, you had to do it."

"Now they're sure to launch an attack against us," Carol pointed out. "The vigilant must have radioed Loran Base when you destroyed the other guard ship. Even now they're probably on their way, thinking we're in league with the enemy. When they get here, they're bound to shoot us both to pieces without even comming us first."

Stella nodded at her weapons officer. "You're right, but we have to deliver the Slug ship to Loran Base." She pressed her lips together, fighting a wave of almost unbearable frustration. "I know I can do it. I've acquired many of the alien's skills through some kind of memory transference. It's like I'm half Slug myself now."

Seeing the shock on her officers' faces, Stella followed with a brief summary of what she had discovered about the Slugs, the All-Mother, and of what it was like to pilot the alien craft. In the process, she was also able to clear up a long-standing mystery.

"So you see," she concluded, "the reason the Scaleys always troubled us was that they were soulless drones who masked the real enemy beyond them. In a sense, they were never even alive."

When she was finished, George returned to the statement which had astonished them. "You said you feel you're half Slug. If that's so, isn't it dangerous to continue piloting his ship, Stella? What if the Slug part of you acquires ascendancy and makes you fire at us?"

She suppressed her irritation. As psyche-physician, George was only doing his job in establishing that she was mentally fit to command.

"It's not like that, not mind domination," she said. "It's more like knowledge and memories that wax and wane, such as how to bring you up on the vid sector of the panel."

"The enemy never used it to communicate with us," Lee said. "We never saw their faces or received one word from them."

"That was part of their psychological warfare. It's easier to defeat an enemy if they don't know what you look or sound like. The unknown can be terribly demoralizing and frightening. Besides that, there's another reason. The Slugs' general, the All-Mother, sees us as a vastly inferior species. So why bother to show herself?"

"Why didn't she do it just to get attention?" George broke

in. "You said she wants to be adored and venerated by the Slugs and that the Scaley drones also worship her."

"You're not listening," Carol said, her habitual animosity toward George hardening her tone. "Stella said that the Scaleys worship the Slugs, not the All-Mother."

"Yes, that's correct," Stella said. "It's all line of command. The Scaleys provide the attention and ego-gratification the Slugs need, and the Slugs do the same for the All-Mother."

"Didn't the Slug disobey the All-Mother by extending his boarding tube?" George asked. "You said he was lonely, bored by being alone so long."

"Yes, even his imager, the Scaleys, and other amusements wore thin after"-she sifted through the Slug's memories-"three hundred centuries."

"That long?" Myles said. She watched her security director press his cheek in amazement. "He must have long since been driven mad!"

"A human would be," she said. "But then, we don't live that long."

"Let's get back to the All-Mother," George persisted. "You say her thoughts reached you from far away. How could she have such power?"

Stella sighed. She knew the Slugs, but the All-Mother remained cloudy to her, as she had evidently been even to the Slug. She remembered the Slug saying the All-Mother was blessed. *She does not have a heart but is as different from me as I am from you.* No image of her appeared in Stella's mind. Didn't the Slug know what his own mother looked like, or had the All-Mother purposely prevented her image from passing to Stella from her son? And if so, why?

What was the secret she'd dimly glimpsed about the All-Mother? Something about... Yes! It was...

George's words scattered the insight that had been about to form. "Stella, you said there was something the All-Mother didn't want you to know about her. Can you-"

"She already said she couldn't remember," Carol snapped.

George clenched his teeth. On the alien's screen, Stella could see him trying to be patient. "It's a standard psy device,

Carol. You return periodically to a key question in order to jar someone's memory."

Too bad it just made me LOSE it, Stella thought.

Lee cut short the squabble developing between George and Carol. "Enough, people." His young face turned to her. "Stella, Sloan told me you wanted a conference to determine just what we know about the aliens. Perhaps now is the time."

She shook her head, knowing she was the only one who really understood them. "We don't have it, Lee. Loran Base is nearly three days away, and we must get this ship to them as soon as possible." She leaned closer. "We don't want them to fire on sight when we approach with an alien ship, so here's what we're going to do...."

A day later, when what looked like half the Imperial fleet approached, the Slug ship was fully secured in a cradle behind the *Spaceranger*. Wrapped snugly from bow to stern in virtually unbreakable multifilament lines, the alien vessel, and the Imperial ship that towed her, constituted a standard message. To make sure there was no misunderstanding, Stella also radioed the news. "We have a hostile alien craft in custody. Please provide all available assistance."

The only question was, would they instead both be blasted to atoms? In the past, Imperial ships had hauled everything from pirate cutters to rebel scuts to justice, but never, never, a vessel of the enemy who had all but conquered them.

As she watched, the guard ships fanned out and surrounded both the *Spaceranger* and the alien ship, the *Pregnant Song*. She started counting the vigilants in an effort to relieve her tension, but gave up when she reached twenty.

At least we're alive, she thought. I wonder how long that will last?

On a bridge monitor, Lee turned a dial to just over twenty-seven megahertz. Nothing. She watched him adjust the instrument some more, knowing it would work only if the person in command wanted to establish contact. Whatever the case, Stella kept the *Pregnant Song* off-line. Better to have them think the enemy ship was captured than to advertise that a cyborg-human had 'mutated' enough to fly and control it. The latter possibility was one that would conjure dark dragons of suspicion and fear that the enemy controlled her mind and would use her to attack them.

In the *Spaceranger's* bridge, images abruptly appeared above a holovid. To Stella's surprise, the view was not that of a vigilant cockpit but of a neat office. Behind a desk sat a small, tight-lipped woman dressed in a starched, much-bemedaled uniform.

"This is First Officer Lee Song of the Imperial cruiser *Spaceranger*," Lee said. "Commander McMasters and our crew have captured a Scaley vessel and request permission for both ships to dock."

Three seconds elapsed before the reply came, indicating a distance of nearly one million kilometers. "I'm General Gage, commander of Loran Base, First Officer. Please report about the guard ships patrolling the singularity Charybdis. One was reported destroyed by a Scaley ship; the other's status is unknown to us. Can you explain this matter, First Officer?"

"Regrettably, I can, General Gage," Lee said, not missing a beat. "Commander McMasters ordered me to proceed down the singularity first in order to prepare the guards for her emergence in the enemy craft. Unfortunately, her ship was ejected in a vector that impacted one of the guard ships. In the confusion that followed, with Commander McMasters relentlessly fired upon, I was compelled to take action."

General Gage stared grimly at him. "You destroyed the vigilant?"

Lee swallowed, his face working. "Yes, ser, and our comrades upon it."

General Gage was silent for several seconds, her eyes unblinking. "So you claim you have captured a Scaley ship."

"Affirmative, ser. Commander McMasters presently occupies the ship directly astern of us." Stella noticed that he did not say she 'pilots' the ship. "We have killed and thoroughly destroyed the Slug-uh, Scaleys, General, and I assure you that everything is fully under our control."

A voice urged General Gage to be cautious. Stella saw a hawk-nosed man with Colonel's wings on his shoulders step forward and stoop to speak urgently into her ear.

"First Officer Lee," Gage said. "Colonel Powers would like to know how you managed to neutralize the Scaleys. This has never been done before."

Lee responded with the prearranged story. A fierce battle in space, malfunction on the Scaley ship, their enemy's docking bay opening to Imperial soldiers who board and manage to defeat the enemy. During his summary, Lee said nothing about the enemy's extended boarding tube, the Slug commander, and, most importantly, nothing about his mind-meld with Stella.

When Lee was finished, Stella watched Gage chew it over.

"How did Commander McMasters learn to control the enemy craft?" she asked. "Equally important, why is she flying it and not you? After all you are the chief navigations officer."

Daunting questions, but ones which Stella and her officers had anticipated. As the *Spaceranger* hovered in space, Lee spun out a rehearsed web of circumstance. Commander McMasters did have previous bridge and navigational experience aboard the *Imperial Star* and the *S.S. Kolanera*. Besides that, she had displayed a surprising intuitive grasp of the drive apparatus of the Scaley vessel. She had consequently deemed it wise to pilot it herself.

Watching, Stella saw that the story held together, but barely. Gage leaned forward on her desk.

"If that is so, why isn't Commander McMasters herself addressing us from the enemy ship? Why are you serving as intermediary?"

Lee answered smoothly, his youthful, sincere manner commanding belief. "Commander McMasters felt it might be alarming if she commed you herself," Lee said, giving Gage a boyish smile. "After all, it is a Scaley ship."

A voice near Gage but off-screen purred agreement. Stella saw the general's expression soften.

A moment later someone entered Gage's office and delivered a sotto voce message to her. Head turned away, she listened to it. When she swung back, her eyes were flint.

"First Officer Song, you are to stay where you are. Our files show that Sloan Williams, not you, is first officer of the *Spaceranger*."

"First Officer Sloan lost his life in the confrontation, General."

"On the Scaley ship? I find that highly unlikely. Why would a first officer risk boarding an enemy vessel?"

"He didn't board, ser," Lee answered promptly. "A laser barrage just aft of the bow made him fall and strike his head. He died instantly."

Gage's jaw hardened. "So McMasters chose you, is that correct? Well, ser, we have your file too. Please explain why the commanding officer of an Imperial cruiser would choose a Level Two, Battle/Nav/Comm tech with thirty-seven months experience who's only twenty-one years and two months old."

Oh shit, Stella thought, glancing at Thunderheart. Though she and her officers had anticipated such questions and Lee's responses were well-delivered, they sounded increasingly implausible. Piled layer by layer on top of each other, they created a fragile tower that trembled in the relentless gale of Gage's interrogation.

"I was Sloan Williams' personal choice," Lee answered, his voice ringing with sincerity. "He communicated his preference to Commander McMasters shortly before the engagement."

Abruptly, Colonel Powers reentered the picture. "First officers don't advise commanders to jump a snot-nosed junior tech six levels. That's third-rate pula shit, son."

Despite Gage's sharp look at Powers for interrupting, her face indicated her agreement. "Colonel Powers is correct, Song. At the very least, your appointment violates established procedure."

Stella saw Lee glance briefly at fellow officers in the bridge. "With all due respect, General, I believe my promotion does fall within a commander's discretionary wartime powers. But aren't we all overlooking the important issue here? We have a fully operational Scaley ship."

"I will determine what's important and what's not," Gage snapped. Her eyes boredd into the camera. "How do we know your crew haven't mutinied, killed, or imprisoned your commanding officer and taken control? That would explain why she hasn't communicated with us."

Double shit. Stella threw Thunderheart a frustrated look,

seeing him scowl at Gage's words. Of all the subjects she didn't want raised, this was the worst. With morale and obedience tattered in the ranks, mutiny aboard ship was a specter that haunted many officers.

A battery of voices from Loran Base overrode Lee's reply. Gage silenced them with a chop of her small hand.

"I'll repeat my question. First Officer Song, how do we know you and your crew haven't committed treason?"

End of the line, Lee. You've taken this ruse as far as it will go. Stella manipulated a vortex and faced Gage's now hostile expression.

"General Gage," she said, "I am Commander Stella Singlethorne McMasters, presently piloting the Slug spaceship they call the *Pregnant Star.*"

Gage and others stared at her for five seconds. Finally... "You mean 'Scaley,' don't you?" Gage said.

"I do not. The Scaleys are puppets created by the Slugs."

Powers waved his hand impatiently. "What do you mean, *'Pregnant Star'*? How do you know the ship's name, much less how to pilot it?"

She sighed, wondering why Gage permitted Powers to interfere. The general seemed to be a strong leader. Could discipline at this base have eroded because of sustained military losses? "I don't pilot it very well, Colonel. I'm still learning, figuring things out. As for the name, it's a long story, ser, and I'd rather explain in person."

On the monitor, Powers' face trembled with anger. "I'm your superior officer, McMasters. If you-"

"That'll do, Colonel," Gage cut in. "Commander, we seem to be at an impasse. I can't allow you to approach until I have satisfactory answers to certain questions."

Damn it, Stella thought, I always hated diplomacy. Never had patience for it at all.

"General Gage, with all due respect I'm exhausted, totally wiped. And I'm getting progressively fricked off. Through considerable valor and as much luck, my crew and I managed to capture an enemy vessel. In addition, we've just jumped a wormie. My sole desire at this time is to deliver the alien ship safely to you so our experts can study it. With what I've learned about the enemy's technology and the tissue samples we have obtained from the alien, I have no doubt that we can turn this war around. But-we-can't-do-it-if-you-and-Colonel-Powers-continue-to-interrogate-us!"

Powers opened his mouth. Gage silenced him with a jab of her finger. "I sympathize with your situation, Commander, but you must realize my concern for base security." She crossed her arms. "I wouldn't be so strict if it weren't for the fact that you might not be what you claim and could destroy this base."

Stella nodded reluctantly. "It's a real nice situation, ser."

Gage ran a hand through close-cropped hair. "I'm glad you understand why I can't allow any risk."

"General Gage," she said, "let me introduce you to someone who feels very deeply about honor and honesty." She beckoned Thunderheart over to stand beside her.

Gage studied him and his uniform. "Ah, a member of the Emperor's Arm. What's your name, soldier?"

"Thunderheart, General." He paused. "I belonged to a dek-path, all sworn to the Emperor's service."

"'Belonged'? Where are the others?"

"They are dead, ser. All nine gave their lives when they boarded this ship."

Gage's eyes softened. "I'm sorry, Thunderheart. My condolences." She pursed her lips. "Thunderheart, has Commander McMasters told the truth?"

Stella saw Thunderheart turn to her and felt his respectful gaze. "On my honor, General, she has. Commander McMasters would never betray or endanger our cause in any way. As one consecrated to defend the Emperor with his life, I swear this as a sacred oath."

Gage's cheekbones worked beneath her skin, and her fingers tapped the table. The silence lengthened. Stella could only wait-and hope.

"Fair enough," Gage finally said. "Here's my order, Commander. You will direct First Officer Song to proceed with you to a distance of exactly one hundred thousand kilometers from this base. At that point, he will remove the cradle that secures you and proceed alone under guard to our docking bay, where he will surrender the *Spaceranger* and its crew to our security police. Commander McMasters, you will wait motionless for a squadron of firedarts that will approach and guide you in. You are to consider yourself under arrest. The slightest sign of resistance or deviation from my instructions will cause you to be instantly treated as one of the enemy. Do I make myself clear?"

"Perfectly, General," Stella said. "I am hereby ordering First Officer Lee Song of the *Spaceranger* to obey and I will obey also."

"Good." Stella heard Gage murmur to Powers that both ships would be carefully scoured for bombs and other hazards. Turning back to Stella, she pulled a handsome officer with sand-colored hair to her side.

"Commander, this is Captain Orian. He will lead the squadron that will direct you in. You are to obey any orders he gives you."

Stella nodded. "I look forward to meeting you, General," she said.

Hours later, as the space station grew in her displays, Stella could not help feeling impressed even though she had seen numerous holos of it. So this was Loran Base, aerial monument to General Ulysses Narraganset Loran, who was not only Defender of the Emperor and Supreme Commander of Imperial Forces but the Conqueror of Rebel Insurgents and a glorious Living Legend. Stella remembered hearing stories as a small child about how he had singlehandedly engineered a strategic withdrawal from rebel hordes at the Battle of Kakkistan, saving thousands of lives.

Above the Slug's holovid displays, Loran Base appeared with a clarity and resolution Imperial technology lacked. Orbiting above Etienne, a cloudy methane world, the base's gleaming, slowly revolving silver globe measured twenty-five kilometers across. Switching to close-up magnification, she was able to make out features of the base's elaborate interior structure through transparent parts of its shielding.

As Gage had ordered, Lee removed the cradle from the

Pregnant Song when they were one hundred thousand kilometers from Loran Base. It was an operation that required an hour and nearly thirty crew, who moved over the ship's hull in expert hops with only slender tethers to prevent them from drifting off into space.

When the operation was completed, the guard ships accompanied the *Spaceranger* to the base for docking, leaving Stella stranded. She was alone now with space, the stars, and Thunderheart, who smiled tightly at her. She managed a smile back, and her thoughts turned to Jason. If only it was he who sat beside her instead of Thunderheart.

Then General Gage came back on. "The *Spaceranger* is now safely docked, Commander. Because of your ship's size, we're assigning you to a berth reserved for one of our hammerhead dreadnoughts. The firedart squadron will direct you there. I want to reemphasize that you are not to move or maneuver your craft in any manner until your escort arrives, and that you are to proceed slowly in the center with them in locked formation."

"Aye, aye, ser," she responded, strangely reassured by this tough little fireplug of a woman. "I do appreciate your situation, General," she said.

Gage smiled. "And I do appreciate yours, Commander. I know you just want to get that damn crate you're toting here so you can get it off your back."

Stella laughed, seeing gray-white blips emerge from stations on the base. The firedarts were on their way.

She sighed. "I could sure use a bath," she said.

Gage's eyes sheared off-screen, and then flicked back. "You'll have it, and I'll throw in some of my choice caviar and vintage champagne to wash it down."

Caviar she had heard of but never tasted. Champagne was unknown to her. As the firedarts approached in two formations of what looked like twenty apiece, she savored the prospect of depositing her burden, telling them everything she knew, and receiving a pat on the head for a job well done. Who knows, perhaps she'd even receive a commendation from the Emperor.

Something streaked by overhead-blips of light. Then more. She blinked, snapped alert.

A blast of flame struck the plexiport, and a monitor signaled a hit. Another blast and then another followed as the firedarts closed quickly toward her, their formations abruptly fanning out.

They were being fired upon!

Her mouth opened in disbelief. Betrayed, and by Gage! The sleek firedarts were mere kilometers away now, and yet she sat motionless, blindly following the general's orders.

Quickly, she reached for her artillery board as frustrated anger ripped through her. It tasted bitter, bitter as dashed hopes.

Damn it, it's not fair, it's not right! she screamed inside as the first firedarts streaked past. I'm on your side. I killed the enemy and brought their ship all this way to help us! But the firedarts didn't hear her. Nor, she knew, would they have listened even if they had. They just came on and on, closer and closer.

And then they were upon her.

CHAPTER THIRTEEN

It was as if she were in a nest of enraged hornets, stung again and again. As the firedarts streaked past the plexiport, shield monitors overhead signaled hits with staccato rapidity. They indicated twenty-two in nine seconds, and even the superb shielding of the Slug ship, which had quickly regained its power after the vigilant's attack, had now lost a third of its capacity.

Reaching into the yellow vortex, Stella wrenched and guided the *Pregnant Song* into full power. At once it rammed forward and shot out of its cage.

As with the vigilants, if she'd had time to accelerate, she could have outrun them. Her tiny attackers, faster and more mobile than the vigilants, swarmed about her, needling her in a barrage that triggered a constant complaint from the monitors. Shielding was now down to half. She was vastly outnumbered, and being overwhelmed only underscored her limitations in piloting this craft. Despite the memory, knowledge, and new way of seeing which she had inherited from the Slug, she couldn't ignore that the drive and weapons controls were meters apart on different consoles. Convenient for a being that acted through thought alone, they were impossible even for a 'modified' human to use when strapped in a chair and surrounded by hostile forces.

Straining forward, Stella reached into another force field and abruptly decelerated. Then, like a whale that seeks to dislodge small parasites that bite and cling to its body, she rolled and yawed and windmilled the craft in crude circles. A green monitor directly above signaled two hard hits as the *Pregnant Song* plunged erratically through space.

Someone was shouting. She turned, seeing General Gage gesture fiercely from the screen.

"You lied, betrayed me!" Stella snarled.

"No! Captain Orian acted without authority. Orian's parents were killed in a Scaley raid, and his brother was on that vigilant you just destroyed. We think he must want revenge."

Now's a great time to find out, Stella thought, swinging the *Pregnant Song* viciously into a swarm of firedarts. A monitor shrieked and she saw one of them shatter into a million pieces. Good, that meant there were only thirty-seven left.

"Commander," Gage shouted, "Orian ordered their comm terminated, so we can't recall them. We're sending a rescue squadron at once. Hold on! I'm sorry!"

Stella had no time for apologies, especially since the base was so far away. The firedarts swarmed upon her; wherever she turned they roared in her face, stirred to a killing frenzy.

Then all at once, it changed. One moment the *Pregnant Song* consisted of mechanical notes; the next it was a symphony that was vitally alive. She blinked at the drive system and artillery board, seeing not a machine of bits and parts but a sensitive life form, a machine raised to such a level that its processes had become dimly sentient, imbued with a deep organic potency. And she...

...was the Slug, the meld and transference of minds at last complete as they reached together into all the vortexes at once and felt the surge and confluence of myriad forces. They twisted, pulled a little here, prodded a little there and the ship leapt forward like their own body in a second skin, as close as Jason ever was to the Spaceranger. No longer was there any thinking or analyzing, only BEING, the blast of verniers on their right side and the hot roar of cannons on their left as half a dozen firedarts flashed out of existence. And they swam and sang through the ebb and flow of a million currents, some unborn and yet to be, deep in the ship's womb as the Pregnant Song yawed, rolled, fired plasma streams, crushed half a dozen more firedarts and speared others with their artillery....

Gage was screaming at her from a holovid. "McMasters, stop! You've won, they're leaving! Don't attack anymore!"

She shook her head, came partway back, finding herself Stella again, not *we* but *me*. The alien's residue of despair and ennui was gone, but his stirring unity with the ship remained.

Scanning the monitors, she saw that Gage was right. The firedarts had been routed, blown to the stars like bits of fluff from a dandelion. None of them was of any consequence.

Except one.

A streak of red on its nose singled it out from the others, and she knew instantly who flew it. Captain Orian.

Stella turned to Thunderheart in the chair beside her. "What do you do to a comrade who betrayed you?"

He drew in his breath, his dark skin gleaming. "You destroy him, Commander."

She glanced at the firedart's shrinking image. "Even if the enemy killed his parents and he thinks they just killed his brother? Even if he bears a deep and secret wound?"

Thunderheart sat rigid. "The Emperor requires strength and justice, my commander. Anyone can be loyal when the guns are silent."

She nodded, his confirmation fanning her rage. "Agreed."

"No!" General Gage shouted. "You can't do that. Commander McMasters, I order-"

Stella deactivated a force field. As Gage's image vanished, she plunged her mind into the yellow vortex, straining for maximum power.

The *Pregnant Song* gathered, and then exploded forward, grinding the harness cruelly into their bodies. As she gripped her chair, Stella's mind entered the drive system through a hundred portals, adjusting and fine-tuning it.

The ship's speed increased.

For a while the firedart outpaced them. Then the vast potential of the *Pregnant Song* began to close the gap, and Orian's ship swelled before them. So too did the distant structure toward which he fled.

Orian was heading directly back to Loran Base.

She checked some readouts. Seventy-two thousand

kilometers to Gage. Thirteen hundred kilometers between them and the firedart. Why didn't Orian bob and turn, double back the way he'd come? As good as she now was at piloting the Slug ship, she couldn't hope to follow him if he used his greater maneuverability. Orian, though, wasn't trying to do that. In fact, he flew like a man possessed by fear and shorn of judgment.

Such thoughts humanized Orian and made him a victim, threatening to dilute her fury and frustration. Grimly she concentrated on honing the blunted edge of her purpose. To come all this way, the alien ship in hand and perhaps the end of the war as well, and to have it all destroyed by this one fool!

Thunderheart was right. The Emperor required strength and justice. There could be no excuses, no mitigating factors. But then she remembered Sloan's betrayal, motivated by an unjust system that never gave him a chance to excel because he was poor. She had snapped his neck but concealed his dishonor. Why had she done that? And more important, why couldn't she now forget her vengeance? After all, despite his actions, Orian had not destroyed their hopes.

Seeing a squadron of vigilants approach the firedart, Stella made her decision. She reduced her speed and let the firedart streak ahead. Let Gage attend to her own, force Orian to surrender or smash him to pieces if she wanted. Unlike the rest in this unforgiving Empire, she herself could show a little heart.

Suddenly the firedart exploded.

She watched the squadron beyond Orian decelerate. Numbly, her mind reached out, bringing Gage back on-line.

"Commander McMasters," Gage's white-faced image said. "Captain Orian has evidently taken his life. We've reestablished communication with the firedarts and they've been ordered not to interfere. Report to base. The crisis is over."

Between Stella and the base, Orian's passing was a fading whorl on the cosmic sea. She stared at the distant, still decelerating ships and turned back to Gage.

"Please," Gage said, "come in and dock." She clasped her hands on her desk. "I swear to you, Commander, that I knew nothing of Orian's intentions."

Stella locked eyes with the base commander, knowing she

was telling the truth but not wanting to give her anything. Thunderheart touched her. She looked down at his armored hand covering hers, an anchor holding her to reality.

She returned her gaze to Gage. "I know you didn't, General. We were both deceived."

Gage visibly relaxed. "Thank you, Commander. And thanks too for not attacking Orian's ship. I will order all ships to return to base." She smiled. "You may dock at Loran Base at your pleasure."

Stella nodded, and a few moments later, as the firedarts and rescue squadron began to return, they took with them the last of her anger.

"Thank you, General," she said. "I'll see you soon." She started to accelerate.

And that was when the All-Mother struck, pouncing across the void of space. *Destroy the base. Attack and drive my son's ship into its sterile womb. Impale and gut it, spin its death song.*

Her will staggered. Stunned, she tried to resist, to regain control of herself as she had while pursuing Orian. But the All-Mother seemed closer, stronger than before. She felt herself weaken. Jason, her mind cried, I wish I'd told you how I felt.

The voice filled her being until there was nothing else.

Attack and destroy it, Stella Singlethorne McMasters. Avenge my son!

Before Stella, Loran Base waited-unguarded, unsuspecting. *Attack. Destroy. NOW!*

As the *Pregnant Song* roared onward, Stella readied its artillery for battle, her eyes glassy with delight as she prepared to obey.

CHAPTER FOURTEEN

The radiant globe of Loran Base hovered before her, a world waiting to be destroyed, just ten thousand kilometers away.

"Commander," Thunderheart said, "shouldn't you decelerate? At this rate, we won't be able to dock."

Instead of slowing, the *Pregnant Song* accelerated. Like a Scaley, she possessed no will or volition, existed only as her master's tool. When Thunderheart gripped her shoulder, she barely felt it.

"Commander, what are you doing?"

The base was centered in her scopes now. Submerged in hundreds of force fields, she awaited her master's call.

And then it came: *FIRE on the base. Avenge my son!*

Thunderheart's grip tightened. A rebel pocket of Stella's mind stirred, struggling to free itself. Ahead, blinding white blips shot for the base, now less than two thousand kilometers away.

And missed, continuing on into space.

You missed on purpose! The All-Mother railed in her mind. *I order you to avenge my son!*

To hell with your son, Stella's mind managed to reply. Bent, but still struggling against her oppressor's will, she savagely worked the weaponry. More tracers shot out, missing the base.

Nine hundred kilometers away now. A tongue of light streaked narrowly past them. Loran Base was retaliating.

Despicable, inept human...Do not dare to resist! Yet there was surprise in the imperious tones. *Unleash my vengeance upon this frail egg of your species' technology. Impregnate it with death!*

Instead of a ruined globe, Captain Orian's exploding firedart filled her vision. A shroud of radioactive iodine. Orian's murdered parents and dead brother. Despite what Thunderheart said, was there really any difference between her and Orian? Weren't they both victims? Yet before she'd held back, she had been about to fire upon him.

I will not fire, she resolved despite a thought-numbing haze. You can't make me!

The All-Mother's voice sliced through Gage's and Thunderheart's shouts. *Very well, if you will not fire upon your precious base, then RAM it. Impale and stave it in. Let the sterile vacuum of the void spin its death song.*

Directly before her, the base's colossal structure loomed. She couldn't miss hitting it, even though Thunderheart had unlocked his harness and labored to free her from the chair. A blast struck their bow, casting him to the deck. She aimed the *Pregnant Song* at the globe's equator, torn between the desire to obey the All-Mother and the need to resist her terrible order.

At the last moment, something inside her unfolded throughout the bowels of the drive system and the ship reared up in a steep trajectory. Dazed, she banked the ship around and headed back.

"What's going on?" Gage shouted. "I gave you free passage."

She blinked and shook her head, finding the All-Mother gone. She had managed to resist her.

"A mistake," she said, staring past Thunderheart's arm at Gage's face. "As I told Colonel Powers, I've just started learning how to fly this ship. I've got it under control now."

On the holovid, Colonel Powers leaned over Gage's seated figure. "Destroy her," he said.

Gage snapped her hand up. *Silence.* Opposing forces warred on her face before she spoke. "I think I believe you, Commander. You could have raked us a dozen times over." She rapped the desk. "Can you control the ship now? We have a berth prepared for you."

Stella sighed, feeling as if she'd just escaped from a nightmare. "General," she said, "you don't have to tell me twice."

Gage was waiting for them in the docking bay when they left the ship. Even more amazing, there was no one about. Marching toward her, Stella realized that the commanding officer of Loran Base had chosen to meet her alone and without protection.

As she drew near, she assessed Gage. Small and tough, she was the kind of person who would never be intimidated. Or lie. She knew that now.

Halting, she and Thunderheart snapped Gage a sharp salute and received one in return.

"Thunderheart," Gage said, "would you excuse us?" She pointed. "Head that way. Someone will meet you and take you to your quarters."

Thunderheart hesitated. "Yes, ser."

After his footsteps died away, Gage turned to her. "Commander, did you really lose control a few minutes ago?"

She considered lying, and then rejected the idea. "No."

"What happened?"

Stella hesitated. Perhaps Gage was screened and half the base was listening in. If so, a few comments about the All-Mother might have her arrested, killed on the spot.

But you had to trust somebody. Sometimes you just had to tell the truth.

So she did, boiling the crucial information down to two minutes and trying to present her fantastic discoveries in matter-of-fact terms. Scaleys had been created by Slugs who were created in turn by the All-Mother, an enigmatic horror who could control one's mind from a galaxy away and make one do almost anything.

"But you didn't," Gage said when Stella was finished. "You resisted, which means humans can."

Stella frowned. "I barely resisted, and I was aided by Thunderheart. If the All-Mother were closer..."

Gage locked her hands behind her, medals gleaming on her green uniform. "So, you're saying you're dangerous. She could interfere again." Her jaw hardened. "Could the All-Mother possess any of us?"

"Perhaps, but I think she's only interested in me because I bonded with her son. Which means I'm the one threatened by the All-Mother."

"She could have you sabotage this base," Gage said.

"Or kill you," Stella replied, surprised at her honesty. "So you see, it might not be a bad idea to neutralize me. Or strand me on some asteroid."

Gage's lips curled in a faint smile. "Oh, our hospitality's better than that. Besides, you're the only chance we've ever had to win this damned war." She exhaled loudly. "In my opinion, you're worth the risk."

"Would your security officers agree?"

Gage raised an eyebrow. "You won't wear a weapon. And you'll be watched closely."

Stella leaned forward. "General, there could be a hundred sharpshooters following my steps, and I could still snap someone's neck before they knew it."

"Oh, yes, you're cyber-enhanced. I've scanned your compfile." Gage rocked on her heels, head tilted up as if in challenge. "What about it, Commander. Will we have to watch our necks with you?"

"No," she said. "At least I think not."

"Then let's not worry about it. You'll have to go through a debriefing, but as for now, we'll keep the restrictions mild." Her eyes flashed. "In case I forget to tell you, Commander, well done. You've accomplished what no one else has ever managed, beaten the bloody Scaleys. At the very least, you should get an Imperial Medal of Honor and your comrades' eternal gratitude."

Stella dipped her head. "Thank you, ser. Right now, all I want is a warm bath and a little rest. By the way, I think we'll have to stop saying 'bloody Scaleys.'"

"By God, you're right," Gage said. "It's not the Scaleys at all, is it? Or even the Slugs. From what you've said, it's this confounded All-Mother who's our real enemy." She shook her head in amazement. "A lot of old ways of thinking will have to change." A troubled expression settled over her face.

Stella waited. "Is anything wrong?" she said.

Gage struggled with something, her fingers burnishing her

chest nameplate as if to hasten the process. *A. Gage.* Wonder what the "A" stood for. Alice? Alicia? Ann? None of them seemed to fit.

"You've been honest with me," Gage finally said. "Let me reciprocate and confide in you." She glanced about the huge, vaulted docking area as if searching for spies. "Matters were tense here even before you showed up."

"I don't follow."

Gage rubbed her shoulder. "Commander, the Emperor himself is due to arrive at this installation in less than twenty-four hours after completing a state visit in which he reviewed Loran's forces."

Stella blinked at her. "Kolanera?"

"Affirmative. He will be accompanied by Regent-Protector Malek, a personal staff, and a coterie of New Son devotees." Her mouth twisted sourly. "In case you haven't heard, the Emperor is the idol of this new millennialist cult."

"Yes, I'd heard something about it." Stella grunted, trying to harvest this revelation. Kolanera was coming here. The Emperor himself!

"As if the Emperor's visit is not enough," Gage continued, "the situation's complicated by another factor."

"What's that? What could be worse than having the Emperor and me here at the same time?"

Gage wet her lip. "Surely you're aware that discipline and morale are suffering throughout the Empire? Well, it's especially true here because of our glorious eponym. Loran Base is an emotional symbol because it's named after the great commander who's supposed to save us all. After countless defeats, so many of our soldiers have given up. Pride has crumbled, as well as the will to obey superiors without question."

Remembering her first encounter with George, Stella nodded. "Colonel Powers. He second-guessed you when we talked."

Gage nodded. "Powers is head of security, and he's far from the worst. His main problem is that he's two-dimensional. He sees chaos growing, disobedience and insubordination spreading, and all he can do is look for scapegoats, suppress all weakness and destroy all threats. When a crisis develops, he wants to attack first and ask questions later. I have to keep directing him to use moderation."

Stella tapped her foot against the bay's metallic floor. "He advised you to shoot at me without even listening. That's what one of my officers would call 'jumping the gun.' He didn't even care what I had to say."

Gage nodded. "He's far from alone. I've got others like him on my staff. Some I've had to reprimand, but..." She turned away, and then whipped back, a stubby turret besieged on all sides. "Commander, they didn't even want me to come here to meet you, especially without a screen. You should have heard the grumbling. Powers and Lovejoy wanted to seize the enemy ship at once, and you with it. If someone who followed regular procedure were commanding this base..."

Stella mentally completed the thought. If someone else were in command, they would have. Perhaps I'd even be dead by now. "I didn't know discipline was so bad in the ranks," she said. "Of course, I've heard stories."

"Up to now," Gage said, "I've been in control, though it's been a struggle. But with your arrival, and the Emperor's tomorrow..." She jabbed the air. "Several of my officers feel you should be killed or incarcerated, especially because you seemed to attack us. Others are plotting how to ingratiate themselves with the Emperor and take credit for your achievement."

Stella was dismayed. "In the end we could destroy ourselves, couldn't we? It wouldn't require the enemy at all."

"That's right," Gage said. "It wouldn't be the first time an empire's crumbled from within. It's happened before." She folded her arms. "Fortunately, there are some pluses. The Emperor's much beloved, a unifying symbol that can bring us all together. I've seen him, and he's a sweet, beautiful little boy who should make a good ruler one day, despite some things I've heard about him lately. And then there's you."

Stella shrugged. "I'm not the Emperor."

"Maybe you're even better: somebody who's finally done something, kicked the enemy's ass and found a way to win this war." She stepped close, her head not even reaching Stella's chin.

"Commander, there are fifty thousand personnel on this base, not to mention families and dependents. Except for second-guessers on my staff, they're predisposed to love you. You're on the brink of becoming the greatest hero we've ever had, a savior they'll leap in desperation to embrace. They've been praying for someone like you for a long time, and I'm going to ride you to the hilt in this crisis, use you to improve morale. All right?"

Stella grinned. "Ser, I try not to disobey superior officers, especially those three ranks above me. You use me any way you want." She hesitated. "You said 'families and dependents.' Did Captain Orian have a family?"

Gage sniffed in displeasure. "A wife and son. I've already reassigned them to Q-deck."

Q-deck. That referred to quarantine for pariahs, those who had shamefully disgraced the Empire and who bore ever after the stain of ignominy. Stella cleared her throat. The terrible threat of the last five years had exacerbated the worst tendencies of a militaristic system, but had it reached the point that the families of failures were stigmatized so blatantly? Apparently it had, at least at Loran Base.

"I hope Orian's family is all right," Stella said.

Half a dozen expressions flitted across Gage's face, none of them pleasant. "A member of it tried to kill you, Commander."

His family hadn't. She thought of Sloan, whom she had killed in order to save him and his family from disgrace, and then of Lee, whose sin was that he had been born poor. Why was there such prejudice? She could understand, perhaps, making scapegoats of traitors and those who had failed, but why visit their sins upon their families and descendants? How were they guilty?

Gage moderated her tone. "I didn't mean to be harsh, Commander. It's just that treason is something I will not tolerate."

But you'll be as rigid and two-dimensional as Colonel Powers in handling it, even when it involves innocent wives and children. Stella rubbed her neck, wearied and dazed by all that had happened. "General, I'm concerned about my crew."

Now that she had chosen a more acceptable subject, Gage's

attitude changed and she assured Stella they were being well provided for. "After you've rested and been debriefed, you can visit them. I've already taken measures to see that some of your personnel and mine remain onboard for essential maintenance. I'll be glad to show you the list."

Stella declined the courtesy. "I'm sure you've chosen well." She shifted her weight. "I assume you're sounding my ship for explosives?"

"Yes, as we'll do for the Scaley, uh, enemy vessel." Gage clicked her tongue. "I'm afraid it's more than routine. Some of my officers are deathly afraid one or both of them will blow up. To soothe them, I've ordered that every cranny be searched for bombs and pathogens, and that certain systems be neutralized so they can't monitor this base." She snorted. "Hell, they're soiling their pants right now waiting to hear from me, partly because they fear you might injure me."

Reaching into her pocket, she produced not the comlink Stella expected but a large red whistle. She held it before her lips. "Time to call in the dogs," she said.

Stella smiled, finding she liked this woman very much. "They can search the *Pregnant Song* till hell grows icebergs, General. But I'm the only one who has some understanding of how it works. If you want your search to be thorough, ask me."

Gage hesitated. "I'll remember that," she said.

An instant later, a shrill blast shattered the air. Within twenty seconds, the place swarmed with personnel. Some immediately stationed themselves before the enemy vessel with rifles held at the ready. Others, carrying rad counters and anti-demolition devices, disappeared into the *Pregnant Song*.

Other personnel, though, seemed to forget their purpose. At least a dozen saluted her.

One member of the crew, his face streaked with tears, rushed forward and pressed her hand.

A few minutes later, Stella realized she wanted to see her crew, especially Jason, before taking a bath and getting some rest. By then she and Gage had been joined by Colonel Powers and Major Lovejoy, Gage's Communications Officer responsible for propaganda and the base's public image. Lovejoy himself was a man who seemed misnamed, judging from his marble expression and the hawk-like glances he gave her.

"General," she said, "do you mind if I check something on board the *Spaceranger*? It will only take a moment."

"That should be no problem." Gage gestured at a circulator and they cut across the corridor they'd been walking. Once they were inside and the doors closed, the carriage glided smoothly around the base's perimeter. It was a breathtaking sight. One way was the vast, multi-tiered, interior structure of the base, some levels gleaming, some masked in darkness, with the methane-swaddled globe of Etienne far below. Another way was only stars and infinite space up, down, around and everywhere.

She pulled her thoughts back to the circulator as it coasted around the base's circumference. Gage rocked lightly on her heels, arms locked behind her in a gesture Stella could already see was characteristic. She looked like a monarch surveying her dominions, and Stella half-expected her to whip out her red whistle again and blow it in celebration.

In contrast, Colonel Powers and Major Lovejoy stood rigid, trying not to look as if they were watching her. Both had nodded when they'd met and spoken brief greetings. Lovejoy's had been particularly curt.

The circulator stopped. Leaving it, they crossed another docking bay which Stella estimated was located about one-hundred-eighty degrees from their starting point, on the other side of the base. She paused outside a hatch just behind the *Spaceranger's* bow, where two guards were posted.

"I'll make it quick."

"Please do," Gage said. "A welcome gauntlet is scheduled along the main concourse. Half the base is waiting there to greet you as you pass them on the way to your quarters." Her eyes swung to Powers and Lovejoy. "It's a tradition here at Loran Base, a rare honor we accord heroes. And you, Commander, are our greatest yet."

Stella nodded, aware of the subtext of Gage's remarks, which were addressed as much to her officers as to her. "Be right back," she said, and entered the *Spaceranger*.

Moving up the port-side corridor to the bow, she listened eagerly for Jason's greeting. Had he missed her as much as she had him? She blinked in surprise when she saw Dr. Wynn heading her way in the dim light. The beautiful, auburn-haired woman wore a white lab coat and Stella remembered the cryogenecist's absorption in Jason as they peered together into his tank. As they drew nearer to each other, she felt her face flame in embarrassment, though she knew it was her imagination.

What was Wynn doing coming from the bow? Evidently, she was one of the personnel Gage had permitted to remain onboard, but shouldn't she be in the cryotank ward, looking after Jason?

When they reached each other, they paused, and then moved together in almost conspiratorial silence.

"How is he?" Stella whispered, wondering if Jason was observing them now in this darkened, minor corridor. But then, he couldn't notice everything, could he?

"He's fine," Wynn said. "I just thought I'd..." She let the sentence lapse.

Stella reached out and touched her shoulder. As on their first meeting, she was painfully aware of the other woman's greater attractiveness and desirability. "How is he doing?" she whispered. "Do you think he'll get bored now that we've docked?"

The cryogenecist's breath fanned Stella's face, and she found herself wishing she could breathe again, fill her lungs with sweet air.

"Not at all. He works equations and we play tri-chess together. That and talk."

"Talk?"

"Yes." A quick breath, a pleased smile. "In a few weeks we'll change pilots, won't we, Commander? Then we can return his brain to his body."

"Perhaps." Stella forced down a keen surge of envy and pulled back. "Well, you'd better carry on," she said.

Watching Dr. Wynn leave, she cursed her own weakness. What was she doing here, keeping the base's commanding officer waiting while she pursued a schoolgirl's infatuation? And that's all it was. Despite George's affection for her, she was still a warped, distorted thing, a fool pursuing a younger man she barely knew. What did she really know of him? She had never touched him or been touched in return, had never seen him smile or his eyes light up at her presence. It was all a puerile fantasy, and she was stupid, immature, irresponsible! She sat on the crucial cusp of great events, and her duty was to devote every effort to helping Gage use what she'd learned to defeat the enemy, not indulge in personal obsessions.

Silently, Stella leaned against the wall. In her chest her heart beat calmly, as it would for three hundred years.

What the hell, she thought. I'm only human. I think.

She straightened and entered the bow, hoping no guards were posted there. Where was Jason? Why hadn't he spoken? Perhaps he was absorbed in a tri-chess problem. She glanced around, tense with dread and excitement. Maybe he didn't care any longer, had chosen Dr. Wynn. She told herself she was being irrational, but couldn't help herself. Then she remembered that Gage had ordered certain systems neutralized as a safety measure. That must be why Jason hadn't contacted her.

"Hello, Stella."

When she heard his voice, nothing else mattered. Not Gage, not Powers, not Lovejoy and his loveless face. Even the All-Mother faded to a distant dream.

"Hello, Jason," she said. "I thought you'd speak up before this." It seemed so long since she had heard his voice.

"I thought I'd wait till we were alone." The purple command chair reclined. Unsurprised, she moved to occupy it, accepting the gesture as an unspoken understanding between them. Leaning back against the cushion, she felt his excited words wash over her.

"Thank God you're all right! After I docked I didn't know what happened to you."

She felt her eyes moisten. "I'm fine, Jason."

"And you've done such great things! Jumped the Slug ship down Charybdis, learned how to pilot it."

"I could have done without hitting the guard ship, though."

"An accident! A terrible, one-in-a-billion accident! Luckily, it turned out all right." Pause. "It did turn out all right, didn't it, Stella? They've stripped most of our crew and posted guards inside and out. I count sixty-three at seventeen different stations. Is everything-"

"Everything's fine. At least I hope it is," she qualified after a moment. "Some of the high muckamucks are unsure of me, and not just because the Emperor's due to arrive."

"The Emperor?" Jason said. "He's coming to this base?"

"Yes, quite soon, according to Gage."

Jason digested the news. "That's amazing. The Emperor coming here. And you said they're unsure of you. What do you mean?"

"I'm unsure," she said, playing on the word. "But let's not talk about it now." She closed her eyes, liking it best that way. With her eyes shut, she could imagine him lying on the chair beside her, though there wasn't room. "I can only stay a minute," she said. "I've got some important people waiting."

"So I see. The short woman who looks like a bulldog. That's Gage, isn't it?"

She giggled, amazed at the sound. "She does not look like a bulldog."

"Well, then, like Uxman's pyota goat, the one that almost chewed his foot off."

Stella tried not to laugh but failed. Jason joined her in high, almost childish tones. Thinking of the fierce pets her security officer kept, she fought against admitting that Gage resembled them. The comparison seemed so unflattering.

When their laughter died away, the quality of Jason's voice changed. "I notice you went aboard the Slug's ship with Thunderheart."

"Yes."

"Was there any particular reason?"

"I don't know. Is there any particular reason Dr. Wynn plays tri-chess with you?"

As soon as she said it, she hated herself. "I'm sorry," she said, "I guess I'm just jealous."

"Maybe I am too." Jason's voice was hurt and sullen now,

sounding different than she'd ever heard it. "I told you before she means nothing to me."

"I'm sorry."

Jason's voice cracked, the computer that translated his brain waves into spoken words achieving novel effects. "There's something I never told you," he said. "I've never mentioned it before to anyone."

She waited. "What is it, Jason?" she finally said.

"It..." He stopped, and then started again. "It happened when I was twelve. My father died shortly after I was born, and for as long as I could remember, there had been only my mother and I. Now and then a man would be interested in my mother, who was a beautiful, graceful woman. She never showed any interest in return, and he'd move on. It was as if she kept my father alive for both of us, as if we were all we needed."

His voice stopped, and Stella listened to the near-silence of the bridge.

"Then one day a man came," Jason continued. "He had red hair and a fiery beard and charm that swept my mother right away. Overnight, it seemed, it was no longer just the two of us. Before, we had been together, played together, laughed together. Now, he was there between us, always thrusting his voice and body where they didn't belong. When we were alone, my mother would laugh and kiss me and say it wasn't serious, that it was still just the two of us. I wanted to believe her, wanted to so much. Then one night..."

He broke off. Stella rubbed the chair's arm back and forth, back and forth. "Yes?" she finally said.

"One night..." Jason faltered, and then plunged hoarsely on. "It was a tape on astronavigation she'd bought me shortly before for my birthday. I wanted to show her something on it. I forget what it was-something to do with pilots, neurological implants, which I was interested in even then. Mother's door was ajar, and I was so eager, I just rushed right in."

Silence. "What did you find, Jason?" Stella asked softly.

"First there was only the smell of perfume, the soft, exotic kind my mother always wore. And there was moonlight, a gleaming shaft of it right across her room, silvery-blue like Tuax that time of year. Then I heard jangling, the musical sound of the bracelets and hoop earrings she liked to wear, and turned. They...they were there together on the silk sheets, and she was moaning beneath him. Her eyes were closed, her nails gripped his back, and the smell of jasmine perfume was everywhere. Her room rang with the sound of her bracelets and earrings. I can still hear them! They sounded like wind chimes."

Again, silence. Stella trembled, and then parted her lips. "What happened then, Jason?"

No response. For several heartbeats, she thought he wouldn't answer. She asked again.

"I ran," Jason said. "But they were so lost in each other, I don't think they even knew I was there. Not that it would have mattered, of course, since from then on, my mother never really saw me again. The one time I told her how I felt, she just laughed at me. Laughed! Then she called me a little boy who needed to grow up."

He hesitated. "It was always him, you see, his feelings that mattered, and always just the two of them. Suddenly I was a memory even less real than my father, a distant one she had little use for."

"I'm sorry," Stella said.

"I know it may sound like I was a selfish kid who wanted his mother all to himself, but I can still hear her laughing, and I still feel she deserted me. She was hardly there anymore, and she had no time for me at all. It was always him. A few weeks later, the hovercar they were riding in malfunctioned and leapt a cliff. My mother was killed instantly."

"Oh, Jason," she cried. "How terrible."

"Since then," Jason said, "since she died, I guess I've just used women. Or had them use me. In some way, I feel it's all had something to do with my mother, but I'm not sure how." He hesitated. "Let me be honest, Stella. George was right in what he told you in sickbay. I must have had a thousand women. I've never enjoyed them, not really. And I've lied and cheated most of them, even said some of the same things I've said to you. But I swear, Stella, I never cared for anyone until I met you."

She gripped the chair. "Jason, we've never met, never touched! It's just a fantasy."

"I don't care," he said. "I know I love you, even more than George does."

She touched her face. "You can't. I'm a cyborg."

"Ah, but you've got the cutest little upturned nose. Did you know it's turned up, Stella?"

Her laughter erupted again, along with hope. "It's synthetic," she protested, glad that he sounded happier and had turned from his past back to her. "They grew my whole face in a vat. It's a complex polymer of some kind."

"Well, it's still cute. Stella, when we finally meet in the flesh, or whatever you want to call it, I'll show you that I don't care two overcooked beans what you're made of or what's real. It's you I care about."

She smiled, eyes closed, and reached up as if to embrace him. "Would you mind saying that to me once more?" she said.

Leaving the *Spaceranger* ten minutes later, she felt restored, buoyant and washed clean. It had felt so damned good to laugh.

Gage was right where she'd left her, as were Powers and Lovejoy. Their stone faces exuded all the warmth of obelisks.

"Well," Gage said, "should I inform the waiting multitudes that we're on our way?" Stella saw that the general held a comlink instead of a red whistle in her hand.

"Not yet," Stella said.

"Oh?"

"No, there's something else I have to do first."

Powers and Lovejoy cocked their heads like bird dogs. "What is it?" Gage said.

Stella squeezed her fists. Something was growing in her, had been growing all along. She told them.

"No," Gage said. "I can't let you do that."

She smiled. "Yes, General, I think you can."

The guards at the door saluted smartly when they approached. "General Gage!" one said.

Stella saw Gage thrust a hand into her pocket, obviously displeased with their destination. "Admit us, soldier."

"At once, Commander."

The guards moved to open the door, which bore two locks instead of one. They weren't palm locks either, but old-fashioned key locks she'd considered obsolete. Each guard had a key to only one of the locks, so it took two to open the door.

Isle of the damned, Stella thought, remembering a phrase from some vid. She glanced about the silent corridor they stood in, wondering how many people were confined here.

The door swung open. Gage and the others waited. After a moment, she entered first.

Inside, a slender woman rose quickly from a couch in alarm, her face red and swollen from crying. A little boy of about three remained sitting.

The woman's fingers worried each other, picked at her dress. Stella smiled. "Tessa Farron?"

"Yes."

"I'm Stella McMasters."

Snuffling, the woman blotted her eyes, then took the boy's hand and pulled him to her.

"I'm sorry. I don't know who you are."

"I was piloting the enemy ship when your husband approached with his squadron," she said gently. She hesitated, seeing Orian's firedart in her sights again, and felt profoundly grateful it hadn't been she who had taken his life. How must Lee feel after killing the entire crew of a guard ship and strewing their bodies in space like garbage? She wet her lips. "I just wanted to tell you how sorry I was that he died and express my deepest sympathy."

It was a lot for the woman to digest. As someone gasped behind Stella, Orian's wife clasped her heart. "You flew the ship Jack attacked? And you feel sympathy for me?" She shook her head, clutching the little boy who clung to her side. "How can you feel that? My husband is a traitor!"

Stella took a step forward. "But you aren't."

"No, I'm guilty too. I knew how Jack felt. It kept eating at him, what the Scaleys did to his parents. He couldn't sleep, had terrible nightmares. Today, when he heard about his brother getting killed, it must have been too much for him."

Behind Stella, Lovejoy-she could tell it was he-made a sound of disgust. Stella took another step forward.

"But you never suspected he was capable of such a thing, did you?" Stella said.

"No! But I should have informed Colonel Powers." She motioned meekly at the base's security officer.

"Yes, you should have," Lovejoy said. "It was treason not to."

Stella studied him, and then turned back. "Tessa," she said, "General Gage informs me there's a reception waiting for me."

Tessa wiped her eyes. "Yes, we do it for honored dignitaries. Most of the base should be there."

"So I've heard." Stella glanced at the little boy, who had delicate features. "General Gage didn't tell me what your son's name is."

"It's Ulysses."

Ulysses. Fabulous voyager. Probably named after General Loran himself. "Well, Tessa, would you and your son like to accompany me and these comrades when we meet them? I'd be honored."

"Bloody damned Scaley!" Major Lovejoy said. "Why in hell would you want to take them?"

Good question. Why was she doing it? Was it the accident in the turbine building that made her sympathize and stand up for the despised and downtrodden, or her essential nature? She wanted to believe it was the latter but couldn't be sure.

"Why do I want to take them?" she said. "I'll tell you why." In two strides Stella stood before Lovejoy, her face hard as she fought the desire to break his neck as she'd broken Sloan's to save his family from precisely this. "I want them because we've got to stop fighting and hurting each other. If you must have scapegoats, make them the enemy, not grief-stricken women and children."

Lovejoy stabbed his finger at Orian's widow. "You heard her. She knew Orian was unstable. It was her duty to inform Colonel Powers."

"It's so easy for you to know what's right, isn't it?" Stella snapped. "You're like a stiff reed that will break in the river before it bends, Major." She drew herself up. "Maybe I can't prevent you and others from continuing such stupid persecution, but I can refuse to accept it. For me it stops, right here and right now."

Lovejoy sneered. "Spoken like a freak grown in a lab vat. You're not even human!"

"Major," Gage said, "that's enough! You will apologize!"

Stella raised a hand. "Quite all right, General. Let him say what he thinks. It's about time we allowed a little honesty." She nodded. "Go ahead, Major, let me have it."

Lovejoy's lips slid back from his teeth. "I already have. After you rest, I want to personally take part in your interrogation." He looked at Gage. "That is, ser, if I have your permission."

Gage stared at him for three seconds. "Request granted, Major, but only if you remember it's a debriefing, not an interrogation." She looked at Stella. "Commander McMasters has a point. Tessa Farron's not the enemy. The Slugs are."

Powers, Stella saw, was looking at her differently. "Do you really believe what you said?" he asked. "We need strength and discipline, especially these days, when there's so much disobedience."

"Have they been enough?" Stella answered. "Yes, we need strength. Yes, we need discipline. But we need something more: a willingness to accept the fact that those of us who falter and break in this terrible war aren't the enemy, but our comrades."

"Compassion," Gage said. Her eyes moved to Orian's widow and son, and then slid away.

"No, not compassion," Lovejoy said. "Sophistry. A specious, sentimental rationale for treason and weakness." He glared at Stella. "And all of it spoken by a mechanical soldier with a duroplast heart."

"But a soldier nonetheless," Stella said. "And one better than you." Seizing Lovejoy's belt in both hands, she lifted him half a meter in the air.

"Hey! What…" He sputtered in shock.

"I may be duroplast, major," she said, "as well as some components you've never even heard of, but I urge you to remember that it was I who defeated the enemy, I who flew the enemy's ship here. When you debrief me a few hours from now, be sure to include that in the report."

Above her, Lovejoy's obelisk face was now wonderfully expressive, with intriguing shades of color. He opened his mouth, seemed to reconsider, and closed it.

"Commander," Gage said, her voice not quite concealing her pleasure, "I'd appreciate it if you'd be kind enough to put Major Lovejoy back down."

Stella smiled up at Lovejoy, tempted to lift him still higher, through the ceiling if necessary. "I'll be glad to oblige, General," she said. "By the way, do you think you might ask the good major to personally invite Tessa Farron and her son to join us?"

She walked down the massive, sixty-meter-wide concourse, holding Tessa Farron's hand on one side, and her son's on the other. Just beyond Tessa, General Gage marched with them, her face sending ambivalent signals.

When Stella glanced behind her, Colonel Powers' expression seemed similar-troubled, no longer so certain. Only Major Lovejoy looked unchanged. Clearly, he was not happy to be with them.

Stella smiled at Tessa and her son, trying to coax a smile out in return, but they both looked crushed and overwhelmed. As they should be, Stella thought, especially the boy, who was too young even to understand. Stooping, she picked him up in her left arm and cradled him against her.

On the walls of the concourse, large oval holos of a silver-haired, handsome man appeared at regular intervals. He bore many rows of medals on his chest, and his slate blue eyes gazed off into a distance beyond their ken.

"He's a good-looking man," Gage said, following her eyes. "He visited here once."

"Really?" She adjusted the boy's weight in her arm. "What's he like?"

Gage considered. "Greatness and pettiness rolled into one."

"I see." She peered ahead at the corridor's foreshortened horizon, seeing the beginnings of crowds massed against both sides. "What did he have more of, greatness or pettiness?"

Gage shrugged. "I could never decide."

The beginning of distant cheers half-drowned out her answer. Soon they could no longer speak, for the numerous people waiting had started to clap. It sounded wild, joyful, unrestrained, as if they had been waiting a long time.

Would they still applaud when they realized who was with them, when they saw the traitor's family? Glancing at Tessa, Stella saw the dread in her face, the fear of public disgrace that would crown her already staggering loss. Was she doing this woman a kindness in taking her on this march? Even if the people didn't revile her and she stayed as a guest in Stella's quarters, would anything really change? After she left, wouldn't Tessa be returned to the room with two locks and as many guards?

Against her cheek, Ulysses Orian had fallen asleep and was beyond such cares. But she knew that someday he would have to face them.

Soft words at her back, Lovejoy's voice: "They will cast curses, Commander. Despise them for what they are."

"It appears I have a higher opinion of our comrades than do you, Major. I say they won't."

Lovejoy didn't answer.

And now, with Loran's regal features gazing down upon them, they reached the first of the people. The applause swelled, the cheers rising still higher.

Then, abruptly, they faltered. Stella saw people nearby turn silent and stop clapping. Some pointed at Tessa and her son and spoke quickly to those standing next to them, who stopped clapping too. The effect rippled ahead through the people waiting, and their enthusiasm diminished, though they didn't know why. Stella looked past Tessa to Gage.

"I would have told you," Gage said, "but you wouldn't have listened."

She glanced at Tessa, whose twitching, wet-eyed face showed that she was fighting hard to keep her head up, and felt a dagger of doubt. Was it just pride and vanity on her part to believe that she could change people's hearts? Maybe she was just as closed-minded and arrogant as Lovejoy.

"You said it yourself," she said to Gage. "We have to change the way we think."

Gage scanned the people with her eyes. "I didn't mean this."

The people were almost silent now. Their faces were riveted on Tessa and the child. Looking closely, she saw revulsion, contempt, and hatred, but here and there she also saw flickers of pity and compassion.

Raising her hand and Tessa's together, she stopped and the others did also. Turning to both sides of the concourse, she looked at the silent rows of people, then at Lovejoy. "At least there are no curses."

Lovejoy smiled. "This is even worse. They give you nothing, only the silence of their contempt."

And indeed, they were all silent now. They just stared and stared, vast walls of contempt that could never be climbed.

No, not just contempt, she thought. She saw hints of fellow feeling in their faces. It was buried perhaps, and deeply conflicted, but it was there. That black-haired woman with trembling lips in front, for example. Perhaps she was a mother like Tessa.

Gage stood shifting her feet, apparently uncertain what she should do. Tessa herself stood erect beside Stella, tears glistening on her cheeks.

Lovejoy, Stella saw, was smiling directly at her. He looked smug and satisfied, totally vindicated.

It can't go on any longer, she thought. Not this silence, this cruelty.

Hardening herself, she removed her hand from Tessa's and stepped away from the others. She opened her mouth to speak.

Then a hand gently touched her shoulder as someone moved past her. At first she thought it was Gage, but the figure was too tall and the wrong sex.

Colonel Powers raised his hands and started to clap. The sharp reports filled the concourse, echoing off walls, off General Loran's stately face. Again and again the security officer of Loran Base brought his hands together, producing explosive sounds as if to herald the birth of a new tradition. Stella's hands tingled in sympathy, but no one else was responding.

Then, to her surprise, someone to their right clapped. Soon there was another and another and another. Cheers stirred and whistles as the applause grew and gathered, rising from a murmur to a swell, from a swell to a roar, and finally to thunder that deafened them all. They stood there, pounded by an ovation that seemed to go on and on forever.

At one point, laughing, Stella turned and looked at Lovejoy. He was clapping too, mechanically, but his eyes bored into hers like pistol sights, as cold and unforgiving as ever.

CHAPTER FIFTEEN

The "debriefing" started badly and got worse. Sitting in the stiff-backed chair, Stella quickly reached the conclusion that while everyone else at Loran Base might love her, this group of officers most definitely did not. They seemed harsh, devious, and above all, suspicious, seeing alien treachery in her slightest word or gesture.

There was another quality too, one which took longer for her to identify. She saw it in subtle things, in shared whispers and mutual glances. Her questioners seemed to have ulterior motives, to be playing some kind of game in which she was an important piece. The only trouble was, she was a passive one.

Major Chong, an Intelligence specialist whom Powers had chosen to lead the questioning, sat at a table before Stella, flanked by Colonel Powers and another officer. Chong had flat eyes that never blinked and a soft voice that struck like a cobra. It occurred to Stella that Lee Song might look like him in thirty years if he lost his soul one piece at a time.

"How did you know how to pilot the enemy ship?"

"I already told you."

"Be so kind as to tell us again."

"During the mind meld with the Slug, a sharing of memories and knowledge occurred. After he died, it ebbed and flowed, but basically it grew stronger, until I was able to interface my mind with the ship's complex drive system."

"Just like that. Poof."

"Yes."

"And you were able to do this even though you're human?"

"Also yes."

"I see. And therefore you would be able to teach the method to someone else?"

She shook her head. "No."

Even though he was sitting still, Chong seemed to eel his way closer. "I don't understand. If it gave you its-"

"He, not it."

"Ah, yes. If he were able to pass this talent on to you, why can't you do the same with one of us?"

"Because I'm not an alien." She considered saying more because there was more to it, but their hostile stares kept her silent. Despite herself, she felt her frustration and rage rise. Why didn't they want to believe her and take what she had to offer? Instead of pats on the back and a hearty "Well done," there was only Major Chong's unblinking face.

"Is that true, Commander McMasters? You're not alien in addition to being 'cyber-enhanced'? Your loyalties and identity haven't been subverted and compromised by another allegiance?"

"No, they have not."

"But if you're not alien, why did you fire at the base and almost ram it? Such behavior indicates that you're a terrible risk to this base and to our beloved Emperor, who is soon to arrive."

"As I told you before, the ship malfunctioned. It was an accident. I remain as loyal to the Emperor as you are, Major Chong."

At that moment, Major Lovejoy, standing against the back wall, played his trump. "That's odd, Commander. According to some of your officers, you claimed to be 'half Slug' during one of your conversations."

She could have bitten off her tongue-or Lovejoy's head. "It was just a figure of speech."

"Really?" Lovejoy glanced at some fellow officers with a faint smirk. "It sounds pretty plain to me, subject to only one interpretation."

Easy, Stella. Stay calm. "I meant that I had acquired some of his abilities, not his allegiance or values. Once again: I remain a true and loyal subject of the Emperor." She moved in her chair with growing unrest. If any of her officers had mentioned the All-Mother, that would make things even worse. Why hadn't she thought to prepare for such questions? For that matter, why had she told Gage in the first place? If the base commander disclosed the All-Mother's ability to control Stella's mind to just one of these vultures, they might execute her. But she didn't think Gage would tell anyone. No, she was sure of it.

With a smile, Lovejoy passed the questioning to another officer, who Stella remembered was a highly regarded xenologist. Captain Starkey was a fat woman with a double chin and a fair mustache. "Commander McMasters," she said, "are the Slugs the final link in the enemy's chain?"

Though she understood the metaphor, she pretended confusion. "What?"

Starkey smiled and straightened her snug jacket. "Let me rephrase. Is there any force or power beyond the Slugs to which they, in turn, are psychologically subject?"

It was quiet in the room. She raised her head and stared at General Loran's handsome, avuncular image on the back wall. After a moment, she lowered her eyes.

"Yes, there is. She's called the All-Mother. She seems to function as their 'overmind,' I guess you could call it. Their commanding and coordinating intelligence."

"It seems odd that you held that information back, Commander," Starkey said. "Are you trying to hide something?"

Stella shifted in her seat, wondering if one of the reasons she hadn't mentioned the All-Mother was that she was afraid she herself might be dangerous to the Emperor. After all, the All-Mother had almost made her attack this base.

She cleared her throat. "No. I'm not hiding anything."

Starkey made a rude sound. "Oh, come now, Commander...."

"That's enough," Colonel Powers said. He rose to his feet at the table. "You all know there's such a power because you questioned her officers and learned about the All-Mother." He turned his head, looking at Lovejoy and the others in the room. "I think we should stop trying to catch Commander McMasters in some lie and treating her as if she's the enemy. She's not."

"I agree," a dark-faced captain said. Several other officers murmured assent.

As Stella watched, the room seemed to split in half and she saw smiles turn in her direction. A few officers lightly applauded Powers' words even though he had earlier urged Gage to destroy her and her ship.

Gripping the table, Chong gazed up at Powers with a look that bordered on outrage. "As this base's security officer, you're completely satisfied, Colonel Powers? You don't think there's any chance at all that she poses a risk?"

"No, I don't."

"You say this even-"

"Don't question me, Major Chong. As security officer, this session continues only as long as I want it to." He turned to Stella, brushing his close-cropped hair with his hand. "I do have one last question, however. It's peculiar that no one thought to ask it. Commander McMasters, is there a name for our enemies? I mean, what do they call themselves?"

"The Slug we killed said they call themselves the 'Seeds of Time,'" she said.

"The 'Seeds of Time.'" Powers frowned at the words.

"That's a very strange name for any species to call itself," Starkey pounced. "Especially a militaristic one like the Slugs. Suppose we explore right now the implications-"

"I think not," Colonel Powers said. "The Emperor's due in less than twenty-four hours and we must prepare." He smiled at Stella. "For now, our distinguished visitor needs to visit with her crew. Later, she and her officers will dine with General Gage as her personal guests." He nodded crisply at those assembled. "Thank you for your assistance. The meeting is adjourned."

Escorted from the room by Colonel Powers, Stella waited till they were out of earshot before glancing at him. "Do you mind telling me what happened in there?"

"I don't understand."

"I'll make it clearer," she said as they turned a corner into another broad corridor. "On my approach to the base, you counseled General Gage to blast me to pieces. Now you halt an inquisition designed to expose me as some kind of alien traitor and practically proclaim me to be a hero. Do you mind explaining the sudden about-face?"

Colonel Powers marched at her side, his back ramrod straight and his eyes directed straight ahead. "General Gage ordered me to stop the meeting if it seemed to be getting too adversarial."

"I see. And the officers who seconded your defense of me-were they ordered to do so also?"

"Yes, though they were glad to do it."

"Why did General Gage order it? If, as you said, your decision to stop the meeting was sufficient, why should she arrange for additional support? Unless..." She thought of some of the things Gage had told her. "Unless your authority alone may not have been sufficient."

Powers stopped and turned to her as she also halted. "There is opposition," he said reluctantly. "General Gage felt it might be necessary to broaden my support."

"Colonel Powers, are you implying that otherwise they might have disobeyed you and continued the meeting?"

Powers' expression remained unchanged. He turned.

She caught his shoulder, stopping him. "No, please. I've got to know. Tell me."

"It's not your-"

"It is. I'm at the center of this. How can I know what to say or how to act if I don't know what's going on?"

Powers hesitated, clearly reluctant to discuss the matter. What had Gage called him—"two-dimensional'? For such a man, Stella thought, discussing his fellow officers' potential disobedience with an outsider must be difficult indeed, especially since he was the one in charge of security. Remaining silent had to be standard policy.

But this situation was unique, and she could see Powers' grudging agreement with her question even before he answered. "Your arrival just before the Emperor's visit has complicated affairs even more. Some of my fellow officers are competing with each other, maneuvering for position in an attempt to curry favor with the Emperor." He glanced away, trying to conceal his distaste. "Unfortunately, his arrival provides them with an unprecedented opportunity to exploit your visit for personal gain."

"You mean to help their careers?" Stella almost stamped her foot in exasperation. "How would discrediting me do that?"

"You don't understand, do you?" Powers said. "If they ask the question that exposes you as a traitor who's been corrupted by the enemy, they can receive Kolanera's blessing for saving the Empire from a disastrous mistake."

"Don't they care that our capture of an enemy ship can turn this war around and save the Empire?"

"To them, it's your capture of the ship," Powers said, "not theirs. The only way they can get credit for it is if you can show them how to pilot it and employ its ordnance. And you just said you couldn't."

"So it's easier to promote their careers by tearing me down than by building on what I know? General Gage mentioned that some officers might try to ingratiate themselves with the Emperor, but this behavior is selfish and unconscionable. Even worse, it's treason to oppose what can help us."

Powers' mustache twitched. "To be fair, the matter's not quite as clear-cut as you suggest. They do have doubts as to whether or not you can be trusted, as to whether or not you are what you claim." He looked away. "Since I've defended you, I too am suspect. Major Lovejoy, in particular, is not pleased."

"He didn't like your defense of Orian's family either," Stella said. "I know General Gage didn't order you to do that. Do you mind telling me why you did?"

Powers took a deep breath. "Some of the things you said made sense. Punishing a family for another's failures..." He closed his eyes and rubbed them with his fingers, then returned his hand sharply to his side. "It's always seemed like a necessary thing to do. In order to assure your soldiers' loyalty and obedience during a terrible war which you were losing, you made certain the penalty was severe enough that it touched not only them but their loved ones as well. I always believed in that principle, but maybe it's flawed."

A 'two-dimensional' soldier? Not quite. Or perhaps he was a rigid, narrow one who was capable of change. "Is that the only reason you clapped for Tessa Farron?" she said. "It took considerable courage."

"There was something else," Powers said, ignoring the compliment. "Virtually every person on this base was inclined to love you, and believe it or not, that includes most of the officers. After all, we've all been praying for a deliverer for a long time. But there was another thing I didn't quite expect."

Stella frowned. "What was that?"

Powers motioned toward a set of large double doors guarded by soldiers and led her to them. "When the *Spaceranger* docked," he said, "I supervised the transfer of personnel. Almost without exception, the crew's primary concern was about you, not themselves. They all seemed worried about your safety and welfare."

"So?"

Powers squared his shoulders. "Love and respect are seldom won by traitors. In all my twenty-six years as a soldier, I've never seen a crew that feels the way about their commanding officer as your crew does." Lifting his hand, he gave her a crisp salute, and then nodded at the guards to open the doors.

In reflex, she returned his salute, searching in her mind for something to say. But the doors were opening, and the people in the great hall beyond exploded in cheers when they saw her. George and Thunderheart were the first to rush forward, their lips parted in giant grins.

An hour later, when she walked through other doors with Tessa Farron and her son, the reception was more restrained but still warm. "Commander McMasters," Gage said, "it's good seeing you again. Tessa and Ulysses, I'm so glad you could come." She shook hands with both of them and smiled down at Ulysses, who still clung to his mother's side. "You're not afraid of me, little soldier, are you?"

A thumb found its way into Ulysses' mouth. Fabulous voyager.

Gage laughed, squatted before him, and produced something from her pocket. A small prism hovered a few centimeters above her palm, each of its many facets a different color. By turning her hand, Gage was able to make the shimmering object revolve.

Ulysses stared down his thumb, mesmerized by the dazzling device. He giggled, and then reached out. The prism settled to his hand and then rose again.

"That should make you happy." Gage chuckled as she rose. She ushered them toward a table covered lavishly with canapés and exotic hors d'oeuvres.

"Thank you," Stella whispered as they walked.

"I've made arrangements for both of them after your departure," Gage whispered back. Then, louder: "How are your quarters, Commander? Comfortable, I hope?"

"Excellent. They sure beat the casket I sleep in on ship." Aware that the last ship she had occupied had been the *Pregnant Song*, she quickly changed the subject. "This is an extremely beautiful room."

Gage nodded in pride. The chamber resembled a small, sumptuous ballroom, and when Stella looked up, she saw the stars through a transparent ceiling. "We reserve this room for our most illustrious visitors."

"Loran dined here, I assume."

"Oh yes. He had three helpings of Lei-on-a sprayfish with white mint sauce."

Stella smiled, liking this woman and grateful for her treatment of Tessa and Ulysses. The informality of this gathering was another kindness. There was no long reception line, no pomp and pageantry. Glancing about, she could see that all her main systems officers were present with the exception, of course, of Jason. George, Myles, Carol were watching her. And Lee, by far the youngest, who outranked them all.

Smoothly, Gage arranged that Stella and her guests received exquisite crystal plates. There were cookies and pastry and nine kinds of flavored ices for Ulysses and even more exotic choices for the adults. Placing a small mound of purple-black substance on a cracker, Gage proffered it to her with a wink.

"Try this."

"What is it?"

Gage rolled her eyes wickedly. "Caviar. Food of the Gods."

Oh yes, Gage had mentioned it when she'd been piloting the

Slug ship. She took a tentative bite, then another.

"Well?"

Stella rolled it around in her mouth. "I'm sorry," she said, "it just seems bitter. Maybe it's my synthetic taste buds."

"Oh, that's right." Instead of acting embarrassed, Gage turned, took two long-stemmed glasses from an attendant's tray, and handed her one. "Perhaps you'll like our champagne better."

Stella sipped and found to her surprise that it was delicious, dry and bracing with a subtle and resonant undertaste. She hummed to herself in amazement.

"Like it? It's a New Bordeaux from Lotus, vintage '98."

"Oh, yes. It's superb. Ambrosia! Do you know"-she took another sip-"this is the first food or drink I've been able to really taste?" She held up the delicate glass, studying the tiny bubbles in the pinkish liquid. "Usually it's bland or just bitter like the caviar, but this..."

Gage rolled her glass beneath her nose and took a sip, savoring it. "Some things are just a mystery, Commander. Miraculous as the fact of life itself." She waved a small hand out at the cosmos. To quote a fourth millennium poet, "Life's a mystery in a mad god's dream/Even our thoughts aren't what they seem."

Stella savored her own drink in deepening amazement. What was Gage? A crusty, hardnosed general or an erudite connoisseur-philosopher? Obviously both, and perhaps more. As Gage took her arm and steered her away from the table, Stella noticed that a woman officer had deftly assumed responsibility for Tessa and her son. Apparently this occasion was all carefully orchestrated. There were no hostile officers present and, as if by an understanding, Gage had her all to herself.

They approached a broad, closed panel in the wall. Gage pressed a button and it rose.

Inside, behind a plastene screen, were books, not vidtexts or sensies, but actual bound volumes which you held in your hands to read. There must have been at least twenty.

"Didn't know there were so many, did you?" Gage said.

"That's an understatement. I saw a few in a museum once,

but nothing like this." She peered through the screen. "What's that one bound with, Eptex?"

"No, leather."

Stella *ooohed*, scanned the titles. Shakespeare-she had heard of him. Confucius, Dante-nothing. A title on a particularly ancient volume caught her attention. *Medea*.

"It's a play from Terra written in ancient Greek," Gage said in response to Stella's look. "It's about a brilliant, fearless woman known for her cleverness and witchcraft. But perhaps you know the story?"

"No, I don't."

"Hmm. I found the book at an outpost on Lotus. It's one of the most valuable volumes in my collection." She shook her head. "Poor Medea, she betrays her country and gives all her love and assistance to Jason, who ultimately betrays her for another woman, one who just happens to be younger and a princess."

Stella gazed down at her empty glass, feeling as if she needed another drink. "What did she do when she found out?"

Gage whistled softly and pressed the button. The panel closed, shutting the past from view.

"She arranged for the princess's death by sending her a poisoned gown and diadem which also killed the king when he tried to help her. Then she killed her two children, who happened to be Jason's as well."

"Seems awfully extreme," Stella said.

Gage shrugged. "Some women you just don't want to cross."

Midway through the banquet, Stella found herself staring at the general's nameplate again. *A. Gage.* "General," she finally said, "do you mind if I ask you a question?"

Sitting next to her at the table's head, Gage spread her arms. "You're the guest of honor. Ask what you damned well please."

"All right. Just out of curiosity, what is your first name?"

Halfway down the table, Colonel Powers and another officer chuckled.

"That's a sore spot with me," Gage replied. "My officers have been trying to find it out for years without success." She glowered half-seriously in their direction. "Had to block my own personal file to stop them from raiding it. Heard they'd set odds and placed bets."

"Hmm." Stella stroked her chin. "Is it Ann?"

Gage frowned. "No."

"Alicia?"

"No."

"Annabelle?"

Gage struck the table. "Most emphatically, no!"

An officer near the other end of the table laughed. "We've all tried to finesse it out of General Gage one way or another, Commander, but she's too wise for us." He raised a glass as if to toast her. "We've guessed everything from April to Aphrodite, Ashley to Ariadne. All the general's ever allowed us is that she'll sign the manifest if we ever deliver the right one."

Stella winked at Gage. "So life's a mystery, eh, General? What's the matter, don't you like your name?"

"You wouldn't like it either if it was yours," Gage snapped with a rueful smile. In the resulting laughter, she frowned at Thunderheart, who sat beside Stella. "Something wrong with him?" she said.

Stella turned to Thunderheart, seeing that he had barely touched his Elano sunfowl and wild rice with spiced almonds. Instead, he stared with an avid yet desperate longing at the attendants who waited on their table. The seven young men and women flowed efficiently about the diners, pouring wine and bringing trays almost before they were needed. They seemed so smooth.

Stella leaned toward Gage. "Are they empaths?"

"Why, yes, they're a hep-path. Bioengineered and specially reared for such functions. They-Oh!" She looked at Thunderheart in sudden understanding.

Stella did too. However, it didn't seem to matter that they stared, for Thunderheart was oblivious of them. His eyes followed the hep-path hungrily as they glided about the banquet table. Thunderheart-a piece of a broken puzzle forever without a place.

Stella took his hand and squeezed it. *You've served me. Now let me serve you and take away some of your pain.*

Thunderheart started, and then turned. Seeing her smile, he slowly smiled back.

"Better?" she whispered.

"Yes. Commander, I'm sorry."

"No need to be," she told him. Watching an attendant fill Thunderheart's glass, she found herself questioning for the first time the practice of creating empath groups. Was it right to start determining people's destinies almost at birth, especially since the danger always existed that all but one might die and leave the last an orphan?

"If you stare any harder, George, your eyes'll spang right out of your head."

Carol's voice made Stella look across the table at George, who tore his gaze from her and Thunderheart's clasped hands. "Do you have some kind of problem?" George asked gruffly.

"Not particularly," Carol said. "But when a grown man stares at someone for five minutes straight without even blinking, I'm inclined to wonder."

"Hardly that," George said in embarrassment. He rubbed his beard and took a gulp of water.

"I once used to feud that way with a man," Gage told Carol. "We did it all the time. Or to be more precise, I did." She sat, apparently waiting for a response.

Stella's weapons officer returned the general's gaze, and for the first time, Stella saw how alike they were. Both were small, tough, outspoken women.

"You started most of the arguments?" Carol finally said.

"Yes." Gage ran her fingers softly along the tablecloth. "You see, I loved him, but he did not love me."

Carol blinked, then reddened and looked away. Stella saw her tremble.

So that's why she keeps picking on him, she thought in surprise. Or at least it's part of the reason. She took a sip of her fourth glass of champagne, and then realized it was going to her head. Carefully, she set the glass down.

Gage, who seemed to have a sixth sense for detecting weaknesses in people, now honed in on Lee, who sat beside Carol. "First Officer, you seem awfully quiet. Is something wrong?"

Lee smiled. "Everything's fine, ser."

"That's good, because if you're brooding about destroying our guard ship, it's wasted sentiment. You did the absolute right thing, son."

"Thank you, ser," Lee said. "But with all due respect, you weren't the one who gave the order."

Gage's mouth popped open. "No, I wasn't," she returned after a moment, "but I respect you for it." She studied Lee as if seeing him fully for the first time.

Stella turned to Gage, feeling she needed to steer the conversation in a new, crucial direction. With the base commander, it seemed one had to expect a revelation every other minute.

"What's the situation with the Emperor?"

Gage checked her cronex. "He and his sizable retinue are due here in just over nineteen hours. We should spot him shortly after he comes through Scylla."

Scylla was the black hole located six hours away, on the opposite side of the base from its twin Charybdis, down which Stella had traveled. Between them, the two singularities bracketed the base, though at markedly different distances.

"That's interesting," Stella said. "My orders are to dock briefly here and then pass through Scylla on my way to rendezvousing with General Loran's forces." She leaned forward. "With all that I've learned, General, I find it more important than ever that your experts help me clarify and utilize what I know so that I can do just that."

Gage indicated that they should leave the table. They rose and moved off several paces, ignoring the others' stares.

"Commander," Gage said, "things are in turmoil here. With the Emperor's imminent arrival and a captured enemy ship..." She laughed deep in her throat. "Hell, if it was up to me, I'd say Godspeed. But you must understand that I can't make any promises. From what I've heard about the Emperor's enthusiastic nature, he'll be very eager to meet you and reluctant to let you go. After all, it's not every day one of our officers manages to defeat the enemy and bring back proof of it."

Stella stepped closer and drilled her with her eyes. "General Gage, there may come a time when I'll have to ask you for a favor, a huge one of unprecedented dimensions."

For the first time, Gage seemed surprised. "I-I'm not sure what you mean."

How do YOU like being jolted for a change, General? Slowly, Stella reached in her pocket for a handkerchief and removed a speck of food from Gage's suit. "Desperate times require desperate measures, General. Sometimes the ends justify any means."

Gage swallowed, staring up at her. "My God, you're the toughest damned bitch I've ever met. I thought I chewed rock but you shit diamonds, don't you?"

Over Gage's head, Stella saw a young male officer approaching them. At the table, Tessa Farron watched her in concern. Stella forced herself to smile back.

"A message, General," the officer said.

"Thank you, Marquez." Gage took the note and read it, then read it again before flashing Stella a taut look. She turned and approached the table.

"I have news," she announced.

They all stared up at her. Stella saw Tessa reach out and silence her son.

Gage locked her hands behind her back. "I've just received a message. Our Emperor, Kolanera the Fifth, is due to arrive much earlier than expected. Two minutes ago, we scoped his ship on this side of Scylla." She gave Stella a short look, and then turned back. "I'm happy to say that he should be here in less than six hours."

CHAPTER SIXTEEN

Standing stiffly in the buzzing Control Center, Stella riveted her eyes on the crackling image of the *Imperium* as it swelled like an exploding star above the holovids. She gripped the cold edge of a console with mounting hope and apprehension as the ship and its all-important passenger neared. The Emperor was less than an hour away now, barely two million kilometers out.

The sprawling complex bristled with activity, the crew incessantly feeding data into the AI that would guide the ship in and making constant adjustments on computer astromaps. Being responsible for the Emperor's safe arrival clearly instilled a tense concern for detail in those responsible, and Stella found their energy nerve-wracking.

Not General Gage. She stood with legs spread and arms locked behind her, calmly surveying the scene. Or was she calm? Stella wondered too about her own officers. To her right, Colonel Powers and Myles Uxman were conducting what seemed to be a close, cordial conversation, and she almost smiled at the two security officers' apparent friendliness. As she watched, Myles came toward her, pulling one of his earlobes in excitement. Stella prepared herself for something important, as befitted the occasion.

"I think it's Amaryllis," he said.

"What?"

Myles' soft lips curled in a smile. "It's the worst name I could conjure up. Colonel Powers says it hasn't been used yet."

Amaryllis Gage. The combination was mind-boggling. "What about Agnes, or Anastasia?" she said.

Myles stole a look at Gage. "I think they've both been asked. But I'll check with Powers."

Shortly after he left, Carol arrived. A certain tension pervaded Stella's relations with her weapons officer after Gage's comments at the banquet.

"I'm sorry about what happened at dinner," Carol said.

"It's all right."

"No, it's not. Gage nailed me cold. The only thing is, I don't understand why I didn't see how I felt about George, especially since I served on a crew with him before." She sighed, her small face puzzled. "What an obstinate, impossible man. I don't know why he gets inside me."

"Maybe now that he knows, you can make it mutual."

"Are you serious? Stella, you've got his heart locked in your pocket." She glanced away in embarrassment. "Maybe that's why I'm so fricked."

"Carol," she said, "I don't want him."

"Not at all?" Carol's eyes searched her own. "You don't even find his interest flattering?"

"I'm only human," she allowed. "Any woman would feel pleased to have a man like George interested. But, no, I don't want him, at least not that way."

Carol gave a shrug and touched Stella's hand. "Thanks. Unfortunately, he's not yours to give."

As she left, Lee approached with a boyish smile. "I wanted to thank you," he said. "For Tessa Farron and her son."

"It seemed the right thing to do."

"Yes." He glanced around and lowered his voice. "Commander, will you be able to tell the people here what you know? Will they even listen? Perhaps they'll just appoint a committee."

She hardened her lips, and then shrugged.

Lee nodded. "Let me know if you need me," he whispered.

As he left, Stella half-expected another officer to approach, but none did. She smiled at Thunderheart and returned her attention to the Emperor's approach. Lee was right. What if they kept her here and tied the matter up in bureaucracy, perhaps appointed a committee or two to study the enemy ship and her testimony? That could take months or years, and in the meantime Loran would fight his great battle and lose it, five thousand light-years away.

"Commander."

She turned to see Gage. Lovejoy and another officer stood beside her, holding a softly glowing, green body-cuff in their hands.

"I'm sorry," Gage said. "We've just briefed the Emperor and his advisors. Regent-Protector Malek ordered this precaution."

"What?" She stared at the restraining device.

Stella's officers immediately pressed forward. "This is intolerable!" George said. "You've already taken away our weapons. You can't do this too!"

"I have my orders," Gage said. "I was directed to do this."

Carol, Lee, and Myles started shouting. Stella raised her hand for silence.

Then Thunderheart leapt forward, making Lovejoy and the other officer retreat. "Touch her and you're dead," he said.

"No, Thunderheart, it's all right." She motioned him back, not wanting to unleash a member of the Emperor's Arm here in the Control Center. Thunderheart obeyed, his eyes fastened like death on Gage's officers. One signal from her, Stella knew, and the two men would be killed, though it would cost Thunderheart his own life.

George's voice rose in outrage, his great body trembling as he pointed at the body-cuff. "Commander McMasters defeats the enemy, brings their ship here, and you do this to her?"

"Hopefully," Gage said, "I'll be permitted to remove it soon." She glanced at the device in apparent disgust, and then motioned to Lovejoy and the other officer.

Stella let them slip the glowing body-cuff around her and tune it as tight as they could so that her arms were pressed against her body. Lovejoy grinned slightly as he adjusted a seam.

The body-cuff was made for someone of more-than-superhuman strength. Despite her augmented abilities, Stella's arms felt sealed in cement. Even her legs were partially restricted by the device's lower extension.

"It's a special model," Lovejoy said. "Nonflexible, electrically-generated superpolymer gryptite. I've been informed it's state of the art."

Stella ignored him, turning to Gage. "One thing's for sure," she said. "Your first name's not Angel."

"I have my orders," Gage repeated.

"Yes," Stella said. "And we all know disobedience's a problem in the ranks these days, don't we?"

Gage turned to George, who stood glaring at her. "The Emperor's Regent-Protector issued another order. The pilot of the *Spaceranger* is to be disconnected immediately from all ship controls. Life-support, of course, will continue."

George rubbed his thigh. "Am I supposed to restore his brain to his body?"

"No. His brain is to be disconnected from all attachments except the nutri-cell and left in place, exactly where it is."

That means sensory deprivation, Stella thought. She imagined Jason trapped in the dark without any stimulation, and her heart twisted in anguish. "You can't be serious," she told Gage. "It would not only be cruel, it could drive him insane."

Gage didn't reply.

George moved forward like a man wading through a turgid stream. "Stella's right. It's worse than performing a lobotomy. The procedure is known to cause psychosis within eight to twelve hours because there's no sensory input."

Gage locked her hands behind her. "Other comrades have managed to tolerate it. At the Academy, I once floated for thirty hours in an SD tank without any harmful effect."

"It's not the same thing!" George spread his great arms as if to describe the size of the problem. "Even with an SD tank, there's minimal sensation. With Jason, there'll be none! While erasing the interface between a housed brain and a ship has never been done before, there are preliminary indications that its effects would be far more damaging than any SD experiment we've ever tried. We'll lose a perfectly good pilot for no reason at all."

"I have my orders," Gage repeated.

"Your orders stink!"

Lee stepped forward. "General Gage, may I ask you a question?"

Gage nodded. "Proceed."

"Very well. In your opinion, is the latter order a good order or a bad one?"

Gage colored. "It's not my privilege to judge."

"If the order were to blow up this base, would you obey it?"

Gage stiffened, and then nodded at the monitors. "Comrades, we have a docking procedure to perform. Permit us to do it, or you'll all be asked to leave the Control Center."

An hour later, when the *Imperium's* enormous bulk slowly entered its designated berth, Stella could think only of Jason. George had left the Control Center fifty minutes ago accompanied by two of the base's medtechs, and by now they should have begun to detach Jason's brain from the ship. Or was the process completed? Was Jason already reduced to thoughts imprisoned in a void, confined in limbo? Jason's situation was far worse than hers. He would have no sensation whatsoever, would be unable to feel his metallic skin and multi-engine heart, the people in the corridors that were his arteries. What must it be like to be totally bound and circumscribed by your thoughts, to feel yourself already going mad?

Stella looked at Gage, who returned her stare with difficulty. She sensed that Gage hated her orders, yet as a soldier was compelled to obey them. But that didn't make Stella's anger any less intense. Grimly, she worked her muscles beneath her body-cuff and managed to achieve a millimeter of movement. Lovejoy took a step back, bumping into Colonel Powers, who seemed unable to take his eyes off her. Stella's officers, in turn, glanced alternately between the monitors and her, their expressions a mixture of rage and shame.

On the monitors, base personnel unrolled the plush purple carpet down which the Emperor would pass. Within minutes, Gage and most of her main officers arrived and stood in the foreground, waiting to witness and greet the Imperial procession. As Stella watched, the electromagnetic grappling clamps closed on the *Imperium's* bow and the ship finally settled fully into its berth.

Minutes passed. Gage and her officers waited. In the Control Center, Stella and her crew waited, guarded by Powers and the personnel Gage had posted.

Then the *Imperium's* hatch sprang open, and realms of fantasy emerged.

First came beautiful dancing girls and boys clad in wispy, diaphanous veils that scattered flower petals, sequins, and white doves, the latter soaring up into the vaulted docking area above. Others led peacocks on jeweled leashes whose gaudy feathers vied for supremacy with the lithe, gleaming bodies of dancers. These Stella recognized as devotees of the 'New Son' sect which borrowed its tenets from ancient, contradictory religions and believed that the ninety-ninth incarnation of Jesus-Buddha was imminent. The last messiah would bring enlightenment, free the empire from alien infidels, and usher all true believers into Nirvana. To many, Kolanera himself was the savior, but judging from the dancers' sensual movements and the pounding, orgiastic rhythm of harps, pipes, and drums, the Enlightened One's message pertained more to the body than the spirit.

At last, triumphant, came twelve-year-old Kolanera the Fifth, borne aloft in an elaborate sedan chair with rich, brocaded curtains parted to reveal his Magnificence. Stella was half-surprised he wasn't nibbling some delicacy like minced peacocks' brains.

"What is this? What are they doing?"

Stella turned in her body-cuff. The incredulous outburst came from Thunderheart, staring at the idol to which he'd sworn and consecrated his honor. He looked like a man whose faith was shaken.

Stella swung back and inspected the boy whose curly, dark-haired face rose from his neck like a beautiful flower. Perhaps it was the angle, but at the moment it looked like a decadent, diseased one, and she felt her spirits sink. Turning, she stared at Colonel Powers until he finally managed to tear his gaze away and look at her.

"Tell me, Colonel Powers," she said. "Who's going to clean up all the bird shit?"

An hour later, Powers relayed a message: the Emperor wanted to see her.

Despite being treated as an enemy, Stella felt anticipation wash through her. A year before, she had been a token supervisor on a third-rate world at the tag-end of a mediocre career. Now, through a series of fantastic events, she had been catapulted into an audience with the Emperor. Though she knew she was overreacting, her stride felt springy-body-cuff and all-as Powers and others led her and her crew to the royal chambers.

When she entered, the Imperial party knelt in deep meditation on a platform at the front of the room. Kolanera sat perched on a pile of satin cushions in a full lotus position. To his right, Malek, the Regent-Protector, emulated him, his neat goatee pointing down like a dagger at his hands. Others, the almost nude dance-singers Stella had seen before, clustered about them within an emerald triptych screen with an overarching canopy of splendid flowers. Incense filled the chamber, its scent so intense even Stella could smell it.

Before the Emperor, people lay prostrate on the synmarble floor. Gage, Lovejoy, and others were on their stomachs, outstretched hands cupped upward in the symbolic gesture of supplicants.

To her right, another door opened and George was escorted inside. His eyes found hers across the ten meters distance, and she suppressed an urge to shout out a question about Jason's welfare. A moment later, a guard indicated that George should prostrate himself like the others, and he obeyed. So too did Stella and her crew when Powers nodded downward. With Thunderheart's help, she lay down beside him, cursing the suit which neutralized her abilities. She couldn't even lie down by herself!

Time passed. A soft breeze stirred the air.

"You may rise," a deep voice proclaimed.

Thunderheart assisted her to her feet, and she faced Malek, a tall, sharp-featured man who strode a few steps forward in a resplendent robe. With a grand, sweeping gesture he indicated those assembled. "Oh, Omniscient, behold the loyal faces of your subjects."

"Where is General Gage?" the boy asked in a soft, beautiful voice. "I wish to see her again."

The commanding officer of Loran Base stepped forward and bowed. "I am here, Enlightened One."

Kolanera's eyes turned. "And that nice major. What's his name? The one who gave me the jeweled model of this base?"

"Major Lovejoy, Supreme Incarnation," Malek supplied as Lovejoy bowed deeply.

The Emperor's eyes settled on Lovejoy. Kolanera smiled, raised a large, gleaming model of the base in both hands, and shook it. "We are most pleased, Major Lovejoy."

Lovejoy bowed again. "I am joyful beyond words, Enlightened One."

A toy, Stella thought. It's like the bauble Gage gave little Ulysses. Something for a child.

"I've saved the best for last," Kolanera said. He craned his neck, looking about the room. "Where is this Scourge of the Scaleys," he called, "the bold commander who has routed the enemy and captured their ship?"

CHAPTER SEVENTEEN

Stella braced herself and bowed her head, aware that everyone in the large chamber was staring at her. "Oh, Omniscient, I stand here unworthy before you."

"Unworthy!" the Emperor piped. He all but scrambled to his feet in eagerness before his beautiful features clouded. "Why are you bound? You are a hero of the realm, not a prisoner."

Malek glided quickly toward him, dipping his head in obeisance. "You remember, Supreme Incarnation, the data transmission concerning her actions? This officer, Stella McMasters, not only managed to pilot an alien warship all by herself, but personally attacked this base. You decided, Son of God, with my humble counsel, that it would be wise to confine her in a body-cuff lest she do you harm."

"If she had really attacked this base, it would be a gaping ruin." Kolanera turned from Malek, who towered over him, and frowned at Stella, then swung back to Malek. For a moment he looked only like a little boy.

"May I speak with her?" he said.

You don't ask, Stella thought. If you truly are the Emperor, you tell. But of course he was only a twelve-year-old boy who would not legally escape Malek's control and assume his full powers until he reached nineteen.

Malek bowed deeply before he replied. "Your slightest wish is our command, Supreme One."

Kolanera gathered his purple robe together and stepped off the dais. Stella started to kneel, but the Emperor stopped her, actually laid hands on her cheeks. She heard the room murmur in awe.

"Your face, Stella McMasters," Kolanera said, "it feels a bit strange."

Stella looked down at him, wanting to kneel. "I'm cyber-enhanced, Son of God. Nearly seventy percent of my body was destroyed in a fusion-reactor meltdown."

"Oh yes, I recall. It's one of the reasons my Regent doesn't trust you."

Stella glanced quickly at Malek, catching a fleeting look of embarrassment. She smiled.

"Omniscient, you have only to ask for my life and it's yours."

Kolanera waved his hand. "Oh, but I want you to live! The Empire needs a great hero like you."

More murmuring. Kolanera ran his eyes over her body. "My science advisors tell me that a few such as you are capable of great things." Hero worship stirred in his eyes. "Can you really jump ten meters high in the air and crush men with your bare hands?"

He's just a little nip. If I could only get him away from Malek and the rest, he'd have a chance. "Yes, Supreme Incarnation." She hesitated, and then made her decision. She had to try it now, for if she didn't, she might never get another chance.

"Enlightened One," she said, "while I can perform such feats, there are more important matters to consider. Because of what my crew and I were privileged to accomplish, it now lies within your power to turn the tide against the enemy."

Malek instantly stepped forward. "There'll be none of that! The matter will be decided later in proper-"

Kolanera raised his hand, and Malek ceased. "This is true? We can actually win?"

"Yes." She panned the chamber with her eyes. Everyone was watching her-Kolanera's retinue and Imperial and base guards, Thunderheart and her officers, Gage, Colonel Powers, and the detested Lovejoy. "Omniscient, may I be permitted to make a suggestion?"

Malek opened his mouth, and then closed it when Kolanera flicked his hand. "You may say anything," he said.

Stella licked her lips. "Son of God, in our conflict with the enemy, I was granted an unprecedented advantage. My mind and that of the 'Slug' that guided the alien vessel merged. He didn't control or manipulate me in the slightest, but as a result of the interchange I was able not only to pilot his craft and employ its superior weaponry, but to improve quickly at both operations. I am now able to pilot and navigate the enemy's ship and use its weapons as well as he was."

"You can?" Kolanera said. "Please continue!"

"I propose that we establish an immediate Priority-One program to study and harness what I know. Under your authority, Supreme One, we should have all experts here examine myself, the alien ship, and the enemy's tissue cultures. If we proceed quickly enough, there's an excellent chance we may be able to aid General Loran in his massive campaign just a few weeks away."

"We can also give you the glory and attention you so obviously seek," Malek sneered. "But the fact remains that you are deeply suspect. You're a cyborg-human who not only can pilot an enemy ship but who actually used it to attack this base. Isn't that so, Colonel Powers?"

Powers stiffened. "Yes, she did, but-"

"So you see," Malek continued, "the Enlightened One is not about to be bedazzled by any high-sounding recommendation you make." He straightened his crimson robe. "After the New Son and his servants have rested following their onerous visit to review General Loran's forces, we can establish judicious procedures for setting up a system of committees that will examine the evidence and make recommendations."

"That could be too late!" General Gage blurted. "With all due respect-"

Malek cut her off. "The Omniscient One is far too wise to plunge down a black hole of emotional rhetoric into a hasty decision." He looked smugly at Stella and made what looked like symbolic hand gestures. "As it is written, 'Enlightenment does not come to those whose mouths are open while their eyes and ears remain sealed.'"

"Why don't you let him speak for himself?" Stella snapped.

Malek's jaw sagged. "What?"

Stella squirmed, her anger increased by the fact that she couldn't even raise her hand to scratch a maddening itch on her nose. She glared at Malek's neatly clipped goatee, wanting to tear it from his face. "What are you afraid of anyway?" she said. "That someone might penetrate the web you've woven about your Emperor and do something that's actually good for the Empire? Don't you see that we've lost this war and that we'll all be destroyed if we don't do something?"

Malek sputtered. Stella knew that her words could cost her her life, but plunged on before the Regent-Protector could reply. "Enlightened One, I beseech you on the behalf of our comrades. In the final analysis, it is they and they alone whom we serve. No matter how high our station, we are nothing without them, for our only purpose is to serve their best interest."

"This is outrage-treason!" Malek gestured to one of his guards. "Remove her!"

Gage, Powers, and Thunderheart moved forward along with the guard. "Regent-Protector," Gage said, "as commanding officer of this base, I request that such orders pass first through me." She glanced pointedly at some of her guards.

Malek's face hardened. "I am the Regent-Protector. It is my duty to protect the Emperor when he's endangered."

Gage locked her hands behind her, gazing up at him with steely eyes. "If I am not mistaken, the Rules of Regency stipulate that you should first offer your recommendation to the Emperor. In the event the Incarnation does not concur, a two-thirds vote of the Regent-Protector's Council is then required."

Malek's eyebrows rose. "They're over two hundred light-years away!"

"Then I suggest you inform them at once," Gage said.

During the tense pause that followed, Stella realized that Malek probably kept the Council under his heavy thumb. Still, Gage had a point.

"I see no reason to have her removed," Kolanera said. "After all, she's already securely bound." He smiled up at her and laid his hand on her body-cuff. "You wouldn't hurt me, would you, Stella?"

Stella. Oh, I bet you'd make a great Emperor, she thought, if we could just hack away the briars that surround you.

"I'd protect you with my life," she said, half-expecting one of his guards to end it from behind at any moment.

Major Lovejoy marched forward and halted, clicking his gleaming black boots together as he bowed to Kolanera. "Promises are pretty, but we must judge by actions." He glanced at Gage. "Though others may disagree, I must state my belief that this officer, Stella Singlethorne McMasters, is a traitor and most unworthy, Supreme Incarnation, to continue in your service. If anything, she should be executed."

Lee, George, and others protested, but it was Thunderheart who stepped forward. He knelt on one knee before the Emperor and reverently raised his hand.

"Ser, I am Thunderheart, bred and led from birth in your Majesty's service. My Emperor, I am your own!"

Even Malek, Stella saw, was taken back. Kolanera's small hand reached forward and gently touched the patch on Thunderheart's breast pocket which bore the official emblem of the Emperor's Arm. His finger lingered on his own image, placed against the background of a burning lightning bolt.

"Yes, you are," Kolanera said. "You are my highest soldier, the best and most noble."

"Ser," Thunderheart said, "I'm a plain man, not one given to fine and eloquent words." He lowered his head. "Excuse me if I don't know how to address you."

Kolanera chuckled and glanced at Lovejoy. "It might be nice not to be called 'Your Omniscience' or 'Supreme Incarnation' for a change. I especially hate those two." He studied Thunderheart, whose head was nearly on a level with his. "Speak as you feel, Thunderheart."

"Ser," Thunderheart continued, "Stella McMasters is the finest officer I have ever been privileged to serve under. Major Lovejoy has called her a traitor and said she should be executed. In my opinion, anyone who says such things is a fool. She alone has managed to defeat the enemy and present you with the means of victory, and how is she treated? She is thrown into chains and soldiers who ride desks and shuffle papers are permitted to vilify her."

"Hear, hear!" George cried.

"Take off her suit!" Carol shouted.

As Stella marveled at Thunderheart's words-a plain man, not eloquent indeed!-Myles and Lee moved forward to remove her body-cuff as if they'd been given permission. A few moments without interference could make all the difference. If she could just be allowed to remove this thing...

Lovejoy shoved them away, then went to the platform and snatched up the glittering model of the base he had presented the Emperor. He returned and held it toward him. "Please heed, Oh Omniscient. She schemes to destroy your Empire beginning with this very base! Already she has pardoned a traitor who lived here!"

Suddenly it was very still. Kolanera's eyes widened. "Pardoned a traitor?" He turned to Gage. "General, you did not mention this in your report."

Gage sighed. "I felt it could wait, Incarnation. The fire-dart squadron leader fired on Commander McMasters against orders. He later took his own life."

"And later still," Lovejoy sneered, "she absolved him and extended her liberality to his widow and son." He almost beamed at Stella in vindication. "I'm pleased to report that they now share her quarters as her personal guests."

Kolanera blinked up at her. "Is this true?" His skin suddenly broke out in a fine sweat and he wavered on his feet. Malek moved forward to steady him.

He's only a boy, Stella thought. Good as he is, this is too much for him.

"Enlightened One," she began. "I..."

She stopped as Malek half-carried Kolanera to a cushioned chair. "The Incarnation is fatigued from his recent travels," he said. "I'm afraid this last excitement has been too much." He and Kolanera disappeared from view as attendants surrounded them.

When Malek reappeared a minute later, he had a slight smile.

"Is everything all right?" Gage asked.

"Yes, perfectly. There's no need to worry," Malek replied.

"It's merely a slight indisposition. Ah, I see that the episode's already subsided."

Like curtains, the attendants parted, revealing the Emperor sitting in the chair. A male dancer waved an embossed fan near his face.

"Your Majesty..." Thunderheart began.

Kolanera smiled, his eyes glassy. "I declare a period of celebration before we attend to more serious business." His eyes swung about, finally locating Stella. "Is that all right, Stella?" he laughed.

Stella watched as an almost naked girl caressed the Emperor's thigh. The young man who fanned Kolanera bent forward and kissed his cheek.

"You've heard the Enlightened One," Malek said. "Let the days of sacred revels begin!"

Instant jubilation broke out. Some of Kolanera's party raised instruments and launched into a sensual, grinding rhythm. Stella saw three girls dressed only in veils bound down from the platform and seize Thunderheart. "I want you," one said. "Rut with me first."

"No, with me," a shapely, well-endowed blonde dancer insisted. She clamped herself tightly about one of Thunderheart's thighs. "Help me worship the lusty God Jesus-Buddha-Kolanera the Fifth who will save us from the Scaleys. On his cross we will burn in desire together and enter Nirvana!"

Caught tight, Thunderheart turned to Stella with pleading eyes. "Commander..."

"Relax," the blonde girl chided.

"No, Kama," another girl laughed, "we want him stiff!" Deftly, she opened Thunderheart's jacket and started to unbutton his shirt.

"Commander," Thunderheart said, "what should I do?"

Stella glanced at Gage, who stared grimly at the chaos raging about her, then shrugged. "That's up to you," she said. "I'm not sure it really makes any difference."

A sharp crack made her turn just in time to see a dancer's foot smash through the model of Loran Base which Lovejoy had presented to Kolanera. The dancer laughed, scooped it up, and tossed the shattered structure into the air. Stella heard it crash somewhere.

Afterward, escorted back to her quarters by a base and an Imperial guard, Stella was joined by George who ran to catch up with them. "You're not being guarded?" she asked.

"Not right now, apparently," George said. "Guess it's the excitement." He glanced at the guards. "Mind if I walk with her?"

"You may do so," one answered, distracted by some revelers up the corridor. "But don't interfere."

"I won't." George moved closer to Stella as they walked. "There's been some trouble with Jason."

"Oh?" Fear gripped her throat.

"Yes. It looks like a psychotic episode caused by sensory deprivation. Gage gave me permission to play with his chem feed. I was watched by two of the Emperor's goons."

"Will he be all right?"

A shout of laughter came from behind them, followed by a series of whoops. "I hope so," George said. "Gage said I can return there under guard and monitor him."

Shrill feminine laughter erupted behind them as a figure rushed past. It was Thunderheart, his uniform in disarray and his pants down to his buttocks. They watched him yank them up as the three girls from before padded after him, their gauzy garments streaming behind them in the air.

"I don't believe it," Stella said. "For a man of few words he was a master orator with the Emperor. Hell, for a moment I thought he could even make the difference." She nodded at the dancers who chased Thunderheart. "Now he's got half the females on this base panting for his body." She smiled despite herself. "Poor Thunderheart. He can kill dragons with his bare hands, but no one ever prepared him for this."

"Horny wenches indeed," George said, "As long as I've known Thunderheart, he's laid down pheromones like road signs. The reason this hasn't happened before is that he's always had his family to shelter him and provide such things."

In the distance, Thunderheart turned down a side corridor.

He seemed to be gaining, though Stella didn't feel sanguine about his chances.

"You mean women have always found him attractive?" she said.

"You seem surprised."

"I am. It's strange.... I think of him almost as a mother. I never thought of him as being…"

"Not at all?" George said. "Really? You're not even a little jealous?"

"What of?"

George smiled at the dancers, who were just rounding the side corridor after Thunderheart. "Of them."

Stella started to answer, and then reconsidered. "Why, I guess I am a little," she said in surprise. "But I imagine that's normal for a mother."

"Only a mother?" George pressed. "I know he's not Jason, but aren't you interested in him at all?"

How could I be, with Jason? she almost cried, but the naked pain in his eyes stopped her.

"This is good for Thunderheart," Stella finally said. "He's lost so much. He needs something for himself, a little pleasure."

George started to reply but was bumped by several members of the Imperial party as they moved past him. They were sharing a bottle and laughing loudly. Stella heard one of them tell a crude joke whose punch line was instantly rewarded by guffaws.

"I wonder how the hell Gage is going to keep a lid on this," George said with a rueful expression. "How do you tell a drug-addicted Emperor to keep his entourage orderly and stave off state-sanctioned anarchy?"

"Drug-addicted? What makes you say that?" She tapped her forehead. "Wait, he did sweat and sway on his feet."

"Right. When he learned about Tessa and Ulysses."

"But the boy's only twelve, too young to be doing such a thing!"

"Apparently Malek disagrees. Did you also notice the glassy look in Kolanera's eyes just before he called for the revelries? That meant he'd gone into systemic shock. Malek's got the kid addicted, probably gave him a shot to supplement his implant. Also, the bastard's using sex to influence him, warp his judgment."

"I saw that," Stella said. "Does Malek think he can get away with it?" She slapped her thigh. "But hell, he already is. I bet he told the boy to 'declare a period of celebration' in order to seize control here. Gage can't resist when she's fighting chaos."

"Malek. That degenerate's corrupted and perverted the boy." George hissed and glanced cautiously at an Imperial guard. "If only Kolanera's parents hadn't been killed! A child like him doesn't have a chance."

Poor kid. He might make an excellent leader, Stella thought. If only I could help him.

George nudged her. "This is why I questioned our orders at the beginning. Why I gave you so much trouble. It wasn't just that the enemy was so superior. The Empire has become decadent and irredeemably corrupt. You see it now firsthand, Stella. It's a dying animal whose final trump will be blown by that pompous ass Loran."

"You can't mean that," she faltered. "You're saying it doesn't make any difference who wins, that what we're fighting for isn't worth it?"

George sighed, his great chest heaving. "Is what you just saw worth anyone's blood? Could the enemy possibly be any worse?" He shuddered, his breath hitching. "For a while you almost had me believing otherwise, but I can't defend this. God in heaven, our rulers see the truth. They must see it. Yet they do nothing."

"If Malek-"

"It's not just Malek," George said. "The Empire's a vast, barren pigsty, Stella. Malek's in power because he's a representative hog, or perhaps even the best we have to offer. He's exactly what we deserve."

Stella felt her will weaken. Maybe George was right. Look at what had happened: she'd beaten the enemy and captured their ship and yet no one believed her, no one would even listen. Instead, they cast insults, called her a traitor. And Jason was...

What was the point in continuing? George was right. Let the

Maleks and Lovejoys prevail and the All-Mother triumph. And she would, of course. In the end she would conquer the galaxy, abetted by their own stupidity.

She gripped herself beneath the tight green cocoon they'd wrapped her in. *It is when we are most opposed and cruelly tested that we discover our truest self. Pain and failure and crushing adversity shall sound the dirge of our spirit's death, or be the crucible from which, phoenix-bright, it soars anew into the sky.*

Sentimental crap...where had she read such tripe? But she felt herself harden, pull together inside into a hard knot. She couldn't give in to George's cynical defeatism. She was still the Commander. Even though she no longer had a ship, her crew still looked to her.

"There are reasons we should fight," she said. "I can give you hundreds why our side is better than the enemy's and why we shouldn't give up."

"Hundreds?" George laughed bitterly. "Let's hear 'em. This oughta be good."

"All right." She gazed ahead at the guarded door of her quarters as they neared it. "George Darron. Lee Song. Carol Wayne. Myles Uxman..."

"Stella," he said, "this isn't..."

"Jason and Thunderheart and his dead family," she continued. "Brett Duvall, Nick and Morner and over two hundred brave crew who died in battle and whose names I still don't know even though I was their commander. They make it worth it, damn it!"

George coughed. "I'm sorry. I should have thought."

"For God's sake, help me," she said.

"Help you? How can I?" George raised a fist then lowered it when a guard grunted behind them. "I hate to say this, Stella, but I expect that bastard Malek to assassinate you."

Stella swallowed. "That possibility had crossed my mind. But I'm not dead yet, George." She hesitated. "Please, find a way to help."

George sighed. "Stella, we're in prison here, freaking helpless." He nodded at her body-cuff. "You more than anyone should know that."

"I'm not helpless as long as I don't think I am," she said. "Don't go belly-up on me, George. Damn it, find a way to help."

They reached her door and one of the two guards stationed there stepped forward with an instrument to remove her suit. She stared at George, feeling the body-cuff slacken about her and grow loose beneath the guard's hands.

"All right," George said aloud, "I will."

She nodded and stepped inside her quarters, hearing the door slide shut behind her.

"Stella," Tessa Farron said urgently as she came forward. "General Gage just called you. She's on the cen-scan now."

She looked at the bubble-shaped booth against the wall near her bed. *Gage!* Maybe the disastrous audience with the Emperor had made her realize something had to be done. Maybe she wanted to help.

Quickly she went to it and slipped through the door, pulling it shut behind her. Turning, she faced Gage's face on the screen.

"Go ahead, General," she said. "And for the Empire's sake, you better have some good news."

CHAPTER EIGHTEEN

"Affairs," Gage said, "are in a fine mess."

"Is that why you called me?" Stella said. "To tell me what I already know?"

"You left at an opportune time," Gage continued as if she hadn't heard. "Dancing and drinking I could stand, but not an orgy." Raising her hands, she massaged her temples. "I don't think I'll ever forget the madness I've seen. If anything, Colonel Powers is even more upset than I am."

Remembering Thunderheart clutching his pants as he ran, Stella could sympathize with the security chief's situation. "Are all your officers and personnel acting this way?"

"Some are engaged in meditation, worshipping the New Son in silent groups."

"They sound like sincere believers. Can't you get some of them to help settle things down?"

Gage lowered her hands and stared at her. "They're useless, Commander, lost in mystic communion with who-knows-what. As for others like Lovejoy and Chong...hell, half my officers are probably getting their engines tuned at this moment. As they see it, when the Emperor throws a party, you don't sit on the sidelines."

"We both know the Emperor didn't throw it," Stella said. "Malek's the one. And unless your eyes were sealed shut, General, you know how he's corrupted the heir to the Imperial throne."

Gage winced. "Commander, let's not talk about that. If we

do, I'll..." She fought for control. "The reason I've contacted you is to tell you that at the earliest opportunity I will use all my authority to arrange the investigation you want. Even if the Regent isn't interested, we have our own experts here. You'll have their complete cooperation."

Stella stared at her in disappointment. Was this the best Gage would do?

Gage spread her arms. "Well? Why don't you say something?"

"What is there to say?" Resisting the urge to smash the cen-scan to pieces, Stella leaned toward the screen. "Do you really think Malek will let you? Or that Lovejoy and some of the others won't squeal when they find out?"

"I'll order them not to."

"Oh, come on, General!" she said, slapping her thigh. "Here's another chunk of reality to chew on. Sooner or later, and it'll probably be sooner, Malek's going to remember my disrespect, and when he does, my ticket will be cancelled for good. If you don't believe me, go take another look at Kolanera."

"You're right," Gage conceded. "As one of the books I showed you says, 'The insolent menaces of villains in power.'"

"General," Stella answered, "they stay in power only as long as we permit them." She had a thought. "By the way, is this line secure?"

"Yes, and your quarters too. I still have some power around here."

"Good." She straightened in her chair and crossed her arms. "At the banquet I told you there might come a time when I'd have to ask you for a favor. That time is now, General."

Their eyes locked. Long seconds passed.

"You're talking treason," Gage whispered. "The Emperor would never-"

"It's not the Emperor, it's Malek," Stella corrected. "And even if it weren't, it would make no difference."

"You're asking me to defile my command, authorize an operation in direct opposition to Malek." Gage rubbed her eyes and glanced distractedly about her office, for the first time showing serious signs of strain. "I'll be branded a traitor, despised and remembered only as an officer who dishonored her uniform by flouting an Imperial order, and never mind what he's done to the boy."

"Think about the boy, General, your duty to save him."

Gage jabbed her finger at Stella. "History won't know anything about that, or even care about the fine points. And that's not all! Though I'm not married, I've got a family." She counted them off on her fingers. "A mother, father, and two sisters. Even if I didn't care about myself, think of what people would do to them."

"General," Stella said, "this one's a bitch. It doesn't get any harder."

Gage rolled her shoulders, squared her chin. "Anyway, you can't guarantee you could actually beat the Slugs if I arrange for you and some crew to leave, can you? This All-Mother you mentioned, do you even have a rudimentary plan to beat her, any idea at all how you'd accomplish that?"

"No."

"So it all seems very doubtful, doesn't it, that you could be the mighty hero you claim. And yet, you're asking me-"

"In a way it's doubtful and in a way it's not, General," Stella said. "No, I'm not certain I can defeat the All-Mother. Hell, all I have is a vague feeling that I might be able to see how I can possibly do it when the time comes. But I'll tell you one thing that is certain. If I don't make it to Loran's big show, the Empire will be flushed down the toilet bowl of history and it won't make a goddamned bit of difference what anyone thinks of you. Because they'll all be dead!"

She fell silent, waiting for Gage to decide. Despite her last words, she knew it was a terrible decision for any officer to make. Gage herself looked chipped around the edges and no longer certain at all. Was it fair to expect Gage to make the right choice when her family was involved? Could she herself even be sure it was the right choice? She had generated this 'fine mess' like a spider did a web. It had come from her, been spun out of her guts and actions, and now she was caught in it. But was it sensible or ethical for her to expect Gage to see that sometimes an officer's highest duty was to disobey her orders, even if they came from the very top?

Gage sucked in her breath and pulled back. "I can't do it," she said. "I'll arrange for that investigation you want. Be back on-line with you soon."

After the screen winked into black, Stella sat staring at it. It was, she thought, not unlike the black hole of a singularity. The only difference was that there was nothing at all at the other end. Nothing to go to, nothing to hope for.

Sitting in the darkness, she realized she had never been so miserable, her brave, inspiring words to George returning to mock her with all their pathetic inanity. Even the accident and its aftermath paled compared to the way she felt now. This was the absolute nadir, the floor of hell.

Do you hear that, All-Mother? I'm beaten. I'm never going to make our rendezvous for that last dance of death. Someone else will spare you the trouble of killing me.

But there was no answer. No spiteful response from five hundred light-years away to mock her or sting her back to life. She was alone.

Rising, she dragged herself out of the booth, blinking against the brightness. Tessa had retracted the divider between her room and theirs. On the floor, Ulysses sat playing with padded blocks that Gage had sent over, the gaudy toy she had given him forgotten. His mother stood midway between Stella and her son, watching her anxiously.

"Is anything wrong?" Stella said.

Tessa's hands worried and picked at each other. "You were in there so long."

Stella shook her head leadenly. From somewhere, she dredged up a little spirit.

"I'm all right." She smiled down at the boy. "What are you doing, Ulysses?"

The boy looked up. "Building very big blocks. Can you play with me?"

Why not? She went over and sat down, picked up a red and green block and turned it. *A*. Yes. *A* for *Averse* Gage, *Abstain* Gage, or *Affrighted* Gage. But the last, she knew, was unfair. Why, though, did Gage keep her name a secret? Was there some awful truth connected to it? Did her name have some deep significance or reveal something she didn't want others to know? Puzzled, Stella placed the block in the top row and leaned back to see the word she had helped spell.

TMOHRE.

It was gibberish, like her life, like all that had happened. But the giggle and grin Ulysses gave her was a package that made it worthwhile. Reaching for another block, she noticed something and changed the letters' order.

MOTHER.

"What do you know?" Tessa said. "You made a word."

An hour later, she rose to help put the blocks away. Suddenly she heard a sound outside the door.

She dropped a block, fear singing fire through her body. What if it was Malek? He had ordered her death, and assassins were here now to carry it out. If so, Ulysses and Tessa could be in danger too.

She had only a second to act, perhaps less.

She darted across the room, knowing she must be faster than ever before, and grateful that when her death came, she hadn't been caught waiting for it in a body-cuff. As she neared the opening door, she saw a figure slip through. George.

She ground to a halt, stabbing her feet into the carpet and falling to one knee to avoid a collision. George looked down at her.

"Hey, Stella, I'm glad to see you too."

She rose as the door slid shut. "Oh, George." She went and put her arms around him.

"Hey there." She felt the soft bush of his beard on her cheek and a light kiss. After a reassuring squeeze he stepped back, eyeing her critically.

She hoisted her chin. "I'm doing fine. How's the base?"

"You mean Malek and his goons?" George arched his heavy eyebrows. "It's a three-ring circus. Like New Year's Eve and an Imperial coronation rolled into one. I saw Powers-he looked like he was having a fit. I can imagine how Gage is taking it. Her base could sail clear out of orbit if this celebration soars any higher."

Stella managed a smile at the hyperbole. "I'm glad you're here, George."

"I can't stay long." He rubbed his brow. "I wanted to tell you about Jason."

"How is he?" she asked anxiously. "You said before there was a problem with his chem feed, that he'd had a psychotic episode."

"It's fine now. I got it under control."

She trembled. "Thank heaven." She glanced at Tessa, who discreetly pressed a button. The divider slid across the width of the long room, giving George and herself privacy.

George cleared his throat. "I knew that Jason's next episode would be worse, that it was just a matter of hours before he went insane. I had to act. I asked for an audience with Malek, said it was urgent."

Stella blinked. "You asked to see the Regent-Protector?"

"Yes. And he granted my request. I told him Jason had barely survived a psychotic episode and that if I didn't operate, the Empire would lose an excellent jump pilot who was innocent of any offense against him. What's more, I pointed out that if he was restored to his body, Jason couldn't pilot a ship effectively anyway. Malek conceded my points and gave me permission to perform the procedure."

Stella felt stunned. "He did?"

"It wasn't just logic that convinced him." He hesitated. "Somehow he learned about your feelings for Jason. When Malek gave his approval, he was amused. He smiled and said, 'Tell her to enjoy him while she can.'"

Stella considered the ominous implications. "Sadistic bastard."

"An arrogant one too. He also said to tell you he doesn't need your experience, that he'll soon have a team of his experts examining the alien and scouring every atom of his ship to see what makes it tick. He's confident they'll succeed."

"Stupid."

"You sure there's no chance? At least he's trying."

"It's a huge problem, George, and he's trying to do it all by himself. He should be using Gage's men as well and most of all, me. Without my knowledge, they'll accomplish nothing. At worst, they could blow up the base."

George touched her shoulder. "Stella, aren't you going to ask how Jason's doing? After all, I've already performed the procedure."

She gasped. "You've already performed it?"

"Yes. Wynn, myself, and a couple neurotechs did it over three hours ago."

For a long moment she could only stare at him. "How did it go?"

"It went fine. He's only had ninety minutes rehab with his body, learning to use it again, but there should be no problems. He's done it before." He paused, his eyes intent on her face. "He's waiting outside the door now," he said softly.

"Outside the…" She turned and looked at the door. "Jason's out there?"

"Yes," George said, his voice cracking.

He walked to the door and raised his hand to press the button that would open it. Before he did, though, he turned to face her, his eyes wet with tears.

"This one's for you, Stella," he whispered. "Besides saving Jason, I wanted to keep my promise to help you. This is the best I can do. Knowing Malek, I doubt you'll have long."

He straightened. "I wanted to see that one time, just once, you got what you wanted."

She swallowed, seeing his tears, his naked, blasted face.

George smiled and pressed the button. A moment later, when the door slid open, she felt as if her calm, efficient heart were wrapped in ice.

CHAPTER NINETEEN

Beyond the open door, a guard stepped aside so that Jason could enter. He did so slowly, not quite sure of his body. Behind him, the door slid shut.

Jason stopped two meters away in his Imperial uniform and they gazed at each other. She could see his chest rise and fall as he breathed.

"Jason?"

His mouth crinkled at the edges, then opened. "Stella?" His voice was rich and resonant.

Her knees turned to liquid and she teetered, as if she were going to pitch over on her face.

"Stella," he said in alarm, "are you all right?"

"Yes...fine." She held her hand up, both to ward him off and to maintain her balance. "It's just meeting you. Your voice sounds almost the same, but you're taller than I expected."

"I am?"

She thought of him lying in the cryotank when she and Dr. Wynn watched him. He'd been naked. "You're as tall as Thunderheart, almost as tall as George."

"Is that all right?"

"Of course!" I wouldn't care if you didn't reach my chin, she thought, though she couldn't imagine Jason like that.

His eyes moved over her body, cataloging each flaw, each synthetic mockery of a feature. She could already see the beginnings of disgust.

She stiffened her shoulders, stepped forward, and stuck out

her hand. "Well, I'm glad you could come, Jason. Thank you."

His dark eyes swept down to her hand and then rose to meet her gaze. "What?"

She pushed her hand forward. "Thank you for coming," she said. "I appreciate it."

"You appreciate it?" He raised a hand and ran it through his long black curly hair, almost poking his eye as he did so. "What's wrong? Aren't you happy to see me?"

She opened her hand, closed it. "It's not that. It's just-"

"I've dreamed of you," Jason said. "The warm solar wind on my panels, the surge of my engines and guns…these were all sweet. But do you know what I kept thinking of more than anything else? The one thing I would give it all up for?"

She shook her head, unable to speak.

He raised his arms, trembling with emotion. "The feel of you in my human arms, your lips against my own. Damn it, I was willing to fly through hell and down the All-Mother's throat for that."

"Excuse me, Stella." Tessa's soft voice interrupted them as she opened the divider. "Ulysses is hungry." She gave Jason a shy glance and moved past them with Ulysses. "We'll be back later."

As the door shut behind Tessa and her son, Jason moved forward, not giving Stella a chance to speak as he threw his arms around her and pulled her to him, his lips, his blood-warm lips pressing down upon her own. She stood there in his arms, passive as she'd been with George, a stunned spectator whose synthetic blood ran cold as ice.

Then, between one heartbeat and the next, she thawed. She raised her hands and pulled him to her, feasting on his mouth, his sweet breath. She let it go on till she felt dizzy, then softly pushed his head back from hers, studying the handsome features, the straight nose, the dark pools of his eyes.

"What are you doing?" he murmured.

"I'm memorizing you," she said. "I've thought ten thousand times about this moment, and I'm not going to let it get away." She moved her hands over his face like a blind person, learning him forever through her fingertips. Her thumb lingered on a small scar below his lip.

"How did that happen?"

"Marion Colchis threw a stone at me when I was seven." He moved his mouth to kiss her thumb. "I deserved it. I was being very mean to her."

"I don't care. If I ever see her, I'll break both her legs."

Laughter coursed down Jason's body, ripples that swept into her and came out her mouth. The sound of her own laughter was a revelation.

Abruptly, Jason stumbled. She reached out.

"Are you all right?"

"George says the body-mind reknit takes a while, so I'm a little weak. Besides, this happened my first two times." He swallowed, studying her. "If it weren't for George, I'd be gibbering madly away in my nutri-cell by now. We owe him a lot."

She remembered George's tears and nodded. "More than we can ever repay. But you've tried to readapt so fast. Doesn't it usually take a couple days?"

"Even weeks sometimes before the crossover is complete and the pilot feels fully at home again in his body." He shifted his feet, looking at her bed beyond the cen-scan booth. "I wanted to recondition fast so I could see you, Stella. It seems we have so little time."

Yes, so little. No time at all, she realized, for tea and teasing and prolonged mating rituals. Raising her hands, she fumbled with the buttons of her uniform jacket and let it slip to the floor, not letting herself reconsider or question what she was doing. Then she stooped to take off her boots and stockings. Watching him closely, she stripped her shirt and pants off next, then finally her underwear, which fell softly to the floor.

She stood there naked before him.

Jason grinned. "Such a cute upturned nose."

She trembled. "It's synthetic."

"Oh, Stella!" Raising his hand, he gently touched the long scar on her side, which she had kept because in some small way it kept her human.

"You remember," she whispered. "A Scaley did it."

Half-comically, Jason hardened his face. "How could I

forget? I'll break both his legs!"

"George already did it for us," she mock-chided. George again.

A little clumsily, Jason removed his clothes. Kneeling, he kissed her scar, running his lips along its length as if to touch every molecule. She felt his tongue's moist caress, his hands on her back and buttocks. Then, to her surprise, he slipped his arms behind her back and knees and picked her up in the air. He swayed briefly.

"Are you sure?" She gripped his shoulder.

He kissed her, and she caressed the skin over his sternum, the taut muscle of his biceps. "Oh yes," he whispered hotly when their lips parted. "Oh yes, am I ever."

He carried her to the bed, which proved broad and comfortable. Jason kissed her lips and eyes, then ran his mouth down her body. She stroked his back, then reached down to caress him. His mouth, warm and demanding, found hers again, and she felt herself open to him.

Entering her, Jason quickly showed that he was all right indeed, despite his new body. Holding her close, he started to move, his lips murmuring in awe as if he saw an undiscovered country that transcended description.

And despite all her doubts, all her deepest fears, she found that she went there with him.

Afterward, they lay tangled together. She ran her fingers lightly over the damp hairs on his chest, not wanting to think of anything but the two of them together.

"Are you sure you aren't pushing things to do this so soon?"

He smiled. "No pun intended."

"No!" She laughed. "I'm not so clever as that."

Jason wiggled his nose, looking almost like a little boy. "You aren't, huh? Even after all you've managed to accomplish? I disagree. By the way, if you'll take a look, you'll see I'm not pushing things too fast at all."

"Ohhh," she marveled. "You're ready again."

"Uh-huh. Or you might say that I'm prepared to fire my engines for another launch."

"But your engines are back on the *Spaceranger*."

"I'm still able to use them." He winked, and then turned serious. "I'm going to be different with you," he promised. His hand caressed her cheek. "There isn't going to be anyone else."

She moved her hand down his body and fondled him. "How old are you, Jason?"

"Twenty-eight."

She sighed. "I'm be thirty-eight."

"So what?"

"So don't promise undying love and fidelity, especially to an older woman."

He kissed her, kissed her again. "I mean it, Stella. I'm going to change."

She sighed as he bit her earlobe, feeling his long hair brush her cheek. "If you say so. But I'll expect it in writing."

"I-"

There was a sound at the door.

They sprang apart, Jason covering himself with the blanket and Stella freezing in terror. She knew there was no time to act, even for her.

The door slid open, and General Gage entered the room.

Turning, Gage saw them and came forward, her face doing a double and triple take as she registered the situation. She halted a meter from their bed, shaking her head in amazement.

"Well, at least there's only two of you in bed together. That's refreshing."

"General," Stella said, "what are you doing here?"

"We have to move quickly," Gage said. "Now. You were right, Commander. Two of my officers reported our plans to Malek and he forbade the investigation. You're in danger. We have to move now!"

Stella and Jason scrambled out of bed and yanked on their clothes. Stella was ready before Jason was even half finished.

"I've arranged for some of your key officers and crew to join us on the way," Gage said. "We're taking a rather colorful route. It may seem strange, but it's fast. And don't be surprised by anything you see, just keep moving." She headed toward the door, anxious to go. "There's only one problem. Since your pilot's been disconnected, who's going to pilot the *Spaceranger*?"

"I am," Jason said, buttoning his shirt. "It'll be harder but I can do it."

"General," Stella said, "can't you get us on the Slug ship? It would be much better."

Gage shook her head. "It's harder and longer to get there, far more dangerous. Besides, it's more heavily guarded. You'll have to go this way or not at all." She snapped her fingers at Jason. "C'mon. The shit's about to hit the vents and every second counts."

The door opened and someone entered. Gage's hand slapped her holster and rose with a weapon trained on Tessa and her son.

"You're leaving, aren't you?" she asked Stella.

"If God's willing," Stella said.

"I haven't really thanked you for all that you've done." Her pale face twitched with emotion.

"Stella, now," Gage said.

"It's all right," Stella assured Tessa. She pressed Tessa's hands and then knelt and embraced Ulysses. "Grow tall and strong and true," she whispered, kissing his cheek.

"Hurry!" Gage snapped.

She rose and turned. Jason was ready.

Gage checked them both, then jabbed the wall button.

Oh God, Stella thought as the door slid open. Hold on tight 'cause here we go.

CHAPTER TWENTY

Outside her room, Jason almost hit the guard when he put the body-cuff back on Stella. However, Gage silenced him with a look, and after a couple minutes they were on their way down the corridor.

"First chance we get, we'll try to pop you out of that suit," Gage said.

"That would be nice," Stella answered. "By the way, I saw your gun. It looked old-style, driven mass to me."

"That's right," Gage said, eyes trained straight ahead. "This station's tough, but it's SOP to use only metal-alloy projectiles. We don't want to risk any damage to the outer surface."

I hope Lovejoy and those on the other side use similar restraint, Stella thought. 'The other side'...it seemed so strange to think that way. Damn it, they all belonged to the same side and she shouldn't have to do this!

As they walked, Jason's physical presence became more and more of a distraction. It was so hard to believe he was actually beside her, she wondered if she were dreaming. The feeling only intensified when Gage waved her to a door and she passed through it to see Lee and Carol hanging onto each other in apparent drunkenness at the bottom of a stairway. Their disheveled appearance and gaudy robes made them look like they'd joined the revelers. Stella felt surprise, then hot anger. Had her crew given in to debauchery?

Before she could speak, Lee moved forward, slipping the ornate robe off his shoulders and over her own, then another robe onto Jason. He wore yet another robe beneath them.

Carol placed a brown wig on Stella's head, tucking in some hairs. "Don't want them to spot your blonde locks."

"We're revelers," Gage said, "part of the celebration. If we act festive but not too boisterous, we should fit right in." She started up the stairs as Carol poured a glass of champagne from a bottle and gave it to Jason.

With Gage in front, Lee and Carol behind, Stella and Jason proceeded up the stairs. A little champagne slopped over the rim of Jason's glass, and he steadied it. He seemed bemused by his glass, and Stella wondered if he'd eaten or drunk anything since being returned to his body. Did he have to relearn how to swallow and take nourishment? She felt a thrill of embarrassment as she remembered Jason's recent skill at love-making. No, it probably hadn't taken him long at all to reacquire his basic functions.

At the landing, Jason cautiously took a sip and held the glass to her lips. She drained the rest in two gulps. Lee instantly gave him a partial refill from his own bottle. "Get in the mood," he advised. "But don't get squigged!"

Gage, who was already halfway up the next flight of stairs, glared down at them. "Hurry up!"

They followed her up the stairs, out a door, across a concourse, through another door and into the mezzanine of some kind of theater. Stella felt soft plush carpet beneath her, and Jason put his arm around her shoulders at a suggestion from Carol. That way they'd look more like another carousing couple and people would be less likely to notice her arms were confined.

The move came none too soon, for two couples with arms flung around each other half-stumbled past them from the other direction. Stella saw a heavily painted woman's face, mouth wide open in mid-screech. For a moment they looked directly at each other.

It was Major Stuckey, the fat xenologist who had interviewed her so rudely.

The champagne soured in Stella's stomach. Would Starkey have a delayed reaction, recognize her despite the disguise? Long seconds dragged as they continued on with no sharp cry of "Wait!" from behind. Before them, Gage's small, tough figure was a beacon she clung to with her eyes.

Jason's lips brushed her ear as they moved. "I love you," he whispered.

Behind them, glasses clinked and Lee made a mock toast. She heard them laugh.

"I love you too," she whispered back before faking a laugh. God, she had to be dreaming!

Or maybe it was a nightmare. They might fool a drunken Starkey, but what about Lovejoy, Chong, or a hundred other of Gage's officers? What if Malek and a death squad were already on their way to kill her?

"Hi, Stella," Myles Uxman said. Stella saw him rise from a theater seat with Brett Duvall held in his arms. Brett's soft features were flushed, and she clung tightly to Myles' neck. The strength required for him to stand while carrying her made Stella reassess the plump, unmuscular man. The orange lipspan smears on his face were a surprise too. From the looks of things, the two had been doing more than just play-acting.

Brett slipped drunkenly from Myles' arms to the floor, but Stella could see the sober precision in the move. Glancing quickly around, Brett scooted close. "Hey, we First Contact Heroes gotta stick together, right?" She took a glass from Myles and frowned at Jason before they all continued on. Stella was at the center of a growing company, and more concealed than before.

Through a door and out the theater. Then down a broad corridor to a smaller one and a panel on the wall. Gage checked both directions, and then opened it. "Used to be a clothes chute," she said, climbing inside. Perched on the edge, she looked back at Jason. "Hold her going down."

Jason looked at Stella. "All the way."

Gage nodded. "It's a low ceiling. Be sure to keep your head down, and last one in closes the panel. I don't want any arrows pointing our way."

She turned, ducked her head, and slid from sight.

Stooping, Jason picked Stella up and set her on the edge, then maneuvered himself up till he was sitting behind her. He held his arms tightly around her waist and his legs pressed against hers and the narrow walls of the chute. "Head down?" he asked.

"Yes."

"Then here we go," he breathed against her ear.

And down they slid, down into darkness. She felt Jason's arms around her, his breath on her cheek. Then the dark flicked into light and George Darron was at the bottom, waiting to catch her. She saw him give Jason a quick, probing glance as he helped them up.

As others slid down, Gage handed out guns and ammunition from a hidden cache. "Remember the recoil," she warned. "Projectile weapons will kick your hand off if you're not ready, so brace one hand with the other and squeeze smoothly, like this. Got it?"

"Let's get you out of that thing, Stella," George said.

He found the seams and pulled, his face turning red.

The device wouldn't loosen. "Shit," he said. "Might have known I couldn't open it if you couldn't."

"Lovejoy said it was an electrically-generated polymer," Stella said. "One of the guards used a field disrupter or something to open it."

Gage cut short a gun demonstration and came over to check the body-cuff. "Damned thing's super-tight," she said, tugging at it. "We'll have to get you out of it later."

George gripped the green suit and his great arms strained again to open it without success. Sighing, he closed the robe about her and tied the belt. "Sorry," he said, "you'll have to wear it."

Stella stamped the floor and strained against the body-cuff herself, grunting with effort. Nothing. She was sealed tight.

They were in a corridor that had either fallen into disuse or was being renovated. Moments later, they took off at a slow run and were joined at various points by members of the *Spaceranger's* crew. Nick and Morner appeared, and Stella realized that five of the six surviving members of what Brett called the 'First Contact Heroes' were now present. Only Thunderheart was missing. As she moved, she counted nine other crew as well, including

O'Bannion, the red-haired bridge tech.

She feared they were getting too numerous to escape detection, but they passed other groups almost as big as theirs. Not all consisted of raucous celebrants. Stella saw worshippers kneeling in silent communion. Their faces bore beatific smiles, as if they beheld the face of God.

At the head of Stella's group, Gage reached another panel and stood before it with her finger held to her lips.

"This is our next-to-last destination," Gage said. "We pick up our last members here before advancing to the docking area and the *Spaceranger*. It's possible that area will feature even heavier traffic, especially since the revels are in high gear. I want you all to be sure Commander McMasters is shielded as well as she can be. Do I make myself clear?"

Stella heard them murmur assent. As Gage and four others entered first, she crouched and again tried to loosen the body-cuff, straining till her eyes bulged. The others watched her. Gritting her teeth, she braced herself and tried again, contorting herself in what felt like nine different directions.

Nothing. It was like she was buried in solid rock.

Jason touched her. "Stella," he said, "we have to go."

Swearing softly, she turned and slipped through the panel.

On the other side, she saw a wall of lush green fronds. Gage called her softly from beyond, so she slipped through and looked around.

They were in the botanical gardens.

She caught a glimpse of exotic flower beds and a blue lily pond into which a small silver waterfall splashed. Pebbled paths wound here and there and something darted overhead in the warm, fragrant air, followed by a sharp *caaw!* Glancing up, she saw a bird with brilliant green and gold plumage settle on a branch.

They all clustered about her, covering most of this Eden from sight, and started down one of the pebbled paths.

With Jason's arm around her, she continued to fight the suit, squirming within it. How much stronger was she than before the accident-fifteen times? Twenty? Yet it was as if she were a powerless child, like Thunderheart when he tried to crawl from the Slug's dead body. Jason touched her cheek and bent down.

"Take it easy, people coming."

She relaxed and huddled against him, hearing drunken greetings from outside the group which those around her answered. Gage said something which drew coarse laughter in their wake. They wound onward along the path.

Just ahead of her, George caught his breath. "Jesus-Buddha on a primrose pogo stick," he said, "I don't believe it!"

What did he see-some danger? Were Powers and Lovejoy closing in? The people to her left parted slightly.

And there was Thunderheart, Thunderheart as she'd never seen him. The three girls from before were all hanging onto him with sated, contented smiles, their makeup and hair in disarray. Thunderheart himself was barefoot and half-naked, his head erect and his shoulders thrown back. His black skin glistened with sweat and honed muscles rippled as he moved. He wore what appeared to be an animal skin draped over one shoulder and carried a large tankard of ale. As he strode forward, his deep rich laugh burst out.

Thunderheart and his harem flowed into the small gap before her, and within seconds, she was even more concealed than before. Stella saw him recognize her despite her disguise before turning to Jason. "You're..."

"Jason, the pilot. George Darron reimplanted me."

A look passed between the men, then Thunderheart's eyes dropped to hers and he smiled. I'm glad for you, his expression said.

"Let me tell you something," one of the girls chirped, looking possessively up at Thunderheart. "They oughta call this man 'Thunderstud'!"

The blonde girl slapped the other girl's hand away and stroked Thunderheart's chest. "Umm, I just love him. He's such a brave and tireless warrior."

"Especially 'tireless,'" the third girl giggled. "I think I'm going to be sore for a week."

Thunderheart nuzzled the girls and beamed like a galactic conqueror. Looking at him, Stella saw that he had changed, been transformed in some irreversible way. Could something as elemental as sex with these simple-minded pets of the Emperor's court account for his new vitality? Whatever the case, the dek-path soldier who had died in the Slug's body was gone. He had evolved into an independent spirit. Her 'child' had begun to transcend not only the family that had nurtured and narrowed him, but herself.

Seeing Thunderheart laugh, she felt joy for them both. Her bleak despair of a few hours before seemed drenched in the fertile hopefulness of this place. Like Thunderheart, she too had been transformed, and as she moved on beside Jason, she knew that these danger-filled moments were among the happiest of her life.

All too soon they were over. They passed through doors and the pebbled surface beneath her was replaced by flat metal. The next corridor led to the docking bay. Through her group's bodies, she caught a glimpse of the *Spaceranger's* bow and two guards standing at the closed hatch just behind it.

They continued on, passing broad columns that supported the upper level. Purposely, her crew raised their level of gaiety while Thunderheart's adoring companions prattled on and competed for his attention.

Suddenly they stopped. Stella heard a clear, sharp voice, evidently one of the guards.

"Ser!"

"I request entry," Gage's voice said with just the right mixture of stern confidence and in-her-cups good cheer. "We wish to bring the sacred revels to those poor soldiers confined to ship."

A pause. One beat, two. "General," the guard said, "we have our orders. Regent-Protector Malek has expressly forbidden any unauthorized personnel to board this ship."

"That's true, ser," the other guard said in deference. "The order was quite clear."

"'Unauthorized personnel'?" Gage's voice rose, its festive tone hardening with outrage. "Soldier, I am the commanding officer of this base. You will let us enter at once!"

Another pause, longer this time. Stella could sense the guards' discomfort at being caught between Malek and their commanding officer. Jason smiled and touched her cheek.

"Ser," the first guard said, "if you'll just-"

"Enough of this!" Gage raged. "Out of the way!"

They all surged forward. Stella heard the guards say something and then came a metallic sound she had heard a thousand times. The hatch was being opened.

For a tense moment she thought they would be allowed to enter. Then the second guard cried out. "General Gage, Colonel Powers is on the comlink. Please wait."

Their momentum died. Stella heard the comlink crackle, followed by the guard's crisp reply.

"General Gage," he announced, "Colonel Powers is disembarking from this level's circulator and he and his detail should be here promptly. I'm sorry, but we can't permit you and your company to enter until you're authorized."

Stella pieced it together. Powers obeyed Malek because he outranked Gage. What's more, Malek had sent his killers to her quarters and been informed she was gone. So he had immediately ordered a base-wide search and dispatched Powers to ensure the *Spaceranger* remained where it was.

Footsteps left the ship and approached. Through a rift in the bodies, Stella saw Gage standing parallel to her, watching something. Her lips moved.

"I count thirty, half with rifles," Gage said softly. "Lovejoy's with them, but I don't see Malek."

Bitter irony edged Stella's heart. "For a moment there, I thought we were in real trouble."

Stella's crew reached for their weapons, clutching them under their robes and dresses. Jason held her with one arm and gripped his gun with the other. He looked down at her with a tense smile.

Footsteps approached, sounding like an army.

Stella watched Gage's face between two of her crew's bodies. It was as hard as granite.

The footsteps echoed loudly, rapidly growing closer. Gage raised her arm. "Halt!"

The footsteps stopped. A moment later, she heard Powers' voice. "General Gage, this sector is restricted. Regent-Protector

Malek has ordered that only authorized personnel be permitted here."

"I am the commanding officer of Loran Base," Gage said.

"Excuse me, ser," Powers replied, "but according to official policy, the Regent-Protector may assume command during wartime."

"I demand a hearing first."

Stella heard an argument break out near Powers. Lovejoy's voice urged that Gage and her party be arrested at once. Powers silenced him and addressed Gage again.

"Ser, surely you know the Regent-Protector's orders take precedence. They're backed up by Imperial authority. I must respectfully demand that you leave this area."

Stella's crew tensed. She saw several guns catch the light as they emerged from clothes. Furiously she strained against the body-cuff. If only she could get out of it!

Gage glanced aside at them, and nodded. "Well, Colonel, there's only one thing I can say to that."

Reaching to her holster, she pulled her gun and fired.

The scene dissolved into chaos. Some of Stella's crew pressed against her, trying to push toward the hatch, but the guards there drew their own weapons. Stella heard shots ring out and saw the guards fall, one landing half in and half out of the open hatch. A fusillade of shots followed, ricocheting off the bulkhead and preventing them from entering the ship. Someone rammed her from behind, and she was torn away from Jason and carried off as if on a raging river toward one of the broad columns that supported the upper level.

Thunderheart's girls screamed, their mouths opened wide in panic. Near Stella, one of her crew gasped as a bullet struck him. He collapsed, causing others to trip over him. Thunderheart threw his tankard and an officer dropped his weapon as it struck his head. A bullet ricocheted off a column, and someone cried out.

Then she was behind a column with Gage and Lee. Kneeling clumsily, she glanced around. The broad support structures gave them a temporary advantage in case of attack. Judging from what she heard, Powers was holding his fire and pulling his forces back. With his rifles, of course, he had greater range and could pick them off one by one.

"Stella," Jason called, "are you all right?"

She swung. Five meters away, behind the column to her left, Jason stood next to George, who sat with Carol's head in his lap.

"I'm fine." She looked at Carol's chest as it rose and fell. "How's Carol?"

George raised his head and looked at her. He didn't answer.

"General Gage," Powers called, "I order you to surrender!"

"I can't do that, Major," she answered.

"I don't understand!" Powers shouted back. "This is insane. Why are you doing this?"

"What difference does it make?" another voice said. Lovejoy again. "She's disobeyed an Imperial command. She's a traitor!"

"Call me what you want!" Gage shouted. "But the fact remains that we only have one chance to win this war and that's to get Commander McMasters to General Loran-alive. I'll do anything to achieve that."

Lovejoy started to reply but Powers cut him short. "General," Powers shouted, "you have no choice. You're pinned down and a small army will arrive shortly. You'll all die unless you surrender."

Gage spat on the floor. "I'll see you in hell, Powers."

Stella could hear the circulator open behind Powers. She risked a glance around the edge and saw a mass of soldiers slip quickly from it and take up positions. Some darted behind columns while others threw themselves prone and squinted through their rifle sights.

"I'll give you two minutes!" Powers called. "Then we're coming in."

Stella sighed and looked about. She counted at least a dozen bodies, most of them Powers' soldiers. At the *Spaceranger's* hatch, two guards ducked their heads out and were driven back by shots from Jason, who quickly reloaded.

Behind the next column, George clutched Carol's hand in his own as if he were trying to hold her to life. Her chest rose and fell, rose and...stopped.

Stella closed her eyes, hearing George sob.

"You know something?" Gage said to Stella over her shoulder. "You were right. Disobedience is a definite problem in the ranks these days."

Stella smiled bitterly. "It seems to be getting worse."

Gage grunted, her face pressed near the column's edge. "You know something else? This is my birthday."

Stella glanced at George, who was easing Carol's head gently to the floor and slipping free in preparation for the assault to come. Jason leaned against the column beside him, his gun raised. She saw him glance at her in concern, then peer around the column.

"What about your family?" Stella asked Gage.

Gage turned to her, but didn't answer. Instead, she laid her gun down on the floor. "I'm sorry," she said. "I tried my best."

Stella bit her lip. A few columns to her right, one of Thunderheart's girls broke into a shrill wail of terror. Glancing over, she saw him press her head against his chest to comfort her.

"Not your fault," Stella said. "George would say it just wasn't in the cards."

Gage checked her cronex. "Thirty seconds left, Stella." She coughed. "I want to tell you something."

"What?"

Gage reached out and touched her shoulder. "My first name. I've always hated it but I never changed it. Somehow, it always seemed right for me even though I..." She coughed again, her eyes bright with fierce tears. "I've kept it secret, removed it from records and never told anyone, not even my two husbands. But I want you to know, Stella."

Stella swallowed. "All right."

Gage leaned forward, opened her mouth.

Suddenly rifle fire burst out, spraying walls and columns. The attack was on.

They came like the sea in remorseless waves. Stella saw Myles clutch his throat and die on his feet. O'Bannion had half his head blown off, splattered against a column. Morner collapsed, striking Nick as he fell. They came on and on and she watched in helpless rage, unable, despite her great strength, to do anything. At the next column, George knelt on one knee, calmly squeezing off shots as soldiers swarmed toward him. She saw bullets strike the column near his head, shearing off pieces and revealing a lighter-colored substance beneath.

Beside him, Jason spun sharply and fell to the floor, dropping his gun. She saw him reach for it and rise to his knees, clutching his shoulder. He began firing again at the charging soldiers. George himself was reloading, his quick physician's fingers inserting the cartridges as attackers swarmed toward him.

Other soldiers now moved toward her. Gage grunted. Grabbing Stella's shoulder, she yanked her to the floor and stepped before her with her gun raised.

Lying there, Stella watched Gage in dread as she screened her from attack and fired at her own soldiers. One of them went down, then another. Gage's uniform appeared to be plucked by unseen fingers as bullets whipped past. An instant later, a bullet took her and she staggered back. Still, she kept her body in front of Stella. Trembling in anguish, Stella saw Gage swing her gun and another soldier scream and clutch his chest. Gage shot again, and then again as the stench of macrocordite filled the air.

Then Gage's body seemed to dance as bullets found her. One cut her leg out from beneath her. She pulled another weapon from her belt as she swayed on one knee, her body gushing streams of blood. Gage raised the weapon and fired yet again, sending a bullet into the soldiers' midst.

A moment later, a broadside of bullets blasted her. Stella saw Gage shiver, then topple to the floor and lie still, the gun still gripped in her hand.

Fighting back tears, Stella forced herself backward with her legs, trying to escape a death that was seconds away. The docking bay was a bleeding, reeking, smoke-filled battlefield, the scene of her final defeat. Fifteen meters away, an officer turned slowly, peering through the smoke. His eyes found her.

Lovejoy.

He started toward her, his pistol held upright in the air, his face a twitching mask of hate. A smile stained his features as he neared, widening into a savage grin.

She drove herself backward, unable even to get to her feet. Oh, Gage...she was just getting to know her! And Jason, he must be dead by now, the lips that had caressed hers forever still. She would never... Straining, torn by grief, she saw Lovejoy close to ten meters, then five, his face cold, white, and filled with ferocious anticipation.

Finally, he stopped. With a fierce grin, he lowered his gun and pointed it directly at her face. His finger tightened on the trigger.

A flash of movement to the side caught his attention. He turned.

And toward him, in the air, came Thunderheart, his gleaming body horizontal as he shot his foot out at Lovejoy's face. The blow caught Lovejoy with split-second accuracy, crushing his nose and chin and reducing his neat, regular features to jelly. Lovejoy's body flew through the air and Thunderheart sprang up, placing himself between the approaching soldiers and Stella. He crouched and spread his arms.

Bitterly, Stella fought the body-cuff as never before, driving herself back against the floor—writhing, twisting. She heard something crack and the green polymer loosened, strained again and it parted against her breast. When she bent herself almost double, the suit snapped sharply and gave way. She struggled to throw it off, only to feel both it and the robe slide upward-over her chin, over her face. Gripping it from inside, she strove to cast it off.

It wouldn't go. The body-cuff closed and settled tightly over her head, trapping her arms. She struggled on in darkness, her heels viciously pounding the floor.

She was caught, couldn't get out. She would die this way!

Someone seized the suit and pulled...pulled again. The body-cuff began to open. Another savage effort and light blazed in. She saw a pair of black hands rip the fabric and robe apart and cast them aside, bringing her back into life.

Above her, Thunderheart knelt, still alive amid the din of death, and kissed her cheek. Then he was up and the guns flashed. Stella rose to follow, but two soldiers rushed toward her. A bullet whizzed past her cheek. She clubbed one, then the other, a heavy man who fell on top of her and carried her to the floor. She killed him with another punch and threw him off her.

Before she could rise, a soldier aimed a rifle directly at her. "Don't move," he shouted, "or I'll shoot!"

Weaponless and on the floor, Stella was unable to help Thunderheart, surrounded by soldiers ten meters away. A bullet took him pointblank in the chest, yet he closed with his attacker as if he had missed. A quick chop and the soldier dropped like a stone. Thunderheart whirled, taking another soldier out with a flashing kick to the chest. As he spun back, another bullet struck him, but he only leapt through the air and delivered a series of lethal punches in lightning succession. She saw two more soldiers fall, then a third as they closed in about him, firing again and again until he could not rise.

It was over. Within seconds, the docking bay was secured, the soldiers in full control. Staring at the floor in misery, Stella saw a pair of black boots obstruct her view. She looked up.

Colonel Powers gazed down at her with a strange expression. In her present state, it seemed sphinx-like or mystical, a mandala she couldn't read.

"Congratulations," she rasped. "You have just lost us the war."

Footsteps approached in the distance, clear and coldly distinct. Through a surreal haze, she saw the tall figure approach in its magnificent crimson robe. She laughed weakly. Hail, the Angel of Death.

The footsteps stopped. His face taut, Regent-Protector Malek held out his hand. "Colonel Powers, give me one of your pistols."

Powers frowned. "Ser?"

"A pistol, Colonel. At once."

Powers looked away, perhaps hoping that the Emperor would arrive and stop this. But the Emperor, of course, was only a little boy, probably unconscious in a drug-induced sleep.

Powers drew his pistol and gave it to Malek.

"Thank you." Malek, whose eyes had never left hers, raised the weapon and aimed it between her eyes. "I should have ordered this done when you dared offend the Imperial Court."

"No!"

To her right, Jason lunged forward with a bloody arm, only to be seized by soldiers. Malek didn't even look.

"Traitors without honor who disgrace their uniform and defile their sacred vows deserve to die on their face in the dirt. But in your case, I'm willing to make an exception." He flicked the barrel. "Get up. I want to see if you have the guts to take it on your feet."

CHAPTER TWENTY-ONE

She rose, facing the barrel pointed between her eyes. Slowly, so there was no chance Malek would think it a threat, she raised her hand and saluted him.

Malek's lips hardened. She saw his finger start to move.

"Ser," Powers said, "don't you think we should take her to the brig?"

Malek didn't answer. His finger tightened.

The gun exploded in a loud discharge, but the bullet missed her head.

Stella didn't flinch. "It's you who are the traitor, and you who have betrayed your trust," she said. "Worst of all, you have willfully failed your own Emperor."

Malek's head snapped back in surprise, and the gun sagged in his hand. He would like her to crawl or at least cringe, so she smiled instead. She would give him nothing.

As Jason strained in his captors' hands, others protested too. George and Lee-still alive!-pressed forward, only to be seized.

Farther off, Brett Duvall was cursing with an imaginative richness that rivaled Thunderheart's. Malek listened to none of it. Instead he raised the gun again. Stella stared at the barrel.

There was a streak of movement as Powers drew his gun and pressed its barrel to Malek's temple. "No," he said.

Stunned seconds passed. "C-Colonel," Malek finally managed, "what are you doing?"

Powers' Adam's apple bobbed as he swallowed. "With all due respect, Regent-Protector, I think we should take Commander

McMasters to the brig to await her court-martial."

Malek's face reddened. "This is treason!"

Other officers advanced. One, Stella saw, was Major Chong, who had led her interrogation. "Colonel, you're the security officer. Holster your weapon at once!"

Powers' eyes dropped to the pistol in his hand. He stared at it in confusion, as if he had awakened from some dream and couldn't believe what he saw. Stella watched his resolve waver.

"Colonel Powers," Lee cried, "I know how you feel. I had to destroy a guard ship carrying several of our own comrades in order to save my commander. I hated to do it and it's going to hurt a long time, but I knew it was right no matter what others would say."

Chong sneered, the cast of his features identical to Lee's, but his voice icily different. "Sheer sophistry! It's only a cheap rationale for treason."

"No," Powers said, "it's not." He stared at Malek, pressing his pistol harder against the Regent-Protector's temple. "I serve a higher good too."

"What higher good?" Chong laughed mockingly. "Killing the Regent-Protector? Where in your vows does it say you should do that?"

Lee squirmed, his arm locked behind him by a soldier. "I'll tell you where! It says in the third paragraph of the Imperial Oath that any enemy of the Emperor, no matter what his side or how high his position, shall be your enemy, and his orders rendered null and void." He glared at Chong. "Try reading it sometime, Major!"

Before Stella, Malek trembled in fear and rage. "All this stupid talk. You're nothing but a damned traitor, Colonel."

Powers stiffened, cocked his pistol. "I'm getting a little tired of that word. It seems only those with the most power feel they have the right to use it."

"Colonel..." Major Chong began.

"Regent-Protector," Powers said, his voice sounding different than she'd ever heard it, "I want you to drop your gun and tell these soldiers to withdraw."

Chong sneered. "We'll do no such-"

"Shut up, Major." Stella saw Powers press the barrel so tightly against Malek's temple that he winced in pain. "Regent-Protector Malek, if you don't comply with my wishes, I believe I will blow your brains out. I sincerely think this is true, ser. And ser, though I respect your high office, it is also my conviction that you are a turd-filled son of a bitch who will soon be worm meat if you don't relay my request to our comrades."

Malek's lips twitched and the gun clattered to the floor. "M-Move 'em out, Chong," he croaked.

Stella watched them withdraw. Chong shook so hard he looked like he was having a stroke.

As the soldiers pulled back to where they'd been before, they themselves moved behind the columns. When they were concealed, Powers turned to Stella, his hand gripping Malek. "What do we do now, Commander? Even with him, they won't let us leave."

Stella rubbed her arms, still a little numb from the suit, and looked at Jason. He was gazing at all the dead bodies, grief in his eyes. There was Carol near one of the columns, and what remained of Gage, who had defended her with her own body. A little beyond her, Lovejoy's ruined face gazed blindly up at nothing.

Farther out, surrounded by soldiers he had taken with him, Thunderheart lay on his back with outstretched arms. He had died nobly, upholding his creed, and he had spent his very last breath in the Emperor's service. Was there any better way for a soldier to die?

But, Stella thought, he had only begun to grow and explore, discover who he was, his ultimate potential.

She fought back a tear. There was no time for such thoughts.

"We have to reach the ship," she said.

Malek sneered. "They'll kill you first. The best thing you can do now is surrender."

George seized Malek's collar in one hand. The other pulled Malek's goatee so hard that he screamed. "Let me make this plain, you puffed-up bastard. If we die, you go too. That's a promise you can count on."

Malek's complexion went chalky, and he closed his mouth.

Jason clicked his tongue. "He's right, though. It must be sixty, sixty-five meters to the *Spaceranger's* hatch. Maybe they won't charge us, but will they let us leave with him?"

"There are also guards on board," Lee said from the next column. "Even if some of us make it, we'll have them to worry about."

"So you're saying we're at an impasse?" Stella said. "They'll starve us out?"

"Or get us when we're sleeping," Lee replied. He looked up. "Maybe they'll pick us off from another level."

George poked Malek hard. "Stella, he's our ace in the hole. But if we play him, we lose him. Once he's dead, they'll come down our throats."

At the word 'dead,' Malek paled. Stella turned and moved near the edge of the column. "Major Chong," she called, "we're taking Malek on board the *Spaceranger.*"

"You will be fired upon if you do!" Chong called back.

She frowned. "Even if the Regent-Protector's with us? You'll kill him too?"

A long pause. "The first person who shows their face anywhere will be cut down," Chong answered. "That means anyone!"

Stella turned back. "Hear that, Regent-Protector? He's willing to sacrifice you like a hog. Does that make him a traitor too?"

Malek hyperventilated, his skin pasty-colored and wet. "Major C-Chong," he quavered, "I order you to let us go!"

No answer. They waited.

"Major Chong!" Malek delivered the order again, his voice cracking.

Still no answer. "Aw, that's a shame, Regent-Protector," Stella sympathized. "But you know that disobedience is a definite problem in the ranks these days." She gazed at the hatch door behind the *Spaceranger's* bow and the soldier who lay in it. If one of the guards on the ship pushed him out and closed it, they were finished.

"You know," she said, "we don't all have to reach the ship. Just one of us. One who knows how the weapons work."

George's eyes widened. "The bow plasma and laser weapons!"

"Especially the plasma, which has broader effects at close range. Whatever they choose, there's enough power there to cremate Chong and gut this complex."

Lee pounded the next column with such excitement he hurt his hand. He clutched it and did a quick jig of pain. "I get it, ser! One of us blows the enemy kaplooey and we all slip aboard in the confusion!"

Enemy. Kaplooey. For a heartbeat, the whole universe tipped sideways and went insane. Jason touched her, and she struggled back.

"Stella," he said, "it would take a very fast runner." He measured the distance with his eyes. "Even then, there's not a man alive who'd stand a chance. He'd be cut down before he got halfway."

"What do you mean, 'he'?" she said.

Jason and George both sucked in their breath. "You can't go," Jason said. "We need you!"

"He's right," Colonel Powers said. "If what you say is true, Commander, the only chance we have to win this war is if you get to your destination. The rest of us are expendable. Besides, the one who goes will still have to deal with the soldiers on board to get to the weapons station."

Lee broke in again. "Ser, we've got a galactic-class runner here. Nick Flynn. And he's a gunnery specialist."

Nick stepped forward. "Let me go, ser." He patted a pocket. "I've got a laser."

"Sorry, I can't let you do it."

"Remember last time, ser?" Nick said. "You wouldn't let me rush the Scaleys but went yourself. Things are different now. You're the one person we can't lose."

Stella heard a chorus of agreement but held firm. He was so young, and enough had died.

"Nick makes sense," Lee said. "Ser, you can't risk it yourself. You're irreplaceable."

Stella gazed at Nick, winner of the diamond novaburst at the Olympiad. But this was no game. Turning, she glanced at Malek's lean, hard face, knowing that he wouldn't think twice about sending a man to his death.

She swung back to Nick. "Are you sure?"

"Yes, ser." Nick removed his shoes and handed something on a chain to Brett. His code tags. Nick wanted Brett to give them to someone-perhaps his parents, or a girl.

Along the line, Stella's crew passed the word and readied their weapons. Powers gave her one of his pistols.

Nick assumed a sprinter's crouch. "I'll see you soon, ser."

"Godspeed," she said softly.

Then he was off and they all leapt out from behind the columns, firing not so much to hit anyone as to distract them with an abundance of targets. As her finger pumped the trigger, she tracked Nick with her peripheral vision, seeing him streak forward and his body rise as he settled into a full stride. He had run ten meters, fifteen...

Shots came, a solid, sustained blast. Nick raced on.

Then his chest and stomach heaved like he was crossing a finish line and his arms flew up as if in celebration. She stopped firing and turned. Nick's momentum carried him on a few steps, but he soon pitched forward on his face.

Jason had been right. Nick had made less than twenty-five meters.

They hid behind the columns again. Two more members of her crew had been shot and killed in the effort.

She handed Powers' gun back and did a few quick deep knee bends, then rolled her neck from side to side to loosen it. "Colonel Powers," she said, "when I blast Chong's men, I want you all to run for the ship. Be sure to bring Malek too. He might prove useful later."

"No, Stella," Jason said. "You can't...you'll be killed!"

"You said it yourself," she said. "We need a fast runner, and without making too fine a point of it, there's no one in the Empire who can match me." She shook off George as he tried to restrain her, and then felt Powers touch her shoulder. "We'll cover for you," he said, raising his hand to pass the command on to others.

Stella turned. Jason was staring at her in desperation, his wounded shoulder still bleeding. She put her arms around him and pressed her lips hard against his own; wanting to take him into her, wrap her body and soul around him. Then, because she couldn't make it last forever, she pulled back from his tight embrace and dipped her finger in his blood, painting her forehead and cheeks in quick swipes.

"Stella..."

"Goodbye, Jason," she said. "I take you with me."

Turning, she fixed her eyes on the hatch and was off.

CHAPTER TWENTY-TWO

As Stella started running, it seemed to her that someone was always either pointing a gun in her face or making her run for her life. She saw Sloan in her cabin, telling her with a laser in his hand there'd been a change in command...Lovejoy and Malek looking at her over their gun barrels. Now here she was, dashing toward the hatch just as she had charged the Scaleys on the enemy ship, endlessly determined to make long odds longer by placing herself in impossible situations.

Her boots pounded the floor and she cursed herself for not removing them and taking a gun instead. But she reached Nick and passed him, driving herself on with every fiber of her being. No full-body servos in her armor this time. She'd have to do this on her own, with only her enhanced abilities and no duroplast shielding.

She had passed halfway! Ahead, the hatch loomed.

Shots sounded. Something nipped her sleeve, whined off the hatch door. Just twenty meters left.

A bullet took her in the shoulder, two others in the leg. She lurched and swerved onward as hundreds of others struck and cracked around her. Another bullet slammed into her back, almost driving her from her feet. She forced herself on. Please! Just ten meters...five...

Just as she reached the hatch, yet another bullet tore into her side. She fell to her knees, reaching up for the door. She was finished. She couldn't make it.

Then she thought of the All-Mother, and hate surged

through her like an electric charge. She rose, plunged inside, and started up the narrow corridor to the bow.

And stopped.

A half-dozen guards stood three meters before her with drawn weapons, obviously determined to prevent her from reaching the bow.

She screamed and charged.

Shots went off but her scream startled them just enough to let her cover the distance without taking another hit. Then she was among them, striking to kill. She pulverized faces, smashed chests, even rammed two heads together. In close quarters, no one could shoot, but she felt a gun butt bludgeon her skull from behind. She sagged toward unconsciousness but fought it off, turned, and cut her attacker down with a vicious punch that knocked out half his teeth.

When they were down, she leaned against the wall and looked at them. All dead or unconscious. She shoved herself from the wall and started toward the bridge.

Before her stood one last man, dressed like the others in the olive green uniform of an Imperial guard. He was young and looked nervous, but he held a pistol pointed right at her face.

And there was no chance-no chance at all-that she could beat him.

She tucked her head in and snarled. "Get the freakin' hell out of my way!"

The guard screamed and bolted past her, his gun clattering to the floor. She watched him fall once in his haste and stagger up, casting a frantic glance back over his shoulder before running on.

Stella tottered toward the bridge.

She must have blacked out for a moment, because she came to draped over the weapons control panel on the command console. Before her, above five vid displays, floated overlapping views of the docking area in mid-range magnification. When had she activated them?

Fighting dizziness, she zoomed in on Chong. He'd set up a barrier of refractory combat bunkers, and was talking to a subordinate behind them. What if he decided to rush her crew because she'd gained access to the ship?

That was exactly what he was going to do. She saw him rise with a comlink held to his mouth and glance to left and right as his soldiers climbed to their feet. Protected by duroplast shields, they moved forward with their rifles.

Think again, Chongee. She centered the target grid on his chest and placed her fingers over lit buttons marked PLASMA-ON.

The soldiers kept marching, nearly two hundred against barely a dozen. Talk about overkill. Fortunately, even with their shields, her advantage over the enemy was greater than theirs over her remaining crew.

Enemy. There was that word again. She had to remember that they weren't the enemy. It was the All-Mother who had done this, the All-Mother who had hurt and divided them. The figures now approaching her crew were merely taking orders.

From Chong.

Steeling herself, she pressed the buttons with one hand and worked the target grid with the other.

Two burning white rods of ionized gas speared Chong and a dozen others in mid-stride. Stella swung the beams from side to side, decimating his forces before they got halfway to her crew.

Powers and the others ran toward her. She raised the plasma jets to the far wall of the docking area and strafed it from left to right. Unlike Gage, Stella had no compunctions about risking decompression, even if it involved destroying an entire sector and venting it into space. All the people on the base she had ever cared about were either dead or about to board.

Not so. What about Tessa and her son? The *Emperor?*

She had no choice. It was imperative she continue. If she caused enough damage, they might not be able to launch a pursuit ship.

Gentle hands took her shoulders and assisted her to the battle harness. When had she called that up? She must have blacked out again while holding the buttons down. Jason lowered the affixed helmet over her head and grimaced in pain, then slipped into his own seat where he repeated the process. The tripod structure beneath his seat shot left, then right in the cogged floor apparatus as he pressed buttons and adjusted dials. She caught bits of exchange between him and Lee, seated behind her.

"Retros up."

"Check."

"Shields on."

"Check."

"All compartments sealed."

"Check."

She struggled to remember what such things meant. Turning her head, she saw Powers give her a concerned smile. And Brett was watching her too. Where were Myles and Carol?

A harsh curse sounded. George slammed Malek down into a seat and rudely strapped him in. A hypospray rose in his hand. He rolled up the arm of Malek's luxurious robe and unceremoniously injected him. "That should keep you quiet," he said, heading toward his own seat.

She glanced over at Jason, who seemed to have injured his shoulder. How had he done that? And what was it she wanted to tell him? She knew it was important.

"Jason," she said.

He flicked a switch. Turned. "Yes, Commander."

She opened her mouth. "When we launch, blast the docking bays to hell and back. I don't want anyone to follow us."

He grinned. "Aye, aye, ser."

Seconds later, or minutes, a tremendous hand seemed to press her down in her seat. She blinked at the bodies strewn in the base's docking area, seeing them dwindle as the ship rose into space. As they left, plasma jets and laser beams, all the ship's available artillery, scorched and crisscrossed the base's structure.

The last thing she remembered before she lost consciousness was seeing Loran Base from five hundred kilometers out, its outer shell breached and broken in at least a dozen places.

When she awoke, George was tending to her head. She groaned, her eyes asking ten questions at once.

"Welcome back, Stella," he said. "We've been out an hour

and there's no pursuit. The ship's secure. All told, we've got seventeen crew on board, including Colonel Powers. He salted Malek away in the brig and got two guards to cooperate. We had to shoot some others, though, and took four casualties ourselves."

She rolled her head on the pillow and spotted Jason. He sat all the way across the room on a gurney and was being attended by Dr. Wynn. As she watched, Dr. Wynn almost reverently wrapped Jason's arm in gauze. He was naked to the waist.

Well, that answered her next question. She was in the infirmary.

"I've removed the bullets and used nine kinds of healant," George said, "but you're banged up pretty bad. Ideally, you could use a new body."

Stella managed a small smile. "Next time I'm near a state-of-the-art cyber lab, I'll make an appointment."

"It's your head I'm worried about," George said, ignoring her irony. "Despite your frills, you've still got a standard issue brain, and it's just withstood a major league concussion. You need to take it easy for a few days."

"As you would say, 'fat chance.'" She squeezed her eyes shut in sudden pain. "Ooooh! I've simply got to find a new form of employment."

"Well, I'll say one thing. Traveling with you is never dull."

"No?" Stella scanned his body. "Why is it that every time we go to the wars, I get my ass shot off and you don't even get your hair creased? I could have sworn when Powers' soldiers came at us that your ticket was going to get punched."

"Maybe I've got nine lives." A sudden thought erased the smile that had formed on his face.

She touched his hand. "I'm sorry about Carol."

He looked away. "Before she died, she said she loved me."

Stella was silent.

"Maybe if things had been different, if I hadn't met you, she and I..." He shrugged and popped a mint into his mouth. "To quote an old proverb, 'If wishes were horses, beggars might ride.'"

"You're no beggar, George."

"No, I'm not," George said. "As a matter of fact, for a long time I thought I was something infinitely worse."

"How could you be?" She squeezed his hand. "You've got to be about the finest person I know."

"Aw, I bet you say that to every guy who pulls bullets out of your hide." The attempted joke fell flat. "Remember your asking me why I quit being a soldier? It had to do with some incidents on Baxter."

"Oh yes," she said. "Baxter used to be controlled by rebels. Ithaca the Pretender's, I think."

"Yeah, he wanted to depose the present Emperor's daddy and we ran his forces out of there." His face twitched. "It was nasty. After we were through, the colonel in charge tortured a few of the men. Their women met another fate."

She could imagine. "Is that why you gave up fighting and became a psyche-physician? Because of your association with that?"

George shook his head, and she saw him grip the side of her bed. "No. God help me, I knew I couldn't stop it. I had heard that such things went on."

"Then why? I don't understand."

A shudder passed through him. "Because I liked it," he said. He closed his eyes. "Even worse, after a while I did it."

She tried to think of something to say, but couldn't.

George released her bed and straightened. "What do you think of me now? Still think I'm so fine?" He snorted in self-disgust. "I warn you about Jason's indiscretions while my own past is excrement."

Across the room, Dr. Wynn stood directly in front of Jason, hiding him from view. Her voice was so low Stella could barely hear it. "War makes us do terrible things, George," Stella said. "You can't atone the rest of your life for what your superiors condoned."

"Stella, war hasn't made you do terrible things," George said. "Instead, it's only brought out the best."

She closed her eyes, seeing Nick die as he ran, Gage erupt in blood. Thunderheart...

"Commander McMasters."

Stella opened her eyes. Colonel Powers stood beside George, looking neat and handsome with his pencil-thin mustache.

"Hello, Colonel," she said. "George tells me you've been a big help in getting the guards' support."

He nodded. "Most of them were accountable to me back on the base anyway, ser."

Ser. He had called her ser. "How would you like a new job, Colonel?" she said.

"New job?"

"I know you're two ranks above me and technically in charge here, but we have a couple of crucial posts open. I thought you might do well at Myles Uxman's position." She waited. It hurt to say Myles' name.

"Internal Security?"

"The responsibilities are similar to those you had on the base." She searched his expression. "Besides, I got the impression you liked him."

"I did. Very much." Powers removed his hat, and then carefully replaced it. "It's just that I didn't do a very good job in my last position."

"Colonel," she said, "you served a higher security."

"I don't know." He rubbed his brow. "It bothers me, goes against all my training, everything I've valued."

"You could always talk to Lee," George said, stirring briefly.

"Maybe I will." His eyes shifted to Stella. "Could you trust me, Commander? What's to stop me from committing another act of betrayal?" He squared his shoulders. "If I decide you're a traitor, I might put a pistol to your head."

"Colonel, I'll trust your judgment." She raised her hand. "Come here and we'll seal the deal."

Powers did so, gently pressing her hand. She read his nameplate. *P. Powers.*

"Most of my officers, including myself, are on a first-name basis," she said. "I'll call you Colonel if you want."

He smiled. "It's not necessary."

"What does the 'P' stand for?"

He looked at his nameplate. "I don't really like my first name."

Oh no. Not another Gage. Sensing her thought, he waved it off. "It's not that. I'm not paranoid about it like she was. Usually friends just call me Pierce."

"Perce?" George said. "P-e-r-c-e?"

"Not quite." Stella saw Powers actually blush. "It's P-i-e-r-c-e. I shortened it from uh, 'Percival.'"

Oh shit. Percival Powers. With great effort, she kept her face straight.

George smiled and slapped him on the back. "Well, what's wrong with that? As a great bard once wrote, 'What's in a name? that which we call a rose/By any other name would smell as sweet.'"

Across the room, their conversation had finally caught Jason's attention. She saw him push Dr. Wynn aside and rush over with a huge smile, delighted that she was awake and all right.

Four hours later, with the black maw of Scylla rapidly approaching, Stella walked down a corridor past the officers' quarters. Beneath her uniform, the bandages felt thick as boilerplate. Her body itself had become stiff and clumsy, though there was no pain.

Why was she here? She could still see and hear George's indignation when she'd told him to send for her other uniform and help her to dress. For the first time ever, he'd called her 'stupid.' She couldn't blame him.

She stopped outside a door. Twenty-eight. That was, let's see, Carol Wayne's.

She tried the palm lock. The door was sealed tight and could only be conveniently opened by Carol. But Carol wouldn't be around to press it.

Gently, she placed her forehead against the door, feeling its hard finality. Goodbye, Carol, she thought. Now you won't ever have to fight with George again.

After a moment, she moved on.

A few steps later she heard a sound, a barely audible rustling. She moved to the nearest door and pressed her ear against it. It was coming from here.

One of her crew, a security guard, was just approaching. "Your name's Girault, isn't it?" Stella said, noticing her cheeks were wet.

"Yes, ser," the woman said with a salute. "May I be of help?"

Stella returned her salute. "I hear a sound coming from these quarters. Do you hear it?"

They listened together. Stella picked it up immediately, a low, barely perceptible sound like leaves whispering in the wind. Or dreams being broken. She tried to stop the morbid flow of her thoughts but death seemed like a swollen river she was drowning in.

"No, I don't, Commander," Girault said.

Well, that was to be expected. It was her imagination, that's all. Then again, though inner-ear technology had lagged behind other areas, she had been assured her hearing would be at least fifty percent better than normal. She thought of asking Girault for her gun.

A fresh tear ran down Girault's cheek. She pulled out a handkerchief and honked loudly into it. Stella found she could smile at the sound.

"It's hit us all hard," she said. "We're going to have to stand by each other in the days ahead."

"Yes. Well. It's not just that." Girault folded the handkerchief and put it in her pocket. "That's Lieutenant Uxman's room. He was my systems chief."

"I'm terribly sorry." Stella remembered what it had been like ten years before when her maintenance head had died. She smiled again. "Myles Uxman was a good comrade."

"Yes, he was, ser. The very best." With a crisp salute and a last glance at Myles' door, Girault left.

Stella turned back to Myles' door. Raising her hand, she checked the lock.

It was disengaged from the jamb. Myles had closed but not locked his door.

She pushed the door open and entered, closing it behind her. The lights automatically came on, not knowing or caring that Myles himself would never return.

On the floor near the back wall, she saw a cage. Snuffling

sounds came from it. How could I forget Myles' pets? she thought. Someone has to look after the poor things.

She sat down beside it and opened the small door. To her surprise, she didn't have to reach in because the scrunched-faced, furry creatures scampered eagerly out and ran over her body. Stella knew pyota goats were an unpredictable species and that these particular ones had even bitten their owner, but at the moment they seemed overjoyed to see her. They made high, squeaky sounds that sounded like *yipt!* and *yawp!* and licked her face with silken tongues. They flowed around and around her, pressing and molding her with their soft, warm bodies. If she hadn't known better, Stella would have sworn she'd just made new friends for life.

She picked the larger one up and studied its homely face. After a few seconds, something broke inside and the hot tears came, raining down her cheeks. Sobbing, she pressed her face against the animal's fur.

Damn it, Jason had been right again. General Gage did look like a pyota goat. The spitting image.

The swirling interior of Scylla waited just ahead. Stella sat in the command chair, wishing she had never reported to the base but had proceeded directly on to Loran himself.

"All systems go," Lee said.

"Take us down, Lee," she said. "Out."

"Aye, aye, ser."

The ship trembled, then leapt forward like a giant animal into the vortex. Stella noticed tiny, sparkling lights inside it that Imperial experts were unable to account for. As Gage would say, some things were just a mystery, as miraculous as life itself.

Down they went, and this singularity passage did not elicit old memories like Charybdis. Instead, Loran Base lived again in vivid reality. She re-experienced scenes, felt them with her body. Jason was there, his arms extended to show how he wanted to hold her. Gage handed her a glass of champagne, then died while protecting her. Thunderheart pulled her back into life from the body-cuff, kissing her for the first and last time before marching to battle. Nick promised he'd return soon, only to die.

Tessa Farron's hands were there, picking at each other as always. She felt Ulysses' cheek press against her own. In the royal chamber, the Emperor asked if she would hurt him, smiling as he touched the suit that bound her.

And above, the smashed globe of Loran Base spun, glittered in the air as she slid down a chute with Jason's arms close around her. At the bottom George waited to catch them. Only it wasn't George, it was...

...Clear, open, star-flung reaches as they shot out of Scylla and coasted through space on autopilot, gradually slowing as reverse thrusters kicked in. Removing her seat belts, she rose and gazed out the plexiport.

Three weeks to rendezvous with Loran's forces, give or take a few days. She pressed her hands together, hoping there'd be no more trouble, just smooth sailing. And Jason, of course. Jason with his soft lips and gentle hands.

Greetings, Stella McMasters.

The All-Mother raged through her mind and drove her to her knees, not with the diluted force of a will sent from a remote realm, but from much closer. In shock, Stella realized the All-Mother lurked a mere light-week's distance away, where she waited to meet Loran's forces. Swaying, Stella stared blindly up at the ceiling, her neck straining as if caught in an unseen fist.

You have passed the test and escaped the base. The All-Mother laughed darkly. *But how, oh how, Stella Singlethorne McMasters, will you ever resist me NOW?*

CHAPTER TWENTY-THREE

There was no escape from her, no way to turn. Every exit was only an entrance back into her presence. The All-Mother filled the universe, God and Satan combined. Love, death, pride and honor were nothing before her, did not even exist.

And the most amazing thing of all was that the All-Mother wanted something from her besides revenge.

She glimpsed it in snatches, along with yet another revelation the All-Mother didn't want her to know. The knowledge instilled a tiny seed of hope in her, for if the All-Mother needed her for something, and also possessed yet another secret she didn't want her to know, then she was not all-powerful, not omniscient, and not all-seeing. Before her, a puny human, a cyborg human, stood some small chance.

Then desire for the All-Mother flooded her being, an unbearable, irresistible yearning to be with her...for what? Her enemy did not permit her to see that. As if the All-Mother were regulating Stella's intense longing, she felt it subside. Still, it remained too great, would drive her mad if it continued.

The All-Mother knew and released her, sending a parting thought that pierced her mind with a new and different message.

When we meet, you will want only me. And then, frail human, we will spin your death song together.

She opened her eyes. George knelt over her with a hypospray, his face etched with concern.

"Are you all right?" he said. "You should take a jump better and recover quicker than any of us." He touched her cheek. "You must have blacked out again. Your concussion."

"It wasn't that," she said. "The All-Mother. She came to me."

George's heavy eyebrows rose. "She was that strong?"

She nodded her head weakly against the floor. "We're so much closer than before. She's just weeks away, where the big battle's going to be. She's been waiting there to meet Loran's fleet." Stella swallowed. "The All-Mother was like...God."

He exhaled slowly. "Then we don't have much of a chance, do we? Even the rebel angels got cast out of heaven when they challenged the Almighty."

"There may be a chance," Stella said. "It seems God has not one secret but three."

"Three?"

"Yes." She gazed out the plexiport, toward their ultimate destination. "Two of them concern her nature, what she is. The third..."

"Yes, Stella," he prompted. "What is it?"

She swallowed. "The third is what she wants and must have from me."

The next two weeks were uneventful only in that no one was shot or attacked, though Malek threatened reprisals and complained about his confinement. George's healants knit her wounds and his team installed the brain of Jason's replacement pilot.

The man, Peter, had an apparently insatiable craving for vid and mental games. It seemed strange to hear his high, synthesized voice fill the bridge with blithe comments on telemetry and the Ro-Two Gambit in tri-chess. Every time Stella looked at Jason's 'place' above the holovids, she found it difficult to believe he wasn't there.

Instead, he was right at her side whenever they had some free time. Not that there was much. The *Spaceranger* was desperately short in personnel, and Jason, like the others, helped wherever he could. It was good for him. Jump pilots who had been restored to their bodies during a mission often felt demoted and virtually useless, without anything to do.

One day, during a calm stretch when there were no pleas

for assistance from Hydroponics, or endless reports from the enthusiastic weapons tech she had appointed to fill Carol's slot, she found herself heading for Jason's quarters. There was a warm yearning in the pit of her stomach and she had to keep herself from running. Though their love-making had deepened and she glimpsed vistas of what a more mature, profound relationship between them would mean, her body still overrode her mind. It was, in fact, as if it were only complete when she was with him.

She laughed when she reached his door in the officers' quarters. Jason was forgetful like Myles and hadn't engaged the palm lock. With a mischievous grin, she pushed the door in, hoping Jason was there.

He was.

He lay on his back in bed with Dr. Wynn straddling his middle, her head tilted toward the ceiling as if in prayer. Stella saw at once she was adept and practiced at love-making, for her naked pelvis rolled smoothly in an endless flowing cycle. Also apparent was Jason's own active involvement. He held one arm extended, fingers lightly caressing Wynn's full breasts and erect nipples. His face looked mesmerized, and his breathing was loud.

She took a step into the room. Another.

Dr. Wynn was nearing a crisis, and Jason, she saw, was concerned about helping her reach it. Both were intent on each other. To both, she didn't exist.

She stood there as Dr. Wynn moaned and her skin broke out into a bright flush. Afterward she bent and whispered endearments to Jason as she kissed him. Through it all, their bodies continued to move.

How they became aware of her, Stella didn't know. One moment they were joined together; the next they sprang apart. Dr. Wynn stooped and snatched up her clothes, murmuring an apology. Stella ignored her, staring at Jason as he sat up and gazed down at the floor. He remained that way as his partner, half-dressed, quickly left. Stella heard the door click shut but not locked behind her.

"Why?" she finally said.

Jason shook his head. "I don't know," he said.

Stella kept her eyes on his face, not wanting to see his body. "Do you remember what you said to General Gage when she asked you to hold me going down the chute?"

He lifted his eyes to hers. "I said, 'All the way.'"

One moment she wanted to kill him, the next she wanted to weep at the sheer sordid banality of it. It was so cheap, so tawdry. The worst of it all was that she should have known it was coming. After all, George had warned her.

She turned to leave.

"Please, wait!" Jason moved past her to the door. "Give me a chance," he said. "Let me explain."

"Explain?" She felt her control crumble. "What is there to explain, Jason? You saw a chance to get a little extra action behind my back and you took it. You don't have to explain that. It's perfectly obvious."

"No, that's not it at all." Jason pressed her hand in both of his. "I...I love you, Stella. I'm sorry. I never meant to hurt you."

She looked at his hands holding hers. She could break both of them, but all she could think of was the rapt look on his face as he caressed Dr. Wynn.

Pushing him aside as if he were made of straw, she left his cabin.

George Darron came up to her a few days later as Lee was showing her some data on the bridge.

"Stella, may I see you?"

"Sure, George." She handed a printout to Lee and went to George. "What is it?"

"Can we speak privately?"

She frowned. "Okay. Is it important?"

"I think so." He indicated the bridge portal. "Perhaps in your quarters."

On the way Stella informed him they were only seventy-two hours from the flagship *Victory*, which was General Loran's headquarters and command center. George murmured an indifferent response.

When they were in her cabin, he came to the point. "Jason told me what happened."

Stella let her face freeze over. "Really."

"Yes. He's very upset, Stella. He came to me in a frenzy. I had to sedate him."

"I presume there's a point to all this?"

"He told me about his mother dying," George said quietly. "About the man who came between them. He said he'd only told it to one other person before and that was you."

She folded her arms, trying to seal the hurt in, not let it erupt. "Is this all supposed to excuse what he did? Or make me feel sorry for him?" She managed to smile even though it felt ghastly. "Congratulations, George. You were right when you warned me about him. Jason's a womanizer, and that's all he is."

"Stella, when Jason's mother died, she took his childhood with her. I haven't run a psy-con on him, but it doesn't take any deep insight to see that he distrusts women because of what his mother did. He sees her absorption in the man as a betrayal, and her laughing at him and calling him a little boy as proof that she didn't love him. The fact that she died soon after only makes it worse. It explains why he runs from woman to woman to avoid being hurt again."

She lowered her arms, feeling her control go. "What is this, instant diagnosis? Psycho-babble?" She stepped forward and tapped George's chest. "Let me tell you something. You didn't see his face when he was rutting Dr. Wynn. His mother wasn't there, and he enjoyed every moment of it."

"I know you've been terribly hurt," George said. "Ordinarily, you'd have every right to shut Jason out. But Stella, this is war. You don't have time to adjust, don't have time for personal concerns. We could all be dead soon, blown into atoms amid the stars. If you lived and Jason died without you seeing him one last time, imagine the pain you'd feel." His mouth twitched. "Believe me, I know all about remorse."

"What are you saying, George?"

"I know it's a lot to ask, but would you consider talking to him? Perhaps give him a chance to explain?"

Explain. She couldn't even think of seeing Jason, much less talking to him about why he'd broken every promise he'd made to her, all the way back to their first meeting. To seek him out, to ask him why he had taken something that was so beautiful and spat on it-no, she just couldn't do it. Nor could she bear the thought that Jason and everything they'd shared had been an illusion, a glib lie. How could she have been so stupid, and how could she ever trust any man again?

"I know how you feel," George said.

"You know how I feel?" She snorted. "Believe me, George, you don't have the faintest idea!"

"Then maybe I don't," George said. "Maybe you can explain it to me. It has something to do with your accident, doesn't it, and your feelings about your...body?"

She stiffened. "What do you mean?"

"Just that if it hadn't happened, you might feel a little differently about Jason and his actions the other day," George said gently.

"I see," Stella said, her voice hardening. "Let me try to guess the rest. You're going to say that if I hadn't lost my body in an accident, I wouldn't take his rejection so badly. Or maybe it's not a rejection at all. Maybe you think we're both sick or wounded inside. Is that what you feel, George?"

"Look," George said, "I'm not trying to minimize what Jason did. It was a terrible betrayal. If this was peacetime, you'd be justified in freezing him out. But this is war, Stella, and we're fighting for our survival. As Commander, you must be logical, analytical. You can't allow anything to cloud your judgment. You can't make decisions based on anger or rage or personal feelings. Too many lives depend on your being in complete control."

"I'll tell you what I think," Stella said. "I don't want to talk about this anymore." Despite herself, she continued. "Damn it, he didn't lose most of his body, I did. He can slip back into his nice beautiful hide any time he wants. But me-what can I go back to, George? Believe me, you'll never, never know what it feels like."

"You could tell me," he said softly. "I'd be glad to listen."

She stepped back. "I don't want to talk about myself. I've already done it enough."

He extended his palm. "Then what about Jason? We could talk about him."

"Why would I want to?" she said. "Why should I want to at all?" She ran her hand through her hair, seeing Jason in her cabin after Wynn had left. *Please,* he had said. *I love you.* She pushed the memory away, hardening herself. "Why should I even care? Don't you remember that it was you who warned me about him in the first place?"

"Yes, and I was wrong," George said. "I've watched you both the last couple weeks and if any people belong together, it's you two."

She reached out and touched George's hand. "If I hadn't been so blind, I'd have picked you instead of him."

George's face twitched. "No, not me." His eyes moistened. "I've loved you, Stella, but I've had no right. Not after what I did as a soldier. Compared to me, Jason is a saint."

"That was when you were young," she said. "You've changed. Unlike Jason, you've grown, matured. Besides, there were extenuating..." An insight broke upon her with such force that she trembled. "My God, we're both similar. I can't bend with Jason even though it's war, and you can't forgive yourself because in your heart you'll always be what you once were."

George smiled painfully. "You would have made a good psyche-physician, Stella."

She sighed. "It doesn't matter. I can't change the way I feel."

George stared back, and then shrugged. "Well, there you have it," he said.

Her comconsole beeped. She went and tapped in to Lee.

"McMasters here," she said.

"Commander," Lee said quickly, "we've got a ship coming up on us fast. I've boosted power, but it's still gaining."

"Ship?" She flashed George a look. "Is it a pursuit ship from Loran Base?"

"Negative. It looks like a rebel scut, ser. And its message..."

"Yes, what is it?"

"Commander," Lee said, "its captain sounds determined. He's ordered us to surrender at once."

CHAPTER TWENTY-FOUR

When they reached the bridge, George announced at once that they weren't rebels. "See those ventral fins, the pointed bow and overall streamlining? They're Denzee pirates, and those ships are cutters."

"What are they doing here?" Stella said. "Pirates usually haunt the trade runs, dart in and sting us before our police can arrive." She waved at the open space before them. "There's nothing out here but void."

"Ser," Lee said, "there might be more. It's common knowledge that in a week or two the greatest battle of the war will take place here."

She nodded. "Yes, I see. These are the vultures who will feast on the remains, no matter what side wins."

"They don't know the Slugs would eat them too," George said.

Stella nodded and checked their velocity. "Are they still gaining on us?"

"It's leveled out, ser," Lee said. "They're twelve thousand kilometers behind, and in a minute we should start to gain."

"They haven't fired," George pointed out.

"We're probably outside their effective range," Stella said, "and in any case, they'd want us as undamaged as possible." She gnawed her lip, studying the control panel. "They haven't commed us again?"

"No, ser," Lee said.

"Try to reach 'em. See if you can get some vid so we can see what we're dealing with."

She watched Lee run the frequencies, tightbeam to broad. Nothing. Only static and white noise on the bands. Then came a flash and a face appeared.

"Ser," Lee said, "they're sending again."

"Shh." She studied the face, which was swarthy and wore a broad-brimmed, tall crowned hat tied under the chin. The man was small and gave them a wide, toothy grin.

"Ah, *buenos dias, amigos*. It's so good to see you!"

She stared at him. "I'm Stella McMasters, Commander of the *Spaceranger*. Who are you and what do you want?"

"*Mis companeros*," the man said with a smile. "I am Pancho Villa of *La Libertad*, and I am proud to inform you that I am the spiritual reincarnation of that great revolutionary leader of old *Mejico*." He crossed his arms. "I demand your unconditional surrender at once."

Stella glanced at George, who covered his mouth with his hand. "I've seen his compfile, Stella. He's a sombrero-wearing crackbrain, and he's not even of Mexican descent. Don't be fooled by the skin treatment and dyed beard. His ideas are a mishmash, like that crazy religion Malek hooked the Emperor on."

"*Mis companeros*," Pancho rumbled. "Please, do me the courtesy to speak to me. And do so *muy pronto*, eh?" He glowered at them. "Now, be so good as to tell me if you will accept my terms."

Terms? He was asking for unconditional surrender. Stella leaned forward. "Ride off into the sunset, *amigo*. And do so *muy pronto*."

Pancho's face darkened and he rattled off a string of language she didn't understand. She looked at George.

"Old-style Terran Spanish," he said. "I'm no expert, but most of it's pretty bad, especially the accent."

Stella turned back to Pancho. "Look, let me explain something. You and your ship tried to sneak up on us and it didn't work." She glanced at a vid that plotted the distance between them and their pursuers. Fourteen thousand, seven hundred kilometers. "We're rapidly leaving you behind in our dust."

"Ah, it is all so *mucho triste*." Pancho's fingers stroked the drooping ends of his mustache, and he gave them a hangdog look that made Stella smile.

George placed his lips to her ear. "What are we talking to

this clown for? Let's break contact and tend to business."

She nodded and started to order Lee to do just that.

"*Mucho triste*," Pancho said. "It is *muy* hard to serve the little *nino* these days."

"What was that, Pancho?" Her mouth quirked as she realized she'd just called a hostile pirate by his first name.

"What did I say?" Pancho said. "I was merely stating that these are bad, sad times for *un hombre* who loves and serves his *Emperador*. The war has made his merchants so *muy pobre* that they have put me in a *casa de caridad*."

Stella heard laughter. She turned, seeing several crew members clutching their sides at Pancho's woebegone expression. Even Colonel Powers was trying hard to contain himself. Beyond him, she saw Jason entering the bridge. She turned quickly to George.

"I think that means 'poorhouse,'" George chuckled. He leaned toward Pancho's image. "You say you have no *dinero* for your *companeros*?" he asked. "You are what they call, *los pobres*-the poor?"

"Ah, *si*," Pancho nodded vigorously. "It is *muy mucho triste*. My *Emperador*-may the saints protect him!-has been unable to look after his servants in his war."

To Stella, it would have been comical if it weren't so infuriating. This ugly little rascal claimed to be patriotic. Did he actually believe his screw-brained statement?

"Let me get this straight," she said. "You say you love your Emperor, Kolanera the Fifth."

Pancho's dark face bobbed up and down. "Ah, *si, muy mucho!* As I loved and revered his *padre y madre* before they died. *Tanto trajico. Tanto trajico!*" She watched Pancho cross his heart with two quick gestures. "Such a sweet little *nino* he is. He will make a *muy grande Emperador* one day."

"I don't understand," Stella said. "If you love your Emperor so much, why do you steal from his merchants and representatives? Why have you come here, if not to be scavengers who will plunder the Emperor's ships after they've been destroyed by the enemy?"

There. That should prick anyone's conscience. But Pancho's eyes only widened at her apparent obtuseness. "Ah, *Senorita*, even a dog has its fleas, no? You can't have one without the other. It is the way of things! Through it all, I remain *el Emperador's* loyal *pirata*." He struck the surface before him. "I love my *Emperador muy mucho!* I steal, yes, but I never, ever touch his personal ships or molest his, how you say it, his *ambassadors*." He wagged a chastising finger. "If I was asked, *Comandante*, I would gladly lay down my life for him."

Stella considered this outburst then felt an amazing idea take form. If Pancho was genuinely loyal, perhaps she could have two ships to use in case General Loran rejected her plan. If he didn't agree to withdraw his forces while she faced the enemy alone, she would have Pancho threaten to kill Malek.

There were only two problems. First, what if Loran refused? Second, could she be sure Pancho wouldn't run off with Malek and hold him for ransom? After all, Pancho was a pirate. Perhaps she could arrange for an exchange of crew so her watchdogs could be in two places at once.

What else? She gnawed her lip. Loran knew Powers, so Powers should accompany her to Loran as Gage's representative. But what would she say when Loran asked why no one had radioed the news first? Hmm, perhaps the enemy had blocked the transmission.

"Pierce," Stella said, "have Malek brought here at once."

Powers frowned, then lifted a comlink and spoke into it. "He'll be on the bridge in two minutes," he told Stella.

"Good." She smiled at Pancho. "*Capitan Villa*, would you mind, *por favor*, if we terminate contact for uh, *tres* minutes to discuss your terms?"

"Ah, *por favor*," Pancho said, obviously pleased. "Of course, *Senorita*."

Lee pressed a button and Pancho flashed into black. "All right," Stella said to George, Lee, and Powers, "I want you over here. And Peter," she said, addressing the jump pilot, "I want you to keep a close watch on that ship. Let me know if they do anything suspicious."

"I will, ser," Peter said. Ignoring Jason, who stood near the bridge's entrance, Stella smiled at George.

"Well, George, have you figured it out yet?"

George made a gesture to show he was completely lost. "All I know is that you're not about to surrender this ship to that cut-rate *bandido*. Why do you want Malek here?"

"I think I know," Lee said.

George put his hands on his hips and jabbed his chin out. "Perhaps you'd be so kind as to let the rest of us know."

"Of course, Dr. Darron," Lee said. "Commander McMasters, I believe, feels that we need an extra ship."

"'Extra ship'?" Powers said. "For what?"

Stella saw Lee smile. "To hold a hostage, Regent-Protector Malek," he said.

George was about to reply when Peter's voice swept the bridge. "I get it! That's a brilliant move, Commander. You're going to see General Loran and if for some reason he won't agree to your plan, you'll have-"

"An ace in the hole," George finished. He placed the heel of his hand against his forehead and ground it in. "God-talk about strange bedfellows! And you think since this Pancho claims to love the Emperor so much that if you show him this bastard Malek..."

Powers, who had been following the exchange in confusion, suddenly stiffened. "You're going to put the Regent-Protector on a pirate ship?" He gripped his hat as if to keep it from flying off. "What the hell's going to keep them from just flying off and ransoming him themselves?"

Stella looked at Lee, who seemed to be right in tune with her. "An exchange of crew," he said.

"That's right," Stella said. "A good will swap. We give them say, half of ours and they can do the same."

Powers stared at her, then turned to George with a stunned expression. "Is she often like this, George?"

"Oh, *si*," he nodded. "Things are always *muy interesante* with our commander."

Footsteps. Stella turned to see Malek, his arms bound behind him, ushered by two guards onto the bridge. He looked considerably chastened as a result of his confinement during the past two weeks.

When Malek was standing with them, she nodded at Lee, who reestablished communications with Pancho.

Pancho's face quickly filled with disgust. "*Mierda!* The *Emperador* I love but not this dog."

"You know this gentleman, *Capitan?*"

"Know him?" Pancho broke into a string of guttural Spanish.

"Please, *Capitan*," Stella said. "Use English!"

Pancho cursed and thrust his finger at Malek. "This gentleman, *Comandante*, this dog of a whore, he killed my blood brother Ramos."

Malek stiffened, trying to recover some dignity. "If I did," he said, "then he deserved it. It's my sworn duty to protect the Emperor."

"Protect what? A shit-filled, third-rate merchant scug that wasn't worth the money to blow up? I heard all about it from some of his crew who escaped."

Stella, noting that Pancho was no longer speaking Spanish, gave Malek a nudge. "He's done more than that, *Capitan*. At Loran Base, which we recently visited, he was responsible for more of your brothers dying."

Pancho's eyes narrowed to slits. "So that's why he's on your ship. You take him captive, eh?"

George leaned forward. "We're starting *una revolucion, senor.*"

"*Una revolucion?*" The word seemed to hypnotize Pancho. Stella saw him repeat it silently.

She shook her head. "No, not just *una revolucion. Una GALACTIC revolucion.*" Pancho's eyes got wider and wider. Stella continued. "It will be *una revolucion* that is worthy of a great leader like yourself rather than a cut-rate *bandido.* And you know why we will fight for it, *Capitan Villa?* Because this dog of a whore has betrayed the *Emperador* you love so much."

"That's true," George inserted. "He has him addicted to drugs. I saw it myself."

"Drugs?" Pancho said.

"Probably *meroxadex*," George continued. "We all saw

el Emperador forced to take it. But there is something even worse, my loyal *pirata*. Though *el Emperador* is but an innocent, vulnerable child, this dog has grown men and women use him, if you know what I mean."

Pancho's mouth sagged open. "He has done this to my *Emperador*, my little *nino*?"

"*Yes!*" they all chanted.

Pancho's face hardened and he studied Malek, whose face twitched guiltily. "Regent-Protector Malek," he said in a glacial voice devoid of accent. "I would give my family jewels to have your own in my hands."

Stella smiled. "Pancho," she said, "it's odd that you should say that."

Pierce Powers, efficient as ever, handled the mutual transfer of personnel through the *Spaceranger's* boarding tube as *La Libertad* hovered alongside. During the procedure, Peter kept his artillery trained on the cutter.

When Pancho was escorted onto the *Spaceranger's* bridge, Stella saw he barely reached her chin. Pancho, though, grinned confidently and embraced her like an old lover.

When he finally released her, she found they were on a first-name basis. "So, Stella, this All-Mother sounds like a real dog of a whore, yes?"

"She sure is, Pancho," she said, determined to appear confident.

For Pancho, there were evidently a lot of dogs and a lot of whores, but at the moment it seemed like a fair description of her ultimate opponent.

"You have a good plan to beat this bitch?"

She nodded sagely. "It's a secret."

"Ah, *excelente, muy bien!*" Pancho stroked his mustache, his Spanish mysteriously back. "Stella, after this *revolucion* of yours, you have an important *posicion* for me in your *administracion, si?*"

The question made her turn from the vid showing Pierce and others in the docking area and look at Pancho. "What?"

"I was just asking if you have an important *posicion* for me in your new *administracion*."

"Oh…of course." Was that a lecherous wink the strange little man just gave her? If she ever got out of this, she'd have to ask him if he really thought he was the spiritual reincarnation of Pancho Villa.

Pancho grinned. "So, what is my *posicion*, Stella?" Judging from the way he talked, Pancho felt that Malek's forces and the All-Mother had already been vanquished.

"We'll think of something." An idea struck her. "Perhaps you'd like to be the official Director of Police. You could chase down pirates in my uh, *administracion*. After all, who else is better qualified?"

Pancho's eyes gleamed. "And my share, how you call it, my *percentage* of what I save from these *piratas*?" He rubbed his hands greedily. "Sixty percent seems reasonable, does it not?"

She shook her head, going along with the charade. "No. *Muy* high. Ten percent."

Outrage and indignation. "Ten? For a man of my greatness?" He thumped his chest. "To an Imperial *Director de Policia* you want to give *pesos*?" He calmed, evidently liking the title. "Fifty percent."

"Fifteen," she said. "And that's payment in Imperial chit rather than contraband."

"Agreed. Forty-five."

"Twenty."

"Forty."

"Twenty-five."

"Thirty-five."

"Thirty."

"*Bueno!*" Pancho slapped his knee. "We have a deal, *amiga*."

A crewman led Malek to Pancho, who greeted him with robust delight. "Ah, *senor* Regent-Protector. I am *muy mucho* happy to meet you." He embraced Malek, then vigorously pinched and shook Malek's cheeks. "What a sweet looking *hombre* you are. We make you *muy* comfortable during your *visita, si?*"

Stella savored Malek's expression. He looked like someone who found himself submerged in filth up to his goatee.

"Remember our deal and what you've promised to do," Stella

cautioned. "It's no good if he suffers an accident."

"*Un accidente*? I would not let such a thing happen to my fine *amigo* here." Pancho patted Malek on the cheek.

Stella shifted her eyes to the view of the docking area, which was as bizarre as that of Pancho embracing Malek. Brett and other soldiers Stella had chosen entered the same boarding tube that Pancho's grimy pirates were exiting. She saw a dirty man in a sombrero and crisscrossing bandoleers strut up to Powers and pump his hand. The impeccable Colonel smiled awkwardly, blinking as his greeter pulled a cigar from his mouth and blew smoke in his face. Stella laughed softly.

Her laughter died as she noticed Jason standing near the bridge entrance. He was gazing directly at her. Suddenly she couldn't bear to see him anymore.

"Jason, you go too."

He took a few steps forward, his face uncertain. "What?"

She pointed. "I want you on their ship too. Get your gear and board it."

George came toward her. "Don't do this."

She gazed at Jason, her face giving him no sign of recognition. "That's an order."

He returned her gaze for a moment, and then nodded as if it were his due. She watched him leave, feeling as if he took her heart with him.

"Stella..." George began.

"You can go too," she said.

He touched her arm. "You don't mean that."

"That's where you're wrong," she said. "I do. When we first met, you started by questioning my orders. Don't do it again."

"You're becoming as rigid as Malek and Lovejoy," George said. "Stella, you can't afford to be. Too much depends on what you say and do."

She turned to him, knowing she should reconsider but unable to. "If you like him so much, why don't you go with him? I can certainly do without you here."

George stared at her for several seconds. "I'll get my armor," he said.

Four days later, they reported to Loran's command center and settled into the vast armada of ships assembled in space a light-day from Cygnus X-1. Even as they entered their designated sector, Stella saw two other ships arrive.

Inside, she felt a gaping and guilty ache. She wasn't surprised that she found Jason's absence painful. What did surprise her was George's. His absence on the bridge left a void that no one else could fill. She kept turning her head to see him, expecting to hear his voice.

Powers turned to her with a crisp nod. "They're patching us through to Loran now, Stella."

She thrust Jason and George from her mind. "You say you and the General are good friends?"

He smiled. "Not exactly, but when he visited the base, we got along well. I found him quite cordial."

A vid flickered, and Stella found herself facing a strikingly handsome man with silver hair. He smiled.

"Pierce, it's good to see you again."

"It's a pleasure to see you, General Loran," Powers said. "We just arrived."

"So I've been informed."

"General," Powers said, turning to her, "may I present Stella McMasters of the *Spaceranger.*"

Loran shifted his eyes to her. They were intense blue, as striking as the rest of him, and Stella remembered the holos she'd seen of him at the base. Good as they were, they didn't do him justice.

"Commander," Loran said, "it's a pleasure."

She bowed slightly. "I'm honored, General."

"General Loran," Powers said, "may Commander McMasters and I meet with you at your earliest convenience?"

Loran sat back in his chair. "Is it urgent, Pierce? I'm in a swamp at the moment."

"Ser," Powers said, "it's of the utmost gravity." Stella saw him glance at her. "Commander McMasters may have found a way to defeat the enemy."

Slowly, General Loran sat forward. His gaze was riveted on her.

"I want you both here immediately," he said.

In the shuttle port, Stella saw Dr. Wynn waiting. "May I speak to you, Commander?"

"I'm in a hurry," Stella snapped at her, and then stopped. "How'd you know I'd be here?"

"Chatternet, ser. The whole crew's laid bets on whether or not, and how soon, you get to meet Loran."

"I see." Rumors spread quickly on a ship, and often there was more than one means of communication. Thinking of the days before she'd been an officer, Stella was reminded that sometimes, those without rank heard things the officers didn't.

As Stella started to step into the pod, Dr. Wynn touched her shoulder. "Please, ser, can't you get him back?"

Stella brushed her hand away. When she'd found them making love in Jason's room, her anger had been directed almost solely at Jason. Now it was an effort not to hit Wynn.

"I'm afraid that's not possible," she said.

Dr. Wynn started crying. "I don't know why, but I feel I'll never see him again."

I'll never see him. Stella gave her a broad smile. "You'll get over it," she said.

"You shouldn't have done it, ser. We could have shared him." She wiped her cheek. "A man like that can never be faithful."

Stella heard Pierce climb discreetly into the pod behind her. Raising her hand, she wiped Wynn's other cheek.

"I never share," Stella said.

As the flagship *Victory* grew before them, Powers turned to her in the shuttle pod. "Since the General was friendly, it appears that Loran Base was damaged too much to send a pursuit ship through Scylla to contact him by now. Of course, he could have been bluffing, and there's no guarantee a ship won't come through later and radio *Victory* on this side of the singularity."

Stella glanced about at the thousands of ships gathered, thinking of those yet to come. "Just before we left, I thought of that. I told Pancho that if he doesn't hear from me, it'll probably mean Loran's thrown me in the brig. In that case, Pancho will contact Loran and arrange for an exchange of prisoners. He'll give them Malek if Loran lets me and the crew return in the *Spaceranger*."

"Let's hope it doesn't come to that," Powers said. "The big issue is whether Loran will let you meet the All-Mother alone." He shook his head. "I've never known Loran to run from a fight. To be honest, I doubt he'll do it even for Malek. Since he's a prisoner, his orders are probably invalid anyway. In any case, with the enemy's forces fast approaching, the coming battle has gone far beyond anyone's ability to stop it."

Jason, she thought, will I ever see you again? Will you be all right? She gripped her knee, disappointed in her own weakness. At the same time, she was glad that her rash decision to banish Jason and George to Pancho's ship would keep them out of Loran's reach. "All I know is I must convince the good general to take all this hardware home, or at least far enough away so I can joust with the All-Mother on my own terms. If he doesn't listen to reason, I'll have to use Malek as a hostage. It's our last resort, the only other way I know to get Loran to agree."

"And if it doesn't work?"

Stella shrugged. "I don't know. As George would say, I'll just have to cross that bridge when I come to it."

CHAPTER TWENTY-FIVE

When they docked at the *Victory*, they were met by the security officer, a strikingly beautiful major named Day. She welcomed them while a team of guards searched their bodies with hands and scanners. Stella was grateful that she didn't have to strip and be probed as well.

"We regret the necessity of this," Day said. "But there have been some incidents lately. I hope you understand."

"It's perfectly all right," Powers said. Since he outranked Stella, he spoke first and assumed the lead. "You can't be too careful."

"That's quite true," Day agreed. When the search was completed, she escorted them to a lift tube.

Watching Day's hips sway, Stella recalled chatternet about Loran liking to surround himself with beautiful women. She straightened her uniform and patted her hair, wishing she had spent more time with her appearance.

With their guards, they entered the lift tube and rose silently. Levels flashed past, some dark, most light. She gave Powers a covert glance and saw that he looked poised and calm.

What am I going to say to Loran?

The problem was, she knew what she wanted him to do but not how to present it. Making speeches and offering proposals had never been her forte. Now she had to convince a man known throughout the galaxy for a lifetime of fighting to withdraw from the greatest battle of his career. How was she going to manage that?

She had to think of something, find the right words.

All too soon they left the tube and walked down a corridor. A door slid open, and they entered.

And there was General Loran, rising to greet them. Stella, who had never seen him in person, knew instantly that he was the most handsome man she had ever met. He was tall, silver-haired, and had intense, piercing blue eyes. As he approached with a smile, she thought of Jason and his charm, and felt a barb of self-anger. Why was she thinking such things now when she needed all her wits?

Fortunately, Loran addressed Powers first. "Pierce, you're looking great! Your duties must agree with you."

Powers smiled. "Thank you, General."

Loran turned. Stella could see him size her up in one quick glance and find her wanting. Or was George right in thinking that she tended to see rejection everywhere because she was a cyborg? But no-she remembered Lovejoy's and others' insults.

"Commander McMasters, it's a privilege to meet you." Loran shook her hand and gave her a hint of a courtly bow. Enthralled, she mumbled something in return.

It was only when they were seated that Stella realized Major Day-along with the guards—was still with them, standing beside Loran's desk. She wondered if other people forgot things in the Great Man's presence. Judging from the steady gaze that Day gave Loran, she was distracted too.

Loran seated himself behind a huge silver-metal desk and leaned back. Behind him, a large circular window gaped into space. Stella could see scores of ships-some near, others more distant.

"Well, Pierce," said Loran, "perhaps you'd better explain what you meant when you said Commander McMasters might have a solution to the war."

Powers crossed his knees. "First, ser, I must report a grave and tragic event." He hesitated. "Three weeks ago, Loran Base was severely damaged in an enemy attack. General Gage despatched the two of us to report directly to you. We were terribly fortunate to escape. Unfortunately, we don't know if anyone else did, including our Emperor."

Loran sat upright in his chair, his handsome face stricken. "My base!"

Powers coughed. "You've heard nothing of this, General? We tried repeatedly to radio you, but the enemy must have blocked our transmissions."

"No, I've heard nothing." Loran launched a series of questions. What had happened? When had the enemy appeared? Did Powers think the base had survived? Quietly, Powers answered him. Stella found herself wondering how she would feel if a massive base named after her had been attacked and possibly destroyed.

At a certain point, Powers adroitly shifted the focus to Stella, informing Loran of how she and her crew had captured an enemy ship and brought it to Loran Base, thereby provoking the attack. Loran's eyes shot to her and he pressed a button on his comconsole. "Get my top command and tech staff here at once." He looked at Stella. "Please wait, Commander. I want them all to hear this."

Minutes later a dozen people entered and stood silent. Some were officers, others wore tech coats.

Loran pressed another button. "Go ahead, Commander. I'm recording this meeting. Please tell us about your experience."

Stella gripped the arms of her chair. "Yes, ser," she said. "After we lost the first battle with the hostile ship, I had no choice but to board it myself with a handful of comrades. Colonel Powers has briefly summarized the events, but I can tell you that when George Darron, Brett Duvall, and a few others accompanied me onto the vessel, I had all but given up. To me it was as if we were already dead."

At his desk, General Loran leaned toward her. "I've had that feeling too, Commander."

"And then," Stella continued, feeling herself swept away by the memory, "I saw a stricken comrade lying in a corridor of that ship, buried beneath dead bodies. His hand reached for me, ser, and his face pleaded."

Stella swallowed, and her grip tightened on the chair.

"Commander, are you all right?" Loran asked.

"I don't think I was consciously aware of it then," she

recalled, "but at some level I felt that if I could only save that one comrade, we could win the war. I promised him we'd return even though our chances seemed nonexistent. Promised him that I'd save him."

Loran coughed, his eyes wet. "I know what you mean," he said gruffly.

Stella smiled, her own eyes moist. "And so, General, aided by a few comrades, I went forth to keep my promise against an unbeatable foe. And with God's help, I did."

As Loran wiped his eyes with a handkerchief, Stella heard others murmur in emotion. Eager now, she leaned toward Loran to tell him what she had experienced.

The words came smoothly, and for the first time in her life she felt eloquent. When she told how George had killed the Slug with a Scaley weapon, people gasped in amazement. Loran stilled the voices and she continued, describing everything about the All-Mother because this time she felt she must. The only thing she avoided was the truth about Loran Base, and since Powers had already covered that subject, she barely needed to mention it.

When she was finally finished, the room was silent. Loran's staff looked dazed and overwhelmed.

Loran folded his hands on his desk. "And you say this All-Mother, this...mysterious being who's in charge, wants to meet you for some undefined purpose, that she has some kind of a perverse bond with you?"

"Yes," Stella said. "At first she hated me for killing her son, which made her attack your base. After she did that, though, she changed. When she contacted me again, she seemed to want something more."

Loran's nostrils quivered, and he looked about the room. "Reactions?"

Major Day frowned. "General, there's a lot to accept on faith. We have to examine it more closely."

"I agree," said a lean man whom Stella recognized as a renowned xenologist and Scaley expert. "This is all so hard to accept." He jammed a notebook under one arm so he could have all his fingers free to count with. "One, she says Scaleys are puppets controlled by something called Slugs. Two, all these

Slugs are males and have only one mother. Three, she says she has had a 'mind meld' with this Slug and they were able to share each other's thoughts. Four, she manages to master the totally alien drive system and pilot this ship, which we've never even seen...."

"That will do," General Loran said. "Dr. Eisen, are you saying that both Colonel Powers and Commander McMasters are lying to us? That they're traitors?"

Dr. Eisen shivered. He opened his mouth but nothing came out.

Major Day eyed him. "I don't believe Dr. Eisen is saying that, General Loran. It's simply that this is all much beyond anything we've learned or expected from the enemy, that we need time to study and assess it. Perhaps we should appoint a task force."

"We don't have time for that, Major," Loran said. "You've seen the data, reviewed the maps. The enemy have gathered and are approaching us on a direct vector. They could reach us in a week." Loran swiveled around in his chair to gaze out the window at his fleet. "We have to decide now," he said.

A squat female officer advanced a few steps. "General Loran. You know yourself, ser, how there are too many incidents of disobedience in the ranks these days?"

Loran spun quickly around, and the officer fell silent. "I'll tell you what there's too much of in the ranks these days. Too many mealy-mouthed, weasel words, too many indirect and roundabout ways of calling someone a traitor." He rose to his feet, and suddenly Stella was staring at the hero of Kakkistan, the awesome living legend she had heard about all her life. "Damn it," Loran said, "if you think they've fed us a dung heap of lies, then say it!"

The offender was silent. Loran swept the room with his eyes. "I think they've both told the truth," he said.

Stella almost collapsed in gratitude. Glancing at Powers, she saw vast relief.

"General," Major Day said, "there's something else we should consider." Stella saw the woman's eyes slide to her. "Perhaps it means nothing, but Commander McMasters is cyber-enhanced. We don't know-"

"Major," Loran said, "I think it does mean nothing. If Commander McMasters has done what she said, we should all be very grateful that she is cyber-enhanced." He turned and smiled at Stella.

Stella smiled back, remembering that Gage had said Loran was a combination of greatness and pettiness and she didn't know which predominated. At the moment, Stella could see only greatness.

But what would Loran say when she asked him to leave the fighting to her?

"Commander," General Loran said, "what would you recommend?"

She considered rising, then rejected it. She didn't want to upstage the general or make anyone think she had that intention. Better to appear as humble as possible when she dropped her bombshell.

"General," she said, "this may sound incredible...."

Loran managed a weak laugh. "Commander, after what you've said, I doubt it."

"What is it?" Major Day said. She glanced at Loran. "Perhaps you want General Loran to turn the command and leadership of this operation over to you?"

The atmosphere in the room turned poisonous. What Day had suggested amounted to sacrilege, the defilement of an idol.

"General Loran," Powers said, "Commander McMasters doesn't want that at all, nor do I. Even to imply such a thing would be a gross and treasonous presumption. You, ser, are our leader, and there is no other."

"Then what are you suggesting, Commander?" Loran said.

Stella gazed into his intense blue eyes. "General, I suggest that you withdraw your forces five light-days and let me try first."

"'Try first'?"

"Yes, face the enemy alone."

Eisen couldn't contain himself. "Preposterous! You're going to face five thousand Slug ships and this All-Mother with just your crew?"

Stella turned on him. "I thought you felt it was all lies. If there are no Slugs and there is no All-Mother, what difference does it make? Ser, you can't have it both ways."

Loran gazed at her. "Commander, how do you possibly expect to win? You've only one ship."

"I'm not sure," she admitted. "It's just a feeling. I don't even know what I'll do exactly, but I feel this may give us our only chance to win."

"This being you call the All-Mother," Loran said, "she'll just hold all her Slugs and Scaleys at bay and let you come peacefully to her because she wants something from you?"

Stella held his eyes. "Yes, and I believe that somehow I'll know what to do."

Loran raised his hand, touching the rows of medals on his chest. "Commander, do you know that I have fifty-six years of military experience, in all situations? That I started as a sixteen-year-old apprentice cook?"

"Yes, ser," she said, not adding that she had started in the same position at seventeen.

"Ever since this foe appeared, I have fought them," Loran continued. He put his arms behind him and seemed to gaze off into the distance. "Even before we were invaded, I defended everything the Empire stands for. Kakkistan, Beiruta, Tanzangla, Molerta… I've never voluntarily run or avoided a conflict. In just the past five years, I've spent a lifetime studying and hating the enemy, leading armies and fighting battles."

He lowered his eyes to hers. "Now you ask me to run, tuck my tail between my legs and leave the battle to you alone."

She said gently, "In myself I am nothing. It was only an accident that I happened to be in the right place at the right time with a ship of brave comrades willing to fight and die for us all. If there were any justice at all, ser, it would have been you who were there."

Loran nodded at the xenologist. "We already have a plan. Dr. Eisen's studied the enemy a long time, built on what we know, and with his assistance we've devised a daring strategy. It's a multi-staged, ingeniously constructed offensive that's absolutely brilliant."

"General," Stella said, "based on all your years of experience, do you really feel it will work? Do you think it can possibly prevail against our adversary?" She saw Loran's eyes drop and pressed her advantage. "Besides, what will be lost? If I fail, you simply engage the enemy five light-days away. Your plan should work just as well there."

Loran stood so still he resembled a statue. Stella could feel him weighing what she'd said and imagined looking at the situation through his eyes. What way would he go? What choice would she make if she were in his place? Surely, she'd never let her ego get in the way of what was best for the Empire.

Or would she? She'd already let emotion rule her head twice. Hadn't she let a personal involvement with Jason cloud her judgment when she'd banished him to the pirate ship? Hadn't her ego been involved both there and in her similar treatment of George?

"General," Major Day said, "there's no hard evidence that she's done anything she's claimed. We haven't seen any captured ship or even one tissue sample from the enemy. Yet we're expected to accept on faith that there is, or was such a ship, and that its occupants were all destroyed in a single clash, and accept as well everything else that she's told us."

Loran seemed introspective. "Sometimes all you have is faith, and it's the only thing that keeps you alive and going. If it weren't for faith, I'd be long dead by now." Stella saw him turn to her and smile. "It's all she has," he said. "All she has is her faith that when she meets this All-Mother, she will know what to do."

She smiled back at him. "Perhaps a little hope too."

"Oh yes," he nodded. "Always a little hope." He moved around the desk and came up to her. Stella rose to face him, as did Powers. She could hear everyone in the room snap to attention.

General Loran, the Supreme Commander of Imperial Forces, reached out and shook her hand. "Commander," he said, "we will do as you suggest. I'll order my ships to withdraw five light-days from here and let you be our front line."

Stella trembled, not believing her ears. Powers grasped Loran's hand. "Thank you, General."

"Pierce, it's my pleasure. Who knows? Perhaps history will remember me for pulling off the most strategic stroke of the war." Loran managed a small smile. "Or that I was bright enough not to say no to Stella McMasters."

Suddenly Stella found people clustering about her as if to lap up Loran's blessing. Even Dr. Eisen forged a smile. Stella felt someone squeeze her hand.

"General Loran!"

The voice cut the air like a laser. Everyone silenced, and she saw Loran turn to Major Day, who stood behind the desk studying the comconsole.

"What is it, Major?" Loran said.

"Ser, a message just arrived. It's from a ship that came through Scylla a few days ago. "

"So? It's no doubt joining our fleet."

"Ser, it's come from Loran Base."

"*Loran Base?*" He turned, looked at Stella. "Thank God-that means someone else survived!"

"General," Day said, drawing her pistol and pointing it at Stella, "the ship is commanded by a Captain Starkey and her account does not coincide with theirs." She paused as the guards swiftly drew their weapons. "Starkey says that McMasters and Powers severely damaged the base and threatened the Emperor's life, not the enemy. According to her, they are both traitors."

CHAPTER TWENTY-SIX

General Loran's eyes bored into her. "Is this true, Commander? Did you damage my base?"

Stella exchanged a glance with Powers. What could she say? All her eloquence had vanished even though she had known this might happen.

"I had to do it to escape the base and reach you with what I knew," she said. "No one would believe me there."

Major Day was reading the comconsole. "Captain Starkey reports McMasters kidnapped Regent-Protector Malek and killed nearly two hundred comrades," she said.

Loran's face was empty. "You lied to me."

"I was forced to," Stella said. "Would you have believed me if I had told the truth? If I had come here and told you I crippled your base because I had to, would you have listened? They certainly didn't listen at the base."

Loran's face twisted. "You attacked my base!" He thrust his arm out. "Put her in the brig. We'll await the arrival of Captain Starkey to dispose of her." He glanced at an officer. "Major Rockford, see that the *Spaceranger* is seized and swept clean. Search for Regent-Protector Malek and arrest everyone on board."

A stocky officer with black hair saluted. "Yes, General."

"General Loran." Stella tried to move forward but the two guards intercepted her. "Please, I told you the truth when I said I was the only one who could help. I-"

"Ha!" he mocked. "'The only one who could help'!"

"Yes," Stella said. "Please let me face the All-Mother alone. If you attempt to fight her, you'll all die. Deep down, I think you know it."

"Don't tell me what I think!" Loran moved toward her, spittle flecking his lips. "You damaged my base, and I was going to let you..." He glanced about at the others, and Stella saw humiliation and shame on his face. None of the greatness and magnanimity she had seen before remained.

"General," Powers said, "Commander McMasters is telling the truth. Please listen to her. In five years we have never once won a contest with the enemy. It was only when she-"

"That will be enough! Lies lies lies, that's all you two miserable traitors can do!" Loran ran a shaking hand through his silver hair. "Colonel Powers, your name will live in infamy and you will be remembered only as a soldier who disgraced his uniform." He stepped close and slapped him.

Powers' face rocked with the blow. Stella saw him swallow.

Loran swung to her. She watched his eyes rise from her feet to her face. His face twisted again, no longer handsome.

"You freak. You lab vat monstrosity! You dared to hurt my base?" He made a rude gesture of dismissal. "Get them out of my sight at once!"

They took her to a cell on a different level. Locked inside, she paced the floor as they proceeded on with Powers to another cell. She hoped he might look back at her once before he passed from sight, but he didn't.

She sat down on a thin bed attached to the wall, wishing they hadn't taken her cronex. It would have helped some, enabled her to mark the hours and minutes. As it was, she could only sit and watch the wall.

Traitor.

She closed her eyes. She had been so close.

Hours later, they came for her and marched her and Powers to a lift tube. This time their destination was the General's legendary war room, the site of his historical decisions. As she entered, she saw at least thirty officers present, including Major Starkey, who looked just as unpleasant as she remembered.

At the front of the room stood a large vidscreen that showed Pancho Villa standing with his arm around Regent-Protector Malek. Pancho wore colorful clothes, crisscrossing bandoleers loaded with what looked like outmoded ammunition, and a huge sombrero. Malek, in turn, was dressed in a plain white robe that was none too clean, and his earlier defiance was gone. His once neat goatee was shaggy and ill-tended.

"Ah, Stella, you are here, *si*? I waited just as you wanted, but you did not report."

General Loran glared at her. "What is the meaning of this?" he said.

"General Loran," Pancho said. "Please be so good as to speak to me. I am *el hombre* who's in charge." He laughed coarsely, obviously delighted with his role, and made a sweeping gesture toward Loran. "I have long admired you, General Loran. You are *un muy grande hombre, un muy magnifico general.*" He thumped his chest. "I, too, am a leader of men, *senor.*"

Loran's lips were a bloodless white. "You are pirate scum," he said. "A parasite who sucks our Emperor's blood."

Pancho's smile died. "You would be wise to watch what you say about the Emperor and myself." He lifted a pistol and pressed it to Malek's head. "Very careful, General Loran, or my trigger finger might slip."

As the room's occupants gasped, Stella realized that Pancho had dropped his bad Spanish. She hoped it was for good, because it might make Loran take him more seriously.

Loran nodded to Major Day, who moved toward Pancho's image.

"*Caramba!*" Pancho grinned at her and smacked his lips.

"Captain Villa," Day said politely, "what is it that you're asking?"

Pancho smacked his lips again and eyed Day's body. Stella tensed.

Fortunately, Pancho pulled himself together. "Here are my terms. You will return Commander McMasters and Colonel Powers to the *Spaceranger* and let it and its crew go free. At the same time, I will approach and release the Regent-Protector into your custody." He smiled at Malek and patted his cheek. "Perhaps, my *grande hombre*, you can find a little boy there to enslave by drugs just as you did the Emperor."

Captain Starkey stomped forward. "This is a foul lie. The Regent-Protector's done no such thing." She braced her hands on her ample hips. "Listen, Villa, you've forgotten something. You're within an hour of us. We could chase you down and capture you."

Pancho looked horrified. "Ah, who asked this big fat pig to insult me? Come give our blessed Emperor a drug scan, then say Pancho lies." He flapped his hand. "Go, sow. Snort up another sty."

As Starkey retreated with a red face, Pancho grinned at Loran. "Here's my answer. You come within fifty thousand kilometers of me and I kill the Regent-Protector. Just one *click!* and he will be *muy* dead."

Tense silence. When she'd made this emergency plan, Stella had assumed Loran would be willing to make the trade because Malek was virtually the Emperor. But with every passing second, she grew less certain. Malek's exalted status was clouded by the desperate situation. Also, judging by Loran's anger, he would be reluctant to free any "traitors."

"Here are my terms," Loran finally said. He stalked forward, eyes hard. "We give you back these two traitors and you surrender Malek to us at the same time. But the *Spaceranger* and its crew stay here, under arrest." He gave Malek a pale smile. "I'm sorry, Regent-Protector. I can't release a rogue ship even for you."

Malek's cheek twitched, but he said nothing.

"General Loran," Stella said, "there's one correction. The people I brought with me on the *Spaceranger* will leave with us."

Loran's eyes flashed. "That is not satisfactory."

Stella met his steel-blue gaze. "It will have to be," she said.

Loran inhaled deeply, then turned to Pancho. "Very well. We give you back all these traitors in exchange for Malek alone. But their weapons and the *Spaceranger* remain here."

Stella waited. When she had discussed this plan with Pancho, she had told him, as a negotiating strategy, to demand the release of the *Spaceranger* and its crew even though she had doubted Loran would agree. The question now was what would she do on a pirate ship. More than once, she had wondered if she was crazy even to think of trusting an outlaw like Pancho.

Pancho grinned and waved a hand expansively. "General, it's a deal. And here's how we're going to work it."

When *La Libertad* extended its beat-up boarding tube, the vigilant guard ship cautiously approached. It housed Stella, Powers, and the *Spaceranger's* motley crew of soldiers and pirates. About them, there was no other craft for a million kilometers in any direction. The two ships seemed alone, specks in the infinitude of space.

Pancho's boarding tube drew within an arm's length of the vigilant, whose docking area was too small to admit it. Wearing armor to facilitate their transfer, Stella and the others were all assisted into the tube by two armed guards. The guards appeared reluctant to touch them, as if they feared the taint of treason might seep through even duroplast shielding.

As they moved through the rickety tube, Regent-Protector Malek approached with two guards of his own. The four guards all halted halfway to arrange the transfer.

Stella's crew shifted their feet. The pirates, especially, glanced nervously at Malek as if they feared he would reacquire his lost power. No one, Stella reasoned, would fire lest Malek be hurt. As soon as the procedure was completed, both vessels would streak off in opposite directions.

Malek glared at her through his faceplate, his features chalk white and filled with maniacal rage. "I swear you will pay for this, McMasters," he said. "For what they did to me, for the unmentionable indignities, you shall pay!"

Stella murmured in surprise. Evidently Malek had arranged to be on her frequency with a compatible unit so he could address her.

"Congratulations, Regent-Protector. The greatest battle of the war approaches, and you will have the honor to die for your Emperor."

Malek's eyes bulged. "I will order Loran to transport me elsewhere."

"Will you?" she smiled. "I doubt he can spare even one ship. Besides, before I left, he claimed that your continued presence would be an inspiration to our soldiers, a sign of your confidence in them." She winked. "You can hardly run out on your comrades like a traitor now, can you?"

Malek stared back, but it was clear he was seeing only the dimensions of a new and unforeseen problem.

"I hope you found your host warm and cordial while I was away," Stella said. "If you think about it, you were treated better than you and your associates treated the Emperor. By the way, General Loran seemed a bit concerned when he learned about the boy's addiction to drugs. Perhaps you can explain it to him."

"You're vile," Malek said. He swept Stella's crew with disdainful eyes. "If I had my way, you and all these traitors would die slowly, piece by piece."

"Ah, but you don't have your way, Regent-Protector." Grinning, Stella glanced at her crew and moved on with the guards' assistance.

Then they were all aboard *La Libertad* and rushed to prepared seats in the docking area. Even as they strapped in, the ship accelerated, leaving the vigilant, which she glimpsed through a porthole, heading back to the fleet. No tricks or deception. Her plan had worked.

Shortly afterward, when they were clearly out of danger, Pancho rushed in with some of his crew and unbuckled them so they could stand. After Pancho's men helped her remove her armor, he proved ecstatic. "Stella, ah *Senorita*, you are here!" He embraced her lustily, standing on his toes to kiss her cheek. She smiled and returned his pressure, careful not to let him near her lips.

When Pancho realized she was a cyborg, he caught his breath. For a long moment Stella hoped that it might reduce his ardor, but it only enhanced it. Now his eyes gleamed like she was a special prize he wanted to claim.

She deftly eluded another kiss and slipped past him, wondering why she seemed to attract men she didn't want. Looking up, she saw George enter the docking bay. Just behind him came Jason.

She hurried to George and threw her arms about his neck. He grunted in surprise as she kissed him, then briefly returned it before trying to pull back. She held him in place easily for several more seconds before releasing him.

"Stella," Jason said. He moved forward.

"Hello, Jason." She nodded and glanced away. Spotting Brett, she laughed and called her name. Moments later, her whole crew poured in and victory shouts sounded. She was kissed and hugged a dozen times as Jason looked on. Powers, she noticed, was greeted almost as enthusiastically.

"Stella," Brett said during a lull in the celebration. "Pierce told me that if it hadn't been for Starkey, you would have gotten Loran to agree. Now he's going with his old plan." She went to Jason and pulled him forward. "The big question is, does Loran have any chance at all?"

Stella struggled to appear calm. Did Brett, and perhaps the others, want her to take Jason back? For all she knew, her whole damned crew knew what had happened.

For the first time, she met Jason's eyes. Pain and hate and love milled inside her. She wanted to kill him; she wanted to run to him, she wanted to hide. In the end she did nothing, even though part of her wanted to.

"Does Loran have any chance at all?" she said. "Brett, it would take a miracle."

She spent the next ten days getting used to *La Libertad's* routine, which consisted of avoiding detection and capture by hiding in a gas giant's atmosphere. Whenever possible they tried to intercept Loran's encrypted messages. What was Loran doing? If only she could prevent the colossal catastrophe she felt was imminent. Despite her dread, she tried to open her mind to the All-Mother, wishing her enemy would contact her again, call her to battle so Loran's vast forces could be spared. Damn it, anything was better than this waiting, especially with Pancho underfoot half the time.

At first she was intensely aware it was *Pancho's* ship and that he was in command, but he acceded to all her wishes, speaking constantly of his role in her new *administracion*. If he was the captain, she was the general, and he didn't protest when she asked for a work detail to scrub the grimy decks and cabins. Now and then he'd make an effort to seduce her which she always declined. Sometimes he accepted it cheerfully, other times with a glum expression that almost moved her. After three or four of these attempts, she realized he did it because he felt it was something a hot-blooded *pirata* who was all *hombre* would do.

One of the first things she did was go to George and apologize for what had happened between them. He accepted her apology but told her it was more important that she make peace with Jason. She cut that conversation short and returned to her cabin.

To her surprise, the dead Slug's mind touched hers there and she was stirred anew by his memories. She yearned to plunge her mind into a vortex again and be one with the *Pregnant Song's* artillery and drive system. She caught glimpses of his home world, a place of swamps and green skies. But the link was weak, and she doubted it would return.

On the eleventh day, when she stood on the bridge, the All-Mother visited her again.

She came this time not as a conqueror but as a lover. Dimly, Stella heard George call her name, but she was beyond his reach. Pancho, Powers, and the others faded into the distance.

The All-Mother laid her words like an offering on the altar of Stella's mind. *See, Stella Singlethorne McMasters...do you see what I bring you? All this, all that you behold, is for you.*

As if by a divine decree, it was all there before her. She saw Loran's forces and the All-Mother's converging in space, five thousand ships per side. The greatest battle in history was about to occur, nearly equal sides meeting for an ultimate confrontation. It was Armageddon and the death of dreams. Watching, she wondered how Peter, her game-loving pilot, would have felt. Because of the surgery required to reintegrate him with his body, he'd had to remain with the *Spaceranger* and General Loran.

See Stella, see what I give you.

She throbbed with love and gratitude for the All-Mother, who for once was blessing her with a wondrous gift. Stella cast the feelings of appreciation out, only to feel them creep back. Before her, the advance forces of the two armies were about to meet.

Beams of light speared her vision as the ships began to fire. She watched Loran's forces closely to detect what he'd called their new strategy and saw a complex pattern unfold in overlapping swarms of attackers. She called out, urging them on to victory as the ships made contact. Rods of flame shot out, and she saw metal blasted to pieces and thrown off into space.

"*Comandante*," a voice shouted faintly, "I'm picking something up. It sounds like fighting, some kind of battle."

"*Battle?*" Pancho's voice said. "Can you get it on vid?"

"I'm trying, *Comandante*. I think...yes! They quit blocking us!"

Blind to what happened on the bridge, Stella watched the two vast armies collide, her view incomparably better than that of the crew, which saw only tiny patterns of distant ships. Still, she was dimly aware of their shock, of their gasps of horror and amazement.

"Shit, I've never seen so many! There must be thousands!"

"It's the big one!" Pancho cried faintly. "It's happening just as Stella said it would. General Loran is fighting this All-Mother!"

"And getting his ass smashed!" said a high-pitched voice. "Hey, did you see that? Six or seven of the Emperor's ships just-"

No, Stella cried. It can't be! Unknowingly, she clutched a console before her.

"Stella," Pancho said, "what's wrong? Are you all right?" Dimly, she heard George and others express concern.

"Leave me be," she said, "all of you." She focused on the battle, praying that Loran's plan would work.

It didn't. The next two hours, in the All-Mother's grasp, she watched and heard five million comrades die. The ships perished singly and in groups, during gallant charges and from behind. A spidery network of tracers spanned an area that must have been twenty-five kilometers across. The plasma jets and laser beams of her comrades challenged the superior weapons of the enemy, and were destroyed.

See Stella, all this is for you. Is this not a beautiful death song I have spun for your comrades? Is it not glorious?

For a moment Stella saw it almost as the All-Mother did, as if she were, in fact, inside her enemy. The glittering, radiating tracers did look like a web, a web of singing death spun by a titanic, peerless artist. And yes, it was lovely, glorious beyond description.

No. It was ugly. And she hated the All-Mother!

The All-Mother withdrew but more confidently than before, a lover who was slowly winning Stella over. As Stella watched, a group of Imperial ships in the rear pulled away and started to flee. They were pursued immediately by enemy vessels.

"*Comandante,*" a gruff voice said, "I think they're finished."

"General Loran and his protectors," Pancho's voice said. "Mother of God, they never had a chance."

Do you see what I give you, my Stella? the All-Mother sang in Stella's mind, her voice sweeping everything away so that there were only the two groups of ships-the one fleeing, the other growing ever closer.

Searing light. Blinding explosions. Borne on lightning wings to the scene, Stella saw a massive hull ripped free and bodies spewed into space. Hundreds of them-some in spacesuits, far more who were not, men and women who must have died instantly. And coming her way...

So close she could have reached out and touched them, two figures drifted past. One was Regent-Protector Malek; the other, General Ulysses Narraganset Loran. Malek was already dead, his eyes bulging like marbles. Just behind him, General Loran struggled feebly to seal his helmet, his handsome features contorted behind his faceplate. Stella saw his gloved, bloodstained fingers paw weakly at his throat, then fall away. Slowly, they rose again.

As if the All-Mother had willed it, the helmet was torn off, and Stella saw the General's distinguished features explode into gore in the vacuum of space. Loran's hands fell lifeless and he drifted away, becoming smaller and smaller until he was only a speck of debris lit by star shine and the blaze of artillery.

Shuddering, Stella covered her eyes, trying to blot out the terrible carnage. The All-Mother would not permit her to escape. Ship after ship after ship erupted and died, and as Stella dug her hands into the console, the last feeble resistance of the Empire winked out one by one in brilliant bursts of metal until nothing remained except the untouched hordes of the enemy.

In their center hovered a ship three times as large as the others. A ship she hadn't been permitted to see until this final, climactic moment.

The All-Mother's ship.

Are you ready? The All-Mother's whisper caressed her mind. *Are you ready for the last dance of all, my Stella? The Dance of Death?*

"Last dance, All-Mother," she said and woke up.

They were all staring at her. George, Brett, Pancho, and a dozen others. Jason, she recalled, had not been permitted on the bridge.

"Stella," George said urgently, "what is it?"

She stiffened and looked at their stricken faces, which reminded her of Loran's before he'd died.

"It's time," she told them.

CHAPTER TWENTY-SEVEN

*L*a *Libertad's* armor room was ten meters long, little wider than a closet, and the armor itself hung from rusted pegs in open lockers. Stella found it hard to imagine these pirates ever boarding another vessel to take it over. Yet Powers assured her Pancho was adept at his craft, and that his crew had clambered onto more than one trader and merchant scug. Smile as she might at his seeming ineptness, she could not ignore the fact that he was also a ruthless and efficient leader.

By the time others arrived, all she needed was to have her comm leads connected. George and Brett seemed to have other things in mind, though, for they started to suit up.

"What do you two think you're doing?" she said.

Brett turned, her face drawn. "We're going with you."

"What? Oh no, you're not. The All-Mother just wants me."

"You might need us," George said.

"Don't you remember what you just saw? Thanks to the All-Mother, I saw it all a thousand times better than you!" She raised her fist. "Our army is dead and the same will happen to you if you attempt to board her ship. So stay here."

Other crew packed into the narrow room, an incongruous mixture of pirates and Stella's comrades. She saw them head to their lockers, begin putting on armor.

"Stop!" she shouted.

They all froze, looking at her. Most of them still appeared stunned after watching the recent battle.

"Let's get sensible, people," she said. "Our enemy won't

permit this ship to get within range. The All-Mother wants me to use the shuttle pod, which can only carry six persons. Maybe it can stretch to eight or nine, but I count over forty here."

George touched her shoulder. "Then you can take eight of us."

She jerked away. "No. I don't want you. You'd just get in the way. Besides, the All-Mother only wants me."

Brett reached into Stella's helmet to connect her comm leads. "You can't be sure. We could be the difference that counts."

Stella turned away. "You don't know what you're saying. You'd only get killed. You have to stay here!"

Brett moved forward, her eyes bright and insistent. "Please, Stella, let's not end it like this. Let's finish it the way we started. Together."

Stella returned her gaze. "First Contact Heroes, Brett?"

"Yes." Brett smiled sadly. "There's just you, me, and George left now. But we still gotta stick together, right?"

"That is right," George insisted. "Like Brett said, you don't know for sure that we can't help. Who knows-we could make the difference."

Stella sighed, realizing they wouldn't listen. "All right," she conceded. "You two go with me." She scanned the room. "Who else wants to go?"

Immediately, everyone raised their hands and shouted eagerly. It was a sight she had never imagined: her crew and these scruffy pirates united by a common cause.

"Please, Stella," Pancho said, pressing forward. "Take me."

"I can't," she smiled, not wanting him to die. "You're going to be too valuable in my new administration. Besides, if my mission fails, you'll have to take over and keep these people alive."

She looked at all the upraised hands. She didn't want any of them to die. "I can't take all of you," she said. She pointed at random, choosing four pirates as well. "You and you and..."

"Me," a voice said.

She turned her head. Jason stood in the room, his jaw thrust out.

"I'm going too," he said.

She shook her head. "Oh no, you're not."

"You'll have to stop me, Stella," Jason said, "and by God, you'll have to kill me to do that." He turned and went to his locker.

She moved toward him in hot fury. She would not let-

George caught her hand. "Stella," he said, "let him come."

She glared at him, and then watched as two female pirates in leather shorts and halters helped Jason suit up. Yes, she thought bitterly, it would be women, and half-naked ones at that.

"All right," she said. "It doesn't make any difference anyway."

After a tearful, clinging embrace from Pancho, Stella managed to board *La Libertad's* tiny, much-dented shuttle pod. The pilot, a female pirate, waited till they were all securely seated, then fired the retros that thrust them into space.

"Stella," George said, "are you sure we'll be able to board? You seem to feel the All-Mother will practically invite us on."

"Remember the Slug ship, George?" she said. "The one with the extended boarding tube?"

"Oh," George said. "I see."

"I miss Myles," Brett murmured.

"For me it's Carol," George said heavily. "Somehow it's not the same without her cussing and dressing me down all the time. I never realized I actually liked it."

"We miss all of them," Stella said. "All the comrades we've lost."

They nodded, looked down at their hands as the pod streaked on.

"Loran Base was the first time we'd ever been together," Brett said a minute later. "We always spoke casually before." She sighed behind her faceplate. "Myles was a good kisser, held me like I was part of his body. I wish..."

Before them, space stretched into infinity. Stella gazed out the small plexiport at the front of the pod. "How far to the battle's epicenter?" she called.

"Almost sixty thousand kilometers," the pilot called, checking a gauge. "It should take nearly an hour. You'll have to direct me when I get close."

"I will," Stella answered.

Two seats to her left, Jason leaned toward her. "Forgive me," he said.

She turned. Jason's eyes were fixed on her face.

"Never," she said.

"Stella," George said, "we'll probably all be dead in a short while."

She leaned back. "If that's what it takes."

Silence, then George's voice. "At some level you're enjoying this, aren't you? You've got your chance to be a martyr and raise the cross at your own crucifixion. Hell, you can even drive the nails in yourself."

Except for the pilot, everyone was watching them. "He built the cross," Stella said.

"And you climbed up on it, didn't you?" George said. "Even worse, you don't want to come down."

His words sank into her, compounding her pain. She gripped her seat and tried to concentrate on her mission.

Jason slapped his knees. "You know something?" he said, "in a way it's kind of funny. All my life it's been women, women, women."

His armored hand rose, pointing directly ahead. "And now where am I going? On a visit to see the freakin' All-Mother, that's where I'm going! She's got to be the biggest damned woman of all."

Hysteric laughter came from some of the passengers. The small pod rang with it. Even George laughed a little, but Stella wouldn't.

The biggest damned woman of all. Perhaps it was an even better term for the All-Mother than Pancho's 'A dog of a whore,' or the one she herself had recently harbored: 'A god with three secrets.' What was the All-Mother, anyway? Would she ever see her? Ever know?

"Stella," the pilot called, "we're reaching the first ships."

They coasted through the greatest graveyard in history, passing endless wrecks of gutted, still-smoking metal. Ship after ship after ship. In some places bodies floated, revolving slowly. She saw one face with its eyes open in death, staring directly at her as they passed.

Now and then, they passed objects floating in the void that were even more disturbing than the blood-drenched remnants of devastation. Stella saw a crystal hologram of someone's smiling wife and children...a delicate pink flower with a long graceful stem...a shimmering green party dress that would never be worn at another Imperial ball.

Mostly splintered and broken ships met her gaze, and a limitless wasteland of bodies, some intact, some ripped to pieces. At one point Stella watched a disembodied leg glance off the shuttle pod and sail lazily on, its boot neatly fastened as if its owner had intended to be prepared.

As far as she could see, blasted hulls and countless corpses stretched before them. It seemed to go on forever.

"Stella!" Brett said, swinging from side to side. "Slug ships up ahead!"

"It's all right," Stella said. "They won't attack. This is the All-Mother's show."

On and on they went, passing charred hulks that represented the death of an empire. She read their names, trying to commit them to a roll call of memory. The *S.S. Kolanera...Atlas...The Intrepid...Valiant...Galactica...*

They didn't see the *Spaceranger*, but at one point they passed General Loran's flagship *Victory*. It was a blackened, gaping, twisted ruin.

Amid such vistas of destruction, the huge Slug ships hovered. In the bow of each, she knew, a swollen alien watched them. Any one could have blasted them to atoms.

"Stella," Brett hissed, "I saw some comrades alive on that ship we just passed!"

"We can't stop for them now," Stella said, hardening herself. "Pancho can pick them up later."

"There must be hundreds, maybe even thousands on ships who are still alive."

"All the more reason why we must attend to business first." She stared straight ahead, remembering the soldier she had saved on the Slug ship. "If we don't kill the All-Mother, none of us will leave this place."

They moved on and on. Occasionally, acting on the insistent

call Stella began to feel within her mind, she gave the pilot directions to change their course.

Finally, like an immense, bulbous seed, the All-Mother's ship came into view. They stared at it in awe.

"You were right, Stella," George whispered.

She watched the extended boarding tube as they grew near, knowing that things were finally coming to an end. Or perhaps it would only be the dawn of a new and more terrible beginning.

Expertly, the pilot extended the egress ramp and maneuvered alongside. They all left the pod quickly and entered the All-Mother's ship.

Stella led them, the All-Mother's call now sweet fever in her blood. The All-Mother wanted her and she wanted the All-Mother, and in dim glimpses she could almost see what it was they both wanted. She turned left then right, guided by her enemy, her plasma jet held ready as were the weapons of her crew.

Closer... closer...

The corridors here were cavernous, far larger than those on the Slug ship. Vast and vaulted, they reminded her of a cathedral. Beneath her, the blue metal floor she had seen on the Slug ship seemed to lure the eye and glow with distant fire.

Right again, then left.

Ahead, rose a huge open portal. She knew it led to her final destination, the bow where the All-Mother waited.

Stella halted and glanced at them, this time meeting Jason's eyes. She wanted to say something to him, reach out.

Instead, she only brandished her weapon. "This is it," she said. "May God bless our Emperor."

"May God bless our Emperor," they repeated.

Stella turned and moved on.

The bow was fifteen meters away...ten...

Suddenly Scaleys leapt from side portals into the corridor, their weapons blazing. Stella seared two and they fell as her crew crumbled around her. She saw George thrown back against a wall and collapse, and then Brett cut in half. She whirled, burning another Scaley's faceplate, then another. There were just too many.

"Stella-to your left!"

Jason's voice rang in her ears and she swung to confront an approaching Scaley. But it didn't want her.

Jason thrust himself before her, his plasma jet burning into the Scaley's armor. The Scaley advanced, its own weapon trained on Jason's chest. A beam licked out.

Jason screamed and spun violently, his weapon pointed up at the ceiling. For a long moment he teetered on his toes like a dancer who had just performed a difficult pirouette. Then he fell, his weapon dropping from his hand.

It was over as quickly as it had begun. The Scaleys inspected the bodies and then left, not even looking at her.

Slowly, she moved to Jason and knelt beside him, peering through his faceplate. Behind it, his eyes fluttered open.

"You damn fool," she said, tears streaming down her cheeks. "It didn't want me. I was never in any danger."

Blood trickled from the corner of his mouth. "Sorry. Guess I mucked up again." His face contorted and he writhed in pain. "Please...forgive me, Stella." He swallowed, and then parted his lips. "I always loved you."

"I know you do," she answered. She took his hand, pressed it against her. "I've always known it."

As she said it, something broke inside her. "I love you," she cried, wishing she could kiss his lips. "Sorry...so stupid. Please forgive me, Jason."

"Nothing to forgive," he whispered. He raised his armored hand and touched her faceplate, and it was as if she could feel his fingers against her cheek. "I'll be with you forever amid the stars, Stella. Somehow, I promise, I'll find a way to wait there for you."

He lowered his arm and closed his eyes. She watched his head roll slowly to the side.

Rising, she examined the others, the sonic cleaners in her helmet struggling to remove her tears. Oh God, they were dead-all her comrades. All except...

George opened his eyes as she knelt beside him. His faceplate was spattered with blood.

"You needed us, all right," George said. He swore. "Guess

we didn't make a difference. It looks like my luck's finally run out. Don't have nine lives after all."

"It was bound to happen eventually," she said. She forced a smile. "Anyway, you're too damn tough to kill."

"I admire your confidence," he wheezed. He closed his eyes, gathering strength to speak again. "You're the last one, Stella. Even if I make it, it's all up to you now."

She touched his shoulder though he couldn't feel it, and rose. Turning, she faced the bow's entrance just a few meters away.

Last dance, my Stella, the All-Mother told her. *I am waiting for you.*

Last dance, All-Mother, she answered. She gripped her plasma jet, aiming it straight ahead. Get ready, you goddamned bitch, 'cause I'm coming to get you.

Bracing herself, she entered the bow of the ship.

CHAPTER TWENTY-EIGHT

The room she entered was vast.

She stopped and looked up, way way up to the hull or ceiling. Only there was no hull or ceiling, just silvery-gray reaches that confused and confounded the eye. She stood with her plasma jet held ready, not knowing what to do. Where was the All-Mother? Where was she hiding? And what was she going to do?

She fought down her uncertainties. The All-Mother was the queen of deception and treachery, and she could undermine one's spirit and resolve in an endless number of ways. She must expect anything, even her enemy's apparent absence. Stella took a step forward, and then stopped. No, let the All-Mother come to her.

No bow is this huge, she thought, gazing up into boundless space. It's too big.

And suddenly, as if she'd been conjured, the All-Mother was there.

She was stupendous, towering a hundred meters high. Great rocklike legs supported a mountainous trunk glittering with countless silver facets, and a dozen arms flashed razor-sharp claws that opened and closed with a vast hissing sound. At the top, far above, an immense head grinned down with fierce, slavering jaws. The eyes themselves were molten suns and in them she beheld her puny form. The All-Mother was God: all-powerful, invincible, unknowable. Compared to her, Stella knew she was less than an ant.

Frail, insignificant human, at last we meet.

Trembling, Stella raised her weapon, aiming at the titanic form. She raked it from side to side, moving her arm again and again. Something's wrong, her mind screamed. If I'm insignificant, why do you want me here? It's a lie!

Back and forth her weapon carved, severing gigantic chunks of the All-Mother's body. It crumbled, then finally collapsed to the floor with a sound like thunder, and lay still.

The All-Mother was dead.

Stella crept forward, still firing at the enormous carcass. Was it possible? Had she actually won? Hope stirred within her. Yes, she had won. The All-Mother was...

The All-Mother vanished.

She cut her power, staring at a vast bow that was empty except for a complex drive system far to her left.

"It wasn't real," she said in boundless disappointment. "You're just a master of illusion like your sons, only more powerful in your ability to deceive. Is that one of your secrets?"

Silence.

Stella moved on, her footsteps echoing in the tremendous chamber. Through the bottom of a sweeping plexiport, she saw the black whirlpool of Cygnus X-1 approaching. How had they traveled so fast? This ship's power must be immense!

When she reached the bow's center, she revolved slowly, looking in all directions. "Are you only an illusion, All-Mother?" she called. "Something that doesn't exist?" How could something that didn't exist possess such power?

I AM THAT I AM, the All-Mother proclaimed.

Stella saw her hand rise, borne by another's will, and cast her weapon aside, leaving her defenseless. *I can do all because I am all*, the All-Mother told her. *Behold, finite being, my very first act of Creation.*

A vision appeared in Stella's mind, and she saw the monobloc of the universe before it was formed. Or perhaps it was the monobloc of the first universe, the primal mass that began the cosmic cycles.

Behold.

The monobloc exploded and worlds and stars formed as the

universe expanded throughout aeons. Then entropy set in and energy died, devouring itself as planets and stars and nebulae and quasars contracted toward the center, toward the original, super-dense monobloc whose womb exploded again, re-seeding the void and finally contracting in yet another hundred-billion-year cycle. Each colossal cycle was but a single heartbeat in the infinite life of the All-Mother who was God, God the Mother and God the Father, God the Alpha and the Omega and the source of all fruitful and teeming life.

If this is you, Stella thought, I myself am nothing.

Of course, the All-Mother said. *But you've always known that.*

Something was still not right. If she were nothing, why did the All-Mother care? Why should her enemy want her?

"No," she screamed, "it's all a lie, just another illusion! For all I know, you aren't even real!"

Rage shot through her like lightning. Her God was angry. The cosmic cycles the All-Mother showed her acquired yet greater gloss and glory, seeming to sing their divine provenance. Who was she to question?

"You're too eager to convince me," she shouted. "Why do you do this? What do you need?"

The cyclic procession grew even more lustrous and sublime, as if her adversary were determined to sweep away her stubborn doubts. As the monobloc exploded yet again in new splendor, the psychic link with her enemy strengthened. Stella glimpsed something she hadn't seen before, something the All-Mother did not want her to know.

"You aren't God," Stella said. "You didn't even have the courage to show me your true form. It must be so monstrous, so hideous that you have no choice but to hide behind llusions."

She reached out and seized one of the All-Mother's secrets, turned it to see its facets. "You didn't cause the birth of the universe at all. You only take your powers from that birth, from the explosion of energy that begins each cycle. Somehow you store it like a battery."

Then she knew and flung her laughter at the All-Mother. You were spewed from the first explosion like a dry, worthless piece of dung, weren't you? Cast out from the womb of creation into your endless, miserable night. You had no father and no mother, no family and no species to call your own. And that's why you call yourself the 'All-Mother' and use such terms as 'seed' and 'fertile womb' and 'Pregnant Song.' You want to embody all life because you yourself are life's antithesis, sexless and sterile and dead. 'All-Mother'-ha! You are All-Dead, not a she but an It, and the first of your secrets is that the only way you can have children is to steal them!

No! the All-Mother answered. *You are misguided, and for your pathetic insolence I shall spin...*

You shall spin nothing, Stella retorted, holding tight to their bond so she could see more. That's why the Slugs call you All-Mother, isn't it? You killed their race, the females, and seized their infant sons whom you reared as your own. You absorbed their history and passed it on to them, but you made a few changes, didn't you? You erased their parents as if they had never been and set yourself up as their only one. I should have put it all together at the beginning, for the son George killed never even saw you, did he? If he had seen how vile and monstrous you are, he would have known you weren't his mother at all. If he had seen you just once, he would have spurned and repudiated you.

Stella turned, seeking her nemesis. "What is your true form?" she cried aloud. "What unmentionable horror are you hiding? Come out and let me see you!"

Silence. About her the great bow waited. Through the plexiport, Stella saw the black funnel of Cygnus X-1 grow as they streaked toward it.

This first secret of the All-Mother...was it the greatest of the three? A sentient, barren being without a single other of its kind. How it must have envied and coveted the abundant life it found in universe after universe! How many species had it destroyed, how many children had it torn from their parents and deceived about their birthright?

Footsteps. Stella whirled, weaponless, to see a naked figure walking toward her. The body was beautiful and the face made her moan. Slowly, she raised her hands to remove her helmet, knowing that when the figure reached her and touched her cheek, everything would be all right again.

She watched the figure stop before her and smile, a lock of dark hair curling over his forehead.

"Hello, Stella," Jason said, his fingers warm upon her skin. "Do you still love me?"

CHAPTER TWENTY-NINE

She tried to retreat, but before she could, Jason's arms were around her body, his lips pressed against her own. For one long moment she forgot everything-the ship, the All-Mother, even the protective armor she wore.

When she finally pushed back, Jason seized her arm, his strength equal to her own. No, it was greater; she couldn't break his hold. He held her like gentle steel whose strength she felt only when she resisted.

"Let me go," she said. "You're just another of her illusions."

"No, Stella." Jason loosened his hold but did not release her. "I'm still Jason," he said. "The man who loves you."

She raised her free hand and struck his face, only to feel it absorb her blow like tar. He took her fist and pressed it to his lips until her fingers opened.

Jason's dark eyes and beloved face-so close, so real. "It is me, Stella," he said. "I've come back."

"How?"

"Listen," he murmured, his breath sweet and warm on her face. "When I was dying, she came to me and preserved all my memories, offered me another chance at life. It's me, Stella."

She looked down at his naked, beautifully molded body, feeling memories of its touch on every part of her. Beneath his lip, she saw the scar a little girl had once given him.

"I can tell you things I never had a chance to," he said. "The name of my favorite aunt, the touch of sunlight on my parents' pond, even how it felt the first time I launched a ship."

"No!" She tried again to pull away. "She stole those memories from you. You're not real!"

He brushed her cheek with his lips. "All my feelings for you are still intact, as well as the memory of the terrible way I betrayed you." She pulled back a little, and she could see his tears. "It is me, Stella. The Jason that you know, the one that you love." He gazed at her and touched her face. "I still think you have a cute nose."

This time she wrenched free, but he pursued her with a speed Jason never possessed and trapped her again with his embrace.

"Stella, we have a chance to be together forever." He smiled. "Do you remember what I told you just before I closed my eyes?"

"You mean just before you died?"

"I said I'd wait for you amid the stars. Do you remember?" He raised his head toward the ceiling. "Do you want to talk about illusions? The belief in some kind of communion in a mystic afterlife is the worst one of all." He shuddered. "I would have died if it weren't for her Godlike power. Thanks to her, I can live forever. And so can both of us, together."

She tried to think, but the passionate cadence of his voice swept her away on a hypnotic stream. Now he held both her hands and was gently pulling her somewhere. Looking down, she saw that she was naked, her bare feet passing through deep grass. When had she removed her armor?

"She admires you," Jason whispered. "Throughout all the universes and a trillion trillion trillion millennia, you're the only being she's admired and respected enough to choose as her host. Take me into you, Stella, and we'll be together forever."

The Slug-dimly she remembered that he had wanted to take her into him. Now the direction was the other way. She would take the All-Mother into herself.

She knew she should resist, but soon found that she was lying on a carpet of lush green grass shaded by a leafy tree. Jason's lips were fire on her skin, and she felt her limbs part and open to him. "Let me come into you, Stella," he moaned, "and we'll be together always."

Caressing her body, he moved himself over her, started to...

With a vicious shove she cast him off and rose to her feet. "I won't be her vessel," she cried. "She won't possess me!"

He rose just as quickly. "It's not that at all! I'm not a parasite. We'd live together so we all could live."

A butterfly darted past, a splash of gold on a fragrant breeze. "It's only another lie," she said. "My body would be an empty shell the All-Mother possessed while I existed in some small pocket of hell in what used to be my brain. And the lie that you are would be there with me."

"But I am Jason! Stella, I told you that she…"

"Damn it, say her name."

Jason hesitated. "All right." He started forward, and then stopped when she stooped and picked up a rock. "Stella, I know you hate the All-Mother, but she's only done what she has out of necessity. Try to see and feel it through her eyes. She's lived virtually forever, and she's been so terribly and cruelly alone. Beyond all that, she's been cursed with a hunger and love for life that mocks her barren existence."

"'Love for life'? Please excuse me if I don't weep in sympathy." She flexed her back. "Besides that, you forget something. I'm barren too."

"She knows that," Jason replied. "But you are what she is not, organically alive. What's more, with her knowledge she can do what humans can't. She can clone your flesh and generate a new womb. Your body can bear children, Stella. Your genes, our genes, can be passed on!" He held out his hands to her. "Stella, she has envied and admired and even loved you as no other. She wants-"

"She wants my soul," Stella said. "She wants to rape and possess all that I am." She paused in understanding. "And that's her second secret, isn't it? Not only is she a sexless, sterile thing that must steal others' children, but she wants to become me and have my children."

Jason's face hardened. "If you refuse, I'll die, Stella. And what we were together will die also."

"No," Stella said, even though part of her yearned for what he offered. "Jason has already died. But my memories of him never will. I'll keep him alive for both of us." She raised the rock. "You aren't Jason."

He moved slightly forward. "What if you're wrong? I think I'm Jason. I still have his memories, and I still love you. What if I am Jason?"

She met his gaze, feeling something heal inside, grow stronger than ever before. "It doesn't matter. At one time all I needed was someone like you who thought I was beautiful, someone who cared for me despite what I was. But not anymore, and never again." Her face hardened. "You're only a man."

Jason took a step, but he was already fading. "Don't...Don't say that."

"I can live without him," she said. "I can stand alone." She smiled. "And you don't exist."

Before her, Jason wavered like a dream, a mirage she could see right through. The thick grass and shady tree were disappearing too, as was the rock in her hand. Bracing herself, she watched Jason slip from existence. His outstretched, pleading hand was the last to go.

She scanned the bow. Ten meters away lay her armor. She had come so close.

Stella faced the way Jason had been pulling her. The All-Mother had projected Jason's image and used it to entice and draw Stella toward her. That meant she should continue in the same direction in order to find her enemy.

"Where are you?" she called, walking slowly forward. "Show me your true form. I've learned your first two secrets; now show me the last and best of all. Show me what you look like!"

She continued on, moving directly toward the huge plexiport and the yawning singularity beyond it.

"Where are you?" she said. "Come out and show me your face. That is, if you have one!"

Stop!

The All-Mother struck, withering her resolve so that she froze. *I wanted you to accept me and what I offered of your own free will, and to help me spin your death song. I wanted this because I've come to respect you as a worthy and resourceful adversary, the only one in all my endless existence. I offered you Jason and eternal life after you had passed from this one, but since you have scorned them...*

For a moment there was only the brooding presence of the All-Mother's mind in her own. *Since you have scorned them, I shall now take by force what I could have taken even before you entered this bow. I shall destroy your mind, Stella Singlethorne McMasters, cast you out, and replace your identity with my own.*

And the All-Mother struck again, this time with all her strength.

Stella fell-first to her knees, then on her face. The All-Mother's will was overwhelming, pounding at her in relentless waves. She felt her sense of identity fade like Jason's image, the All-Mother start to invade her deepest core and claim it as her own.

NO.

Strong her enemy was, and meters away. Still, the All-Mother was not omnipotent. Prostrate upon the bow floor, Stella realized that through repeated exposure, she had become somewhat resistant. While her defeat might be swift and total, it would not be instantaneous.

If she could only find a way to use the few moments she had left to fight back and get closer.

You are mine now, abject human. After I have spun your death song, your brain and body shall be mine. You shall have nothing, not even Jason or your memories of him.

Fading, fading…Stella couldn't even remember how she had come here or what her mission was, only that there was a terrible need to resist this force that crushed her and sought to suck her dry. If there was only something…

Gage.

A name, a feeble flame in darkest night. But she clung to it. The name, damn it. Concentrate on the name. Use it to resist.

Soon you'll be mine, Stella Singlethorne McMasters, all mine. I shall seed the stars with my own children and fill this universe!

Yes, Gage. Her first name, what was it? The initial was A, but what did it stand for? Could it be Antigone or Audrey, Alpha or Ashley…?

Don't try to shield your mind from me, the All-Mother raged. *You cannot keep me out, let alone escape defeat. Indeed, you have already lost.*

Slowly, painfully, Stella crawled forward, her concentration on a name she had never learned.

Perhaps Alvenice or Alicia, Arden or Arnette, April or Astra...

Do not come closer! the All-Mother ordered. *I forbid you.*

Or what about that soldier I once knew named Agrippina? Stella thought. Or other odd names such as Alcestis and Allexandrina? And don't forget Amarantha and Andromeda, Abrosine and Annuncita!

Driving hard, Stella crawled on, her mind screaming a name for each cry of her enemy's.

Ayanna.

Stop!

Adele.

No!

Aurora.

I command you-stop!

The last words stunned Stella and she collapsed on her face at the base of an ornate ivory pedestal. She moaned, tried to rise but failed. So near and yet so far! She felt her consciousness and sense of identity fade as before, and knew that this time would be the last. Soon she would be only an empty vessel for the All-Mother to fill.

I have WON! Triumph swept through Stella's being. The All-Mother sang joyously, gloating in her imminent victory.

Leadenly, Stella raised her head, seeing the pedestal above through a thickening mental mist. At the top of the column perched a shimmering, multi-faceted crystal secured by an intricate harness.

With the last of her will, Stella reached up and struck the pedestal as hard as she could.

Jarred, the alien presence in her mind weakened briefly, and then surged again toward full control. Knowing she must resist both the All-Mother and the tempting slide toward oblivion, Stella raised her fist and struck the pedestal again and again, feeling the hard surface tear her skin and smash her knuckles. Pushing herself up to her knees, she struck the pedestal once more and saw it teeter, fall, and crash to the deck.

No time to rest! Fighting unconsciousness, Stella removed the crystal from its harness and cupped it in her hands. She staggered to her feet, staring in awe at the beautiful object.

The crystal glowed and pulsated with the primal fires of creation, with the measureless energy that had created the All-Mother herself so many times. That energy, Stella knew, was the source of the All-Mother's prodigious powers, and it was wondrous, ineffably glorious to behold. Colors and patterns beyond description surged and danced, creating dimensions that sang within her veins and made her throb with infinite power.

It was like holding the universe in her hands.

But something was wrong, for the cosmic furnace that warmed her hands began to dim. Turning the crystal, Stella detected a hairline fracture on one of the facets, caused by the crystal's fall.

She brought the crystal close to her eyes. "Losing your spark, All-Mother?" she said. "The blaze of new-born suns that conceals you? Come out from behind your veil and hide no longer. Let me see your inmost form!"

The crystal continued to fade, its alchemy reversed. No longer sublime, its fires subsided, dulled to dross and soon to even less. The universe she held was a wasteland about to die, approaching the final stage of entropy.

But not quite. Peering close, Stella spotted movement. What was it? She turned the cold crystal in her hands. "Where are you, All-Mother?" she said. "Let me see you."

Another flicker of movement. Squinting, Stella caught a glimpse of tiny spidery legs and a face so alien, so antithetical to her species that no human mind could ever retain it or even preserve a single feature without going totally and hopelessly mad. Though she saw it only for an instant, the image seemed to last forever, to burn its way into her soul. Such subtle and haunting wrongness, yet, at the same time, such skewed, distorted, and impossible geometry! Why, it was as if...

Then the All-Mother vanished and all Stella could remember was its limitless hate and malevolence, and the small spiderlike legs. But that was enough.

"No wonder you've always bragged about spinning death songs," she laughed, "and no wonder you didn't want me to see you. That's your third and final secret isn't it, All-Mother? Instead of being godlike, you're puny and insignificant."

Rage blasted Stella from the All-Mother. Rage at being exposed and rage at having her third secret uncovered. At this final onslaught, Stella wilted, feeling icy talons claw at her mind. Then the assault waned, trailing a brief fear-filled image.

An ejector tube.

Stella clutched the crystal to her, staggered up and glanced about. Where was the ejector tube? She took a step, then another, seeking the object she had glimpsed in her enemy's mind. But it wasn't here. She must have been mistaken.

Ah, there it was against the wall! Holding the crystal, she lurched toward the ejector tube.

"Still afraid to die after having lived so long, All-Mother?" she said. "Let's see if you'll boast about your godhood after a plunge down a singularity without a ship! As you go, here are some other names to take with you. Thunderheart...Brett Duvall...Myles Uxman...Carol Wayne..."

She found a swirling red vortex against the bulkhead and plunged her mind into it. I learned this from your son! she screamed.

Stop! You must listen!

"Why must I listen?" Stella laughed. She found the core of the force field and prepared to access it. "In a moment, you'll be gone forever!"

"You must listen," the All-Mother cried. "I have a fourth secret!"

Seductive tendrils of thought crept into Stella's mind. Against her better judgment, she partially withdrew her consciousness from the vortex.

"You're only a spinner of lies!" Stella said. "There is no fourth secret."

Yes, there is. And deep within you, you know it.

Curious, Stella withdrew completely from the vortex. She felt certain that all of her adversary's mighty power was gone, that it had slipped through the crack in the crystal. Yes, she was quite sure of that. Since the All-Mother had only this desperate ploy left, since she was reduced to such a pathetic ruse, why shouldn't she play with her a moment longer?

"Very well, what is this fourth secret of yours? You're a sexless thief of others' children; you want to become me and fill the universe with my children; and you're only a pitifully small thing I could step on. What else could you be hiding?"

I have many more secrets yet to tell, the All-Mother whispered, *but it is my fourth one especially that you should know. You see, I don't have to become you, for you can become me. I can make you God, Stella.*

"God?" Stella's lips shaped the word. "What do you mean?"

The All-Mother's words grew silky, soft as a caress. *What would it be like to have immense, unlimited power? To be me? I could give it all to you, Stella, and more!*

"I..."

Think for a moment what it would be like, the All-Mother murmured soothingly. *Unlike those you call 'Slugs,' you are not bored and sated with existence but hunger to embrace it all. You could span the universe and with your infinite life, bring it under your dominion. And even more, you could have children, Stella, seed the stars with the fruit of your womb. I can bring that to pass as well.*

"No." Dimly, Stella sensed that she had misjudged her foe. The All-Mother wasn't powerless, for she was capable of using Stella's own subconscious desires against her. It was as if she were becoming ensnared in a seductive web that she was helping the All-Mother to weave.

Think of your enemies, my Stella. Those who have laughed and opposed you, mocked your greatness and dared to call you names. Imagine the delight of being able to destroy those who offend or revile you as if they were helpless vermin beneath your feet. Think of it, Stella!

Stella was surprised to find that she was thinking of it, thinking of all those who had scorned her like Loran and seen her as a 'monstrosity.' What would it be like to be able to crush such an offender like an insect? And Malek, who had subjected her to the indignity of wearing a body-cuff after she had captured the Slug ship. What outrage, what unbearable insult! If she listened to the All-Mother, she would be able to punish such transgressors, and her retributive justice would be swifter than any sword!

Do you see, my Stella? the All-Mother coaxed. *Do you see what I offer?*

"Yes...I do." Stella gazed raptly into the dead, dark interior of the crystal. "What must I do?"

Not much at all, the answer came. *It is such a little thing. All you must do is turn the crystal over so I can slip through the crack and rest in your hand.*

Stella's hands were already beginning to obey. "But why don't you do that yourself?"

I have been weakened. In time I will recover my powers. But there is no need for me to do so, Stella. All you have to do to seal our bond and embrace your transcendent destiny is one small thing. Just turn the crystal over and hold it in your hand.

Such glory, Stella thought, her hands turning the crystal as if they had a will of their own. All she had to do was as the All-Mother asked and she would be able to span the stars, conquer a thousand galaxies. And her enemies, all those who dared to offend her, however slightly, how she would crush and lay them waste! She laughed, and then felt a twinge of doubt. Was it right to use power so selfishly?

If you like, the All-Mother said, *you could use your abilities for noble causes. You could cure disease, eliminate war, and promote love. The choice would be up to you, Stella, for you would be God.*

She would be God. the All-Mother was right. She could use her powers for good, not evil, make life beautiful rather than ugly. The only problem...

Stella frowned and rubbed her eyes, surprised at how dazed and numb she felt. It was as if she had been drugged, drawn to the abyss by this deadliest, most seductive trick. Swallowing, she gazed at the crystal and gasped. She had turned it almost completely over. Even as she watched, a shadow within the crystal crept toward the crack, getting closer and closer. She saw one of its legs reach the crack, then another.

The All-Mother was about to slip through it and onto her hand!

Quickly, Stella turned the crystal back over and gripped it tightly in both hands.

Shuddering, she peered into the crystal, catching a wisp of movement and a furtive, diminutive face. It was only the briefest of glimpses, but it was enough. She had no doubt about what she had seen, no doubt that the face was different now.

This time, the face was her own.

Why do you hesitate? The All-Mother asked. *Do it.*

Stella blinked and shook herself. She felt as if she had awakened from an insidious spell, a deep, hypnotic sleep in which she would have lost the most important part of herself. Even if she tried to do good, she could not risk being seduced by her enemy and corrupted by such powers. She might seek to conquer the cosmos and crush all resistance while spreading her children everywhere. Her children, born of her own regenerated womb. Yes, she could become what she had not dared even to hope for-a mother! She would be able...

Catching herself, she pulled herself back again. It was all so seductive, so terribly tempting. Even now, despite the horror of what she had almost become, she felt the lure of such power beckon again, begin to pull her back once more.

Stella, the All-Mother soothed in a voice like fragrant moonlight, *don't refuse my gift.*

"It almost worked, didn't it?" Stella said hoarsely, forcing her hunger down. "But you can't have me. I won't let you use my own darkness to destroy me." She trembled, the All-Mother's voice lingering like a narcotic in her blood. "If I can resist your false Jason, I can sure as hell do the same with any shadow trick you conjure up, even if you snatch it from my soul."

Whirling, Stella summoned all her strength and all her resolve. Reaching out, she plunged her mind again into the swirling red vortex that would eject her adversary from the ship. "As I told you before," she said, "I learned this from your son. Don't you detect a note of irony in that, All-Mother?"

Her enemy's thoughts hardened. *You cannot do this.*

Stella raised the crystal toward the vortex. "Watch me."

You must not refuse such power! the All-Mother raged. *I give you Creation to dispose of as you will!*

"It's only another lie," Stella answered. "And even if it weren't, I don't want it-or you." She moved the crystal into the force field.

No, I beg you! the All-Mother wailed. Her imperious tone vanished, replaced now by one Stella had never heard before. *Please, I beg you.*

Stella smiled, holding her enemy on the edge of eternity. Begging at last, Oh Mighty One? She thought. And do you seek my mercy and compassion? Did you ever show such sentiments to the decillions you must have killed in all your universes? Did you bother even to listen to their cries and prayers, their screams of agony and the weeping of their loved ones? The tube opened into space and Stella watched the crystal leave her fingers and slide down the force field toward the black pit of the singularity, carrying the All-Mother's final cry into eternity.

Nooooooooooo!

And as Stella's psychic link with her foe waned, she felt five thousand Slugs die in agony as their sustaining bond with their commander was broken. The All-Mother's passing was far from alone, for she was taking the last of an entire race with her.

Clenching her fist, Stella threw her voice after the crystal in the loudest and fiercest shout of her life.

"Adios, amiga!"

An instant later, just before the ship itself plunged down the gravity well, Stella raced across the bow to the drive system to reverse their course. If George was still alive, he would never survive such a passage. She didn't think she had a chance in the universe to save him, but she had to try.

EPILOGUE

The day of the ceremony dawned bright and glorious, a harbinger of things to come. Before the platform, people stretched far into the distance, their mood joyful and expectant. After one year, the long crushing war was fading from their minds as they turned optimistically to the future. They could do that now, the Emperor had assured them, since human beings were once again masters of the galaxy.

For this one day, though, they would also remember the dead and commemorate the first anniversary of their victory over the All-Mother. When the huge, bearded man rose and advanced to the podium, a million voices cheered. Minicams whirred silently, preserving the event for other worlds. The man spoke quietly, simply, concerned only with introducing the blonde-haired woman who soon rose from her chair. The ovation that greeted her name was deafening, and she paused to smile down at a beautiful boy with dark curly hair. Then she walked across the platform to the podium, accepted the man's embrace, and gazed out at the people.

Raising her hands, Regent-Protector Stella Singlethorne McMasters smiled, and the ovation became still louder. It pounded against her and made even the platform vibrate. She let it continue for a minute before indicating it should stop, but her gestures only served to excite the people more. Accepting what she could not change, she turned to gaze at those on the platform.

There was Kolanera the Fifth, 'Tippi' as she now privately called him, sitting next to her mother who looked both radiant and overwhelmed. The Emperor held her mother's hand fondly, playing the role of Imperial host with a grace and poise beyond his years. Stella chuckled. Even now, after a full year, her mother couldn't quite believe that the Emperor liked to hold her hand.

In the first row sat other people who were important to Stella. George Darron overfilled the seat on the other side of her own. She saw him grin and raise his fingers in a victory sign. To his left sat Lee Song, Tessa Farron and her son, General Gage's family, and selected officers of the *Spaceranger*. Colonel Powers, now General Powers and Supreme Commander of Imperial Forces, sat talking to Pancho Villa, Director of Police. She enjoyed the former pirate's delight in his starched dress greens and regulation spit-shined boots. Though the bandoleers were gone, she was glad he'd kept his mustache, and glad too that despite criticism, this seemingly mismatched pair had already proved remarkably effective in reducing crime and piracy.

Behind them, in the second row, sat her primary enemy. Lord Quinn Regis Hamilton, tall, handsome, and the head of a prominent family, was a fabulously rich and influential aristocrat. Even now, at the peak of her power and with the Empire still recovering from the war, he worked to defeat her vigorous initiatives in human rights and legal equality. Meeting his eyes, Stella knew he hated her and despised being on the same stage with such people as Tessa Farron and her son, Pancho and the equally low-born Lee Song. If he had his way, the punitive policy of exclusion would be returned with a vengeance.

Turning around, Stella faced the people, and this time their welcome subsided when she raised her hand.

"Citizens of the Empire of United Worlds," she said into the microphones, "it seems only proper, on the day that marks the first anniversary of our victory over the enemy, that we celebrate it on the planet that is the birthplace of our race."

Cheers rose as a million throats roared approval. Glancing at the tall, veiled structure beside the platform, she waited for the applause to subside.

"I'm not good at speeches," Stella said, turning her head to gaze at individual faces, "so I'll keep this brief. Since our Emperor appointed me Regent-Protector, I have been privileged to preside at a variety of occasions. I have spoken to you of our dead and wounded, of our gallant comrades who gave so much in the recent conflict. I have officiated at the rededication of our defense complex, which will replenish the thousands of ships we lost even though those who perished can never be replaced. And last, though there are those who oppose such views, I have argued for a fundamental change in human and individual rights, a change that combines compassion with strength, mercy with justice. A change that recognizes that despite our differences in birth and wealth and ability, we are all comrades and members of humanity and deserve an equal opportunity to enjoy the good life."

The people cheered. She smiled, wondering if she was beginning to turn into a politician, and waited until they again grew quiet.

When they did, she gripped the podium. "I am happy to tell you that such a fundamental change in our thinking and values has the enthusiastic and heart-felt support of the Emperor himself and the Regent-Protector's Council. They too share my belief that no child or spouse, no clan or family member, should be forced to bear the shame for a kin person's failures and compelled to face censure and ostracism. Instead, they should be treated with love and sympathy, and with the understanding that the same fate could easily befall us all."

She paused, glancing again at the tall structure beside the platform with its opaque white veil. The applause that came this time was less intense and certain, but it was there. She knew that before the war's conclusion, there would have been only boos and denunciations.

"Today," she continued, "we have gathered here to make flesh the words I have spoken, to embody them in a living monument to one of the comrades who made our victory possible. Like General Powers, who now occupies the office lately held by that great soldier and patriot, General Loran, General Gage too had the courage to do what others said was treason for the good of her comrades. She too had the vision to place conscience before rigid creed, and gave her life so that others might live. Today, I am here to tell you, and the members of her family who honor us with their presence, that if it were not for what some might call General Gage's 'treasonous' actions, we would have lost the war. Instead of being transformed into rulers of this galaxy who have already trebled our technological knowledge as a result of the ships we captured, we would be buried in the final stages of defeat and ruin."

This time when she paused, the applause was the greatest yet. She raised her hands for silence.

"Of all the state occasions I have attended since the war's conclusion, this is the most moving. General Gage loved books and culture, and I'm sure she would have fervently endorsed the words in an ancient Terran book that we should 'beat' our 'swords into plowshares.' It is therefore with deep personal pleasure that I greet you here today at the statuary unveiling and ground breaking for the A. Gage Center for Humanistic Studies."

A million voices swelled. As they cheered, she found herself remembering the All-Mother. They had been enemies but at the same time, so close. If only she had used her vast powers for good rather than evil.

Still, that was the same temptation the All-Mother had offered her, wasn't it? And she had almost accepted it.

After some minutes, she signaled again for silence. What had she been about to say? Oh, yes.

"The A. Gage Center for Humanistic Studies, which one day will stand on the ground where we are gathered, will be dedicated to the millions of comrades who gave their lives in the war. Every single brick will bear a name, and if necessary, every tile inside will do the same." She smiled. "No comrade, however obscure, will be forgotten, and I promise that every name shall be preserved for posterity."

Stella stiffened and placed her hands behind her. "In addition, I pledge to you that we shall do even more. We will take careful measures to insure that General Gage's illustrious name and valiant image are preserved for ages to come, and that this comrade whom we cherish so deeply will never be forgotten!"

Stella nodded at the officials who stood near the covered

structure beside the platform. They stepped toward it, picked up the veil by its edges, and swept it free.

On a duroplast plinth, the statue of General A. Gage rose gleaming in the sun, fashioned of Tiranium blue-veined, glistening white marble. Looking at it, Stella thought that Gage looked just as she remembered. Legs parted, hands locked behind her back, jaw thrust up against a taller world, Gage appeared on the verge of launching a blunt, no-nonsense broadside at a hapless offender. The only thing she lacked was her red whistle.

As the applause for Gage's statue subsided, Stella descended the stairs with the Emperor and headed for the ground before the platform where the culminating part of the ceremony would take place. It was one that she owed to George, for it had been he who had told her of the ancient rite.

She had arranged for Tessa Farron to present her with the iridium shovel, but instead Quinn Regis Hamilton had carried it down from the platform. He stood there in his elegant, purple, ruffled shirt, smiling at her as others gathered around.

Stella glanced at Kolanera. He could order Hamilton to surrender the shovel to Tessa even more effectively than she. But an Imperial directive would leave a bad taste at such an event, especially since there were those who still regarded Tessa as a traitor's widow.

Very clever, Lord Hamilton, she thought. Even here, even this early, you have used your influence to draw the sides. I shall not forget this.

Holding the shovel in both hands, Hamilton gracefully pointed it at the ground. "You have a hard task, Regent-Protector. The sun has made the dirt hard."

Stella looked down, seeing it was true. They had cleared the grass and the dirt that remained had been baked by the sun.

She reached for the shovel and Hamilton gave it to her. He stood watching her with a slight smile.

She turned the shovel in her hands. She hadn't thought of it before, but the square design of the scoop wasn't designed for hard soil. If it were only pointed.

Stella looked at Tessa, who held Ulysses' hand. Both mother

and son seemed anxious, as did Kolanera and her mother. She gave them all a smile and fed it last to Hamilton.

"It's only dirt," she told him.

She raised the shovel in her hands and brought it down with all her strength, driving it deep into the packed dirt. Her hands twisted, her shoulders turned, and with smooth ease she brought the fully laden shovel up just beneath Hamilton's chin. She smiled, seeing that he didn't look so smug now.

"Would you like to try the next scoop, my Lord? It's not as hard as it looks."

Sometime later Kolanera touched her hand as they sat together on the platform. Before it, people in the crowd were now taking turns with the shovel, struggling to widen the hole she had started.

"I thought you weren't good at giving speeches," Kolanera said. "I'd say that was the best one I've ever heard."

Stella squeezed the Emperor's hand. "Thanks, Tippi."

She smiled and gazed out above the people at the turquoise sky. Luna, she saw, was full and clearly visible, and beyond it a whole galaxy waited. Despite enemies, things were pretty fine at the moment. After all, she had her mother, the Emperor, and all her friends here. And she knew that beyond those distant stars Jason waited for her, just as he had promised.

About the Author

John, a retired English professor from Norfolk State University, has published over 300 stories in *The Speed of Dark, Weird Tales, Whitley Strieber's Aliens, Galaxy, The Age of Wonders*, and elsewhere. He's also published twenty books, including SF novels such as *Speaker of the Shakk* and *Beyond Those Distant Stars*, winner of AllBooks Review Editor's Choice Award (Mundania Press), and *Alien Dreams, A Senseless Act of Beauty*, and *The Merry-Go-Round Man* (Crossroad Press). MuseItUp Publishing has published seven SF novels. They are *Dark Wizard, Dax Rigby, War Correspondent*, and five in the Inspector of the Cross series: *Inspector of the Cross, Kingdom of the Jax, Defender of the Flame, Conqueror of the Stars*, and *Skyburst*. MuseItUp also published *The Blue of Her Hair, the Gold of Her Eyes* (winner of Preditor's and Editor's 2011 Annual Readers Poll), *More Stately Mansions*, and the dark erotic thrillers *Steam Heat* and *Wet Dreams*. His time-travel tale, "Killers," was an Editor's Top Pick at Musa Publishing. Some of John's books are available as audio books from Audible.com. Two of John's major themes are the endless, mind-stretching wonders of the universe and the limitless possibilities of transformation—sexual, cosmic, and otherwise. He is the former Chairman of the Board of the Horror Writers Association and the previous editor of *Horror Magazine*.

John welcomes comments from readers at jroseman@cox.net and invites them to visit his web site at www.johnrosenman.com and blog at www.johnrosenman.blogspot.com. His Facebook author page is https://www.facebook.com/JohnBRosenman/